Barbara Taylor Bradford

A Man *of* Honour

HarperCollins*Publishers*

HarperCollins*Publishers* Ltd
1 London Bridge Street,
London SE1 9GF

www.harpercollins.co.uk

HarperCollins*Publishers*
1st Floor, Watermarque Building, Ringsend Road
Dublin 4, Ireland

1st published by HarperCollins*Publishers* 2021

Copyright © Barbara Taylor Bradford 2021

Barbara Taylor Bradford asserts the moral right to
be identified as the author of this work

A catalogue record for this book
is available from the British Library

ISBN: 978-0-00-824252-7 (HB)
ISBN: 978-0-00-824253-4 (TPB)

Set in Sabon Lt Std by Palimpsest Book Production Limited,
Falkirk, Stirlingshire

Printed and bound in the UK using 100% Renewable Electricity by
CPI Group (UK) Ltd

To the memory of my beloved husband,
my darling Bob. Always my joy and
inspiration and in my heart forever.

CONTENTS

PART ONE:
FLIGHT OF THE EAGLE
North Kerry, Ireland, 1899   1

PART TWO:
DREAMS COME FIRST
Leeds, England, 1903   73

PART THREE:
CHANCES WITH CHALLENGES
Yorkshire & London, 1903   209

PART FOUR:
GOOD FORTUNE FINDS ITS WAY
Yorkshire & London, 1903–4   301

PART FIVE:
OTHER PEOPLE'S LIVES
Yorkshire, 1905–6   361

PART ONE

Flight of the Eagle
North Kerry, Ireland
1899

ONE

It was very windy on the top of the cliffs. He hadn't expected that, to be sure. And it was a strong wind that buffeted him forward. It was as if two strong hands were pushing him. Mighty hands at that.

He staggered and flayed about, and attempted to stay upright. Somehow he managed to do so, but he was suddenly afraid. The cliff top was a dangerous place to be on this cold morning.

It was Monday 8 May in the Year of Our Lord 1899 yet, despite the month, the weather was icy. What bad luck he had in choosing to come here. Daft, I am, he thought, that's a certainty.

His bright mind was racing as he continued to be battered about, and so he threw himself on the ground, deeming it the best place to be as this gale raged around him.

Once down on the ground, he began to crawl across the grass, heading for the formation of boulders grouped together. He knew these cliffs well, and there was a crevice between them. He could squeeze in there and be protected until the wind settled down or disappeared. If I be lucky, he thought miserably.

It was some relief when he reached the rocks and managed to get comfortable in the crevice. Sitting back, he pulled his overcoat around him and stuck his hands in his pockets. Although he was still shivering, being sheltered from the wind helped. He warmed up a bit.

His name was Shane Patrick Desmond O'Neill but the whole world called him Blackie. He lived in a hamlet in North Kerry, these days with his cousins Michael and Siobhan O'Brien. They had invited him to come and live with them in their cramped thatched cottage after his sister Bronagh had died a few months ago.

The twins were employed by the wealthy Anglo-Irish Lassiter family, who lived in the mansion up on the hill above the hamlet. Huddled against the rocks, his thoughts stayed with his cousins.

Michael was a gardener and Siobhan a housemaid. They were not paid very much; he knew that only too well, sure enough he did. Yet they managed better than their neighbours. He mentally hugged them to himself, because they were so caring of him in his time of dire need. His heart ached for his sister – his whole family. They were all dead now. Killed by this fearful land they lived in.

How he longed to leave this place. If only he were a bird he could take flight . . . soar up and away . . . be free of pain and sorrow.

Blackie's thoughts shifted to the opportunity he had, and Mrs O'Malley. She was very kind to him. She mothered him and had taught him to read, far better than he had been able to before. She was the housekeeper for the local priest, Father O'Donovan. Both kept an eye on him and were now helping to plan his trip . . . a different future for him, if his Uncle Pat could arrange everything. I know he'll pull it off, Blackie decided. As usual Blackie was full of optimism; a useful trait, he often thought. *Keep smiling* was his motto.

He had been inspired by Father O'Donovan's confidence and filled with excitement about going to England, as thousands had before him. There was no work here, no opportunity for him to earn a few pennies. Even the grown men had no jobs.

The idea of adventure and opportunity overseas was fed by his proximity to the mouth of the River Shannon and the wild Atlantic Ocean beyond.

The wind had finally died down, gone out to sea. Blackie pushed himself to his feet. Stretching, and then pulling his coat around him, he headed for the edge of the cliffs.

He stood gazing out at the rolling waves, tipped with white foam, and felt as if the sea were calling him across the waters. In his imagination, he envisioned freedom from hardship, poverty and loneliness. He was impatient to be gone, could hardly wait for the day he would leave Ireland from the port of Queenstown. It was usually tough, even harsh to cross this dangerous sea. Some did not survive the journey, so he had heard, and he believed it to be the truth.

Blackie knew *he* would. He would will himself to survive, in order to meet his Uncle Pat in Liverpool, from where they would travel on the train to Leeds. He had never been on a train before in his life; the idea of this intrigued him. His uncle had a good business in Leeds, repair work and building for the mill owners and even some householders nowadays. He would teach Blackie everything he knew and make him a partner. One day.

Turning away from the roiling ocean waves, Blackie walked back towards the hamlet, his mind settling on the book he had just finished. Father O'Donovan had lent it to him. It was a book about history and Elizabeth I, an English queen from the past.

Blackie loved history, churches and cathedrals. History fed his keen mind; churches and cathedrals fired his ambition to be a builder, a constructor of *wonderful* buildings. Elizabeth I had been a brilliant queen, a queen who had built a *country* to become its very best, better than ever before.

He smiled to himself, wishing he had lived then. Suddenly he thought of the Spanish Armada, which had foundered on the Irish Sea, in front of the dark eyes of the queen herself. She had been wearing a silver breastplate and was mounted on a white stallion, waiting on Plymouth Hoe for her greatest enemy, King Philip of Spain.

Blackie laughed out loud as he thought of this long-ago event, his brain focused on the queen. He was positive she had been well aware that the harsh wind, which had unexpectedly blown up, had pushed those great Spanish galleons away from the shores of her beloved England. There was no invasion of her land after all.

Her enormous victory had been called an Act of God by the people. He bet she had known the ships had capsized because of a change in the weather, and not Divine Intervention. She was too clever to miss that. A wry smile flickered. The vagaries of the weather were powerful, he knew *that*.

Black Irish, that's what I am, so called because of my black hair and dark eyes, he thought, as he contemplated those Spanish sailors of the Armada who had made it to the shores of Ireland and lived. Hundreds had stayed and married the beautiful Irish girls . . . he truly *was* descended from them and proud of it. Sure and he was, very proud.

Blackie was tall for his age and well-built, with a wide chest and broad shoulders even at thirteen. He had an inbred sense of purpose, which gave him a certain self-confidence, even an air of authority. It would be the underpinning of his life, a blessing.

This young man who had known much sadness, had grieved

for his father and mother, William, his brother, and finally his sister, Bronagh. They were all buried next to each other in the church cemetery; buried in the earth they had been the victim of . . . killed by hunger and grinding poverty.

He sighed under his breath as he walked on. He genuinely understood that life was hard. Mrs O'Malley had told him *that* many, many times, and he had already experienced unendurable pain and sorrow.

It had been terrible to lose first his da then his mam and William. He and Bronagh had tried to keep going for a year after that, but after Bronagh's death he had vowed to himself that he would make *his* life different, whatever he had to do to attain this. Mrs O'Malley constantly called him *the poor wee bairn* under her breath. That was how *she* saw him. Yet he knew he would grow up to be strong, a man of steel. He understood he could erase the past, create a new future for himself. Who could stop him? He had the time. He was just thirteen.

The drizzle started as Blackie was walking down the dirt road that led into the little hamlet where he had been born and brought up. Just my luck, he muttered under his breath, and started to run.

The drizzle became rain and, in seconds, it was a downpour. He was wet through as he jogged ahead, his eyes fixed on the first cottage at the edge of the hamlet. That was where Mrs O'Malley lived.

He glowered at the leaden sky. Thank God for Mrs O'Malley, he said to himself. She will come to my rescue. As she had many times.

He slowed down as he entered the hamlet. Within a minute, he was outside her cottage. He was not a bit surprised to see Mrs O'Malley herself, standing on the doorstep in front of her open door, a look of expectancy on her face, worry in her eyes.

Two

'Well, just look at yeself, standing there, dripping rain and on me clean floor, Blackie!' Mrs O'Malley exclaimed, after she had beckoned him into her cottage.

Blackie, looking down at his feet, murmured, 'Very sorry, Mrs O'Malley, swear I am. If ye give me a cloth, I'll clean it up.'

'Nay, away with ye, lad, I can do that. Take your coat off, and then your boots. That's how a lad gets a cold, standing around in wet shoes, ye knows.'

Moving towards him, she took his coat, which was soaked, and carried it to the sink. After laying it across the top, she went for his boots.

'Go and sit near the fire,' she instructed, 'while I stuff newspaper in your boots. Best thing there is for helping to dry 'em.' She didn't say that they wouldn't survive if she didn't, as cracked and worn as they were.

'Thanks, Mrs O'Malley, for looking after me like this.'

'Been doing it all your life, lad, to my way of thinking. Best take your socks off as well.'

Mrs O'Malley spoke the truth. Ever since Blackie had been born to Ellen O'Neill and her husband Mick, she had been on hand to help them. He was their youngest child, and Ellen was already run-down, exhausted by housework, lost pregnancies, cooking, and looking after her family.

Martha O'Malley had been glad to help. She had been widowed several years when Blackie arrived on their planet. Her own son Dennis had been eight years old. He was her only child and her joy in life. Dennis had grown up well, and now, at the age of twenty-one, he lived and worked in County Cork, where her sister Agatha Nolan and husband Jimmy had a small shop selling groceries in the busy port of Queenstown. Childless, and also fond of their nephew, they had taken him under their wings. Dennis worked in their grocery shop. He enjoyed his job and his life there.

Mrs O'Malley put the stuffed boots on the hearth and turned to Blackie. She reached for the wet socks and placed them next to the boots. Straightening, she turned to Blackie and said, 'Now, how about a cup of nice tea? It'll warm the cockles of your heart.'

'Faith, and it would,' he responded, and flashed her a wide smile.

She smiled back and felt a small rush of pleasure. There was something special and endearing about the boy. Everyone felt his warmth and friendliness and was drawn to him immediately.

His geniality was part of his natural personality, and he spoke to everyone, radiated kindness. These traits never varied, and his dark good looks played into the attraction he exuded.

After taking the bubbling kettle off the hob, Martha O'Malley filled her brown teapot with tea and then poured in the water. She left it to mash for a few minutes. She went to the larder and took out the biscuit tin, well aware Blackie liked her sweet oat biscuits.

* * *

The two of them sat in front of the roaring fire, silent, lost in their own thoughts, comfortable with each other. This easiness between them came from the longevity of their friendship, the middle-aged woman and the young boy. They understood each other perfectly.

Martha O'Malley was pondering Blackie's clothes. The dark coat, drying now, hanging on a chairback near the fire, was threadbare and looked as if it had seen better days. And his boots, drying as well, were in poor shape, but just about held together at the moment. Fortunately the heavy-knit fisherman's jumper was one she had knitted years ago for her son.

As for the long trousers, they were a pair Lady Lassiter, from the big house, had given to Blackie's cousin Michael. They had been too big for him, but they fitted Blackie well. As if made to measure, Mrs O'Malley thought, her mind focusing on Lucinda, wife of Lord Robert Lassiter, the Earl of Harding, who lived in the big house on the hill above the hamlet. Her ladyship was often found giving away cast-off clothes no longer used and worn by her children, or even sometimes by Lord Robert. Blackie had been the beneficiary of her gifts and, before him, Mrs O'Malley's son Dennis had received hand-outs, along with some of the younger village children. She was a haughty woman, and odd, no denying it, but Father O'Donovan had got on to her about gifting unwanted clothes to the village children, and she had hardly been able to refuse.

The Lassiters were an Anglo-Irish family with ancient roots in Ireland. Ancestors of Lord Lassiter had built the large house on the hill two centuries ago, and it had stood fast and strong for all these years.

Lady Lassiter had been born to English parents, herself the daughter of an earl. Her maiden name had been Lucinda Harley, with the honour title of Lady. Her parents, who had been staying in Ireland when she was born, were Lord and Lady Harley, the

Earl and Countess of Carlton. They lived in Skipton most of the time.

Drawn to their daughter's birthplace, Lady Lucinda's parents had brought her often to the Emerald Isle. One day she had been introduced to Lord Robert, and a glittering match was made, though Mrs O'Malley didn't think there had been much love involved. Now they divided their time between England and Ireland, with Lady Lucinda seeming to prefer the Irish mansion.

'What are ye thinking about?' Blackie said, touching Martha's arm.

Startled, she jumped slightly, and then gave him a loving look. 'I was brooding a bit, my lad, thinking how much I would miss ye once ye'd gone off to join your Uncle Pat.'

'I'll miss *ye*,' he answered, and looked at her intently. 'Mam always said ye were like a second mother to us all, faith and she did, and ye were. 'Tis the truth, Mrs O'Malley.'

'Well, your mam is always your mam, but I did enjoy looking after ye all, sure and I did, and I'm proud of ye, Blackie. What a grand lad ye've become, and handsome.'

A blush spread across his face and he mumbled, 'Oh, I don't know about that.'

Martha O'Malley said in a low voice, 'Has Lady Lassiter given Michael any cast-offs for ye, lad?' Her eyes were on his.

He nodded. 'I'm getting an old overcoat, a jacket and another pair of trousers, so Michael told me. I'm grateful, sure and I am.'

A smile spread across Mrs O'Malley's face. 'I have a surprise for ye. I've knitted two jumpers for ye and I found a bag of Dennis's socks that will do ye well.'

Blackie laughed and exclaimed, 'I'll be the best-dressed lad in Leeds, won't I?'

Mrs O'Malley laughed with him, and then glanced at the small clock on the mantelpiece as it struck twelve. 'Goodness me, it's already dinnertime. I hope ye'll stay and have a bite with me, Blackie, sure and I would enjoy that.'

'If ye're sure that's all right,' he said quietly, knowing it was. They often had dinner together, and she always invited him if she ran into him. With his cousins at the big house all day, she knew he'd go hungry otherwise.

''Tis indeed,' she answered, the Irish lilt in her voice apparent. 'It's always been all right with me, sure it has . . . I love ye like my own lad, Shane Patrick Desmond O'Neill, known as Blackie to the whole wide world.'

THREE

T he kitchen was warm, cosy and quiet. Blackie sat back in Mrs O'Malley's chair, relaxed, even a little sleepy, as he gazed into the roaring fire.

The flames flaring and rising up the chimney were vividly pink, gold and deep red. And in them he saw his dreams reflected: this trip to Queenstown, the sea crossing to Liverpool, and the long journey on the train to Leeds.

That city flickered within the flames, many images. A great metropolis it was, his Uncle Pat had explained that in his last letter. He had told him the streets were paved with gold, there were jobs aplenty, and work for everyone who wanted to make money. The right place for him.

MONEY. That word loomed large in his mind. Money made you safe, less vulnerable to the grasping world surrounding you, especially if you were a young boy like he was. No, he now thought, I'm not a *young boy*. I am thirteen, and thanks to my height and strong build, I look much older – sixteen or so at least.

This happened to be the truth. Unlike his brother, William,

and sister, Bronagh, he was a grand specimen of a young man and extremely good-looking. His siblings had been so much slighter and shorter in height. They had teased him, called him *the giant*, and just laughed.

The luck of the draw, he thought, sure and it is. Blackie was well aware he could win in a brawl. He'd knock a man out with one punch. He'd tackle a small group if they came after him intent on trouble. Once his Uncle Pat had come to visit from England, and had said he ought to step into the ring and become a boxer, and that he'd become a champion.

No, not for him. He could not abide violence of any kind and avoided confrontations like the plague. His ambitions were to work hard with his uncle and to learn to be a builder. He didn't just want to repair houses. He wanted to construct houses, even design them. He had the talent. He knew that.

He smiled inwardly and saw the house of his dreams hidden in the bright red flames. It was large and square, with three floors. When he built it one day, it would have tall windows, high ceilings and a fireplace in every room, even in the bedrooms. His feet were always cold and so he loved fires.

He glanced down at them now, encased in a pair of Dennis O'Malley's socks. They were warm wool socks which Mrs O'Malley had given to him earlier. She was so good to him, faith and she was, a loving woman.

She dropped a spoon and bent to pick it up, turning to look at him as she did. A smile slid onto her face.

'Thanks for letting me stay here after dinner,' Blackie said.

'Ye always can and ye always do,' Martha retorted, a grin replacing the smile.

'I know.' He grinned back. It was a ritual.

She nodded and swung back to the bowl on the table next to the sink. She began to knead the dough, pushing her hands into it determinedly.

He watched her for a while, then asked with a puzzled frown, 'What are ye making all that dough for?'

Without turning her head, she replied, 'Rabbit pies. Two rabbit pies.'

'Are ye really?' He couldn't help wondering where the rabbits had come from. He said, 'Who caught the rabbits for ye, Mrs Martha?'

He often called her that, because her first name on his lips made him feel she was family, which she was in his opinion. For all his life, in fact.

'Joe O'Donnell did me the big favour. See, he tries to help me when he can. He found 'em in a warren near the edge of yon woods. Trapped 'em and carried them over.'

Blackie nodded, then exclaimed, 'I hope ye didn't have to skin 'em!' He pulled a face.

She shook her head and smiled. 'I know ye're a bit . . . *squeamish*, lad. Though you won't be when it's your next meal. But Joe saved me the job. He brought 'em last night, skinned 'em right here at this sink and wrapped the skins in an old piece of sacking, sure and he did. Then I washed 'em with salt and put 'em away in yon cold room.' As she spoke, she indicated the larder across the room.

'When will they be cooked? Are the pies for tonight?' He knew he sounded eager, but he was hungry again.

'Aye, they are that! When Siobhan and Michael come to get ye, I shall invite your cousins to stay to tea. And ye are very welcome too, I swear on the heads of the Blessed Saints ye are.'

Blackie wasn't surprised about the invitation, because Siobhan and Michael often stayed when they came back from work at the Lassiters. What intrigued him was Joe O'Donnell bringing her the rabbits. Was Joe after Mrs O'Malley? Why not? Joe's wife had been dead a few years. And how did Mrs Martha feel?

Put that thought away, he instructed himself, alarmed by the idea of Joe and his dearest friend together.

Mrs O'Malley said, 'Come to think of it, I'd better get 'em out, start to cook 'em on the hob.' She pushed the odd pieces of dough off her hands, and washed them at the sink. She then turned to Blackie and said, 'I'll need your help, me lad. Come on over to the cold room. Get me the pot, will ye, please? It's heavy, so it is.'

'Right away.' Blackie jumped out of the chair and followed her across the room. The cold room was indeed *cold*, certainly that was a better name for it than larder.

'That big pot, over there on the shelf . . . do ye see it?'

He nodded. 'Come out, please, Mrs Martha, and then I'll be able to reach it better, take it out.'

She did as he asked. A moment later Blackie lifted the pot with both hands, asking her, 'Where do ye want it?'

'Over here,' she explained, pointing to the sink. 'I've got to rinse 'em, ye see, clean off the salt.'

Blackie stood and watched her wash off the pieces of rabbit. 'I added all sorts of spices . . . pepper, lavender, and nutmeg – just pinches of it. Now I must take out all the vegetables and cook the pieces of rabbit for a bit. Later, ye can help me put the vegetables back in.'

Blackie said, 'I know they can't go in the pot now. They'll become too soft.'

Mrs O'Malley beamed at him. 'I see that ye learned a lot from me.'

He laughed. 'There's no better way than to stand at the knee of the master,' he said. 'And I've been by your side for years.'

She simply nodded. 'I'm going to take the kettle off and ye can carry the cooking pot to the fire. Put it on the hob in its place.'

'I will do that. And when the rabbit is stewed, it will go in the oven, under the dough. And we'll soon have a pie. Correct?'

'Exactly,' Mrs O'Malley agreed, stepping aside so Blackie could have an easy passageway across the kitchen with the pot.

Once the pot was hanging over the fire, Blackie went back to his chair, staring into the flames once more. Within seconds he was daydreaming about his future, wondering how he would fare in Leeds. He was also feeling slightly curious about Joe O'Donnell and the gift of the rabbits.

A thought took hold. Might she not be lonely when *he* left? Perhaps no, perhaps not at all. She *would* miss his presence in her life, and maybe Joe O'Donnell could become her friend, keep her company. Another thought struck him. Joe could already be her friend.

That might not be a bad idea after all. Loneliness was a terrible thing, a burden beyond belief. To be entirely alone in this world made life difficult. He had often experienced this feeling after each member of his family had died.

When Bronagh had passed away, his days and nights had become intolerable. He'd felt as if part of himself had been cut away and there was only half of him left to grieve for her.

They had been the closest in age; his lovely red-haired sister had been seventeen when she had gone to her grave. But, although she was older, *he* was the one who had mothered *her*.

Thinking of her made him choke up, and so he straightened in the chair and took tight control of his raw emotions. Siobhan and Michael were family, as were Mrs O'Malley and her son Dennis. They all helped to lessen the pain of loss, his sadness – that awful lonesomeness that crept upon him relentlessly.

'I have to ask ye to leave yer chair, Blackie,' Mrs O'Malley said, cutting into his thoughts. 'The suet dough is ready.'

'Do ye want me to take the pot off the fire?'

'That'd be a good idea, Blackie, and if ye carry it over, ye can put it in the sink. That's the best spot for it.'

Blackie got up, pushed aside the chair, and found the two thick pot-holders which would protect his hands. Once he had it firmly in his grip, he walked across the kitchen and did as Mrs O'Malley had instructed. 'The pot's in the sink,' he told her.

Mrs O'Malley, who had gone over to the oven built into the fireplace, exclaimed, 'The oven is perfect for the pies. They'll cook fast in this heat.'

Whilst the pies were cooking, Mrs O'Malley cleaned the cooking utensils, and Blackie dried them. At one moment, she exclaimed in her lilting tone, 'Oh, put the knives and forks out, lad. I know Michael and Siobhan will want to stay for tea. Don't the pies smell wonderful?'

Blackie agreed and went over to the small table in a corner of the cottage. He took out four knives and forks and two large serving spoons to set four places. The table was small, but they could sit there comfortably, were not too squashed together.

Within a few minutes there was a light knock on the door. It opened immediately and his twin cousins came into the cottage. Both looked cold and had red cheeks from the wind. They were only a few years older than Blackie and just as thin.

'Hello, Mrs O'Malley,' Siobhan said with a bright smile. 'Oh, it's lovely and warm in here.'

''Tis indeed,' she answered, and looked across at Michael. 'Hello, lad, ye look frozen.'

'Good evening, Mrs O'Malley,' Michael said. 'And it *is* bitter out there. And it's said to be spring.'

'Ne'er cast a clout 'til May's out . . .' Mrs O'Malley said, and went on, 'Take your coats off and come and get warm. I hope ye can stay to eat something. Ye both look as if ye need a hot meal.'

19

'That would be nice, so kind,' Siobhan said. 'If you've enough food to spare.'

'I do indeed.'

'Thank you.' Michael flashed her a warm smile, and then helped his sister to wriggle out of her topcoat, before taking off his own.

'We're having rabbit pie,' Blackie announced. 'A real treat. I watched Mrs Martha making 'em, and they'll be very tasty.'

FOUR

The rabbit pie was delicious. There wasn't much talking done as they ate. The four of them were relishing the meal, the best any of them had eaten in the past few months. All had managed to exist on meagre servings of vegetables mainly and, occasionally, a small portion of fish with a chunk of bread, a piece of bacon or a scrape of dripping. Food was scarce and they were hungry most of the time.

Once the first pie had been well and truly demolished, Mrs O'Malley pushed back her chair and stood. Her eyes swept over them, and she smiled. 'I see ye liked the first pie, so I think we should try the second.'

When no one answered her, just looked astonished more than anything else, she remarked, 'I did make two pies, ye knows.'

Blackie spoke up. 'Are ye sure, Mrs Martha? Don't ye want to keep the other one for tomorrow?'

She shook her head. '*I'm* having a serving, so why not finish it among us? Michael? Siobhan? How about the two of ye?'

Michael said, 'Thank you, Mrs O'Malley, I'd love a bit more, I would that.'

Mrs O'Malley smiled, obviously pleased. Turning to his sister, she raised a brow. 'And Siobhan, will ye take a piece?'

'Thanks, I will, Mrs O'Malley. It's the best rabbit pie I've ever eaten. Delicious.' There was a small pause before she added, 'Rabbit tastes like chicken, at least when it comes out of your oven.'

Mrs O'Malley brought the dish to the table, and each of them served themselves. After giving Blackie the dish to hold, Mrs O'Malley put a spoonful on her own plate, then took it back to the table near the sink.

When they had finished, Blackie and Michael helped Mrs O'Malley carry the empty plates to the sink. Siobhan joined them and within half an hour they were all sitting around the fire, holding a mug of tea, relaxing in the warmth and comfort of the small kitchen. Their bellies were filled with good food, and they were peaceful in their surroundings.

The following afternoon, Siobhan and Michael arrived home early. For once, Blackie was in their cottage and not at Mrs O'Malley's.

When they walked in they found him polishing his boots. He looked up from the task when he saw them, and smiled. 'It's only five, did her ladyship let ye off early?'

'She was away in Tralee for the day, so I took meself off.' Michael grinned and took something out of his coat pocket, then shrugged the coat off his shoulders. After hanging the overcoat on a hook on the wall, he walked over to the fireplace where Blackie sat with his boots and a shoe brush.

Siobhan took her coat off, hung it on another peg on the wall, and hurried to the fireplace. 'Is the water in the kettle hot, Blackie?'

'Indeed it is, and I can make a pot of tea if ye want.' He looked at Siobhan and then Michael hungrily. 'Did Cook send us anything for our tea?'

Siobhan nodded. 'It's in the bag near the door. That's where I put it when we came in.'

'What did she give us?' Blackie wondered out loud.

'A big jar of broth. It's a nice tea, Blackie.'

He nodded. 'Cook never lets us starve.'

'Yes, she's been kind since you came to us.' Michael walked over to the fireplace and sat down opposite his twin. Gazing at his cousin, Michael took the piece of paper he was holding and smoothed it out. After scanning it, he said to Blackie, 'Uncle Pat sent us a telegram today. It came to us at the mansion.'

Blackie dropped the boot and stood up, surprised, staring at Michael, putting out his hand. 'Can I read it, please?'

Michael gave it to him, and explained, 'He's ready for you to go to Leeds. You leave here for Queenstown and go straight to the docks and get on the boat. Uncle Pat will be waiting there at the docks in Liverpool.'

Blackie read every word for himself, filled with relief and happiness. *He was flying away at last!* A thought struck him. 'How do I get to Queenstown? Do I walk there, Michael? Or try for a lift?'

''Course not. I will talk to Finn Ryan. His father bought an old gig from his lordship last year. He – Finn, that is – purchased a horse. He has a . . . a sort of service, taking people where they want to go.'

'I remember. Ye will hire him to take me to the port? Is that it?'

'Yes. With me.'

'I can go alone,' Blackie protested.

'No. I will take charge of things.'

'I'm thirteen. Grown up, Michael.'

'Not quite. Dennis O'Malley will meet us at the docks in Queenstown. He's going to see you safely on to the boat to Liverpool and then Uncle Pat will take over.'

'I am big for me age, and I can look after myself. *Ye* taught me to fight good.'

'I did, Blackie, and I trust you. I know you're capable and all you say is true. But—'

'I'm strong and clever.'

Michael put his hand on Blackie's arm affectionately. His voice was calm when he said, 'Yes, you are, but the world is a weird place, full of strange folk who want to take advantage of a boy.'

Siobhan said, 'We want you to be safe, Blackie.'

FIVE

The following day was suddenly busy, as Blackie found himself running hither and yon, getting ready to leave for the port of Queenstown, in neighbouring County Cork.

Michael had awakened him early and told him to dress quickly. He was to go with them to the mansion when they went to work. When he asked why, Michael explained that there were things there for him, items he would need.

It was cool on this May morning, the mist still rising from the deep green meadows as they walked up the hill. But the sky was beautiful, a deep cerulean blue dusted with sheer white clouds, like puffballs floating across the vast expanse above them. Blackie, glancing up, saw the edge of the sun. It would grow into a pleasant day, he felt certain.

The three of them walked quickly, and it was not long before they reached Lassiter Hall. They crossed the stable yard and, a moment later, were entering the house through the back door.

The warmth of the kitchen, with its huge fire and busy ovens, enveloped them at once, instantly took the chill off them all.

'Top of the morning to ye, Cook,' Blackie said, giving Mrs O'Rourke his brightest smile.

'Ah, there ye are, me boyo,' Cook shot back, a grin on her plump cheeks. They were bright pink from the heat, and her black eyes sparkled. After greeting his cousins, she said, 'Put your coat in the boot room, lad, and come and have a cup of porridge.'

He nodded and followed his cousins, who had already crossed the room ahead of him to hang up their topcoats, as they did every day.

Cups of steaming porridge were waiting for them when they returned to the kitchen. Cook beckoned them forward, and Siobhan and Michael sat down, followed by Blackie.

The cook fussed around Blackie, reminding him there were currants in *her* porridge, unlike the porridge made by others not so talented with food as she was.

'That I know, Cook,' he said, lifting up his spoon. 'And yours *is* the best I've ever tasted.' He began to eat, and Cook went over to the ovens to look inside, nodding to herself before closing the doors. 'His lordship is taking the family to London town tomorrow,' Cook whispered, hovering over the kitchen table. 'So dinner will be one of me best specialities,' she confided. 'Now, what about a mug of tea? Do ye all want one?'

'Yes, please,' the three of them said in unison; a moment later Cook was serving them. She then brought a small plate of three warm teacakes to the table. 'Help yourself, Siobhan,' she ordered, and looked across at Blackie and Michael. 'Don't be shy. Enjoy a teacake, me boyos. I've made a large batch for the family for later.'

They did as she asked, their mouths watering at the sight of the teacakes. This week was turning into a good one for food.

* * *

Once breakfast was over, Michael and Siobhan went to change into their work clothes, and Blackie remained seated at the table.

'I'll join ye for a second,' Mrs O'Rourke said, and smiled at Blackie. She had worked for the Lassiters for many years, and as a local woman she had watched him grow up, and was fond of him and his cousins.

She pursed her lips, and said in a low voice, 'I've a suitcase for ye, Blackie. It belonged to my son, Conor. I don't think ye knew him. He was the one in the Indian army. He got killed there in an accident.' She shook her head, and a flash of sadness slid across her face. 'Not even *fighting* for Queen and country, and he had to go and die like that! In an accident. In a foreign land.'

'I'm sorry, Mrs O'Rourke. Ye have told me much about Conor, and he must have been a lovely young man.'

'Aye, he was that.' She stood. 'Well, we must get on; talking about him won't bring him back. I'm going to get ye the suitcase. Back in a tick.'

Blackie watched her ample figure moving over to a large cupboard at the end of the kitchen. Although she was plump, he thought how graceful she was. And she certainly had a kind heart. She had often spoken to him about Conor, and when he had wondered out loud why he was in the *Indian* army, she had explained it to him. 'It's the *British* army in India, with British officers and regular soldiers, but Indian soldiers as well. Mostly there to keep the peace, I suspect. There's always rumblings in India.'

Mrs O'Rourke returned to the fireside carrying the suitcase. After placing it on a chair, she turned the key in the lock, opened the lid, then glanced at him. 'Look inside, Blackie, it's brand new.'

'I can see that it's as clean as a whistle. Perfect size for me. Thank ye.' He cleared his throat and stared at her. 'Are ye sure ye want to part with this? It's a grand suitcase. Ye might need it.'

'And where would I be a-going, I ask ye that, lad?' She looked up at the ceiling and went on, 'And sure as God made little apples, Conor'll never be needing it, not where he is . . .' Her voice trailed off and Blackie noticed her black eyes were moist with tears.

He was about to comfort her but, before he could, she muttered, 'Silly lad, a-going off like that, and not coming back to me . . . having an accident with his horse and dying on me . . . and in a foreign land.'

Shaking her head, and pulling herself together, Cook closed the suitcase and gave Blackie the key. 'It's strong, well made.'

'Thanks a million, Cook. It's a grand present, and I'll treasure it. I can't believe Conor never used this.' He lifted the suitcase off the chair and put it on the floor.

'He was a soldier,' she said, a hint of pride now echoing. 'They use kitbags, yer knows.'

'Of course. I'd forgotten,' Blackie exclaimed.

'I'm happy ye'll be going ter Leeds,' she said. 'Lots of opportunities there, so I understand. For a bright lad, ye'll do well, Blackie, and especially since your Uncle Pat is there to guide ye. He's clever, but then all the Kennedys are.'

'Yes, I'm lucky, sure I am, having this chance to make me way in life.'

She nodded, sniffed, and went over to one of the ovens, looked inside. 'Oh, that's awright, I thought me cake was burning.'

'I don't smell anything,' Blackie said in a reassuring voice.

'No, a false alarm.' Walking back to him, sitting down at the table, Mary O'Rourke said, 'But I do hope ye'll come back to see us, Blackie. We'll all miss ye.'

'I swear on the heads of the Blessed Saints that I will try to be back here one day, Cook. Siobhan and Michael, well, they're me family . . . I'll for sure be back!'

Mary O'Rourke smiled faintly, her black eyes fastened on the orphan boy in front of her, of whom she had grown so fond. Aye, she thought, they all say that, our young boys when they leave us, but sometimes we never see 'em again . . . some even die in foreign fields.

Six

'You look a bit shattered, lad,' Patrick Kennedy said to his nephew three days later, as he and Blackie settled into their seats on the train. 'I imagine it was a rough crossing on the ship.' His bright blue eyes remained focused on Blackie, his expression full of warmth, and just a little concern.

'It *was* bad, Uncle Pat. I was thankful when it was over, what with having me suitcase an' all to worry about.' His nephew looked pale and tired, an overgrown boy the height of a man.

'A lot of people don't make it in one piece, sometimes even not at all,' Patrick muttered, shaking his head.

Shifting slightly on the seat, he glanced out of the window. The two of them were sitting in a third-class carriage on the train travelling to Leeds and beyond. Its final destination was Scotland.

Blackie explained, 'People were seasick. Many passed out from exhaustion, and some nearly fell overboard when the ship rocked and swayed. Another boy and me, well, we clung together and managed to stay alert, and upright. Still, I'll tell ye, Uncle Pat, we had to use all of our strength to survive the lashing sea. All

I can add is that it was cold, wet and dangerous, but, somehow, we managed.'

Patrick couldn't help smiling when he said, 'Let's face it, you're a young and strong spalpeen. Of course you made it, but I don't fancy it again.'

Blackie eyed his uncle, and shook his head. 'In my opinion ye would've been all right. Mam used to tell me ye were a tough man, strong as an ox, and that I should pattern meself after ye.'

'Ellen was always singing my praises, sure and she was, Blackie. Close we two were, growing up.' A sad smile crossed his face at thoughts of his late sister.

Settling back against the seat, his eyes taking in the train and all the details of the carriage, Blackie considered his uncle for a moment, and then said in a grateful tone, 'I want to thank ye, Uncle Pat, for bringing me to Leeds and offering me a new life. It is right kind of ye.'

'My pleasure, lad, I wanted to do it, and I'd promised Ellen I'd look after you, and also give you a fresh start.'

'I didn't understand at first why Michael and Siobhan said Dennis had to see me onto the ship. But I'm glad he did. The docks were noisy, busy with people getting on ships to America, Canada, all kinds of places. I needed him to survive it.' Blackie paused, and after a moment he added, 'And will ye have to repay Dennis for minding me, a'course?'

Patrick nodded. 'He'd have kept an eye on you, his mother and Father O'Donovan arranged that. But yes, I gave him some money for his trouble. Always pay your debts, Blackie, and be sure to make it earlier rather than later. That puts you on the winner's side, sure and it does. And people will trust you, and favour you.'

'I'll heed that advice, and I hope to learn a lot from ye, Uncle Pat, and in every way, not just about carpentry and building.'

Patrick Kennedy simply nodded, and reached for a satchel on

the seat next to him. Opening it, he took out two bottles and handed one to Blackie. 'Your Aunt Eileen always keeps the medicine bottles from the doctor and, as you see, they come in useful. There's water in there, clean drinking water.'

Next he took out two packets of sandwiches and again gave one to his nephew. 'Sliced ham, the best I could do,' he said, removing the greaseproof paper wrapping.

Blackie thanked him, and said, 'I'm ravenous . . .' He paused, and added, 'But then I always am.'

'I know. None of us gets enough nourishing food. When did you last eat, Blackie?'

'Yesterday. A packet of bread and cheese Siobhan gave me. Same the day before.'

Patrick sighed, thinking of the state of the country – not only of Ireland, but England as well. The greatest empire in the world. The rich lived off the fat of the land whilst the poor had to manage on the scraps carelessly thrown to them. Would there never be a change for the better? There were moments when he thought about entering politics, wondering if *he* could bring about change. But generally he dismissed it before the idea, the thought of it, took hold. He preferred to make money.

Hard work had never bothered him; he went at it with drive, determination and enthusiasm. He sensed the same ambition in his nephew, which was why he had brought him to Leeds, to better himself, to give Blackie a chance to make some good money.

Somebody had once said that money was the source of all evil. In his opinion, it was the source of good health and a secure life. He would somehow manage to dodge the so-called evil.

There was a companionable silence between the two of them as they ate the ham sandwiches and drank the water, and the train rolled on to the north.

At one moment, Patrick said, 'We're lucky to have a carriage to ourselves – because it's Thursday. The weekends are a trial. Too many folk travelling, rushing about.'

'Is that why ye changed the day, Uncle?'

'It is. I didn't want us to have to push and shove our way through the crowds,' Patrick explained. 'Tiresome.'

'I hadn't realized how big the docks would be in Liverpool,' Blackie said, with wonder in his voice. 'And so many boats. It astonished me.'

'*Ships*,' Patrick corrected. 'You can put a boat on a ship, but you can't put a ship on a boat. It's the smaller of the two. Remember that.'

Blackie nodded. 'I will . . . where are they sailing off to?'

'All over the world – India, Africa, America, and even the South American countries. Long voyages, sure and they are, but we've always been the people of seagoing islands.' Patrick smiled at Blackie. 'And perhaps that's because we are islanders, surrounded by the sea, and we want to see the world.'

'Mum told me ye were in the Royal Navy when ye were young – *sixteen*, she said.'

'I was,' Patrick answered.

'Did ye like being a sailor on a big ship, Uncle Pat?'

'Oh to be sure, I did. What a life! I enjoyed every moment I was at sea, and I still miss it sometimes, even now at my age.'

'Mam said ye joined the navy the year before I was born, so ye can't be *that* old now,' Blackie observed, swift as usual with a comeback.

Patrick gave him a long, hard look, then said, 'I'm thirty, lad, and I thought you knew that.'

Blackie shook his head, and after a moment he said, 'Ye don't look it. Ye are still a young spalpeen, Uncle.'

Patrick laughed. 'If only, Blackie, if only.' The laughter stayed; he looked pleased.

'So why did ye leave the Royal Navy if ye liked it so much?'

'*Love*,' Patrick murmured, a soft look slipping onto his face. 'I fell in love with your Aunt Eileen. And after a few years, the loneliness – when I was at sea – got to her. She wanted me with her.'

'And so ye left because of her.'

'Only too true, but why so many questions, my lad?' Patrick probed. He hadn't expected this inquisition.

'I like to know about people,' was the boy's fast response.

'Don't we all,' Patrick chuckled, still amused. 'It's a natural trait of the human being . . . we're all nosy, curious about other people's lives.'

'I suppose,' Blackie answered, wondering if his uncle was annoyed with him for pestering. He didn't seem to be. But Blackie decided to keep quiet, and settled back against the seat.

He couldn't help studying his mother's brother, who had been her favourite. That was not so surprising to Blackie. Patrick Kennedy was a handsome man with the brightest blue eyes, reddish-blond hair and finely sculpted features. He was tall, well-built, and his presence and his looks attracted people to him.

Men liked his easy-going, friendly manner, his vast knowledge of world events and sports. A man's man, his mother had told him once. And a woman's man as well, she had thought to add. They fall at his feet, she had murmured, and he enjoyed every moment.

Blackie now smiled to himself, remembering the day she had said that, and how he had believed she meant they literally fell on the ground at his uncle's feet. It was his older brother, William, who had explained what that meant, and in great detail, not leaving much out about what a man and a woman did in a bed when not sleeping.

Blackie closed his eyes as different memories flooded back. The water and ham sandwich had been restorative, and this, plus the motion of the train, lulled him to sleep after a few minutes.

Patrick Kennedy regarded his nephew for a while, studying him. He was Black Irish to the tips of his toes, just like his own wife Eileen, descendants of those rescued sailors from the great Armada of centuries ago.

He himself was descended from the Norsemen, who had sailed from Nordic lands, going around the top of Scotland, down into the Irish Sea. The Vikings in their long ships with carved heads at the fore and aft, heads of beasties and monsters . . . all that had been aeons ago.

And through all those centuries, the men and women of Ireland had been noted for their fine looks; their colouring had told everyone their true origin. They were also deeply rooted in its Celtic traditions, the Druids they came from, and the history of their ancient island with its multifaceted folklore.

How odd all this was, Patrick suddenly thought, very odd indeed, being able to know a person's country of birth at a glance. Would he be able to pick out an Englishman? *Yes.* A Frenchman? *Of course.* A smile flickered in those deep blue eyes . . . every man had his origins stamped on him, no two ways about it. And clothes told their own story, even if the face and colouring did not. Every country had its own style of dress.

Patrick's eyes focused on his nephew once again. He had been pleased to see that Blackie had arrived off the ship looking neatly dressed, not in rags. For a split second, he had been startled by the boy's height and build, and by those staggering looks.

Shane Patrick Desmond O'Neill, to give him his full name, was one of the handsomest young men he had seen lately. And he looked older than thirteen.

I'm going to have to keep a strong hold on him, Patrick realized unexpectedly. Keep him near me and under my wing. Women will be after him, and women of all ages. A sigh escaped, and Patrick closed his eyes, thinking of his own past and, to be exact, his present. *Women*. Trouble on two legs. Another sigh escaped: I'll think about *that* tomorrow.

SEVEN

It was deep twilight when Patrick and Blackie disembarked from the train in New Station in Leeds. Both of them were glad to stretch their legs and stride out after the long ride on the train.

'This way, Blackie,' Patrick said, taking his nephew's arm, leading him to the left. The boy was gaping, looking up above at the vaulted roof above the cast-iron pillars, trains and noise all around. 'Once we're out on the street, it's only a few seconds away from the tram stop,' Patrick explained.

'I've never been on a tram,' Blackie ventured. 'I can't wait. Do they go very fast?'

'No, no, they push along at a medium speed. You'll enjoy the ride. I know I always do.'

'How do they work, Uncle Pat?' Blackie, as usual, had the need to know how everything worked. He was a stickler for details, the more obscure the better. Even on the steamship over, despite the journey being cramped and often terrifying, he'd been figuring out how the ship operated.

'The trams run on tracks, on large metal wheels. And there

are two levels on some trams, downstairs and upstairs. It's an easy way to get into Leeds from Upper Armley, where we live now. Comfortable they are, too. The great thing is they all come continuously, one after another, with only about fifteen minutes in between.'

He broke off, pointed down the street and said, 'Here comes one now, Blackie. It's a good thing we didn't waste any time getting over here to the stop, didn't dawdle about.'

Within several seconds, the double-decker tram came to a stop and the two men got on. Blackie wanted to be on the upper deck and scrambled up. Patrick followed more slowly, smiling at the boy's excitement and enthusiasm.

Blackie was, quite simply, genuinely astonished as the tram started to move, at first gradually, then increasing its speed as it went along the city street.

Blackie turned to his uncle and asked, 'How do we pay our way?'

'There's an inspector. He punches a ticket and gives it to you, then takes the money.'

'Easy enough,' Blackie murmured. 'That was a brilliant idea, whoever thought of it.'

'Indeed,' Patrick answered, wondering about that himself for the first time. He'd have to be on his toes and have his wits about him when he was with his nephew. He was a mountain of knowledge already, and filled with questions.

Blackie fell silent, gazing out of the window, his eyes wide, as the tram ploughed through the grand new buildings and busy streets of the city centre, past streets crowded with small houses, past tall factory chimneys, and along to Upper Armley and their destination called Whingate Junction. When they finally got there, about half an hour later, it had grown darker. As Blackie stepped off, there weren't many buildings around as far as he could see.

'So much for a great metropolis,' he said in surprise, glancing at Patrick, a brow lifting. His suitcase was heavy now, banging against his leg.

'They're in the city,' Patrick shot back quickly. 'Upper Armley is something like a large village, with lots of parks and green fields . . .' He broke off, stopped walking and swung to his right. 'See that big field behind those railings?'

Following his uncle's gaze, Blackie nodded. 'I do, even though it's getting dark now. What field is that then?'

'It's a football field and it belongs to West Leeds High School for Boys. That's the school just down there. The big black stone building.'

Blackie peered ahead. 'Oh, I see it now.'

'And straight ahead of us is Charlie Cake Park—'

'What a funny name,' Blackie cut in. 'Who was Charlie Cake?'

Patrick chuckled. 'Nobody knows now. But it's said that years ago a man called Charlie sold cakes in the small park, and eventually everyone just called it that.'

'And what's that hut-like thing next to the park?'

'The police box, a sort of shelter for the copper on the beat. He can pop in there for a rest, or to shelter from the weather. Now, come on, my lad, here's Town Street. Let's get us home.'

Patrick and Blackie strode out, heading for the middle of Town Street. This was the main thoroughfare through Upper Armley. Both sides were lined with buildings; on one side, in the middle of the long street that stretched away, there were a few shops in between the houses and cottages. Lower down, Patrick told Blackie, it was filled with shops of all kinds, from the baker's to the ironmonger's, and saw his nephew soaking up all he could of this new home.

Walking swiftly though they were, Patrick started to talk to Blackie as they approached his home. He began, 'Your aunt isn't quite like she used to be, lad. She took a really bad cold in February, and it lingered, turned to bronchitis, which did her in a bit. The doctor was careful with her. Afraid of consumption, you see. Such a dreaded disease—'

'Is she all right though?' Blackie asked, anxious.

'She's better, Blackie. Much, much better. The doctor put her in St Mary's Hospital at Hill Top, that's just above Whingate Junction, where the tram turns around to go back into Leeds. Anyway, Dr Robinson kept her in for ten days, and when she got home she was practically better. Now she's really well, but she's not as strong on her feet, not as vibrant as she used to be.'

'Oh, I'm sorry. I won't be any trouble, Uncle Pat.'

'Goodness me, lad, I know that, and so does your aunt. I was trying to explain to you that she isn't as vital these days.'

'I'll be careful, not rowdy, ye know, Uncle Pat.'

'She's looking forward to you coming to stay, Blackie, and I think your presence will cheer her up.'

There were plenty of tall streetlamps lining the sides of Town Street and, at once, Blackie noticed what a pleasant road it was. The houses were small and stood close together, but the windows were gleaming clean and had white lace curtains, oil lamps casting a yellow glow out into the twilight. It gave him a good feeling. Armley looked nothing like his own local town. Many of the houses looked newly built and there was an order and sense of prosperity with the shops they'd passed, suggesting you could buy most things locally.

When they came to a larger house behind a locked door and tall walls, Blackie looked at his uncle, and asked, 'What sort of place is this? Do the gentry live there?'

Patrick shook his head. 'Lift your eyes and look a bit further down, and you'll see the sign. It has a name on it.'

Blackie did as he was told and read out loud, '*Northcote*

Private School for Girls.' Glancing at Patrick, he laughed and then said, 'It might not be a house but it's certainly *grand.*' He emphasized this last word, and remarked, 'A school for the local gentry, I suppose.'

Patrick said, 'A posh school for the children of the families who are better off, but I wouldn't call 'em *gentry*. More like well-to-do businessmen and the like.'

A moment later, Patrick explained, 'Well, here we are . . . this is my house, Blackie.'

Patrick walked up the three steps to a narrow house and opened the door. 'Here we are, we're home, Eileen!' he called out as he went in. Blackie was behind him.

Eileen was sitting by the fireplace in the small parlour, which had a comfortable and welcoming feeling about it.

She immediately stood up at the sound of her husband's voice, and walked across to greet him and also Blackie, smiling at them.

Her amazement shone on her face as she looked up at her nephew and, in one fell swoop, took everything in. '*You've* certainly grown up since I saw you five years ago!' she exclaimed. She stepped closer and gave him a hug. 'And you're so tall.'

Blackie hugged her back and realized at once how narrow she was, and thin. When he finally released her, he looked down at her, smiling broadly. 'It's a joy to see ye again, Aunt Eileen.'

As he spoke he felt a small surge of relief. Her face was thinner, but she was still a beautiful woman, Black Irish beautiful, without a wrinkle on her smooth face or a white hair in her dark head. But he'd felt her bones when he had held her close. She, who had been so robust, had lost weight. Of course, she had been ill, and she had probably lost her appetite.

'Let's not stand around here,' Eileen said, smiling up at Patrick, adoration reflected on her face. 'Why don't you take Blackie upstairs to his room, Patrick? And I'll go and look in the oven. It's time for tea.'

Pulling her to him, kissing her cheek, smoothing her jet-black hair with one hand, her husband smiled. His love for her flooded his blue eyes. 'I'll do that, my sweetheart, and what's for tea? We haven't eaten all day, except for the ham sandwiches.'

'Then I'll have it ready in a jiffy. You must be ravenous.'

'I can't wait!' Patrick picked up Blackie's suitcase and said, 'See yon door, on the left, Blackie? Open it and go upstairs. That's the bedroom floor above us.'

Blackie did as he was told, and bounded up the narrow stairs, which were actually covered in a patterned runner held down with brass rods. At the top he stood on a cramped landing, waiting for his uncle to arrive.

'This is your room,' Patrick announced a moment later, opening a door. It was a small room, but Blackie liked it at once. There was a single bed along one wall, a chest of drawers against another, a rag rug on the wooden floor and a small polished desk under the window. It gleamed in the light of the gas lamp on the wall, and caught Blackie's eye.

'I can see you like the room,' his uncle said, and placed the suitcase on the bed. 'This door opens on a cupboard,' Patrick explained. 'And your boots can go on the floor in there as well. I think you've plenty of space for your belongings, don't you?'

'Oh, I do, I do, Uncle Pat. Lots. I don't own much, ye know,' he confided and sounded rueful as he spoke.

'You're only thirteen, Blackie. I didn't own much at your age either.' Walking over to the window, Patrick smoothed his hand over the desk. 'I noticed you were impressed with this piece,' he said. 'It shines in this way, looks extra glossy because it's been French polished. That's a special method I will teach you later on.'

'It does look nice, Uncle Pat. And thank ye for everything.' For once, words failed him.

'Pleasure, lad. Now, tucked in here is a lavatory and a bath.'
He went out of the room.

Blackie sounded surprised when he said, 'I'm used to an outhouse.' He followed his uncle as he spoke.

'Everyone is, and I decided I would take a narrow slice out of that room . . .' Patrick stepped forward on the landing and opened a door. 'I did the work in here myself, including the plumbing, all of it. So we are comfortable now, and there's no reason for an outhouse.'

Blackie went inside, guided by Patrick, made a mental note of everything he saw and grinned. 'What a luxury,' he murmured. 'Well, life is full of surprises.'

Patrick chuckled. 'Wash up, Blackie, and then come on downstairs. Don't be unpacking now. You can do it later.'

EIGHT

'I'm not a fancy cook,' Eileen confided to Blackie when he peered into the small kitchen behind the parlour. 'But I try to make my specialities tasty.'

'Food has been hard to come by lately, Aunt Eileen, so I'll enjoy every mouthful.' Blackie glanced at the cottage pie on the table near the sink, then looked at her. He grinned, and breathed in the lovely aromas in the kitchen. 'And I think ye've made something with apples, haven't ye? I smell apples.'

'I concocted an apple-and-blackberry stew, which I'll serve with Bird's Custard. How does that sound?'

Before Blackie could respond, Patrick said, 'A feast fit for kings, Eileen.' Blackie turned and saw his uncle leaning against the doorjamb nonchalantly.

'I love me room, Uncle Pat,' Blackie exclaimed, his genuineness echoing in his voice. 'Thank ye, and do ye know it's the first room I've ever had just for meself.'

'I thought it would suit.' Patrick smiled at his nephew, and then cast his glance on his wife, as usual concerned for her. 'I see you've set the table, Eileen, so can we carry in the food, pet?'

'It would be a great help.'

'So go on, Blackie lad . . . Eileen, give me some pot-holders.'

The two men were deft with the dishes and placed them on the table under the window. Eileen followed with the gravy boat. She served them all good portions and told them to handle the gravy themselves.

Blackie decided her *simple* dish, as she had just called it, was delicious; he wolfed it down and was soon ready for a second helping. He couldn't believe there was enough food for the three of them and worried about whether there would be more the next day.

Patrick and Eileen exchanged glances from time to time. Everyone ate in silence, except for the occasional murmur of pleasure as they savoured the food.

Once the tea was over and all the dishes cleared and washed, the three of them sat around the fire. It was still cool weather, and the flames took the chill off the evening. Blackie felt his eyelids becoming heavy as the three of them relaxed in the main room drinking cups of tea. It was Patrick who broke the silence.

'Tomorrow, I thought I should take you around Upper Armley, show you the neighbourhood. Then, on Saturday, we can take the tram into Leeds. How does that sound, lad?'

Blackie sat up. 'I'd like that, Uncle Pat, and certainly the visit to Leeds . . . the Great Metropolis! I've dreamed of going there ever since the chance of living with ye both was talked about, on the heads of the Blessed Saints, I swear I have.'

'We are happy to have you,' Eileen said, meaning every word. She was well aware Patrick had always wanted a son. A small sigh was smothered as she thought of her two miscarriages, her inability to give her husband the children he had craved. A wonderful, loving man she adored, who filled her heart with joy.

Unexpectedly, Eileen remembered something and sat up straighter in her chair. 'Oh goodness, Pat! I forgot to tell you—'

'What did you forget?' he asked mildly.

'The message from Mrs Burton. She has another job for you, the windows over her garden. The sashes have gone.'

'Oh, to be sure, I don't want to go back there again. I've had it with that house. Do you have the note?'

Eileen said, 'She didn't send a note. She sent her housekeeper, Jeannie Gregson, who explained about the windows.'

Patrick stiffened and looked at Eileen swiftly, but she had not noticed. He attempted to keep a bland expression when he said, 'I suppose I shall have to go around there, but it can wait until Monday. I want us all to enjoy Blackie's first weekend here.'

Patrick Kennedy was unable to fall asleep. He lay on his right side, wide awake, staring at the window. The message from Mrs Burton had surprised him, filled him with alarm. Mrs Burton herself was a fine woman and a good customer. He had been pleased to win her custom. It was her housekeeper Jeannie Gregson he could not abide and hoped never to see again.

She had come after him, thrown herself at him from the first moment they had met. He considered her to be wanton and dangerous, and had always avoided contact with her when working at the house.

Yet there were moments when she would, suddenly, be right next to him, brushing up against him, touching his shoulder or his arm, offering him tea, water, a glass of beer. As if he would actually drink on the job in his client's house. The woman was a fool.

When he knew she was not aware of his presence nearby, he watched her, in particular her behaviour with the other workmen employed by Mrs Burton. Jeannie Gregson was not the same with them. She was remote and had no interest. It was him she was after. So, therefore, he must avoid her at all costs.

Suddenly, his whirling thoughts settled on his nephew. Under no circumstances could she meet Blackie. Firstly, he was a good-looking young boy at thirteen, and that was the inherent problem. Secondly, he looked older, about sixteen, even seventeen, and had an extremely confident manner. These things would make him bait for a woman like Jeannie Gregson.

He knew instantly that he would not accept the job. He hated to turn work down, never trusting where the next penny would come from, but he had plenty on at the moment, and he certainly wasn't going to take Blackie to Mrs Burton's house, expose him to that vulture.

On Monday morning he would write a note to Mrs Burton, telling her he was booked up for months on end. He would send Benny, one of his apprentices, with the note.

Patrick breathed a sigh of relief and settled more easily in the bed. At one moment, he pushed himself up on an elbow and peered at Eileen. In the dim light of the room, he could see she was fast asleep. This further calmed him; he worried a lot about her health and watched her constantly because of her frailty.

Patrick Michael Kennedy was aware of his Irish good looks and that women were immediately drawn to him. He even knew he had a certain kind of charisma which was quite unique.

Yet for all that, he was not vain. He was not a philanderer, nor had he ever taken advantage of women. In fact, he loved Eileen very much and was devoted to her.

Other women he met, when he was out and about and working, held no interest for him. His wife was *it*, and no one else mattered. Except for his newly arrived nephew. Blackie had always been special to him, and after the heartbreak of his sister and her husband dying, and then their poor children William and Bronagh as well, he was thrilled to have been able to bring Blackie to Leeds.

Blackie would be his helper and his heir to the business; he would be company for him, too, and also for Eileen. At last they would be a little family . . . only the three of them, but a family, nonetheless. They were bound together by blood and the past and their ancestry.

By nature, Patrick was a gentle man, kind, thoughtful and compassionate, and always concerned for others. The navy meant a lot to him. He still recalled that day he had gone to the recruiting office in Leeds and joined up. He had wanted to be a sailor for as long as he could remember, and was proud of himself and of his uniform when he had enlisted. He was just sixteen years old. Too young to join, so he forged his father's signature.

The first day he was on duty, he knew he had made the right choice. He loved the discipline, the daily regime, and the camaraderie of his fellow ratings. He found he enjoyed the company of men and worked well with them. He was truly devoted to the drills, the various daily routines, and in general the running of a huge battleship. It took hundreds and hundreds of men like him to properly cope with such an enormous vessel.

He would always recall going up the gangplank, carrying his kitbag and pausing momentarily on that first day. His eyes had lighted on a brass plaque on the wall ahead of him – the words on it: FEAR GOD. HONOUR THE KING. A cold shiver had run through him and settled in his heart, underscoring his patriotism and his desire to succeed. He had both ambition and drive, and fully intended to make the Royal Navy his career. He worked hard, and had focus, concentration and determination. These three characteristics had pushed him up the ladder at a fairly rapid speed.

He not only drew pleasure from his regime on a daily basis

but also appreciated the opportunities of a full education that were offered to him. He concentrated on his reading and writing, studied books on history and geography, and, of course, being clever, he soon improved his manners and way of speaking by observing the way the officers handled themselves. Genial, outgoing and pleasant, he made friends of his mates quite easily, and exercise through heavy work and good solid food kept him strong and in good shape. Patrick had become a highly rated naval man, which pleased him.

The only reason he had left it all behind was Eileen, and her need to have him by her side. Although it saddened him, he had never resented her for changing his life. He was too big a man for that and, after all, it had been his own decision in the end.

Across the landing, in the small bedroom, its occupant was also unable to sleep. Blackie was awake because of his great excitement about being here with his uncle at last, and because of the kind of comfort he was surrounded by. He couldn't get over it, simple as it was.

He had never been in a bed before. When his parents had been alive, he had always slept on a mattress on the floor in a corner, covered by an old blanket. He and his siblings shared two mattresses in a tiny bedroom. Afterwards, he and Michael had done the same in his cousins' two-room cottage; Siobhan had slept on an old cot in the main room.

Now, here he was, tucked up in a bed with a downy pillow, a mattress that seemed to cradle him, and a soft white sheet. He smoothed his hand over it once again. It felt like silk, but he knew it was cotton, often washed, and yet it was so white it was the colour of fresh snow.

On top of the sheet was a large red tartan blanket, which

Aunt Eileen had folded in half earlier, explaining, 'Doing this makes it feel like two blankets, and it's much warmer.'

He liked his aunt, and she had helped him to unpack his suitcase earlier and put his clothes away. He was a poor boy and didn't have much, although he had been unusually lucky this past week. Mrs O'Malley had given him the two jumpers she had knitted for him, as well as Dennis's old socks in a bag. Her ladyship had sent some cast-offs with Siobhan, which had included a nightshirt that fitted him. Michael had told him it had belonged to Lord Robert, who was tall like he was. Cook had given him the suitcase. Brand new, it was, her son's. He felt a flash of sadness again for her as he remembered Conor, killed in an accident in India.

Blackie's eyes roamed around the room, and he took in the lightly patterned wallpaper and the curtains at the window. He noticed the book on the shining desk, *French polished*, his uncle had said.

He smiled to himself. It was Father O'Donovan who had handed the book to him when he went to say goodbye to the old priest, who had christened him when he was born. It was his favourite book about the Tudors, and he had been touched by the gesture.

Those people stayed in his mind for a few moments. That monstrous king, Henry VIII, who thought nothing of killing off anyone who annoyed him, including two wives, many advisors, and even his greatest minister and truest friend, the great Thomas Cromwell, the Lord Privy Seal. He wasn't too enamoured with Mary Tudor either, who had become queen and had the bad habit of killing – her non-Catholic citizens were the victims. But, ah, there was the great Elizabeth, the queen of his delight, the best and the bravest. He loved to read about her.

As these thoughts of the Tudors slid through his busy head, he began to grow drowsy. Remembering the small candle, in the jam jar on the little table next to his bed, he leaned over and blew it out.

And then he pulled the tartan blanket up to his chin and drifted off, feeling as if he were cocooned in soft feathers. Sleep came easily this night, his first in a new country, a dreamless sleep with no nightmares.

NINE

'I thought our first stop should be my workshop,' Patrick Kennedy said, as he and Blackie walked up Town Street the following morning. 'It's not too far.'

'I'll enjoy seeing it, Uncle Pat, and I can't wait to start working there with ye.' His nephew was busy taking in his surroundings in daylight, his head turning to look around him as they walked.

Patrick nodded, gave him a wide smile, and said, 'Likewise, Blackie, and you're fast, have a bright mind, and you'll pick things up quickly – so I think, anyway.' There was a pause. Patrick pursed his lips and said, 'I hope that you had enough to eat for breakfast.' Eileen had commented on how thin the boy was.

Blackie nodded vehemently, and added, 'I had a good breakfast. Thanks, Uncle Pat.'

'Your aunt makes the bread, and it's always good,' Patrick told him. 'She helps out a little at the baker's shop in Town Street, making sponge cakes, pies and tarts. She has quite a talent for cooking and enjoys it. And she likes getting out a bit, going to the bakery.'

52

'I realized she's a good cook, sure and I did. The tea last night was the best meal I'd had in ages, except for the rabbit pies, o' course. They were a treat.'

'And when did you have them?' Patrick asked curiously, giving him a quick glance.

'A'fore I left Ireland. Ye see, Uncle Pat, Mrs O'Malley had two rabbits. Joe O'Donnell caught 'em and brought them to her. Even skinned 'em for her, that he did. And she made two pies.'

Blackie couldn't help laughing. 'If ever ye have an odd rabbit or two, Uncle, I'll make a pie for ye. Mrs O'Malley taught me how.'

'And you can knead the dough, can you?' A brow lifted questioningly.

Blackie laughed again. 'I believe I might need a bit of help, only too true.'

Patrick said, 'Aunt Eileen will teach you. It's not a big job. I look forward to a pie made by your hands. I'm sure it will be excellent.' There was a hint of amusement in his voice.

Continuing to walk up Town Street, Patrick explained, 'As I told you some time ago, I have two apprentices – Benny and Alf – for the repairs and building work, and one fully fledged carpenter, Tom. I am going to bring Alf on more in a few weeks, because he has become very skilled. I myself will train you, Blackie, and I will enjoy doing it.'

'I can't wait, and thank ye for . . . taking me into the business.'

'I promised your mother and, anyway, your aunt and I want you with us, Blackie lad. You're company, and well, family. Same blood. We've got to stick together, move up in the world together.'

'We do, we will,' Blackie asserted. He started to say something else, then stopped. After clearing his throat, he asked, 'How old were ye when you came to Leeds, Uncle Pat?'

'I was six and your mother was ten, four years older than

me. We'd only been here three years when our parents decided to return to Ireland. So they went, but they let me stay behind with my father's brother, Tim Kennedy. He didn't have any children, and he and his wife Kath loved me. They begged for me to remain with them.'

'And ye stayed, I know that. And glad about it, sure I am. Ye have been successful, and I bet Tim Kennedy was proud of ye, the way ye built up his company.'

'He was indeed! He trained me religiously, night and day, months on end, year in and year out. He never stopped instructing me. And that's how it's going to be with you, Blackie, and I hope you will also achieve your dream . . . of being a builder.'

Blackie looked at him in surprise. 'So ye remembered . . . that I want to build houses.'

'Sure an' I did, my boyo,' Patrick responded, allowing his Irish accent to surface. 'And here we are, at Tower Lane, and just ahead of us is my shop. It's part of this warehouse. Let's go inside, and you'll see for yourself.'

It was one large room, with a small office at the far end, and was filled with natural daylight. This came from the many windows on the two long side walls. Underneath some of the windows were workbenches, with tools on top.

Two young men occupied the room, and they turned around and stared at him for a moment. Blackie offered them his widest smile.

Patrick said, 'Morning, Benny, Alf. This is my nephew, Shane O'Neill, come to work with us here. And by the way, everyone calls him Blackie . . . Black Irish, as you can well see from his hair and his eyes.'

The two young men grinned, came forward and shook hands

with Blackie, and remembered, a split-second later, to greet their boss.

'Blackie will start on Monday,' Patrick explained. 'I just brought him in this morning to meet you and see the shop. Where's Tom? Over at Thompson's, I suppose.'

'Aye, he is, Mr Kennedy. He said ter tell yer he'll finish the final work on them doors by ternight,' Benny answered.

Patrick nodded and looked at Blackie. 'As you can see, the lads work at the benches for sanding and polishing the different woods.' As he spoke he beckoned to Blackie, and went on, 'I keep the planks down here. You can see they're different sizes and heights. We make a lot of tables and book-shelves at the moment, oh, and headboards for beds and matching chests.'

'It sounds as if the business is thriving,' Blackie said, realizing there were various pieces of unfinished furniture in the ware-house. 'I think I might have come just at the right time.'

His uncle merely smiled and walked him down to the end of the room. Opening a door, Patrick said, 'I work in here, keep the books, do the paperwork when I'm not at my carpentry.'

He moved on, opened the next door, and said, 'This is where Tom does his drafts of the special pieces he makes. You can learn a lot from him, Blackie. He's a good draughtsman. The last office belongs to my Uncle Tim. He comes in a couple of times a week. He's not got much to do since he retired, and it makes him feel good to be here with us, still part of it in a sense. I'll take you to meet him on Sunday.'

'I bet he's proud of ye, Uncle Pat, the way ye've built his business up, ever since ye were a little lad—'

'Not quite,' Patrick cut in. 'I was away for a while, remember? In the navy. I didn't start to change a few things and encourage him to go into building until I left the military. But, you know, he was always willing and enthusiastic, whatever ideas I came up with, even when he muttered that they sounded newfangled to him.'

A short while later, Patrick and Blackie left the workshop and walked down through the nearby streets. 'I want to show you a bit of Upper Armley,' Patrick explained, as they headed towards another main thoroughfare called Ridge Road.

It was a wide road. On one side was the Co-operative, a large grocery shop with many branches. His uncle explained that everyone used it on a daily basis, since the prices were excellent, and bonuses were given in the form of stamps to buy extra foodstuffs.

'I come here to do the heavy shopping for your Aunt Eileen,' Patrick said as they entered the large, well-stocked shop. 'I get the heavier items . . . like dried goods, canned food, that sort of thing.'

Blackie simply nodded, his eyes wide with surprise at the produce on display. He'd never seen so much food in his life.

After leaving the Co-op, as Patrick called it, they went down Ridge Road, going in the opposite direction from Town Street.

'So where does this road go?' Blackie asked, as usual full of curiosity.

'The main road at the end, which is where we are heading, is called Stanningley Road, and it goes up to Bramley, Farsley, and ends in the City of Bradford. But the reason I'm taking you there is because you'll see some nice houses around this area, and also Gotts Park. That's a nice spot, and on Sunday, a big band plays in the afternoon. We go to listen, or to Armley Park, where there's a band also.'

'A band in a park!' Blackie sounded astonished.

Patrick grinned. 'Oh, there are a lot of things happening in

Upper Armley, my lad. It's a busy place. Dances at the dance hall on Saturday nights, plays at the church hall, and twice a year the Feast comes.'

'Whatever is that, Uncle Pat?'

Patrick chuckled. 'Too hard to explain. However, I think it'll be coming next week, and your aunt and I will certainly take you. We'll all have a bit of fun, the likes of which you've never had.'

Eileen Kennedy was humming under her breath as she stood at the kitchen counter preparing dinner, glad she was feeling better and not so tired. She enjoyed cooking as well as baking, and, most especially, when she was preparing something for her husband.

She had adored Patrick since she was twelve and he was fourteen, and she had made up her mind to marry him at that time. As for Patrick, he had liked her a lot, enjoyed her company. But he hadn't really fallen in love with her until he was fifteen, a year before he had joined the Royal Navy. She had not attempted to dissuade him from enlisting, fully understanding he would pursue his childhood dream no matter what.

Patience, she kept telling herself in those early days of their relationship. And being loyal and supportive had paid off. Three years after becoming a sailor, he had proposed to her and she had accepted. He had fulfilled his dreams of being a naval man, and she had realized her own by becoming his wife.

A little sigh escaped as she mashed the potatoes, thinking of his disappointment in not having children, and the miscarriages she'd had. But her idea of bringing Blackie over to live with them had been accepted by Patrick, and enthusiastically so. Now the boy was here with them, and Patrick hadn't stopped smiling since his arrival.

As she opened the oven to put the bowl of mashed potatoes inside, she couldn't help thinking what a lovely boy he was. 'Boy' was hardly the word to describe Blackie O'Neill. Tall and broad like Patrick, he looked older and acted older. But then perhaps that was because he'd had a lot of responsibility in his family, looking after them in the face of extreme poverty and hunger, and nursing his sister, Bronagh, until her untimely death.

Faith, and wasn't it a pity Bronagh had not managed to find her strength again, to go on living after catching a bout of scarlet fever. Only seventeen when she died, more's the pity, Eileen thought, sadness filling her face. Life is hard, unsupportable sometimes, but we have to live what we are given.

And God doesn't give us a burden we're too weak to carry. At least that's what my mother believes. Oh, and I suppose so do I, Eileen admitted to herself.

Eileen went into the small larder and took out the package of pork sausages wrapped in greaseproof paper. There were four, one for each of them, and the fourth she would cut in half for Patrick and Blackie.

Placing a small pat of butter in the frying pan, she opened the packet of sausages. She pricked them with a fork all over so they wouldn't burst, and put them in to cook. Once they had begun to brown, she placed the chopped onions next to them. Sausage and mash for dinner, a favourite dish of her husband's, which he ate with relish. She thought Blackie would enjoy it too.

A moment later, she heard the front door open and close, and as she moved forward, Patrick put his head around the kitchen door.

'We're back,' he said, smiling at her. 'And famished. And doesn't everything smell good.'

'Sausage and mash,' Eileen murmured and, noticing Blackie

hovering behind Pat, she nodded. 'There you are, Blackie. I bet he's walked you all over Upper Armley.'

Blackie grinned. 'And back again, and I swear on the heads of the Blessed Saints that I've never seen a nicer place. I'm going to like living here, Aunt Eileen, sure and I am.'

TEN

Like all poor, working-class folk, Blackie O'Neill was always preoccupied with food at some time or other during the day, with no exception.

His belly rumbled and he felt the first hunger pangs begin around noon or twelve-thirty – the time of the midday meal, which he and everyone he knew referred to as dinner, but Cook at the big house and the Lassiters called lunch or luncheon. However, no matter what it was called, it was usually the main meal of the day. He and his cousins were convinced that only the aristocracy indulged themselves dining in the evening as well, with Cook working all day sometimes on different courses, or even another meal called supper.

In a sense, Blackie had been lucky. Growing up in North Kerry, there had never been enough to eat for any of them, but he had had several benefactors who had small titbits to give him – Mrs O'Malley and Cook from Lord Lassiter's mansion at the top of the hill. His cousin Siobhan sometimes brought something home with her, sent by the generous cook. Even before Blackie lived with his cousins, Siobhan had tried to share food with his family, much to his sister's gratitude. Bronagh was unwell for a while and did not have a big appetite, but he was much relieved when she managed to eat something, and he could see that she had enjoyed it.

Now, on this cool Friday afternoon, he was seated at the table in Uncle Patrick's parlour, where for the first time in his life it appeared that food was plentiful. His uncle was in the tiny kitchen with Aunt Eileen. The two of them were putting food on the three plates. Blackie's nose twitched at the delicious smells emanating from the kitchen. His mouth watered, and he could hardly wait to eat.

Then there it was, the plate being placed in front of him by his aunt, who said, 'Tuck in, Blackie. I hope you'll enjoy it.'

'Oh, I will, Aunt Eileen, sure and I will. My mouth is watering already.'

Eileen smiled as she sat down next to him, and then accepted her own plate from her husband. Patrick returned with a jug of gravy, which he placed in the middle of the table. Looking at his nephew, he said, 'There are more potatoes and onions in the oven, if you want a second helping, lad.'

'Thanks, Uncle Pat, and ye too, Aunt,' he answered and picked up his knife and fork. With a small and rather shy smile for him, he said, 'I've only ever had sausage once before. What is it made of, Aunt Eileen?'

Startled though she was to hear this, she said quickly, 'Minced-up pork, that's pushed into a thin skin. So it's called pork sausage, but there is beef sausage, too. They make a tasty meal like this with onions, mashed potatoes and gravy. *That* does give it a really special flavour.'

Blackie nodded and munched on the sausage, savouring it, his face filled with happiness. He went on eating, but slowly, trying to be polite, not putting too much into his mouth at once. Oh yes, he decided, I'll have this any time my aunt makes it . . . she's the best cook in the world.

The three of them were all hungry and, although they ate carefully, not wanting to look greedy to finish and have seconds, they were mostly silent. It just so happened they were lost in their own thoughts, preoccupied.

Patrick was reminding himself to go to the workshop after dinner to pay the men their wages for the week. He also needed to write that note to Mrs Burton, to tell her he couldn't mend her window sashes. *That* was most important. He had to avoid the housekeeper.

Eileen was wondering how Blackie had managed to stay healthy and grow tall when he had lived in Ireland. It was obvious to her he had had more food than some because of his height and build, and yet in the two days he had been here, he had always appeared to be very hungry. It struck her then that he'd probably filled up on cheap staples like potatoes, bread, and . . . bread . . . and more bread. That seemed to be the main food of the truly poor. A chunk of bread and a trickle of jam or treacle, and water.

She had been born in North Kerry herself, but she had been brought to Leeds by her parents when she was only two years old. Her father, Mike Loughlin, and her mother, Dervla, had gone to Yorkshire, and to Leeds specifically, to work alongside Mike's elder brother, Cornelius, known to most as Con, or Connie. He had left Ireland years before and had been trained as a mechanical engineer.

Eventually he had opened his own small shop and done well. He was a glutton for work, had immense concentration, focus and strength. He had never married, because he had never met the right girl, even though he was a bit of a womanizer and genuinely *liked* girls.

Yet true love had eluded him. Still, he enjoyed his bachelor life, was gregarious and generous, and helped his brother to become successful by having him also train as an engineer.

Eventually Connie had made Mike his partner in the machine shop.

Eileen, her mind whirling with thoughts of her family, realized at that precise moment that the Loughlins had had luck on their side. She also knew, deep down inside, that her Uncle Connie had always had a soft spot for her. Perhaps even a yen. She let *that* peculiar thought slide away and buried it.

Blackie slowed down, began to eat the last few mouthfuls a little less quickly. He had loved the meal. It had been a feast, but he had cleared his plate before his aunt and uncle. He glanced at Eileen surreptitiously, thinking how kind she was in the way she had divided the fourth sausage between his uncle and himself. She was a good woman.

He switched his thoughts to the following day. *Saturday.* Tomorrow Uncle Patrick was taking him to Leeds to have 'the grand tour', as Uncle Pat had called it. In 1893, six years ago, Leeds had been named a city, because of its size, its growing industries, shopping arcades, tram system, parks and its cathedral. Blackie thought of the other cathedral he wanted to see for himself one day. It was in York, and it was very, very old . . . maybe almost eight hundred years old. The pictures he had seen of it had captivated him. He would go, he promised himself, when he was rich.

Blackie sat at the desk in his bedroom, painstakingly writing letters. He had promised to let his cousins know he had arrived safely, as well as Mrs O'Malley and Cook.

In her thoughtful way, Siobhan had given him a packet of notepaper and envelopes when he was packing to leave, plus a sixpenny bit 'for the stamps', she had explained.

Once the short letters were finished, notes really, he sat back in the chair, glancing around the room. It *was* small, there were no two ways about that, but he could not get over the wonderful thing of the privacy . . . he didn't have to share it. And despite its small size, it had plenty of space for his few clothes, his only possessions, except for his book about the Tudors, given to him by Father O'Donovan before he had left North Kerry. He truly treasured that.

During their walk around Upper Armley, earlier in the day, Patrick had pointed out Armley Library and told him how he could get a library card so that he could take out books to read. Blackie, with his usual string of questions, knew all about the library system in a few minutes. He couldn't wait to join. The thought of shelves filled with hundreds of books thrilled him no end. He was certain he would find some about architecture and engineering, history and maybe even building work. He couldn't get enough of them.

He felt full for once and relaxed. Walking across the room in two strides, he lay down on the bed, sighing with pleasure at the feeling of comfort this gave him. He was warm enough and he couldn't believe his luck.

Well, here he was at last, in Leeds with Uncle Pat, and all set and ready to go. *On Monday morning.* He was happy. Work appealed to him. He enjoyed being busy, and he knew he was lucky to have a relative who was willing to take him into his business as an apprentice and also let him share his home.

Although the house on Town Street was small and simply furnished, it was neat and clean, and had an air of welcome about it.

He had a lot of admiration for his uncle, not only for the things he had done and had achieved, but also the way he carried himself, his good manners, and his inherent kindness. In certain ways he reminded Blackie of his mother. This was partially to do with his colouring, the blond-reddish hair, and his handsome looks . . . Blackie thought his mother had been a female copy of Uncle Pat. He knew he got his Black Irish looks from his father's side of the family, not the Kennedys. Thinking of his mother provoked a familiar wave of grief: he was alone in the world. But now he had his uncle and this new chance at a better life.

His thoughts suddenly ran amok and finally settled on the future. He knew he would be trained as an apprentice first, but when would he start working as a navvy? He thought that would be the second step. That was the work that drew so many men from Ireland.

His uncle had told him ages ago that building canals and railways was a tough job, and he wouldn't consider it until he, Blackie, was older. They would obviously be embarking on this stage of his training in a couple of years, seemingly because of the *money*.

Blackie smiled inwardly, realizing – when he thought of making money – that that particular word was always writ large, in capital letters, in his mind.

Building. That was what he aimed to do one day. Building beautiful houses for those who wanted one and could afford it. It was *his* dream, and he would strive to make it come true.

ELEVEN

I f Upper Armley had charmed Blackie with its country-village appearance, then the city of Leeds bowled him over with its splendour.

On Saturday morning, Blackie and his Uncle Patrick took a tram into Leeds, alighting in City Square, and walked over to the centre of it.

Blackie was much taken with this paved area, triangular in shape, where six roads met. His uncle, glancing around, immediately explained, 'Park Row and Wellington Street, which go east and south, are joined by Infirmary Street, Boar Lane and Bishopsgate Street to the south-east, and Quebec Street is to the south-west. And that big building across there is the new General Post Office, built in 1896. And it was the Lord Mayor of Leeds in 1898 who commissioned William Bakewell to design the square in the style of an Italian piazza, and he did, adding the trees and shrubs. It looks nice, don't you think?'

'I do!' Blackie exclaimed.

Patrick now continued, 'Let's head up to the Town Hall. I do want you to see that, and other places along the way.'

'Oh, yes! Let's go.' Blackie's eyes swept around, taking everything in. He felt as if the buildings had wrapped themselves around him as he moved past them, holding him close. Big buildings, beautiful buildings – the kind he admired. Now he understood why it was always referred to as a great metropolis. It was unlike anything he had seen before, much larger than he had expected and bristling with excitement. He'd never seen so many people, men and women in smart clothes thronging the streets, trams rattling past, prancing horses and fine carriages everywhere he looked and grand buildings as far as his eye could see. The noise was overwhelming, with shouts from the hansom cab drivers, vehicles clattering past and the unfamiliar sound of Yorkshire accents all around.

This was the greatest industrial city of the north, thrilling to him because it was so . . . *spectacular*. There was no other word. He wanted to stroll through every street and see all the sights, take everything in with a big gulp, swallow it whole.

Blackie's eyes were filled with wonder; he was all agog and remained startled by what he saw. Great arcades, with cast-iron and timber trusses supporting dramatic glass roofs, marble-tiled passageways underfoot, were filled with shops overflowing with beautiful things, from dresses and shoes to jewellery and furniture. Elegant women dressed in expensive silks bustled along the passageways gazing into shops through gleaming plate-glass windows, or pushed open the doors to restaurants where, his uncle told him, fancy meals were served every day. Uncle Pat confided there were dance halls, theatres, and a music hall called the City Varieties and, on Fridays and Saturdays, the city was filled with folk out to enjoy themselves, which they did.

At one moment he thought: This is the city for me. I'm going to make it mine. And although he did not know it for certain that day, he would indeed do exactly that eventually, later in his life.

The Town Hall brought him to a stop. He stood staring up at it in total astonishment. It was enormous, made of black stone, built in the Corinthian style, with many steps going up to its wide terrace. And keeping guard were beautifully sculpted lions stretched out on the huge wide ledges, also in black stone. The thing was, the lions looked real, which surprised him. Momentarily, Blackie was speechless, and when, finally, he found his voice, he said, 'What happens inside there, Uncle Pat? In the Town Hall?'

'Lots of things, lad. City business, meetings of city councillors, the courts of law, judges' chambers . . .' Patrick nodded. 'It's a very busy place, you know, full of serious people doing . . . serious things.'

Blackie just nodded, again his eyes still searching around eagerly, missing nothing. He felt an unexpected rush of warmth, knew all of a sudden that it was a sense of pleasure he was feeling, an emotion he had rarely ever experienced in his impoverished young life. And that feeling gave him comfort, and so did the buildings.

To Patrick's surprise, Blackie was somewhat quiet on the tram going back to Upper Armley. Usually talkative, exceedingly so at times, he had lapsed into silence for a while, and as the tram rolled on, he appeared to fall down into himself. There was a thoughtful expression on his face. Silence reigned.

Patrick settled back in the seat, reached into his jacket pocket, and took out a folded piece of newspaper. He began to read it, seeking information about York races. It was the *Racing Form*, and he studied it every day. Too late now to place a bet on a horse; nonetheless, he read on, mentally checking off the good horses from the list. He loved horses and the racetrack.

Blackie was filled with thoughts of Leeds, the city, its people, and the extraordinary buildings he had seen. They were powerful, and, to him, stunningly beautiful. He couldn't wait to come back another day and study them at his leisure. But that would have to be next Saturday. A thought suddenly struck him, and he swung his dark head to look at his uncle. He asked, 'Is the shop usually open on Saturday? I mean, the workshop.'

Patrick glanced at his nephew, shook his head. 'No, I think the men deserve to have a rest on Saturdays and Sundays. They usually have things to attend to at home. Anyway, I certainly get caught up in chores, and I want a rest away from the toil myself.' His focus remained on Blackie. 'Why did *you* want to know?'

'Because I was thinking I need to come back to Leeds as soon as possible. I'm sure there's a lot more to see, and I swear on the heads of the Blessed Saints that it is the city of me dreams. Sure and it is, Uncle Pat.'

'I've no doubt, lad,' Patrick said. 'And there are many more buildings to see, and shops, and I'm certain you want to make another visit to the covered market.'

'Oh, I do, I do, and thank you for the treat, Uncle. I loved the cockles and mussels. I think that stall will become a favourite of mine. I never thought you could have so many stalls under one roof, selling so many different things.'

'I enjoy shellfish.' Patrick grinned at Blackie. 'And I thought you might be getting a bit peckish, just as I was.'

'I was. I still am, a bit,' he admitted.

'Ah never mind, we'll soon be home,' Patrick answered.

Eileen was hovering over the pans in the small kitchen when Patrick and Blackie came walking into the little house on Town Street a short while later.

Patrick swept into the kitchen at once and gave her a warm hug and a kiss on the cheek. She smiled up at him, her love for him always so apparent, shining on her face.

Turning to Blackie, she squeezed his arm, smiling at him. 'Have you enjoyed yourself in Leeds?'

'Oh, I have, sure and I have, Aunt Eileen, and 'tis mighty impressed I am, and ready to rush right back. 'Tis the Town Hall that impressed me the most, Aunt, and City Square. Oh, and the open market. What a treasure trove that is, filled with stalls selling everything from food to clothes and shoes and even bikes! I was *amazed*, that I was!'

He was so voluble and excited, Eileen couldn't help laughing, glad he'd enjoyed the trip.

Blackie confided, 'I am going back there next Saturday. Would ye like to come?'

'I think I might,' she answered somewhat gleefully.

Patrick, still consumed by his *Racing Form*, glanced at her, his attention caught. 'Well, I never thought I'd hear *you* say that. Eileen going to go shopping in the market – that's something for the books.' Laughter echoed in his words as he threw her an affectionate look.

She was laughing herself, and then turned her attention to the pans. 'Dinner's ready. Go and wash up, and then I'll serve.'

The two men left, and Eileen stirred the soup, poked a fork in the carrots and potatoes to check if they were cooked. Yes, they were ready, she knew that. Opening the oven door, she looked at the pie. That needed a few more minutes. Her timing was spot on.

Moving into the parlour, she checked the table she had set earlier. Everything was in its place. Swinging around she went to the kitchen counter and began to slice a loaf of freshly baked bread.

For Blackie, these dinners Eileen made were truly a treat. As he sipped the soup, he marvelled at it. It was flavourful and brimming with carrots, potatoes, parsnips and shallots. The bread was soft, warm and delicious.

Blackie tried to slow himself down, began to eat the soup in small spoonfuls, realizing his aunt and uncle ate less quickly than he did. He felt embarrassed by the way he attacked the food, gobbled it almost.

A few minutes later, Eileen said, 'There's plenty of soup, Blackie love, if you want another bowl.'

'Oh no, thanks, Aunt Eileen, I'm doing well,' he answered swiftly, and put his spoon down, his embarrassment lingering.

'What's in the oven?' Patrick asked curiously.

'Bacon-and-egg pie,' his wife responded. To her nephew she said, 'Do you like that dish?'

Blackie glanced at her and admitted, with a small smile, 'I've never had it before, but since ye're the best cook I know, sure and ye are, I'm certain I'll enjoy it.'

And he did. He also devoured the chunky stewed apples, which Eileen brought out after the bacon-and-egg pie. At one moment, he said, with great sincerity, 'I've never had a dinner like this in my life. Thank you.'

Patrick and Eileen exchanged knowing looks, understanding that he had gone hungry for most of his life. Eileen's food was simple, even plain, but it was like a feast to him. Her style of cooking became his favourite kind of meal, and for him it surpassed the fancy dishes served to him in the world's gourmet restaurants later in his life.

At the end of that day, as his aunt sewed by the fire and his Uncle Pat studied the paper, Blackie knew his luck had once again saved him. Here in Leeds was the opportunity he had dreamed of, to work hard and build a new life. In his uncle's face he saw echoes of his mother's, and was grateful for the bond that had endured, even after they were separated as children. The love between a brother and sister, two people with the best hearts he knew, was the reason his uncle had offered him a home now. He would always be grateful.

Gratitude and memories of his family were in his heart, but in his mind too was his dream of being a builder one day. And he *would* make his dream come true. That was a promise to himself – and to his uncle, silently, too. He might not have a mam or da, but he would make his uncle proud.

PART TWO

Dreams Come First
Leeds, England
1903

TWELVE

When Patrick Kennedy stepped out of his house on Town Street, he automatically looked up at the sky as he usually did.

Today he smiled. This was just the kind of weather he loved: a clear blue sky, no clouds, and the pristine northern light shining down, with a promise of sunshine later in the day. He'd left Ireland when he was six and he was every inch a proud Yorkshireman now.

There was a spring in his step as he headed up the street, making for Tower Lane. When he came to the corner shop, he went in, greeted Mr Brill behind the counter, picked up the racing paper and the *Daily Mail*, and paid. Tucking them under his arm, he went out of the shop and continued on up Town Street.

It was Friday 5 June, in the Year of Our Lord 1903. Three years into the brand-new twentieth century, one which had brought with it better days. At least, so far for him and his little family, including Blackie, who had made his home with himself and his wife Eileen for four years now.

It seemed to Patrick that things had never been brighter in

the country as a whole. England was at its zenith, the greatest empire in existence, perhaps even the greatest *ever*. And while London, the capital, was the centre of everything that was exciting, where it was said anything at all could be achieved, Patrick also believed Leeds could lay claim to be the second greatest city in the country.

The old Queen Empress had died in 1901, after the longest reign of any monarch wearing the English crown, an amazing feat by any standards, although she had been long absent, living in Scotland.

The Prince of Wales was now King Edward VII and, contrary to what had been expected, it looked as if he was good at his job. The newspapers appeared to think that anyway. He hoped they were right.

There was peace in the world now that the Boer War was over. England had lost many men in the fighting in South Africa, but a lot had made it home, much to Patrick's relief. As a former military man, he cared about the veterans who had come back to start new lives after service for their country.

Patrick sighed to himself, thinking of his days in the Royal Navy. Sometimes he still missed being in a ship at sea, serving his King and country. He had liked that orderly life of duty, discipline and dedication, a sense of purpose. It suited his character.

Unexpectedly, his thoughts swung to the prime minister, who was not popular with everyone. Yet he himself had a certain amount of faith in Arthur Balfour. Even so, he wondered how the King got on with him.

His friend, Jack Blane, read more newspapers than he did, and Jack was behind Balfour's policies. Jack also believed the ageing Salisbury was definitely too old now to lead the country. New blood was needed, he said. But Jack had also suggested that Balfour and the King did not complement one another . . .

Turning into Tower Lane, Patrick was unlocking the door of his workshop a few minutes later. It was filled with natural daylight, and he nodded as he glanced at the workbenches. The lads had cleaned up well last night. Everything looked pristine. All was in order. This pleased him.

Once he was in his little office, Patrick put the papers on his desk and then took off his jacket, hung it on a peg behind the door.

It was early, only six-thirty, and the men would not arrive until seven-thirty. In the summer months, they started later, but worked longer, into the early evening. Patrick had instituted these hours, so that in winter they could arrive earlier and go home at four-thirty, whilst it was still light outside. It worked for the men and himself.

Sitting down at the small desk, he glanced at the *Daily Mail*'s headlines, then picked up the racing sheet. When he felt he could afford a little flutter, he would pick a likely winner and place a bet with his bookie, Billy Hill, at the top of Branch Road. He loved horses and the races. But he was always careful with his money, acutely aware of his responsibilities. He must keep a roof over their heads and put decent food on the table, make sure they were safe – protect his wife, and his nephew now.

In actuality, Patrick was not given to self-indulgence, because of his nature and also the need to be frugal, to cleverly manage the money he earned. Nevertheless, he believed he could treat himself to his racing sheet and the newspaper every day.

He was an avid reader of the *Daily Mail*, genuinely interested in the news, wanting to know what was happening in the rest of the world, as well as in his own country.

Information was important to him, and knowing as much as he could gave him a true sense of security. He wanted always to be prepared . . . for just about anything. What had happened to his sister and her family, caught in poverty and ill-health, had saddened him deeply.

Eileen had talked to him a lot, four years ago, just before Blackie had come to live with them. And he would always be glad she had, because she had had more insight into what the boy's presence in their lives would mean than he had himself. She had wanted Blackie to come, but had talked about the ways their life might change – for good and bad – having a lad they hardly knew in their home.

It was true the dynamics of life in their house had changed quite markedly, but in all truth his nephew had brought nothing but a quiet joy to their home over the past four years.

It had been a big change but, even from the start, Blackie had proved easy to live with. After tea, he mostly went up to his bedroom to read, his appetite for learning about buildings and engineering fed by the library books he borrowed. Although he was garrulous at times, he knew when quietness was required, and would slide off to leave them alone downstairs.

The only time they'd found themselves at odds had been when Blackie turned fifteen. Patrick had not been able to stop him signing up as a navvy; his nephew had been determined to earn the lucrative money that the brutal work paid, and for six long months they had only seen him occasionally. When he did come home, he was exhausted from the demanding work on the canals and railways, his thin frame reflecting the harsh life.

Nowadays, he was back working for his uncle and was no problem at all, studying at night school and still determined to build his way to a bigger life. Blackie was seventeen, nearly a man, and had made many friends, and was blessed with a magnetic personality that attracted people to him.

Patrick smiled to himself as he saw Blackie in his mind's eye, singing his heart out, choosing old-fashioned ballads as well as popular songs of the moment. He loved going to the dance hall in Upper Armley, and he was a favourite amongst the girls who went there too. He had also discovered that people loved his voice and encouraged him to sing. And so, whenever they begged him to go up and stand with the band, he did so, his melodic voice breaking hearts with his rendition of 'The Minstrel Boy'.

He gave it his all, and Patrick had soon understood there was a bit of the ham in Shane Patrick Desmond O'Neill. He enjoyed entertaining, and the applause perhaps most of all.

After a quick read of the newspaper, Patrick put it to one side, and took his Friday schedule out of the desk drawer. He only had a few small things to deal with this morning, and then at two o'clock he would be going to Mrs Wilson's house, one of the small mansions in the Towers. This was a row of really elegant houses, behind the high black stone wall that ran all the way up Tower Lane to a moor.

The main entrance to this private enclave was on the Main Road, just above Whingate Junction, where the tram turned around to go back into Leeds. The service entrance was around the corner, just off Tower Lane, and not too far from his carpentry shop. A five-minute walk for him that afternoon.

Patrick sat back in his chair, thinking about the job there.

Blackie was a natural builder, good with tools of all kinds and a hard worker. He could turn his hand to most building and repair work, helping his uncle with the jobs they carried out for the local mill owners and the gentry of the region. But he had been born with a really special talent for creativity and vision, honing his skills over time and with his education at night school. Patrick was sure that Blackie could actually design a house now, and build it himself, if necessary.

He had mastered carpentry and brick-laying very quickly, had strong and nimble hands that proved to be a great asset. Blackie had a precise eye, and could envision whole buildings in his mind. He had been an intelligent apprentice, learning so much from his uncle, but also from Tom Goode, who was Patrick's master carpenter and a talented draughtsman. They had taken to each other, and Tom had enjoyed teaching Blackie.

Patrick was well aware he was lucky to have his nephew with him and, since his arrival, four years ago now, the business had begun to expand. And the two of them grew closer every day. In a sense, Patrick now had the son he had always longed for. He knew Eileen felt the same way.

This job at the Wilson house was Blackie's first proper test. It was carpentry for a kitchen that Blackie was completing. Although Patrick had popped in from time to time to view Blackie's work, he had decided at one moment to stop doing this. He had a strong feeling that Blackie resented these intrusions. And he understood why. His nephew was ready to be his own man now.

Not long ago, Patrick had taken on a new apprentice: Finn Ryan, an acquaintance of Blackie's, who had arrived from Ireland unannounced one day.

Blackie had been as surprised as his uncle by Finn's arrival but, according to Blackie, Finn's father had dropped dead unexpectedly, leaving Finn entirely alone. There were no other Ryans left. 'It was awful,' Finn had told Blackie, and then not long after his father's passing, Finn's horse had collapsed and died. It was the end of the cart service that had taken Blackie to Queenstown. Kerry held nothing for Finn now.

'It was as if God was telling me something,' he had confided to Blackie. 'I believe he was telling me to leave, to go to England. So I remembered what ye had done, and came. And ye are the only person I know here. Can ye help me, please?'

Blackie had asked his uncle, and Patrick, out of the goodness of his heart and his innate kindness, had given the young Irishman a job . . . an apprenticeship. In fact, Patrick was a good judge of character, and he had liked the look of Finn, sensed his sincerity.

Over the past months, Finn had proved himself, and Blackie had taken him under his wing. They had become good friends.

Within a day, Patrick had found a place for Finn to stay for a few nights. And within a fortnight, he had a permanent room at Mrs Andrews' boarding house, two minutes away from Town Street. Finn often worked with Blackie now and the business was growing.

Opening his desk drawer, Patrick put his schedule away, and stood up when he heard the noise of the front door banging. Looking down the workshop, he saw Tom coming in followed by Alf and Benny.

'Morning,' they all said in unison, and Patrick greeted his workmen with his usual cordiality.

The men automatically hung up their jackets and went to their workbenches. Patrick knew Finn would not be here this morning. He was going directly to Mrs Wilson's house in the Towers, helping with the final touches to his work on her kitchen. It would be finished today.

Patrick went and fetched his coat, and focused on Blackie for a moment. He was full of anticipation, could hardly wait to see what his nephew had accomplished. After all, it was his first big job.

THIRTEEN

Blackie O'Neill stood in the middle of Mrs Wilson's kitchen, his eyes focused on the white ceiling. He felt a sudden rush of pride – it gleamed, almost sparkled. Perfect, he thought. *It truly was.*

His gaze settled on the windows at the opposite side of the room. He was glad Mrs Wilson had agreed to his suggestion to make them larger; they balanced the new glass window at the end of the kitchen, which overlooked the garden.

What a problem that huge piece of glass had been to handle and to get into the wall. His uncle had been worried about the idea. But Blackie had been determined, had asked around until he had quickly found men who were the most experienced glaziers, recommended by the manager of the glassworks. And now Mrs Wilson's old, run-down kitchen had brilliant daylight, and something unheard of in these parts: a window so large it was almost a *glass wall*. A faint smile flickered on his mouth. His own invention, plucked from his imagination. He felt proud.

He looked down at the floor and couldn't help admiring it also. A pattern of black-and-white tiles, with the larger white tiles placed to look like a diamond shape, each one surrounded on four sides by black tiles, shaped like narrow bricks.

Unexpectedly Blackie frowned. What was that odd black mark near the wall of glass? A slash of black on a white tile! What was it?

He hurried across the room, the frown intact. He almost slipped, since he had yellow dusters tied around his boots to protect the floor. Instantly, he slowed down and moved more carefully.

It was soot. But from where? The fireplace? Certainly, there was nowhere else to look.

The fire was out, since it was a warm summer day. Puzzled, he shook his head and walked to the kitchen door, looked outside.

Finn was sitting on the stone steps that led to the driveway, smoking a cigarette. He looked up when he saw Blackie, then jumped up when he saw the dour expression on his face.

'What's up?' he asked, walking forward, climbing the steps. 'Ye look as if ye've lost a pound and found a penny.'

Blackie couldn't help laughing. Finn was full of old sayings and phrases. He'd never known anyone quite like him, and those odd expressions were on the tip of his tongue constantly.

'I've found soot! Bloody soot on the floor!'

'From the flue,' Finn muttered. 'I'd better get a cloth to clean it off.'

'There's a clean cloth in one of the drawers,' Blackie replied, and turned to go back inside. Then he noticed the two yellow dusters on the top step, and motioned to them. 'Don't forget to put the dusters on, Finn.'

'Would I ever dare to forget? Ye'd have me guts for garters.'

Still laughing, Blackie went inside, and headed for a drawer in a chest next to the sink. He found a clean rag and handed it to Finn when he came inside.

'It's over near the glass,' Blackie said.

Finn nodded, took the offered cloth, and crossed the floor.

Kneeling down, he carefully rubbed on the soot and, within seconds, the tile was fully white once more. Relief flooded Blackie.

Finn glanced up at his friend. He knew why he was so anxious over every little thing. This job meant a lot. 'I bet yer uncle is going to be . . . *stunned* when he sees this kitchen. There ain't one like it in Upper Armley.' He grinned. 'In the whole country even.'

Blackie nodded. 'Mebbe ye are right. I just know I saw every detail in my head. And with your help, and Benny and Alf from time to time, when my uncle could spare them, we somehow got it finished on time.' Blackie sat down on a kitchen chair near the sink, and continued, 'She loves it – Mrs Wilson, I mean.'

'A'course she does. They say ye can't make a swan out of an ugly duckling, but I think ye have, Blackie.'

'Ye're prejudiced, Finn, but thanks anyway.'

'I like working with ye,' Finn murmured, walking over to join Blackie, sitting down in the chair opposite him. They had dust sheets over them, four surrounding the round table near the fireplace.

A silence fell between them, then a moment later Finn said, 'What was it like working on the canals? Being a navvy?'

'Tough,' Blackie answered at once. 'Very tough. Ye have to master the "graft", that's a drain-digging spade. That's vital and, in a sense, it's become a symbol of the trade. I worked on a canal when I was fifteen, and we lived in huts near the canal. The job has become different over the years. Now navvies work on the railways too, need all kinds of skills. They're very important.'

'What kind of skills?'

'Well, a navvy has to have expertise . . . maybe in joinery, brick-making, laying rails and pipes, building bridges and locks. And there's another thing, Finn, a navvy has to have stamina and great strength. It's punishing work, cutting out the way for the railways.'

Finn looked crestfallen. 'I don't think I fit the bill, do I?'

Blackie shook his head. 'No, ye don't. I was able to do it because I'm tall, well-built and strong. I also look older than my real age.'

'It's good money, ain't it? I heard navvies get paid four shillings per day . . . that's a fortune!'

Blackie smiled. 'It is, yes. I did it for six months, and saved a deal of money, but Uncle Pat came and pulled me out.'

'Because of the difficult work?

'Yes, very much so. But I swear on the heads of the Blessed Saints, the true reason was the men I was working with. He was never happy about it. They were a hard-drinking lot, violent at times. The huts were not very nice, unsanitary. And all sorts of diseases were catching hold; some gangs had typhus, dysentery and even cholera.'

'So he became worried about your health?'

'Aye, he did. Me uncle is the best of men, Finn. I look up to him, respect him.'

'I understand why.' There was a small pause, and Finn said quietly, 'But ye made quite a lot of shillings over half a year. *Money*. That's what I be after.'

'I don't blame ye, Finn. I must admit, I like to make money. And one day I aim to build houses, and become a wealthy man. Not just comfortable, with food on me table. Rich.'

Finn stared at him, obviously startled by Blackie's comments. After a moment, he said, 'What a dream to have . . . I hope it comes true.'

FOURTEEN

Blackie and Finn did one last check of the kitchen, the joinery and the plumbing. They ran the kitchen taps, flushed the modern lavatory newly installed in a small back room, and then they made sure all the doors closed properly throughout the entire kitchen. Mrs Wilson had ordered a modern gas range for her cook to use and the scullery at the back of the house, with its coppers for the washing and deep enamel sink, had new cupboards as well.

'Well, that's about it,' Blackie said, after inspecting some hinges on a cupboard door. 'As far as I'm concerned, it's finally finished.' He put his hand on Finn's arm, and his voice was affectionate when he said, in a quiet tone, 'I appreciate your help, Faith, to be sure, I do. I couldn't have done it without ye.'

'Ye would've,' Finn shot back, ''cos ye're ever so clever, Blackie. I've learned a lot from ye and thanks for having me on the job.'

'I'm famished. Let's go and sit on the steps outside and share the sandwiches Aunt Eileen made.'

Blackie went over to his sack near the sink and took out

several packages and two bottles. Showing one to Finn, he said, with a short laugh, 'Lemonade. Made by my aunt,' as if he were announcing vintage wine.

Finn laughed with him and, a few moments later, the two young men were sitting on the steps in the sun, enjoying their sandwiches filled with thin slices of corned beef, and drinking their lemonade.

His mouth full, Blackie asked, 'Are ye coming to the dance hall on Saturday? I'm planning on that.'

'I was thinking to go,' Finn nodded, putting his bottle down, 'but I'm not sure now. I might go to meet this girl my friend Tommy O'Hara wrote to me about. He's from Galway, but he's down now in London. His friend, Moira Aherne, has come to Leeds. He said I'd like her and that she'd like me, said I should look her up and be a friendly face.'

Blackie nodded. 'Ye well might, and ye should go. Where does she stay?' He raised a black brow and said, with a grin, 'She might live in Upper Armley, if ye are lucky.'

'No, she don't,' Finn said. 'She lives somewhere called the Bank.'

Blackie sat upright, peering at his friend intently. 'Are ye sure? What district did he say again?'

'The Bank, it's between the Selby railway line and the River Aire. That's what he wrote. I've got the full address in me room.'

'The Ham Shank, or Ham and Shank,' Blackie pronounced, and shook his head. 'Ye shouldn't go *there*, Finn. Not alone.'

'Why, what's wrong with it?' Finn asked, his curiosity aroused.

'That ain't such a nice neighbourhood,' Blackie said, thinking back to the time he'd lodged there during his time as a navvy. The Ham Shank was home to many Irish people who'd travelled to Yorkshire, had been since the mid-1800s. But it was dangerous:

the police patrolled there in threes, and the only person safe to walk alone in the nearby streets was a priest. *That's* what it was like; it was a place for the poorest and most desperate. But he didn't want to make his friend anxious. 'Full of roughs and toughs it is!' he told him.

Finn was startled. 'But I thought a lot of Irish lived there, and—'

'They do,' Blackie said, cutting across him swiftly. 'In fact, it's a big Irish colony, so to speak.' He paused, then lowered his voice. 'I had to live there a couple o' times in a boarding house, when I was working as a navvy. But don't remind me uncle about that. There's a lot of violence and heavy drinking. Also, Saturday would be the worst night of the week. It's not the kind of place ye want to be frequenting.' He shook his head once more. 'Ye might be tall, but ye are not as tall as me, and half my weight.'

'Are ye saying I might get into a fight, Blackie? I wouldn't. I'd keep to meself and just go and see this girl, Moira, and that would be that.'

'Drunken men who've been grafting hard all week are often on the edge on a Saturday night,' Blackie told him. 'Boozing it up, letting loose . . .' He paused, cleared his throat, then added in a lighter tone, 'It would be better to go and find Moira during the day. Or ye could send her a letter and ask her to meet ye somewhere. The Bank is not a place to be going at night, to be sure . . .'

'It sounds bad, it does, Blackie. Still, I do want ter meet this girl. I knows I looks like a ha'porth of nowt, but I am strong.' Finn bent his arm, and added, 'I've got ever such strong muscles.' He grinned. 'Awright, Blackie, I'll go to the Bank during the day. I have faith ye knows best.'

'Good lad,' Blackie said, relief echoing. 'I knew ye'd see the sense of it . . .' He paused and waved as he spotted his uncle coming up the drive. To Finn he said quickly, 'Let's keep this to ourselves for the time being.'

'Sure, Blackie,' Finn promised, 'I'll not say a word.'

Blackie nodded, stood up when Patrick arrived at the back steps, and exclaimed, 'Ye've arrived at the right time, Uncle Pat. We've just finished our sandwiches. So come on, let's go inside.'

'Hello, Blackie. Hello, Finn. And yes, I'm right on the dot. So take me to see the kitchen. I'm sure this is special.'

'It's a masterpiece,' Finn said. He then turned to his friend's uncle and said, 'Let me get ye some dusters to tie round your shoes. The floor is all new tiles, black and white. Blackie doesn't want it to get scuffed by our boots.'

Patrick nodded and waited outside on the steps. Finn tied on the yellow cotton dusters that he'd left there earlier.

Blackie motioned for his uncle to enter and they both sat and put the dusters over their boots in silence.

Patrick was eager to see his nephew's work, knowing how much effort had gone into this room. Nonetheless, he was astonished when he stood in the centre of the floor and looked around a few seconds later.

In fact, he was somewhat awestruck by the extraordinary effect Blackie had created: the sparkling white walls, the smart new cupboards, the modern range and the new windows. He exclaimed, 'Lad, you've outdone yourself. The room looks sensational. All this white, and the big window over there is grand.'

'It's really like a wall,' Blackie said. Taking hold of his uncle's arm, he led him over, and continued, 'It doesn't open. There are windows over there, and they open, but not this glass.'

Patrick nodded. 'I understand. It lets so much daylight come in, and what a wonderful view of the garden.' Patrick studied it for a few minutes, then asked, 'It must've been one hell of a job, Blackie.' He looked at his nephew and raised a brow.

'Obviously you had a few men to help you?' It came out sounding like a question.

'I did. Eight men who were strong and, naturally, used to handling glass. They were seasoned glaziers. The secret was simple. I had the glass framed in wood. That made it easier to lift and carry. Once it was cemented into the actual wall, and had dried, I painted the wood frame white.'

Patrick was clearly impressed, beamed at Blackie, and looked down at the floor. 'And I congratulate you on the pattern you've created with the tiles. I should've said I congratulate you on the entire room. It's magnificent. I'm very proud of you.'

'Finn helped me, Uncle Patrick, and I do hope we can keep him on at the carpentry shop. Faith, he certainly deserves that.'

'Of course!' Patrick exclaimed. 'We have work for him.' He turned around to face Finn, who was hanging back. 'Come to the shop on Monday, my lad. I welcome you.'

'I will, Mr Kennedy, that I will. And thank ye.'

Blackie walked over to a bank of low cupboards underneath a set of taller cupboards with glass doors. On the glass shelves were displays of crystal glassware, bowls, jugs and other such items.

But Blackie made no comment about this glittering display. He bent down, opened the door of a low cupboard and beckoned to his uncle.

When Patrick joined him, he said, 'This is another of me inventions, Uncle Pat,' and pointed to the inside of the cupboard.

Patrick frowned, wondering what his nephew was talking about, and then let out an exclamation of surprise. 'Another door inside! A glass door, so you can see all the china. My God, that's a stroke of genius.'

'Not really,' Blackie said, smiling as he spoke. 'Practical, though. I know Mrs Wilson loves it and her cook does too. She can view all her dinner and supper sets of china easily, and the glass door keeps dust out also. And I'm happy ye think I've done a good job.'

'That's a big understatement, Blackie my lad. As I said before, it's magnificent.'

FIFTEEN

Patrick Kennedy gave Blackie a long look, and asked slowly, 'Aren't there enough girls in Upper Armley for him? I would have thought so, if the dance hall on Saturday night is anything to go by. It's packed with young ladies.'

Blackie noticed that his uncle looked more amused than annoyed, and this pleased him.

Relieved that his uncle had accepted his story at face value, Blackie explained, 'Finn knew where she was living, on the Bank on Richmond Hill, but he didn't know what a rough place it was. I had to fill him in, sure and I did, Uncle Pat. I can tell ye Finn was startled, faith and he was.'

Patrick nodded. 'You were wise to give him the true picture, and I suppose his Irish friend in London has no idea about the Ham Shank either. He's newly arrived, didn't you say?'

'Yes, he is,' Blackie confirmed. 'Finn does want to meet this girl, though, and so I said we would go with him *next* Saturday, a week from today. In the morning.' Blackie paused, leaned forward with his arms on the table. 'Will ye come with us too, Uncle Pat?'

For a few seconds Patrick did not answer, wondering what this was all about . . . Finn's obvious determination to meet a girl just come to Leeds from Ireland. He suddenly wondered if Finn was homesick, wanted something from the past. He asked Blackie, 'Who is Finn's friend in London? What's his name?'

'Tommy O'Hara.'

'And who is this girl Finn's so keen to meet?' Patrick's eyes were riveted on Blackie.

'Her name is Moira Aherne, and she must be . . . well, *special*, I am thinking, Uncle, because Tommy was so insistent. Anyway, that was the way Finn did put it to me. He said Tommy was *insistent*.'

Patrick shook his head, a perplexed expression on his face. After a moment's thought, he said, 'I feel sorry for this young colleen. She's come over from the Ould Sod, no doubt with great expectations, only to end up in the Ham Shank, a rat-hole if ever there was one. Not the right place for a young girl.'

'No indeed,' Blackie agreed. 'So will ye go with us next Saturday?'

Patrick did not hesitate. 'Of course I will, and I'll ask Jack Blane to come with us. He can be tough and he's strong. Safety in numbers, I'm thinking.'

Patrick stood and put on his jacket, which had been across the back of his chair. 'Let's go out for a walk, lad. I need to stretch my legs. And your aunt would like us to stop by the bakery shop at noon. She'll be about finished by then. We'll all come home together, and we can carry her shopping bags.'

'Me jacket's upstairs. I'll just go and get it,' Blackie said, and hurried across the room.

'As you well know by now, it's rare I just go for a stroll,' Patrick said with a twinkle as they began to walk down Town Street. 'I need a purpose, or somewhere specific to go. And this morning I need to visit the draper's.'

'As a matter of fact, so do I, Uncle,' Blackie confided. 'I want to buy some underwear.'

'Mr Pinkerton has a good selection of everything,' Patrick said. 'He's bound to have what you're looking for.'

Blackie nodded. 'I must thank ye, Uncle Patrick, for the extra shillings ye're giving me and Finn. Faith, and it's very generous of ye. And thank ye for asking Finn to join us for Sunday dinner. He's so happy to come, he can't wait.'

'He deserves a decent meal in family surroundings. He's a good lad, and I'm happy you've taken him under your wing. I'll be seeing Jack tonight, having a pint with him at the Barley Corn. I'll ask him to come with us to the Ham Shank. It won't be a problem, I know that.'

'That's good to know, Uncle,' Blackie smiled.

Patrick nodded, and stopped suddenly. 'Let's get across the road, if we can. Mr Pinkerton's shop is over there. Lots of traffic on Town Street today. That's normal on Saturdays, I suppose.'

They dodged across the road, and a few seconds later entered the draper's shop to the sound of a tinkling bell announcing their arrival.

'Good morning, Mr Kennedy,' Albert Pinkerton said, smiling, obviously pleased to greet a steady customer of long-standing. He stood behind a long, polished wooden counter, with glass-fronted drawers beneath it and shelves lining the wall behind him. These contained the handkerchiefs, neckcloths, socks and shirts that Patrick Kennedy knew were the best in the area.

'Morning, Mr Pinkerton, and I think you know my nephew, Blackie O'Neill.'

'I do indeed,' he replied, nodding to Blackie in a friendly way. 'And how can I be of help, Mr Kennedy?'

'I'd like to look at some light cotton shirts for my nephew.'

'Oh, Uncle Pat! No, no, ye don't have to buy a shirt for me!' Blackie protested, sounding surprised and concerned.

'I do. Your aunt and I didn't do anything much for your birthday in May.'

'But ye did. Aunt Eileen baked me a lovely cake, and ye had Finn to tea.'

'I wish to give you a present, from us both, Blackie.' Patrick looked at Mr Pinkerton, and said, 'I believe you can gauge my nephew's size, can't you?'

'I can indeed. I shall go and fetch a few of my shirts from a new shipment. I won't be a moment.' The proprietor hurried away, intent in his purpose.

Blackie said, 'Please, Uncle Pat, ye don't have to give me a shirt. Ye keep a roof over my head and feed me, and I am grateful for that, and my job with ye. On the heads of the Blessed Saints, that be all I am needing from ye and Aunt Eileen, to be sure. That's the honest truth.'

Leaning closer to Blackie, Patrick said in a low voice, 'You actually *need* a couple of new shirts. You have very few clothes as it is, and only those worn flannel shirts your aunt has mended more times than I remember. So please accept this gift.' Patrick chuckled. 'Think of it as a necessity, if not a birthday present.'

Blackie nodded, knowing there was no point arguing, and said, 'I thank ye, Uncle. I shall buy a pair of combinations, which I surely need. I took some shillings out of me nest egg.'

Mr Pinkerton came back with a pile of folded cotton shirts and laid them out on the counter, along with the matching collars with studs. Blackie looked at them all, realizing, almost immediately, that his uncle was correct. He did need something new because – if he was truthful with himself – he looked rather shabby.

He hated to spend the money that he was trying so hard to save on clothes. But he realized that to get on in life he could not look poor, like a labourer. His uncle was a working man but always neatly turned out, his clothes tidy and darned, well looked-after.

And Blackie wanted even more from life than his Uncle Pat. He was hungry for a bigger life. To build the houses he dreamed of, using the ideas that filled his mind. BIG *MONEY*. That's what he needed. He would work harder than ever to get it. It was the secret to life.

Sixteen

Eileen greeted them with a big smile when they arrived at the bakery. She had her hat and coat on ready to go; the bakery was full of customers on Saturday mornings, but by midday it was empty, the shelves bare. Everyone had bought up Eileen's Saturday specials and gone home to enjoy them.

Blackie loved the smell of the shop . . . baking bread mingled with the aroma of sponge cake and cream buns, and his favourite apple pie.

Margaret, who was Aunt Eileen's second cousin and owned the shop, gave him a nod and a smile as she came through the back door. She was carrying a tray of pork pies, and Blackie felt his mouth watering. As she passed him, going across to the other long counter, she said, 'You'll be enjoying these soon enough, my lad,' and winked at him.

He laughed, and then went to join his uncle, who was gathering up several brown bags at the main counter. 'Let me help ye,' he said to Patrick, and reached for two more bags. A few seconds later they were out in Town Street with Eileen, walking home together.

Within minutes they were emptying the bags in the kitchen. Aunt Eileen put some of the items in the larder, and said to Blackie, 'Help your uncle to set the table, and I'll have dinner out in a jiffy.'

'Right away, Auntie,' he answered, and did as she asked. As usual, he was hungry and couldn't wait to savour the warm pork pies. They smelled delicious.

Once everything was ready, the three of them sat down.

They both thanked Eileen and she smiled at them, and said, 'Margaret told me today she'd like me to give her an extra few hours every week . . .' Eileen paused, and looked at her husband. When he remained silent, she asked, 'So, what do you think, Patrick?'

'If *you* think it's not too much for you, then it's all right with me. But I don't want you overdoing it, mavourneen. I would be upset if you got ill again.'

'It's just a few hours a week . . . you see my baking is doing nicely. Margaret likes to have the extra pies and tarts alongside the bread and buns. We're selling out.' Eileen laughed, and added, 'And I'll be fine, Pat, I really will. I'm feeling as fit as a fiddle these days.'

'So try it out,' Patrick said, and felt a small rush of pride in his wife's success. She had started by just helping her cousin out occasionally, taking in some pies, and there was no doubt in his mind that she was the best baker there was in Upper Armley. Yet he worried about her health, didn't want the extra work to get her down. Ever since nearly losing her just before Blackie arrived, four years earlier, he had been cautious. And there was no need for his wife to be working. He knew she did it for the love of it.

Blackie reached for the bowl of piccalilli and took a spoonful of the mustard relish with chopped vegetables in it. He liked to eat it with the pork pie, which he had never had until he came to live with his aunt and uncle. Now it was his favourite, which they had every Saturday.

For her part, Eileen was watching the two men, filled with satisfaction that they were obviously enjoying the meal. Her joy in cooking good meals sprang from the pleasure they gave to her 'two lads', as she called them.

Blackie sat on his bed, looking at his two new shirts. How smart they were; he couldn't wait to put one on. Perhaps he would wear one tonight. After all, he was going to the dance hall on Branch Road. He had never worn anything that was brand new before. Well, he'd had the new pullovers Mrs O'Malley had knitted for him, but never any single thing from a *shop*. Over the past few years, he'd had a few more parcels from Ireland of hand-me-downs and cast-offs from the Lassiter house, through his cousin Siobhan, which had kept him going, and also a few things his aunt had adapted for him. She was a good seamstress.

Picking up the two shirts, he opened the wardrobe and laid them carefully away in a drawer. Then he opened another and took out his exercise books from night school. Three years well spent, he thought, as he flicked through the top one, and pulled out a folded piece of paper. It was actually a page he had torn out of a magazine. He stared down at the photograph, nodding his head. It was of a conservatory and he had spoken about the idea to Mrs Wilson.

Blackie was full of hope she would take his advice and decide to add one to her little mansion. And that he would be allowed to build it.

*   *   *

Jack Blane was a Yorkshire man from head to toe. Born and bred in Upper Armley, he was the salt of the earth.

Now, as Patrick went into the taproom of the Barley Corn pub on Town Street, he felt a spurt of pleasure when he spotted Jack leaning on the bar with a pint. The two of them had been best friends since the age of ten, and were still going strong. They spent most of their spare time together, had shared interests and beliefs. And they were both loaded with charm.

He raised his hand to acknowledge Patrick, who grinned as he hurried forward, thinking how smart his friend looked tonight.

Jack was a handsome man with black hair, was thirty-four years old like Patrick, and they made a striking pair. Most people looked at them twice when they were out together, struck by their fine looks and good grooming. Jack was tall and well-built like Patrick, with a chiselled face and dark eyes. Despite Patrick's fair colouring and blue eyes, they seemed like brothers to those who didn't know otherwise. It was true they had a look of each other.

After exchanging greetings affectionately, Patrick called the barman over.

'A pint of bitter, please,' he said, ordering the same as Jack and pushing a few coins over the bar. Once it was poured, he and Jack clinked glasses.

The two men chatted about odd things in general for a few minutes, as they savoured their beer. But after a moment or two, Patrick put his glass down on the bar.

Leaning into Jack, he said, 'I've stumbled into a problem, and I need your help. It could be a bit of trouble.'

Jack frowned and asked in a lowered voice, 'Not trouble with that bloody housekeeper of Mrs Burton's again, I hope to God.'

'No, no, nothing like that. That's long past and, like I told you, I've always declined the work Mrs Burton offered since. It's to do with young Finn, Blackie's friend.'

'What kind of trouble?' As he asked this, Jack glanced around the taproom, saw that it was filling up and growing noisy. 'Tell me what's wrong, Pat. Nobody can hear – a rowdy crowd as usual on Saturdays.'

'It's about a girl—'

'Not that old story, I hope. Don't tell me he's gone and got—'

'No, no, nothing like that, Jack. It's about a girl he's keen to *meet*.' After a long swallow of beer, Patrick told him the whole story about Tommy O'Hara's letter, and, more importantly, about where Moira Aherne lived.

'On the Ham Shank!' Jack was frowning, and after a moment continued, 'Who in God's name would send a young and probably naïve Irish lass to live in that piss-pot? I suppose someone who doesn't know what a hellhole it is.'

Patrick nodded in agreement. 'Look, I said I'd go with Finn and Blackie next Saturday morning, to pick her up and take her to have a bite to eat at a café nearby, if there is one—'

'Best go to the Blue Door,' Jack interrupted. 'You've always liked that place and they know you well.'

'I agree. I was wondering if you'd come with us, bolster our numbers. How about it, Jack?'

'Try and bloody stop me! 'Course I'm going with you. Do you think I'd let you go alone to that bleeding place? Not on your life, Patrick. Even a Saturday morning could be tough to handle. Weekends they're all on the booze, and as violent as hell. There are a lot of brawls.'

'My worry is that the girl is *living* there, apparently with an aunt or a cousin.' Pat paused, shook his head. 'She shouldn't have been sent there, you know that. I can't help feeling we ought to get her out of there, and as fast as we can.'

For a moment Jack was silent, and then he said slowly, 'We would have to get her somewhere else to live, you know. If you're thinking of taking responsibility, you'll have her on your hands, Patrick. Let's really consider this.' Jack gave his friend a long look, his open face troubled. 'Eileen might not like that idea at all.'

'I realize that, and I'm *not* taking responsibility. I'm going to tell Finn he has to do that . . . at least he has to get the girl to safety because she's been sent to Leeds by someone Tommy O'Hara knows, who could have no idea how bad the Bank is.'

'I'm happy you understand what I'm saying – for you yourself. Blackie is a good lad, strong and tough. He'll be of help. Yes, I'll go with you next Saturday, and between now and then we'll think about what to suggest to her. Maybe she would agree to move here. Upper Armley's a safe place, and she could easily find a job, plenty of work at Thompson's mill. Perhaps it'd be easier than in the city.' Jack took a swig of his pint.

'I agree. Or I can ask Mrs Wilson if she needs another maid, and that would be a live-in job. Mrs Wilson has several people in service. A maid, a cook and a butler, as well as outside domestics.'

'That's a good thought, Pat, and I'll talk to my sister. Adele knows a lot of wealthy women, those she makes clothes for. Adele just might have a candidate.'

'It is a good thought. If not, Finn will have to find somebody with a room to let. There are quite a few people looking to make an extra bob or two, renting out in the Greenocks and in the Thorntons.' Patrick let out a sigh, and said, 'I know I'm being a busybody, worrying about a girl I don't know, haven't even met. But I just can't stand the idea of some young woman fresh from Ireland, over here with no protection or family, living in that hellhole. Rape is commonplace and murder not far behind.'

'I don't think you're interfering, Pat. I believe you're a good man who has a conscience and the balls to go on his instincts and step into a situation that is undoubtedly rotten. No two ways about that. And I'm joining you. We'll look like a gang of sorts, but who the hell cares?'

Patrick began to laugh, and then said, 'When we were kids, I used to say there was safety in numbers, but you insisted we could fight the world and win. Just the two of us.'

Jack grinned, his dark eyes full of laughter, and shot back, 'And we bloody well can, even now.'

'We're not that old, mate. Thirty-four, the two of us. We're in our prime, Jacko!'

While Pat and Jack ordered themselves another pint, not far from the Barley Corn pub Blackie and Finn pushed open the door to the popular dance hall at the top of Branch Road.

Ever since he'd first set foot in the place a couple of years after arriving in Leeds, Blackie liked to spend his Saturday nights there. He loved to dance, and, of course, inevitably he went up to the band and sang a few old ballads and popular songs, by request. Everyone who went there enjoyed his singing, and he secretly loved the enthusiastic applause and shouts for another song from him.

It didn't take the two boys long to realize that the hall wasn't so packed tonight, and a number of regulars were nowhere in sight. Turning to Finn, Blackie said, 'Poor showing, I be thinking. I don't know why it's half-empty, sure and I don't. 'Tis joyless, even though the band's goin' strong.'

Finn nodded, also looking around, a dismal expression settling on his face. He said, 'I do know that one of the really popular chaps was in an accident earlier in the week. Ye knows him, Blackie, Andy Paulton. All the girls flocked around him. He was a masterful dancer—'

'Oh, I do know him!' Blackie cut in. 'So what happened? What kind of accident did he have then?'

'He was run down by a horse and carriage, 'cos the horse got startled, reared up and bolted. Andy was trampled on.'

'Oh my God! Is he dead? He must be, surely?' Blackie exclaimed, sounding horror-struck.

'Badly injured,' Finn replied. 'In Leeds Infirmary, so I heard. But ye knows as well as I do, them, these kind of accidents, do a *lotta* damage to a man.'

Blackie nodded, his face sober, concern reflected in his dark eyes. 'Me Uncle Pat stopped one like that only a couple'a years back; had to grab the bridle of a horse that was about to bolt. He got a hearty thank you from the man – proper gentry he was too. Squire Fairley. He's been sending us work as a result.' He spotted one of the girls he often danced with and started to walk towards her, taking Finn with him. 'Look, Sarah Clough will fill us in on Andy, ye knows she always has gossip to share, sure and she does.'

Finn laughed. 'She's better than them there newspapers ye are allus reading. More news than ye can stand.'

Sarah, a nice-looking young woman with blue eyes and blonde hair, smiled broadly as the two young men came towards her. Seated in a chair against the wall, she immediately stood up. After greetings were exchanged, Blackie spoke first.

'It's right nice to see ye, Sarah, and ye look lovely in that blue dress.'

Her face dimpled, and she nodded. 'Thank you, Blackie. And you look smart. I like your smart white shirt.'

He nodded as Finn said, 'That frock matches your blue eyes, right nice ye are, Sarah.' She was wearing a dress with a deep flounce, its gathered bodice trimmed with lace, modelled on the latest look.

There were a few chuckles all around, and then Finn opened

up. 'We heard Andy was in a real terrible accident. Do ye knows anything about it?'

Sarah nodded, her face suddenly sad, and both men noticed she had paled. They gave her a moment, as she seemed about to cry, struggling not to do so.

Taking a deep breath, Sarah swallowed her emotions, and said, 'He was, yes, and I went with his mam to see him on Thursday. He's in a bad way, but I don't think . . . he's going . . . to die.' Her voice trembled on her last words.

Blackie reached out and squeezed her arm reassuringly. Finn asked, 'Is he badly hurt then?'

'Yes,' Sarah answered. 'He got trampled on by one of the two horses. The carriage wheels damaged one of his arms and part of a leg—'

'Oh, I hope he'll be able to dance again!' Finn exclaimed, staring at Sarah in alarm.

'His mam thinks so. His leg and arm are both in casts, plaster of Paris, and the doctor told us he's badly bruised, but nothing else. Nothing hurt inside him.'

'That's good news,' Blackie said. 'How long will he be in hospital?'

'They don't know, but probably a few weeks. He was a bit out of it on Thursday, drugged. Because of the pain,' Sarah explained.

'When did it happen?' Finn probed.

'On Monday of this last week. His mam went every day, and she asked me to go with her on Thursday.'

'So it's gonna be a long haul?' Finn asked in a questioning tone.

'It is, and then he will have to go to a special hospital for recuperation. That'll be a few weeks, too. Poor Andy, he's going to be out of action for ages.'

'All the girls are going to miss him, don't ye think, Sarah?' Blackie asked.

'I do. He loves to dance, and especially with me.'

'I can't say I blame him,' Blackie said gallantly, his dark eyes smiling down at her.

Finn frowned slightly and, staring at Sarah, he asked, 'Were ye goin' with him then . . . courting?'

'Not exactly,' Sarah responded at once. 'But it was heading in that direction. We'd grown to like each other a lot.'

Blackie exclaimed, 'No wonder ye are so upset. Mind ye, most people who know him would be, I'm sure of that, I swear on the heads of the Blessed Saints.'

'You're right,' Sarah answered. 'People have been trying to get to see him all week.'

'I expect that's why this place isn't so full tonight . . . I mean because Andy ain't here,' Finn murmured.

'Not exactly. It's emptier than usual because Billy Flint got married to Lettice Maple today. At Christ Church, and there's a wedding dinner at the church hall, going on right at this moment.'

'Oh really,' Blackie said, glancing at Sarah, thinking she sounded rather bitter. 'I don't believe I know that couple.'

'You've not missed anything,' Sarah remarked, making a face. 'Although they deserve each other, in my opinion.'

'I agree with ye,' Finn jumped in. 'A couple of snobs to my way of thinking. Toffee-nosed, that's for sure—'

Finn stopped as the door flew open and Alf Smithson rushed in, frantically looking around. He noticed his fellow workers from Pat Kennedy's workshop and hurried across the room to join them.

'Finn, Sarah, have you seen Gwen?' he asked in an anxious voice.

'Yes. She's here somewhere, Alf.' Sarah frowned. 'I think I saw her go to the ladies' lav.'

'Can you go and check for me? Please.' As he spoke he glanced around again, and frantically, as before.

'Yes. But is there something wrong?'

'Not exactly. I went to her house to pick her up, and her mother said she'd already gone to meet me here. But our arrangement was to come together.'

'I see. Back in a tick,' Sarah said, and went in the direction of the ladies' room.

Alf Smithson took a deep breath and shook his head, then said in a quieter voice, 'Sorry, mates. I got worried when Gwen had left before I arrived. We'd had a bit of a tiff last night.'

Blackie nodded. 'We understand, don't we, Finn?'

Finn nodded. 'Don't worry about the tiff. Most girls get over 'em real fast.'

'I hope so,' Alf said.

Sarah returned, shaking her head as she came back to the group. 'The room is empty, Alf.'

'Oh my God, where can she be? Are you sure you saw her, Sarah?'

'Yes. We said hello, and then she went to get a lemonade at the bar over there, and sat across the room.'

'Wait a minute,' Finn said swiftly. 'I saw her leaving a while ago. Out of the corner of my eye. I was looking around, thinking how empty this place was.'

'She must've left!' Sarah exclaimed.

'Certainly I don't see her,' Alf cried. 'I must go and look for her. I don't know where she might be, but I'll go through all the streets. Looking.'

'We'll come with ye, Alf,' Blackie said in a strong voice. 'And ye will, won't ye?' He looked pointedly at Finn.

'I will, mate. Try and stop me.'

'I'm coming too,' Sarah told them. 'But just one question. Could she have gone home?'

'No, I just left there. I told you, I spoke to her mother,' Alf answered, the anxiety in his tone apparent, his nervousness visible.

'Let's be off, chaps,' Blackie said, ushering Sarah across the dance floor. The other two followed, all of them going out into the warm June night, wondering where to go first.

SEVENTEEN

By the time the four of them had walked up Branch Road, onto Town Street and headed towards the Barley Corn, Blackie suddenly stopped.

Taking hold of Alf's arm, he asked, 'Why are we doing this? Look around, Town Street is empty.'

Alf nodded in agreement, and replied, 'Better to go into the side streets, don't yer think?'

Blackie shook his head. 'No. Why would Gwen be roaming around at night? She must have gone home, sure and she did, where else?'

'I was just there, talking to her mam, and Gwen wasn't in the house. I know that for a fact, Blackie!' Alf exclaimed.

'Then she must have gone to a girlfriend's house. Yes, I be thinking that's what happened,' Blackie now said, wanting to reassure his workmate. 'Unless she's with . . .' He broke off abruptly, pursing his lips, regretting his words.

'Were yer going ter suggest she's with another chap?' Alf asked swiftly, throwing Blackie a sharp, questioning glance.

'I'm afraid I was,' Blackie murmured in a low voice. 'Ye did say ye'd had a tiff—'

Finn cut in. 'Was the tiff about another lad, then?'

Alf let out a long sigh and was silent. After a moment, he said in a low tone, 'Yes, that's it. Do yer know Ian Craig?'

Finn and Sarah said, 'Yes,' in unison. Then Sarah ventured, 'He's a bit of a chaser . . . you know what I mean; he's always after different women, makes no bones about it.'

'Has he been after *you* then?' Finn asked, giving Sarah a hard stare.

'Yes. And I soon sent him packing. He's not the kind of lad I like. In fact, I wouldn't touch him with a barge pole.'

'That bad, eh?' Blackie said, and then turned to Alf. 'I hate to say this, but I don't think she's wandering around Upper Armley. That's a silly thought, and I can only suppose she's with this Ian lad. I don't know him, sure and I don't. Never met him. Just heard his name.'

Alf looked at Sarah very intently. 'Was Gwen alone at the dance hall, or was she with him?'

Sarah said quickly, 'Alone. I told you, she was sitting alone, drinking a lemonade. Ian wasn't in the dance hall. I would've noticed him. He's always got a swagger to him, makes himself seen, can't help it.'

Finn hesitated for a moment, and then blurted out, 'I told ye I saw Gwen leave, Alf, a bit before you came in. She must have arranged to meet him outside.' When he saw the glowering look on Alf's face, Finn added swiftly, 'There's no other explanation. I'm sorry, but I think I'm right.'

Blackie said, 'I'm afraid I agree with Finn, Alf.' He paused, and his dark eyes swept over his companions. 'It's too late to go back to the dance hall, and it was as dead as a doornail.' He smiled at Sarah. 'Can I be walking ye home . . . it's grown darker, sure and it has?'

'Thanks, Blackie, I'd like you to take me home.'

Finn said, 'I'll walk with *you*, Alf. We're going in the same direction.'

Alf nodded, and they all said goodnight to each other and went their separate ways.

Sarah lived at the top of Town Street, near Whingate Junction, just opposite Charlie Cake Park. Blackie always associated the spot with the memory of his very first day coming to live with his Uncle Pat, and the wonder of that first tram ride.

As they walked along together, Sarah became quite chatty, speaking about Gwen. Looking up at Blackie at one moment, she said, 'Gwen is a nice girl, and I'm not sure she would be interested in Ian. He's just not her type.'

Blackie looked down at her, frowning, his black brows knotting together. 'What are ye suggesting?'

'She might have gone home when she left the dance hall.'

'But Alf would have run into her on Town Street, sure and he would.'

'Not if she'd slipped through St Ives Mount and down to Ridge Road then up to Town Street.'

'I see what you're saying. It's just as easy to go that way.' He shook his head. 'But why would she? Town Street is the direct route from Branch Road.'

'Maybe to avoid Ian, if he's been chasing after her,' she pointed out.

'I see.' Blackie was quiet after that, his busy mind working. He suddenly said, 'Could she have been hoping to avoid Alf? He did say they'd had a tiff.'

'Well, she could have stayed at home, but maybe she just loved to go to the dance hall. We all like that place . . . and there's nowhere else to go for a bit of fun. And flirting.'

Blackie chuckled. 'On the heads of the Blessed Saints, isn't that the truth. Anyway, if ye be wanting my opinion, I think Gwen met someone outside the dance hall before Alf arrived.'

'Oh Blackie, I don't agree. She'd never hook up with Ian.'

'From what ye have told me, I agree. But she could have met another man, sure and she could. There're a lot of nice lads here.'

'Of course she could,' Sarah agreed. 'I'm being a bit daft, focusing on one lad. Oh, here we are, this is where I live.'

Blackie pushed open the gate and went with Sarah down the path of the small garden.

'Silly me, I've forgotten my key,' Sarah muttered as she searched in her handbag. She glanced at Blackie and made a face. 'I'm going to have to knock on the door. My sister Angela is going to be cross, because the noise will wake my mother.'

Blackie nodded. 'Just give a light tap with the knocker. I'm sure she'll hear it.'

Sarah lifted the brass knocker and let it go, lightly so, doing as he suggested.

A moment later her sister said, 'Is that you, Sarah?'

'Yes, it is.'

The door opened and the woman standing there took Blackie's breath away. He had never seen anyone quite so beautiful in his life. He gaped at her as he took in the gleaming light-brown hair, piled up on top of her head, eyes as blue as speedwells, and a face that was exquisite. He couldn't take his eyes away and neither could she.

Sarah cleared her throat and took a step forward, saying as she did, 'Won't you come in for a cup of tea, Blackie? Seeing as the night ended early. And it's turned cold.'

Finding her voice, Angela said, 'Oh yes, do come in. Sarah's right, the evening has grown cooler.' She opened the door wider and stepped back as first Sarah and then Blackie entered the house.

Once Sarah had led him into the parlour, she drew her sister forward and said, 'This is Blackie O'Neill, Angela. He volunteered to walk me home because it had grown so dark. Meet my sister, Blackie.'

Blackie stretched out his hand and Angela took it. Again they were staring at each other so intently, Sarah had to clear her throat several more times.

Swiftly, Angela let go of Blackie's hand and moved away, saying as she walked across the floor, 'I shall go and put the kettle on.'

Once they were alone, Blackie said, 'I've never seen your sister around Upper Armley.'

'Oh no, you wouldn't. She lives on the other side of Hill Top, and she's not often on Town Street.'

'Doesn't she live here with ye and your mother?' Blackie asked, sounding puzzled.

'No, she doesn't. She moved out when she got married.'

Blackie felt as if he had been punched hard in the stomach and an unexpected wave of disappointment flooded over him.

'Who is she married to?' he managed to ask, his voice sounding hoarse to him.

'Let's sit down here near the fire,' Sarah said. 'She got married young, to Anthony Welles. He was in the Royal Navy, but sadly he got killed during the Boer War, in 1901. He was lost at sea. Angela is a widow.'

'Oh, how terrible. 'Tis sorry I am to be hearing that. So young to be a widow,' he said, startled by this news.

'She's twenty-four,' Sarah told him. 'But I know she doesn't look it.'

'Not at all,' Blackie murmured, knowing he had filled with relief at Sarah's words, although a hint of sadness flickered in his mind that she had lost her husband, and she so young.

He knew one other thing. He wanted this woman with a great

fierceness that seemed to overwhelm him. And he meant to have her, whatever it took.

Nothing like this had ever happened to Blackie O'Neill before in his young life. His instant and intense attraction to Angela Welles had startled him. Now he sat rigid in the chair, as if frozen. His eyes never left the kitchen door and, when Sarah spoke to him, he paid no attention.

Sarah grabbed his arm. She said in a low but firm voice, 'You're in some sort of trance. Pull yourself together before my sister comes back.' She tightened her grip on his arm, and finally he turned his head to look at her.

'I'm not in a trance, I'm just taken aback, sure and I am. What man wouldn't be, I be asking ye? Angela has . . . great beauty, Sarah.'

'I know it. Now you do, and so does the entire world. At least, those who've met her do. Men are agog, just as you are. And women, and children, and dogs and horses. And even birds, I suppose.'

There had been laughter in Sarah's voice as she had said these words, and Blackie couldn't help chuckling. 'In fact, she's a genuine knockout, I be thinking. I stared at her, Sarah, and she stared back . . . our eyes met and held.' He cleared his throat. 'Do ye think she would go to the dance hall, if I be inviting her?'

Sarah, looking shocked, shook her head vehemently. 'Oh no, she'd never go there, not be seen dead there. If you ask her out, you'd have to take her out somewhere more elegant. Perhaps the theatre or the music hall. Or one of the nice restaurants. In Leeds.'

'Oh, I see, well, I can do that, sure I can, on the heads of the Blessed Saints, I would.'

Although his prompt acceptance of this suggestion had surprised Sarah, she kept silent for a moment before asking, 'Do you know any of them? What I mean is, are you familiar with any *special* restaurants in Leeds?'

'The Cameo,' Blackie replied instantly. 'And I may be knowing they are expensive, Sarah, but I can afford it.' This was the truth, since Blackie had his nest egg from being a navvy a few years ago, and from the bonuses he'd earned from his uncle. This was why he had not quailed when Sarah had mentioned restaurants. He saved his extra earnings, was in no way a spendthrift, knowing the power of *money*.

Before either of them spoke again, the kitchen door flew open, and Angela came into the room carrying a large tray.

Blackie sprang to his feet and rushed to take it from her.

Angela allowed him to do so, looking into his eyes. 'I hadn't realized how tall you are, Blackie, and strong.'

A faint pinkness flushed his face, but he made no comment, simply carried the tray over to the table in the corner of the room and put it down.

Angela followed him, saying to Sarah, 'I thought you both might be hungry, so I made a few little tea sandwiches and sliced my sponge cake. Come on, join us.' Looking at Blackie, she added, 'Please sit down.'

As she seated herself, he sat down in the nearest chair, only to realize a moment later that he was facing her. There was nowhere else to look but at that extraordinary face.

'It was kind of ye,' Blackie murmured, suddenly feeling more confident about Angela. This was mainly because Sarah hadn't discouraged him from asking her sister out, and also because Angela was gazing at him with a strange expression in her blue eyes. He wondered if it was the *yearning* which he himself was feeling.

Sarah got up, and said, 'I need to go to my room for a hankie. I'll be back in a tick.' She hurried across the room.

Alone, Angela spoke first. 'I know I'm staring at you, Blackie, but I just can't help it. I know it's rude of me . . . but you have such distinctive looks, I've never met anyone with such dark hair and eyes from Ireland—'

'It's not rude of ye,' Blackie cut in. '*I'm* staring at *ye* in turn.' He gave her a rueful smile. 'I am, well, I'm entranced by ye. Ye are beautiful.' It was Angela's turn to blush now and she glanced down while he continued to speak. 'I would like to invite ye out, Angela. Out for a meal, somewhere elegant. We could go next Saturday.'

'Oh, how lovely. But that's very formal.' There was a pause, and she leaned across the table and said, 'I would like to invite you to supper next week. Nothing fancy, just a bite to eat, to get to know one another. Won't you come to my house? I live just across from the Traveller's Rest, the pub at Hill Top. Please say yes.'

'I say yes to ye, Angela.' I'll say yes to anything ye want, he thought, filled with excitement by her invitation.

'Which is the best night for you?' Angela asked, sounding slightly breathless.

'Wednesday would be possible, sure and it would, because I've finished me latest project and will be at me drawing board all day. What time do ye want me?'

Angela stared at him, seemingly transfixed for a moment, before she said, 'I think about six o'clock, if that's all right with your schedule.'

'Indeed it is,' he replied, his voice hoarse. 'I think I know your house. It's standing at the edge of the moor, and it has dark green shutters. Is that the one?'

She merely nodded and gave him a lovely smile, as she picked up the teapot and filled three cups.

Sarah arrived at the table and seated herself between them. As she looked at her sister and then at Blackie, noticing the unexpected ease which now existed between them, she smiled inwardly.

She had noticed the immediate attraction between them, the way their eyes had met. No one could have missed *that* pull between a man and a woman. How right she had been to leave them alone. She was happy for Angela. Her sister's good taste and manners seemed to make it hard for her to meet the right kind of man. She had married up – her husband, Anthony Welles, had been from a good family from Harrogate and, after his aunt had died, he had inherited a small sum, just enough to buy them the little house. But he had loved the Royal Navy, having joined when he was seventeen.

And whilst Angela had put up a good front and decorated their house in perfect taste, she had been very lonely. Sailors at sea did not make good husbands. Also, there had been no children, and Sarah had often wondered about their relationship, the intimate side of their married life, and how much they really had loved each other.

Blackie would pay court to her, assuage her loneliness, put a spark back in her eyes again, Sarah decided, as she sipped her tea and listened to her sister chatting away to Blackie. She noticed the rapt expression on his face, the brightness in his eyes.

Angela was older than him; Sarah was well aware he was only seventeen. Laughter rose in her throat, but she pushed it back. What did age matter? It didn't, as far as she was concerned.

Sarah, now twenty-one, was wise for her years, and she had a knack of sizing people up, understood what made them tick.

Blackie and Angela were attracted to each other and she knew both were good people. They were right for each other at this time in their lives, at least. The future? Who cared about that. Blackie wasn't looking to get married. She wanted a bit of happiness for Angela *now*. And there was no doubt in her mind that Blackie O'Neill, the handsomest man *she* had ever met, would give her sister exactly what she wanted and needed. Certainly Angela's terrible loneliness would be alleviated for a while with this charming Irishman.

Blackie was unable to fall asleep. He lay in his much-loved bed, staring up at the ceiling, seeing only *her* face. It was now imprinted on his brain.

It was a full moon floating high out there in the midnight-dark sky overflowing with stars. The moonlight filtered into the room; he did not need his little candle at this moment. Many thoughts went through his busy mind. Meeting Angela so unexpectedly, being stunned by her beauty, her manners, her refinement. She was unlike every woman he had met so far. He had not had a relationship; he had only danced with gauche local girls at the dance hall, some of them shy, some of them brash and pushy. He was the same way with them as he was with everyone: friendly, cheerful, always looking for the good in people. But in the years he'd been going to the dance hall, he had never met anyone like Angela.

He was a virgin, had never slept with a woman, and for a moment this worried him. Then he shoved the worry away. *He* desired Angela, wished to make love with her, possess her, be possessed by her. On the other hand, maybe *she* would not want to take their initial attraction to that conclusion. He would abide by her wishes.

He felt himself relax. He would be whoever she wanted him to be. That was the only way he knew. A gentleman. His uncle had drilled that into him: don't force yourself on any woman; respect their wishes, and let them take the lead.

Blackie experienced a rush of sudden desire, thinking of Angela's gentleness, and yet there was ardour behind this refined air. He had seen it in her eyes. He closed his own eyes, imagining her in his arms, and groaned with desire, aroused yet again for the third time since he had gone to bed.

He threw off the bedclothes, went and drew the curtains, cutting off the moonlight. Back in bed he let his thoughts drift, his mind going back to the earlier part of the evening when the girl Gwen had gone missing – the event that had led him to walk Sarah home and meet Angela. Whatever Sarah, Finn and Alf thought, he was not so accepting that she had gone off with some other young man. He could only hope he was wrong. Perhaps tomorrow the mystery would be solved. It was a funny world they lived in, a dangerous world.

Eighteen

F inn arrived at Pat and Eileen Kennedy's house for Sunday dinner exactly on time and, as he usually did, he had lots to tell. But in this instance, it was not gossip. It was news, and bad news, at that.

Blackie knew at once that Finn was aching to speak about *something* important, yet was polite enough to greet Uncle Patrick and Aunt Eileen first.

'Welcome, Finn,' Eileen said, appearing in the kitchen doorway, a bright smile on her face.

Patrick shook Finn's proffered hand, also smiling, and then led Finn into the main room. 'Nice to see you, my lad,' Patrick said. 'Come and sit with us.'

Blackie was standing in front of the fireplace, which was not blazing up the chimney today. It was a lovely warm June Sunday, and outside there was a bright blue sky and sunshine.

Stepping forward, Blackie gave Finn a friendly punch on the arm, and asked, 'Would ye be liking a lemonade?'

'Thanks, Blackie, I'd enjoy that.' Turning to Patrick, he went on, 'Thank you very much for inviting me for Sunday dinner.

It's my favourite, but I don't get it very often. I've been looking forward to it all week.'

Patrick added, 'It's mine too, my lad, and Blackie's, and you're in for a treat. My wife's a wonderful cook.' Glancing behind him, and then stepping towards the kitchen, he asked, 'Can I tell the lads what's on the menu, love?'

Eileen came to the doorway. 'Certainly you can,' she answered, laughter echoing. Patrick announced, with something of a flourish, 'First course will be a Yorkshire pudding, one each, served from oven to table as fast as possible, so it doesn't sink. With gravy, of course. Main course is *my* favourite, a leg of lamb, with roasted potatoes, boiled greens and carrots. Gravy, as usual, and mint sauce to top it off.'

'A feast indeed!' Blackie cried and moved across the kitchen. 'Do ye want lemonade, too, Uncle Pat?'

'I will have a glass, please.' Patrick took Finn to the sofa, where they sat together.

Patrick peered at Blackie's best friend, and then frowned. 'Do I detect worry in your eyes? Is something wrong, lad?'

Finn nodded. 'I'll wait for Blackie to come back, then I'll tell ye, Mr Kennedy.'

Blackie heard this, and returned with the lemonade on a small tin tray.

Once they had their glasses in their hands, Blackie said, 'Come on then, Finn, spill it! What's wrong? I can see ye are troubled.'

After a quick sip of lemonade, Finn said in a low tone, 'It's about Gwen. She never went home last night. Alf came to tell me early on this morning, very edgy. Then he went back to get her mother. Mrs Turner was upset, crying and wailing. She and Alf had gone to the police station in Wortley Road. I expect they're still at the station.'

Patrick exclaimed, 'What are you saying, Finn? That Gwen has disappeared?'

Finn nodded. 'In the blink of an eye.'

Blackie said, 'Seemingly into thin air. Ye see, last night, when Alf went to pick her up from her house, to go to the dance hall, her mother explained she'd just left, gone on her own.'

'I see. When the plan was they'd go together, is that it?' Patrick asked.

'That's what Alf told us when he came to the dance hall, looking for her. He looked bothered,' Finn explained.

Blackie interjected, 'She was there at one moment, 'cos Sarah Clough saw her going to the ladies, then later Sarah had spotted her sitting on a bench drinking a lemonade.' Blackie glanced at Finn. 'And ye said, ye saw her leave, sure and ye told me that, and Sarah, too.'

'When did Alf arrive?' Patrick wondered aloud.

'Mebbe ten minutes later. So they can't have met outside, because they'd have come back into the dance hall,' Finn pointed out.

'True enough,' Blackie said. 'And when Alf came in alone, he said there was not one soul on Town Street and he'd have bumped into her if she'd been going home.'

'I understand, and so what did Alf do after that?'

'He said he'd go and look in the streets around Ridge Road,' Finn told Patrick, pulling a face. 'So we volunteered to go too.'

'I see. And there was no sight of her, was there?'

'No, Uncle Patrick, there was no one about last night. Empty streets. So we broke up. It was dark by then and I walked Sarah home.' A deep sigh escaped Blackie and a grim expression settled on his face as he added, ''Tis a mystery to me, on the heads of the Blessed Saints it is, and it don't bode well with me either. Something's amiss here.'

Patrick stared at his nephew, a puzzled look crossing his face. 'Are you suggesting some sort of foul play?' he finally ventured, not liking the sound of this story at all. It alarmed him. And he was concerned about the lad who worked for him.

Blackie took a deep breath and plunged. 'I can't help thinking she was grabbed, taken.'

'By a *stranger*?' Patrick's eyes bored into Blackie. 'But Upper Armley is the safest place *I* know, and I travelled the world in the navy.'

'How do ye knows it's safe, Uncle? These days anything can happen . . . anywhere. Only last week I read in one of your newspapers that a girl had been taken in Harehills. Never seen again, body never was found. So far.'

'I missed that story,' Patrick replied, an undertone of worry in his voice. 'Are you certain she was never found?'

'Sure and I am, Uncle Pat. There are all sorts roaming the streets, weird people in our midst, and ye are the one allus telling me it's a dangerous world we live in these days.'

'Aye, that's true, I am saying that and I mean it.'

Finn now volunteered, 'There is one other thing, Blackie. Don't ye remember Alf said they'd had that tiff the night before; also there was an idea passed around that she might have gone off with another lad.'

Blackie exclaimed, 'That's right! Alf mentioned that lad Ian Craig. Mebbe she's all right. Mebbe she's hooked up with him.'

'So why didn't she go home?' Finn said. 'Did she go back to *his* house? Is she still there?'

'That don't sound like Gwen. She is a nice girl, not a loose woman,' Blackie murmured, and said no more as Aunt Eileen appeared in the main room, removing her pinafore.

She said, 'Will you all come and get yer Yorkshire puddings, please.'

The three men rose, and Patrick said in a quiet voice, 'No discussion about Gwen, lads. I don't want Eileen to be upset.'

'Quiet as two mice,' Finn whispered.

Blackie merely nodded.

*   *   *

From time to time, Eileen and Patrick exchanged glances. They didn't say a word to each other, but their eyes shone with shared pleasure.

They knew how much Finn was enjoying the large, round Yorkshire pudding, now oozing gravy. And Blackie too was engrossed with his food, as he always was.

When they had all finished the first course, Eileen asked Patrick to bring the plates, and for Blackie to refill their tumblers with cold water.

'What else can *we* do, Aunt Eileen?' Blackie asked. 'Can we help some more?'

'Your uncle is going to carve the leg of lamb, and I will serve the vegetables. Once the plates are ready, you can come and carry them to the table. Finn will help you.'

'Sure and we will,' Blackie responded, and glanced at Finn. Leaning closer, he whispered, 'Where did ye get all the information about Gwen? From Alf?'

'Yes, and also from Sarah. I bumped into her on Town Street. She'd been to Christ Church, to the morning service. The neighbours had been talking to each other before and after the service.'

'Was she with her sister?'

'No, she was alone,' Finn answered. 'I didn't even know about a sister. How did ye know there was one?'

'I walked Sarah home last night, remember, and it was the sister who let us in. She was a beauty, believe me, a knockout . . .'

'Are ye interested, eh?' Finn probed, laughter in his eyes.

'No, I am not, believe me . . . she's a widow lady,' Blackie replied quickly, thinking, and a gorgeous widow.

'Oh, perhaps that's why I never set eyes on her. Did ye see her before last night?' Finn continued to press.

'Never. I understand she's a bit of a recluse. Quite refined, like, and . . .'

Blackie stopped abruptly as his uncle appeared and beckoned. 'Come and get the plates, lads, and I'll bring the other two.'

Once they were all settled at the table, Finn looked at his plate, his eyes wide with joy. He hesitated, wondering what to eat first. The slice of lamb with a spoonful of mint sauce or a roasted potato saturated with rich gravy. A moment later he picked up a fork and started with the roasted potato, then cut into the meat, after that a carrot. They were all melting in his mouth. What a special meal, he thought, as he relished the food. I've never eaten a Sunday dinner like this. I hope I get invited again. He knew he must be on his best behaviour today. He ate slowly, savouring every bite.

When they had apple crumble with warm custard sauce, Blackie was in seventh heaven; it was his favourite. But he was well aware that today Aunt Eileen had made it for Finn. He wasn't jealous, he was simply glad his friend was able to enjoy this lovely treat his aunt had prepared.

He suddenly realized, yet again, what thoughtful people they were, knowing they brought kindness and compassion to him, and his friends. Patrick and Eileen Kennedy were truly unique and loving people, who always showed generosity to their family.

NINETEEN

Blackie began to feel nervous as he walked up the hill towards the Traveller's Rest pub a few days later, and this unexpected emotion took him by surprise.

He had always been self-confident, sure of himself, but now he was a little rattled. It was because he was going to see Angela and, at the sudden thought of her, his step faltered, and he leaned against the fence of a house.

An image of her was embedded in his brain and had remained there from the first moment he had set eyes on her. She was a beauty, the kind of woman he had not met before, and he had fallen for her.

This aside, he was a novice when it came to the opposite sex. He had never had a relationship, not even a platonic friendship with a girl. Much less, as in this instance, a woman. An experienced woman, he had no doubt, and a widow. She was elegant, refined and educated.

Stop dithering, he told himself, get a hold of your feelings, and hurry up. He realized he didn't want to arrive late. Pulling himself up to his full height, he now strode on. As he walked at a quick pace, he reminded himself that Angela had issued the invitation. The fact that she was older than he was didn't matter. He was indifferent to age; it played no role in his life.

Within five minutes, he had arrived at the moor, where children played after school, as he himself had once. Glancing across the road, he saw that the pub looked busy, with several men sitting outside with their pints, chatting and smoking.

Walking a few steps forward, he was now at the small, neat house with a dark green door and matching shutters. Angela's house. Pushing open the gate, he walked down the garden path, lifted the brass door knocker and so announced his arrival.

A moment later the door opened, and he was greeted by a smiling Sarah. He forced a smile, but disappointment slid through him. Blackie had believed he and Angela would be alone, but obviously not. Sarah was probably there as a chaperone, to protect Angela's reputation. Even though she was a widow, and would have more freedom than an unmarried girl, she would still need to be respectable. This thought brought a little burst of laughter, as he stepped inside the entrance hall.

'Why are you amused?' Sarah asked, peering at him.

'I'm not,' he announced swiftly, pushing the laughter down. 'I'm just . . . glad to see ye.'

'No, you're not,' Sarah shot back, a smile on her face. 'You thought you'd be having supper alone with my sister, and you are. I just came to bring her a few things. I'll be off soon. So, come on, she's out in the back garden.'

Blackie was thrilled to know he would have Angela to himself, and his anticipation about a pleasant evening was high. As they walked down a corridor to the back door, he glimpsed a room through an open door, with elegant furnishings arranged with taste.

The garden took him by surprise. It was filled with flowers and flowering bushes and the last of the June roses, all surrounded by a high stone wall. Two willow trees brought shade to the lawn.

Angela stood up, as Sarah and Blackie came towards her. There was a wide smile on her face and, when he stopped in front of her, she stretched out her hand to shake his, staring up into his face.

Blackie took it, held it tightly in his own, gazing down at her, savouring the moment. Her blue eyes were sparkling and there was a faint blush on her neck and cheeks. He knew she felt as he did.

She broke the intensity, the silence between them. 'Welcome to my house, Blackie. Come, sit down, and Sarah will help me serve lemonade.'

'Thank ye,' he managed to say, once again overwhelmed by her beauty and her simple but elegant dress. It was a pale lilac colour that accentuated her eyes, cut with a low, scooped-out bodice and loose sleeves, with the slimmer silhouette that was becoming popular. Her skin was pale ivory and he wanted to touch her, love her. He stepped away and hovered near a chair, his heart thudding.

Soon the three of them were sitting together, enjoying the last of the afternoon sun. Sarah was talking.

'So Alf has kept me informed, Blackie. I was just telling Angela, before you arrived, that Gwen has still not come home. Nor has she been found.'

Blackie nodded. 'I had heard that too. 'Tis a true mystery, I be thinking. Apparently the local police have scoured Upper Armley, have gone through Gotts Park and Armley Park, and every lane nearby. No trace of her.'

'This must be quite awful for her mother,' Angela murmured. 'Poor woman, she must be frantic with worry.'

'She is,' Sarah said. 'And so is Alf. He blames himself – well, sort of – because of that tiff they had the night before.'

Blackie said, 'Alf had nothing to do with this situation. In my opinion, I think Gwen had a new chap and either went off with him or she was snatched by a stranger.'

His words startled both women, and Angela frowned and gave him a quick look. 'Who would snatch her, for Heaven's sake?'

'An evil man with bad intentions,' Blackie replied in a low, serious voice.

Angela looked aghast and shuddered.

Sarah said, 'I can't help thinking you are right.' She shook her head. 'I hope it's a new chap, not a bad man out to do her harm.'

'Oh goodness me, yes,' Angela said. After a pause, she went on, 'Let's talk about something less harrowing, please. Is anyone going to the York races this summer?'

Sarah, who always seemed well-informed about what was happening in the streets where they lived, did most of the talking. She was laden with gossip.

Blackie did not mind; he only half listened anyway. He was preoccupied with thoughts of Angela. His feelings and emotions were very new to him, and myriad thoughts swept through his head. His attraction to her was somewhat overwhelming, and little threads of worry lingered. How should he behave? What should he do? Was she expecting him to make a move towards her, or would *she* take the lead? This situation troubled him no end. She was more sophisticated, experienced than he was, and even this house was more elegant than any he was used to.

Suddenly, he had the answer. *She* must make the first move, not him. His uncle had already warned him never to force himself on a woman. He realized it would be out of place if he took hold of her, kissed her as he longed to do. Whilst he believed she felt the same way about him, he could not chance it. Sit back and wait, he told himself. This decision helped him to relax. He had long believed that things happened when they were supposed to happen, and not by chance. Meeting Angela was meant to be.

Now. Not next week or the week after. This was their time to come together. Or not.

He took a sip of the lemonade and settled back in the chair. It was a lovely time of day now, his favourite time. The sun was settling down, sliding over the horizon, and shortly twilight would descend.

A faint breeze rustled through the trees, and unexpectedly a flock of birds flew up into the deep blue sky, forming an elegant V, as they usually did. He heard a scurrying noise and glanced around. To his surprise, he saw a squirrel running up into a tree. A slight smile crossed his face, and then he sat up straight as Sarah addressed him directly.

'I must get off, Blackie,' she said, standing up. 'I have to go and make tea for Mam, her chest's still bad.'

He rose, and replied, 'I hope she's feeling better.'

Angela also got up and went over to her sister, taking hold of her arm. 'I'll walk you to the door. I have a few things for Mam, which I know she'll enjoy.' Looking at Blackie, Angela added, 'I'll be back in a few seconds. Excuse me.'

He nodded and returned to the chair, wondering when they would have supper, as she had called it, and also when she had made it. He had seen no sign of a housekeeper.

Within a few minutes Angela came back, hurrying down the terrace, and he stood up. She stopped directly in front of him, squeezed his arm in an affectionate way and sat down in the chair next to his. 'Sarah's such a chatterbox, isn't she?' Angela laughed and went on, 'But I've always found her entertaining.'

'Yes, she is, and how she does collect gossip! On the other hand, there's nothing malicious about what she says.'

'Very true.' Angela leaned forward, drew closer to him. 'Why do you think something bad might have happened to Gwen?'

'Because of the way she just disappeared. If she had met

some new chap, a local boy, she would have told Alf. Or better still, her mother. That's what I be thinking, Angela.'

'I suppose I agree, and I don't think she would have stayed out all night with a new boyfriend, especially a local chap. Too much gossip.'

'The world is a dangerous place, at least that's what Uncle Pat is always telling me,' Blackie said in a low voice. 'Just recently I read a story in the newspaper about a girl in Harehills just disappearing. Never seen again, and a body was never found. The police were baffled.'

'Oh my God! How awful!' Angela shook her head. 'My Aunt Clarice always warned me about the dangers outside the front door. That was the way she put it when I was living with her in Harrogate.'

'Harrogate! Ye lived there? When was that?'

'Some years ago now. Her husband died when they were quite young. Uncle Oscar was about thirty-nine, forty. My aunt was very lonely, and my mother sent me to live with her sister. The way she explained it was that I could be like a daughter to Aunt Clarice and keep her company, give her a purpose in life . . . *that* was bringing me up.'

'And was your mother right?'

'Yes, she was. Aunt Clarice loved me as if I were her child, and she taught me to be a seamstress like she was, making beautiful clothes for the real ladies of Harrogate.'

Blackie was startled and exclaimed, 'You're a seamstress? Even now?'

'Not now, not really. I do make clothes, but only for Sarah and for myself. I don't work at sewing any more. It's hard work, exacting, and the ladies *can* be difficult at times.'

Blackie nodded. 'I bet they can.' After a moment's pause, he went on. 'So ye more or less lived in Harrogate all of your life . . . until ye came here?'

'Yes, from the age of eight.'

'Didn't ye miss your mother and Sarah?'

'Not really, because they came to stay with us a lot . . . especially for the special holidays, like Christmas and New Year, and in the summer months. My aunt has a house near The Stray, and she was always very welcoming.'

Blackie smiled as he explained to her, 'I love Harrogate. It's me favourite place in Yorkshire. And I swear on the heads of the Blessed Saints that I will build meself a house there one day. That be truly the aim in me life.'

Angela smiled, her blue eyes sparkling. 'A builder, eh? Well, that is surely a good trade, and one day perhaps we could go to Harrogate for a day's outing. And we'll go to Aunt Clarice's house. I, too, love it there.'

'Do ye really? 'Tis a wonderful town. I would like to take a trip there, sure and I would. Thank ye for inviting me.'

They spoke a little bit longer about Harrogate and its beautiful buildings. Then Angela changed the subject and said, 'Here we are, chatting away, and it's already growing late. And the air is becoming a bit chilly. Shall we go in and eat?'

'Why of course, 'tis twilight.'

Jumping up, Blackie offered her his hand.

Angela took it and held onto it all the way along the terrace and into the house.

TWENTY

'I'm going to pop to the kitchen to see what's happening, Blackie. And if you want you can look at these rooms. I believe it's a well-designed house. It might interest you.'

Angela smiled at him, dropped his hand, and waved at the open doors. 'Go on, go and investigate. I won't be long,' she added. 'Builders like to look at houses, I believe.'

'Thank ye,' he answered, and did as she said. Pushing open the nearest door, he found himself walking into a square study, almost like a small library. His face changed, instantly, filled with admiration, as his dark eyes swept over the pine-panelled walls and matching shelves, filled with books. The pale wood seemed to have a silvery gleam to it in the early evening light.

There were only a few pieces of furniture; a small antique desk under the window overlooking the garden, and a rose-coloured sofa and two small armchairs covered in the same rose fabric. All these were arranged in front of the fireplace.

Blackie tried to take in everything at once, the many books, the painting of a bowl of flowers on the wall above the fireplace, and the ornaments placed here and there among the books.

How well she had done the room, small though it was. *If* she had decorated it. Something told him she had. He strolled over to the shelves next to the fireplace, his eyes scanning the books. A lot of history. Biographies of kings.

With a huge smile, he took out the one called *The Six Wives of Henry VIII*. Well, he thought, I've never come across this one in the Armley Public Library. But I'll seek it out, he thought, as he put it back on the shelf.

Turning, he went out into the long corridor which ran from the garden door to the front door of the house. He liked this corridor, and the squareness of the actual house.

He hated what he thought of as 'bits and pieces' – small additions, popping out at each end of a house. Blackie O'Neill's ideal, his true favourite, was Georgian. That was the style he favoured and would build. One day he would own one himself, he was sure. And definitely in Harrogate.

Opposite the library was the drawing room and, like the room he had just left, it was light on furniture and clutter.

How he disliked the ornate style of Queen Victoria's time, so prevalent still. Too much furniture, too many objects, and those ghastly plants in big brass pots – mostly palms squeezed in between small tables.

He walked slowly around, noting the sense of calmness. The walls were painted cream, as were the doors and the fireplace. Two small sofas were covered in cream brocade, and the rug on the floor was cream, patterned with small pink, green and blue flowers. The paleness, the austerity, the smoothness of the room created an atmosphere of tranquillity. He recognized that Angela had good taste and a flair for decorating. A style of her own that was unique.

'Here you are!' Angela exclaimed, coming into the drawing room. 'So, Blackie, do you like my home?'

'Absolutely,' he answered, swinging around at the sound of

her voice. 'The library is a gem, and what a sense of calmness ye have created in here. I like your choices, how ye've been very careful not to fill up space with needless *stuff*.'

She nodded. 'I hate a lot of *stuff*, as you call it; much prefer a sense of airiness, spaciousness. Well, I'm *glad* you approve. So, come along, supper is ready. Claudie is about to put the dishes on the sideboard in the dining room.'

Blackie asked, 'Who is Claudie?'

Walking alongside him down the corridor, Angela explained, 'She's my helper, a devoted friend of many years. Her mother Clara was my aunt's housekeeper in Harrogate, when I was growing up. They lived with us at the house near The Stray. When Clara died, we took Claudie on. She had no other family and nowhere to go, you see.'

'That was kind of ye,' Blackie ventured, a strong hint of admiration in his voice. He glanced down at her, thinking what a nice person she seemed to be, thoughtful of others.

The dining room took him by surprise as they entered. After the paleness of the pine-panelled library and the all-cream drawing room, they stepped into a dark green-and-white room. Green walls and draperies, with white paint on all the doors, wood trim, and the ceiling. The chair frames were also painted white, and all the chair seats were of deep green brocade. It was handsome, he decided, and a nice change.

Angela looked up at him. Observing the surprise on his face, she burst out laughing. 'A bit of a shock, eh, Blackie?'

He nodded, chuckling, and then turned as he heard the click of heels on the wooden floor. A young woman wearing an apron was walking in carrying a tray. He wanted to go and help her, but instinct told him he should not. So he remained put, out of his depth as a guest in this house.

Once the tray was put down on a side table, the young woman turned and nodded. 'Good evening,' she murmured.

'Claudie, come and meet Mr O'Neill,' Angela said, before he could return the young woman's greeting.

She did as Angela had asked and hurried to join them. Angela said, 'Blackie, this is Claudette Bouvier, who helps me in the kitchen.'

Blackie, thrusting out his hand, said, 'I'm pleased to meet ye, Miss Bouvier.'

Claudette took his hand. 'And I am happy to meet you, Mr O'Neill.' With a small nod, she went back to the tray on the table and began to place the dishes on the sideboard. He noticed she was being very careful.

Angela took his arm, guided him to a chair, and then went to the opposite side of the dining table and sat down herself, smiling warmly at him. 'I didn't have any idea what food you like,' she remarked, 'so I just kept the menu simple, just as I like.'

'I'm not a picky eater,' Blackie answered swiftly. 'I enjoy most things.' As he said this, he realized he wasn't hungry at all, for once in his life. At least not for food. He sat staring at this beautiful woman, transfixed.

Claudie walked across and paused at the table. 'Everything is ready on the sideboard. Enjoy supper.'

'Thank you,' Angela said, and Blackie also gave her his thanks.

Once they were alone, Angela pushed back her chair, stood, and hurried to the sideboard. 'Claudie has potato and leek soup for us.' Whilst she was speaking, she put the bowls on a small tray and carried this to the table, placed one in front of Blackie and then the other at her place. 'I think you'll like it,' she said, picking up a spoon.

He did, and unexpectedly his appetite revived. After several mouthfuls, he put the spoon down and looked across the table at her. 'It's delicious. I've never tasted this kind of soup before. Claudie is obviously a good cook.'

'She is. Her father was a Frenchman, Arnaud Bouvier, and she learned a lot from him. You see, he was a French chef by trade.'

'In Harrogate?' Blackie asked, a dark brow lifting.

'Yes. He came to England as a very young man with his brother Jacques. They opened a little shop, and it did well. Jacques handled the business and Arnaud was the chef. His great speciality was confectionery, and he was also a wonderful baker.'

'Well, fancy that. How interesting their story is. I never think of foreigners living in the north. I always think of them in London.'

'I know what you mean, but the man who has opened a café in Harrogate called Hettys is a pastry chef from Switzerland.'

'*Really?*' Blackie stared at her, amazement apparent. 'Ye are a fountain of information, just like Sarah. But in a different way,' he thought to add.

Angela nodded. 'I grew up in Harrogate, as I told you.' Rising, she took the empty bowls away and, over her shoulder, she said, 'Blackie, come and help yourself to the main course. Claudie and I prepared cutlets with new potatoes. There are green peas too.'

Blackie strode across to the sideboard, took the plate she was offering, and gave her an appreciative look. 'It's quite a supper ye planned, Angela. Thank ye for inviting me.'

'I'm happy you're here,' she murmured, looking up into his face, her eyes riveted on his.

'*I'm* happy too, so I am,' he murmured in a low voice, held by her eyes. His heart thudded once more.

Turning away swiftly, Angela began to serve the food to him.

TWENTY-ONE

After supper, Blackie let himself be led into the library by Angela.

The fire had been lit, lamps turned on, and Angela directed him to the sofa. She sat in a chair, and said swiftly, 'Claudie is bringing us cups of tea. We can relax here and let our food digest.'

He nodded, leaned towards the fire, and then swivelled his head as he spoke to her. 'I do like a fire,' he admitted. ''Tis cooler now anyway.'

'There's a bit of a chill in the air, I agree. I hope you enjoyed Claudie's food.'

'The best,' he answered, with a small chuckle. 'Never tasted rhubarb tart like that before. Her flavours are . . . *unique*.'

'She has a secret recipe. It was a pleasure to prepare supper for someone. It's clear you enjoy your food.'

'I do, 'tis true. Perhaps because I often went hungry as a child.'

Angela nodded. 'I guess it was a hard life in Ireland, from what other Irish friends have told me about their early years. Hunger and poverty.'

'Sure and it was tough, and what food I could get was a preoccupation. I was lucky. I had good friends who were happy to share what they had with me.'

'Where do you come from?'

'A little hamlet in North Kerry. It doesn't really even have a proper name. I was born there and left when I was thirteen.'

At this moment, Claudie entered the library carrying a tray, which she put down on the desk. 'Shall I pour?' she asked, looking over at Angela.

'Oh no, that's all right,' Angela responded genially. 'I can do it.'

Claudie smiled at them both and left.

'How do you like your tea? With milk? Sugar?' Angela asked Blackie.

'Milk and sugar, please.'

A moment later, Angela placed the cup of tea on a small table, bending down to do so. She was so close to him, he could smell her perfume, a floral scent, and her gleaming white breasts were directly in front of him. Her closeness made his heart flutter. How he wanted her. He took tight control of himself.

Now Angela moved across the floor and poured herself a cup of tea and went to her chair, moving as gracefully as always.

Blackie tried to distract himself. 'I must admit I am a little confused. Ye see, ye said ye grew up in Harrogate, but then mentioned ye lived in Upper Armley 'til ye got married.'

'Oh, sorry, Blackie, that does sound odd, I suppose. I *did* grow up in Harrogate, and I did come back here to live with Mam and Sarah for a few months before I married Anthony. You see, he was a bit older than me, was in the Royal Navy, and he knew I might be lonely in Harrogate once he was at sea for months on end—'

'But ye had your aunt there, didn't ye?' Blackie cut in. 'Ye could live with her.'

Angela took a sip of her tea, her beautiful face serious for a moment. 'I did, but she was frail by then, and Anthony was truly wise. He was looking to the future. He wanted me to find a nice little house here in Armley so I could be close to my mother and sister, perhaps if we had a family, I mean. And whilst he was on his ship.'

'And was this the house ye found *then*?'

Angela smiled. 'It was indeed, although it did take a long time to find the right one. Months. Still, it did turn out all right, didn't it?'

'More than that. I like this design, that I do. Ye see, I am an admirer of the Palladian style in architecture, and of course Georgian as well – that's my favourite . . . I like symmetry in buildings.'

'And mine has symmetry?'

He nodded, unable to speak. Angela had risen and was walking across the floor to him, a lingering smile on her face, her eyes directly on his. She sat down on the sofa and stared up at him. 'Blackie, I would like . . . us to become . . . friends. Can we?'

Finding his voice, he said, a little hoarsely, 'I want that too. Close friends.'

Drawing nearer to him, she reached out and touched his cheek. 'Very close,' she murmured.

He almost flinched as her long delicate fingers stroked his cheek; he let out a long sigh and closed his eyes. His heart was thudding in his chest.

'Open your eyes, Blackie,' she said in a soft voice.

He did so, and looked at her, his dark eyes full of desire and yearning.

She gazed back, stood up in front of him, leaned forward and kissed him on the mouth. Instantly, he took hold of her arms and stood, kissing her as passionately as she was kissing him. They clung together, pressing against each other. They continued to embrace and touch and kiss for a long while. Finally they stopped, drew apart slightly and gazed at each other, looking a little shocked.

She spoke first. 'Can we become very close now? Intimate? Why do we have to wait until we know each other better?'

'We don't,' he said, his voice hoarse, stroking her breast, leaning forward, one arm still around her. 'Can we find a different room? More private.'

'We can. My bedroom. An intimate room for us to be intimate.' She took his hand in hers and drew him up the stairs, across a landing into her bedroom. After closing the door and locking it, she leaned against it and opened her arms to him.

He rushed forward, embraced her, kissed her lips, her cheeks, and her forehead. When he finally stopped, he whispered against her hair, 'Oh Angela, Angela, let us not waste another moment.'

'We won't,' she whispered back, and slid her hand against his crotch. 'Ah, you see, I knew you felt about me like I felt about you, the very moment I set eyes on you. We are meant for each other.'

'True,' he said, struggling out of his jacket, and then tugging at her sleeve.

'Hurry! We must hurry,' she murmured, and turned her back to him. 'Just open four of the buttons, and I can slip out of it.'

With trembling hands, he did as she asked, then swung around and rapidly undressed, as anxious as her for them to be together. And all the time he watched her, as she stepped out of the long silk dress, threw it on a chair, and then shed her petticoat, her corset and stockings. When she turned to face him, she was naked, as she pulled out pins to release light-brown curls.

They virtually rushed at each other and began their passionate kissing once more, then staggered over to the bed, arms still entwined.

Once they lay next to each other, Blackie pushed himself up on one elbow and gazed down at her.

Her exquisite beauty entranced him . . . the finely crafted, high cheekbones, the arched, darker eyebrows, the perfect nose and a full, rather voluptuous mouth. But it was those extra-ordinary, very blue eyes that dazzled him, held him transfixed. He would never tire of looking at her.

It was Angela who pulled his head down to her face, and they began to kiss and touch each other. Their lovemaking was now in earnest, intense and deeply felt.

Together moving against each other, desire fuelling their emotions, they were carried into another place of lust and sensu-ality, with a hunger to possess and be possessed. Blackie had never known this kind of rapture, this kind of pleasure. But then neither had Angela, married though she had been. In a short time they had become besotted, had lost their hearts to one another, and their lovemaking soared.

They lay together, entwined in each other's arms. Silent. Tranquil. Happy to be together. When Angela began to speak, Blackie changed position and pushed himself up, looked down at her, marvelling yet again at her exquisite face, the bluer-than-blue eyes, the tumbling curls that fell to her shoulders. He took a silky strand in his hand.

'When can I see you again?'

She sighed a little. 'I'm glad you like Harrogate, because I have to spend a little time there in the coming weeks—'

'Why is that?' he interrupted swiftly, taken by surprise.

'Because a lady I used to make clothes for needs me to do quite a few alterations to important pieces in her wardrobe. I feel obliged to agree to do this. Lady Lassiter has always been so kind to me.'

'Lady Lassiter!' Blackie exclaimed, sitting bolt upright. 'Is she married to Lord Robert?'

Angela stared at him, frowning, and nodded, wondering how Blackie knew them – or of them, at least.

Before she could ask this question, Blackie said, 'They live at Bolton Manor, between Harrogate and Ripon. Near Studley Royal, sure and they do.' He grinned at her obvious surprise, and added, 'They also live in me little hamlet in Kerry, in the big house on the hill.'

'What a coincidence!'

'To be sure and it is, and I swear on the heads of the Blessed Saints that I'm as taken aback as ye are.'

'So you actually *know* them?'

'I do indeed, I used to do work in the garden for his lordship sometimes, and me cousin Siobhan is a maid for Lady Lassiter, and Michael, her brother, is a gardener at Lassiter Hall.'

'Of course, I know they live in Ireland for half the year, but I never knew where.'

Blackie smiled at her, bent down and kissed her cheek. He said, 'And so, now ye do.'

'Can you come and visit me in Harrogate on Saturday?'

'I can't. I have to help my friend Finn. I promised. And my uncle is involved.'

'Is Finn in trouble or something?'

'No. But *he* promised his friend Tommy O'Hara to help a girl who came to Leeds, and got . . . sort of stuck with her cousin on the Bank.'

Angela sat up and gaped at him. 'Oh, Blackie, Blackie, that's an awful place! The Ham Shank. Very dangerous.' She grabbed his arm. 'Be careful. You must have your wits about you there.'

'I know that! Me Uncle Pat is coming along. His friend Jack Blane will be with us, sure and we'll be like a little gang. I shall be on me guard, I promise, Angela.'

'Will you come and visit me the following Saturday?'

'So ye will still be there?' His eyes rested on hers, and he frowned. 'Why are ye staying in Harrogate so long?'

'To do the clothes for her ladyship.'

'I don't know what to tell Uncle Pat about going to Harrogate for the day.'

'You could come with Sarah; surely he knows she's a friend.'

Blackie nodded, but there was a worried look on his face, which Angela noticed. She said quickly, 'You could say Finn was going, and you *can* bring him, you know.'

The cloudy expression on Blackie's face faded away. 'Finn would like that. He's never been there, sure and he'd enjoy it. All right then. We'll come with Sarah.'

Angela smiled, her eyes sparkling, and leaning closer, she put her arms around Blackie and held him tightly, filled with a kind of happiness she had never known.

TWENTY-TWO

Patrick Kennedy had travelled the world in the Royal Navy, and during his seven-year service, he had seen and visited many countries: the best and the worst.

Sometimes he had found himself in places which were so rundown and overcrowded they were squalid and almost uninhabitable, and he had turned away in horror and disgust.

Now, on this muggy June morning in Leeds, where he had grown up, he was both startled and sickened as he approached the Bank, nicknamed the Ham Shank in the local vernacular of rhyming slang.

There was a stench in the air and, even from a distance, he realized how foul a smell it was. He took a handkerchief out of his jacket pocket and held it to his mouth, wanting to protect himself from the effluvium of muck and slops and the malodorous stink of rotten food and other rubbish that floated around him. Glancing at his friend, Jack Blane, he raised a brow, and Jack nodded, as he too brought a handkerchief to his mouth. Blackie and Finn, who were walking alongside them, followed suit.

Once they came to the end of the road near the railway line between Leeds and Selby, Patrick stopped.

His three companions surrounded him and listened as he removed the handkerchief, and said, 'It's all round here that they're doing the sanitary inspections and talking about knocking it down. It's just a sprawling and decaying slum. And I want us to go in and out as fast as we possibly can. I don't think we should expose ourselves to disease, and also to the thugs who are bound to be lurking around, intent on making trouble.'

Jack nodded. 'I agree. It's a very poor area, and there are criminals and prostitutes living among the decent people who also live there. Hundreds of houses and cottages were built cheek by jowl, all the back-to-backs, and are still being built today.'

Finn, who had been rendered speechless by the vile stench of the Bank filling the air and its deprived, poverty-stricken, soot-blackened appearance, now said, 'Who in God's name would send a young woman like Moira Aherne here?' He shook his head, frowning. 'We've got to make her leave with us today.' He gazed up at Patrick, and asked, 'Who would do this? Send her to a cesspit, a hellhole?'

'Someone who didn't know what it was really like. And you're right, we must not leave her there. She *must* leave with us. As I told you all on the tram, Mrs Wilson is willing to employ her as a maid, provided her butler and housekeeper are happy with her manner. She will live in, be in service, and Mrs Wilson, a nice woman, will make sure she's looked after properly by the housekeeper, Mrs Caulfield. I got all that finally settled yesterday.'

Blackie, his dark eyes filled with worry, asked Finn, 'She does know we're coming, doesn't she? Ye did send a note, didn't ye?'

'No. The postman told me it wouldn't be received. Ye see, the postmen are afraid to go into the Ham Shank. No post gets there.'

Patrick exclaimed, 'Does she know about us? Does she expect us?'

'Yes, she does,' Finn answered. 'Tommy O'Hara gave a message to a friend of his coming to Leeds several weeks ago.'

'What was the message?' Jack probed, puzzled.

'That Moira was to stay at home on Saturdays, because I would go there the first Saturday I was free.'

Mollified a little, Jack turned to Patrick. 'So, we go into the Ham Shank, find the house . . .' He glanced at Finn. 'You've got the address, right?'

'I have,' Finn replied.

'Then let's go,' Patrick said. 'Here's the plan. We go in, tell her to pack what few things she has and leave, taking her with us. We'll go to the Blue Door Café for a bite of dinner, then take her directly to Mrs Wilson's house in the Towers. Agreed?'

'Agreed,' the three of them said in unison.

'One thing,' Jack began, as they walked across the road. 'Let's avoid trouble. The thugs are bound to shout insults and slurs. Ignore them. Don't answer. Don't speak at all. Keep your eyes open, lads, and be alert, sharp-witted. We must not get into a brawl. Our aim is to rescue that young woman unharmed, and scram.'

'Well said!' Patrick exclaimed, and covered his mouth as he marched forward alongside Blackie.

When they arrived at the edge of the Bank, the four men paused and put their handkerchiefs in their pockets. All of them gagged for a few seconds; the stench was stronger here, almost over-powering. Each wondered how long they would last in there.

Patrick said, 'Let's get this over fast. You take the lead, Finn, and get us to the house. It smells putrid in the Bank. I want us out in a few minutes.'

'I'll take the lead, 'course I will,' Finn muttered, and covered his mouth with his hand.

'There are three chaps in their shirts and braces, sitting just ahead of us on a broken wall, smoking, holding what look like tin cups. Ignore them, walk past them,' Jack warned. 'Whatever they say.'

'I bet that's not tea in the tin cups,' Blackie muttered. 'Booze, most likely.' His head filled with sudden memories of the times he had spent here, relieved to be free of this place once and for all.

The four of them launched themselves into the Bank, moving at a fast pace, staring ahead. Fortunately, the three men ignored them. They looked weary, hungover, and out of sorts. Patrick thought they didn't have an ounce of fight in them. Poor sods, he thought, they hardly have a life. It must be rough for them. Work. Booze. Struggle. They'd never know happiness.

Finn explained, 'Here it is, Green Street! Let's look for number eight.' Within seconds the four of them were standing in front of the door to one of the small back-to-back houses, next to a narrow alleyway.

It was Finn who knocked. The next moment they were staring at the woman who opened the door. Dressed in a black frock, she wore a stained white pinafore.

She was tall, thin, and had faded fair hair and blue eyes. But her face was lined, and she had a dejected air about her. Her eyes were dead and seemed empty of life.

'Are you Finn, then?' she asked, and looked at him keenly. 'Come to fetch Moira?'

'Yes, that's me, Finn Ryan, Mrs.'

'I am Mrs Walton. Come in, then. I'm Tommy's cousin, well, cousin by marriage.'

They all entered the small room and introduced themselves.

'Seems ter me yer've come in ter the Ham Shank like a bloody posse.' She half-smiled. 'Smart of yer, though, it's not particularly safe. Every bloody man that lives here will start a brawl for no reason—'

'Good morning, lads,' a male voice said, and added, 'I'm Stephen Walton, Jane's husband.' A thin, grey-haired man came downstairs and into the room, and went around shaking their hands. He, too, had a careworn face, but his demeanour was pleasant, even welcoming. 'And ye *are* a posse, that's a fact.'

Patrick said, 'We wanted to come with Finn because we'd heard the Ham Shank was dangerous.'

'Aye, it is that,' the man agreed, nodding his head vehemently. 'That's why we haven't let her go outside since she got here.'

'Because of the way she looks,' Jane Walton cut in, grimacing. 'What a face she's got. There's no telling what men out there might do to her. They're easily roused up around the Ham Shank.'

Jack, frowning, asked, 'She's different, is she?'

'I wouldn't say that,' Stephen Walton muttered. 'Just different ter most women we see every day.'

'Ye are goin' ter take her away with yer today, I hope. Whisk her off to Upper Armley, like Tommy said in his message,' Mrs Walton said, sounding anxious.

'Yes, that's what I want to do,' Patrick said, deciding to take charge, wishing to leave swiftly, get away from the Ham Shank more than ever.

'We'll go and get her,' Stephen Walton said and, taking his wife's arm, he led her out of the room and back up the rickety stairs.

Blackie said under his breath, 'This room is clean, and the window and the white lace curtains are pristine, sure and they are. As for the Waltons, they seem like nice folk, friendly.' The house was little more than one room above another but scrubbed and neatly kept.

'I think so, too,' Finn agreed. 'And mebbe younger than we think. Mrs Walton is Tommy's cousin of some kind, so he said.'

'Moira Aherne needs looking after, getting to safety,' Blackie said, glancing at Finn. 'And we'll do that, Finn. I swear on the head of the Blessed Saints I'll do that, and ye all will. Correct?'

'Absolutely,' Patrick answered at once. 'That was the reason we came here . . .' He stopped speaking as footsteps were heard and Mrs Walton appeared, holding the arm of Moira. 'This is Miss Moira Aherne, Mr Kennedy.' She gave the girl a small push.

Moira walked across the floor towards him, her face serious.

Patrick was stunned by her looks and quite speechless when she drew to a halt in front of him. She stretched out her hand to him, and said, 'I'm very glad to meet you.' Her voice was low and melodic.

Patrick took her hand, cool to the touch, and managed to return her greeting. 'And I'm happy to meet you, too.'

He found himself holding onto her hand, gazing at her, mesmerized. She was undoubtedly one of the most beautiful young women he had ever seen. Her hair was an almost white-blonde, her eyes pale grey and translucent, her face exquisite with delicate features.

Finn stepped forward and introduced himself. As she turned to him and took his hand, he felt himself blushing. 'I'm Finn, Miss Aherne, Tommy's friend.'

'Oh, it's lovely to meet you, Finn,' she replied, a smile on her face. 'Call me Moira, please. He's said such nice things about you. And thanks for agreeing to take me away from the Bank.'

Finn swallowed, nodded, and finally said, 'I'm happy to help you.'

Jack Blane, as astonished as the others by the young woman's beauty and poise, came over to join them, followed by Blackie.

'I'm Jack Blane, Moira. Call me Jack, and ask me for anything. I'll do it if I can.'

Once again, she smiled and then thanked him graciously. A moment later, Blackie was shaking her hand and giving her his name.

'And that's a nickname, I think,' Moira said, laughter echoing in her voice. 'What's your real name?'

'Shane Patrick Desmond O'Neill, but the whole world *does* call me Blackie.'

'Because you're Black Irish, descended from the Spanish sailors, who crawled onto Irish soil to survive at the time the Spanish Armada foundered on the rocks in the Irish Sea.'

Blackie chuckled. ''Tis true, to be sure it is, and I want to welcome ye to Leeds. I am at your service, Moira.'

'And now we should leave and be on our way to Upper Armley,' Patrick announced. 'Do you have your things ready, Moira?'

'I do, yes, thank you, Mr Kennedy. I'm packed. My carpetbag is over there by the door. I don't have much.'

Patrick nodded and walked over to Jane and Stephen Walton. 'Thank you both for looking after Moira.'

'Tommy is family,' Jane Walton said, really smiling for the first time. 'I had ter do my duty, and she's a lovely person. But whoever sent her ter me had no idea what the Ham Shank is like, or they wouldn't have.'

'We all realized that, Mrs Walton.' Patrick half turned away, then paused, and asked in a lower tone, 'But why did you suggest she was different in some way, just now?'

'Oh, my God, did yer think that? We was trying ter explain

she was so beautiful we daren't let her go out. These buggers, these rough chaps in the Ham Shank would've grabbed her, mebbe raped her—'

'That's a certainty,' Stephen Walton cut in quietly. 'And probably one by one, taking turns. That's how bad it is here.'

Twenty-Three

O nce they left the Bank, they were able to breathe properly, and made their way towards the heart of the city and City Square.

Patrick and Jack walked on each side of Moira. Finn was stepping out in front of the three of them, carrying Moira's carpetbag. Blackie was striding behind Moira, his uncle and Jack. She was literally surrounded by the men, and well protected. This was the way they left the Ham Shank, Moira safe between them, and they kept this arrangement through the streets of Leeds.

They didn't talk much on their way to the Blue Door, the café they were heading to, just a word or two now and then. Mostly they were lost in their own thoughts. Although they didn't know it, Finn and Jack were both thinking about Moira's unusual beauty, mentally comparing her to actresses on the stage.

Patrick was wondering how old she was, certain she was at least seventeen, whilst Blackie was pondering her personality.

He had been struck at once by her unique looks, her vivid colouring, but he was immediately also struck by the fact she was outgoing and friendly. *Vivacious* was the word that stayed in his mind.

He was most aware that she was well-mannered, and certainly she had self-confidence. He couldn't help wondering about her background and who had brought her up; Moira was no raw country girl like some of those who came over from his home country.

At the back of his mind, there lingered the thought that Tommy O'Hara, Finn's friend, had been concerned enough to make sure she knew someone reliable when she came to England. He had done his best, but sadly he hadn't had the right information about the Bank. Sending her there could easily have been her death sentence.

We probably rescued her just in time, Blackie thought, and shuddered unexpectedly, as dreadful images rushed through his head.

He liked women, got on well with them, and always treated them with respect and deference. A smile flickered on his mouth as he remembered Mrs O'Malley, who had mothered him, and Cook at Lassiter Hall, who had fussed over him and fed him. Good women who had made sure he survived when he was a child. It was because of them he was strong and well-built.

Once they reached Briggate, they were minutes away from the Blue Door. Jack turned around and beckoned Blackie. 'Go ahead to the café, Blackie, with your uncle. They know him well.'

'That's a good idea,' Patrick said, also swinging around. 'They'll give us a good table, I'm sure of that.'

The two of them hurried forward and, once they were ahead of the others, Patrick said, in a low voice, 'Moira's clinging to Jack's arm like a barnacle to a boat. I think he didn't want to upset her by going into the restaurant himself, leaving her side.'

Blackie nodded. 'Yes, I noticed how she's been holding onto his arm tightly. Perhaps she's even more nervous and *afraid* than we realize. The Ham Shank would scare anyone to death, especially a girl from the country. The men are rough and have no respect.'

'I couldn't help noticing how clean Tommy's cousin Jane's living room was, and smelling of soap and disinfectant. And a soup was cooking in that pot on the hob. Homely and clean aromas, I must say, as well as good cooking,' Pat confided.

'Ye are correct, Uncle Pat. And Mr and Mrs Walton were clever enough to understand that they had to keep her inside, sure and they did. 'Tis indeed an ugly place, and dangerous. Everyone living there must worry.'

'I hope I never have to enter that cesspool ever again. And here we are, Blackie, my lad! The Blue Door is right ahead, and we'll receive a great welcome.'

Patrick was correct. Gladys, the waitress who always served them, hurried forward to meet them. There was a huge smile on her face and laughter in her eyes when she exclaimed, 'What a sight for sore eyes yer are . . . the lot of you!' Her beady black eyes settled on Moira and widened as she took in her beauty. The waitress was obviously very surprised.

She glanced at Patrick, whom she knew best, and asked, 'And where did yer find this beautiful package? Under a Christmas tree, that's wot I thinks.'

Patrick laughed, and nodded. 'You've got it exactly right, Gladys love.' He shook his head. 'And if I told you *where* we'd really found her, you'd never believe me anyway.'

'Aye, I would. I've always believed what yer told me. Well, come on then, let's not stand here gawping like a lot of sucking ducks, and looking daft.' With these words she marched ahead, ushering them to Patrick's favourite part of the café.

He took control immediately, seated Moira and Jack together, with Finn on Moira's other side. He put Blackie next to Finn and seated himself on Jack's left. He smiled inwardly as he noticed how pleased his old friend looked to be next to Moira, who was obviously as filled with relief as he was.

It seemed to him that the girl believed she had made a friend and, in actuality, she had. Jack was as steady as a rock and reliable. True blue. Trustworthy. Respectful.

Gladys handed around five menus and said, 'I'll bring two pots of tea, and now yer can give the menu a quick glance.' She gestured to the blackboard on the opposite wall, and reminded them, 'Our Saturday specials are listed over yonder, as yer well knows. Back in a tick.'

'I'd forgotten what a card she is, and then some,' Blackie said, his laughter echoing around the table.

'Yes, she's quite a comic,' Patrick agreed. 'But she's served me for donkey's years, and she's very fast, efficient.' He looked around the table. 'Take a look and decide what you fancy for dinner. And there's food listed on the blackboard too.'

Jack said to Moira, 'All the dishes are good here. We think it's the best place to eat in Leeds, because it's like good *home* cooking. And delicious.'

'Thank you for explaining,' Moira said and looked at each one of them. 'Thank you, all of you, for coming to rescue me. I really am relieved to be out of the Ham Shank. You were brave to do what you did for me – a stranger.'

'Best we could do, time was short,' Finn explained. 'We knew we had to go in, grab ye, and get ye away fast. No time for manners and stuff – smash and grab, sort of.'

She nodded. 'It's a dangerous place. The Wild West, some call it. But it's *worse*.'

'Why did Tommy O'Hara send you there?' Patrick asked, raising a brow.

'He had one person he knew of in Leeds – Jane, his cousin by marriage. And, you see, I don't think he knew how bad it was in the Bank. He'd never been there, or heard much about the place.'

'I'm sure that's right,' Jack Blane said, entering the conversation. 'As you said, how could he know that the Ham Shank is a living hell, a cesspit full of deadly men on the ready to kill and maim.' He grimaced. 'And *this* is *England* – hard to believe, with a slum like *that*!'

'The greatest Empire in the history of mankind, *some Empire* indeed,' Patrick announced, sarcasm ringing. 'Well, my friends, I am going to enjoy the beef stew,' he went on, pushing his anger about the government of his country to one side.

'Moira, what would you like to order? Do you know yet?' Patrick asked, his voice kind. 'It's all on me and Jack, no need to worry.'

The girl blushed. 'Yes, I think I'll have the pie. It's ages since I've eaten that.'

Blackie said, 'It's fish and chips for me.' He turned to Finn. Knowing he was a bit shy, and never wanted to look greedy, he said, 'I know ye like meat, so why don't ye have the liver and onions. I know ye'll enjoy it.'

Finn grinned. 'Awright, and I'll start with the Yorkshire pudding. I hope it's as good as your aunt's, with lots of gravy.'

'It is, yes, ye'll soon see,' Blackie reassured him, and looked across the table at Jack. 'What tempts ye, Jack? Meat or fish? Liver? Steak-and-kidney pie?'

'You've got it, Blackie! Steak-and-kidney pie. Definitely. Goodness, I haven't fancied it for years, not since Beth died, in fact. It'll be a nice change.'

Gladys arrived at the table again, carrying a tray of cups and saucers, which she put down and then arranged around the table. After rushing off, she returned within seconds with two large brown teapots on a tray, as well as a bowl of sugar and a jug of milk, plus teaspoons.

'Shall I pour?' she asked, looking at Patrick.

'No, I'll do it. We're all a bit famished, Gladys. Would you please take the orders from the others? I'll have the beef stew with dumplings, please. Thank you.'

Gladys had already taken her pencil out and was writing his order on her pad. Then she moved on, going to Moira next. Once she had their orders, she hurried off without one of her usual funny comments.

The girl had stunned her into silence. She was almost in awe of her, that incredible beauty was perfection. *Who was she?* She looks like a real lady, Gladys thought. An aristocrat. And her clothes were good. Really fine. Hand-me-downs, mebbe. The mystery girl, she decided. *Who is she?* And that Jack! Well, he was already stuck on her; that was a fact. But then he was a widower, after all. And he had been for a long time.

It was Finn who started the conversation with Moira, asking her about her trip over from Ireland, and wondering aloud if she had come alone. She said she had travelled with someone she knew. Suddenly everyone was chatting with her, obviously taken by the young woman and wanting to know her better.

Only Blackie remained silent, sipping his cup of tea. An observer by nature, he knew that shortly he would have to become the inquisitor.

None of the others were asking her the right questions. At least not the ones he would want answers to. Who had she lived with until now? Who had brought her up? Had she worked?

He had realized, almost immediately, that she wasn't an

ordinary girl from an everyday family. She might be *that* actually, perhaps, but somehow she had acquired a great deal of polish and quiet confidence. A belief in herself. There was no doubt in his mind that she had been tutored by someone, or learned from someone in the upper class, tutored to become a lady in the best sense of the word. But if that was so, why had she been set adrift, sent to England, where she knew only Tommy O'Hara, a poor boy from Galway? Who in turn had sent her to a cousin in the Ham Shank.

Settling back in his chair, as Gladys bustled around, he decided he had a mystery to solve. Later. He was hungry now. Well, that's normal for me, he thought, his mouth watering at the smell of delicious food.

It was during lunch that Moira had a few questions of her own. She addressed them to the four men, rather than individually. Her voice was soft, her Irish accent a gentle one rather than the strong rural accent Blackie often heard from new immigrants from his home country.

'I'm told I'll be living in this place called Upper Armley, just outside Leeds, but who with? And will I find work there?' she asked.

It was Patrick who answered at once. 'I've arranged for you to work for a very nice woman, Mrs Gertrude Wilson, and her husband, Alfred. However, Mr Wilson spends most of his time in London. The Wilsons own a lovely mansion in a small grove called the Towers. There is a housekeeper, Mrs Caulfield, a butler called Harrison, and two maids. You will live in, and be in service. Mrs Wilson will employ you as a parlourmaid. How does that sound to you, Moira?'

'Very nice, Mr Kennedy, and are you quite sure Mrs Wilson will accept me?'

'Lass, who wouldn't? Mrs Wilson is a customer of mine. As I told you earlier, I do carpentry and building work, with Blackie as my partner. She knows us well, and certainly we know her to be fair, kind, and a good employer.'

'Thank you, Mr Kennedy. I am grateful.'

'My pleasure, Moira. Do you have any questions?'

'Several. Do I have a day off, or half a day? Or none at all?'

'You have Saturdays off. And you'll be getting a wage from Mrs Wilson. She did not tell me how much. But no doubt she'll discuss it with you.'

Moira nodded, gave him a huge smile, her cheeks dimpling. 'I am looking forward to my new situation. Thank you again, Mr Kennedy.'

A few minutes later, Gladys returned carrying two plates of food, serving Moira first, and then Finn. Within a short while she was back with plates for Patrick, Jack and Blackie.

There were lots of compliments from the four men, and Moira, as they tasted the food, obviously enjoying it.

Blackie's thoughts ran on as he relished his fish and chips. Once the main course was over, he would insist everyone have a pudding so that he could question Moira. His curiosity about her tantalized him.

Once they had demolished their dinner, Blackie pushed his plate away and said to Finn, 'They have the best pudding here at the Blue Door. I'm going to ask Uncle Patrick if we can see the menus.' Turning his gaze on Moira, he said, 'What about you? Do you like desserts?'

'Sometimes. I'd like to look at the menu, Blackie, thank you.'

'Gladys will bring them, but I can remember several of my favourites. Eton mess and strawberries Romanoff.' He stared at her, noticed how her face changed, and she smiled. 'I like those, too.'

Blackie nodded and smiled back, and waved to Gladys, who was standing near the doorway to the kitchen. As he waited, he knew he was correct about Moira. These two desserts were only served in really good restaurants or stately homes and manor houses. Moira had probably been reared in one or the other.

TWENTY-FOUR

Once everyone was enjoying their pudding, Blackie directed his gaze towards Moira, and asked, 'Don't you have any family left in Ireland?'

Her spoon was halfway to her mouth, but she put it down on her plate, and said, 'No, I don't. My parents are dead.' He saw emotion in her eyes.

'I'm sorry, Moira, for your loss. And no siblings then?' He raised a dark brow, his curiosity most apparent.

'No, I was an only child.'

'I understand, and Tommy O'Hara was a friend in Galway?'

'Yes, I knew him there . . .' Her voice trailed off, and she picked up her spoon and began to eat once more.

So did Blackie but, being so interested in her background, he couldn't help asking about her past life. 'So did they die recently? So that's why ye came to Leeds?'

Moira stared at him for a long moment, and then replied quietly, 'They have been dead for a number of months, and I came to England because I knew there were opportunities here. More than in Ireland.'

'That's true, sure and it is, but why pick Leeds?'

'You know very well that Tommy had a cousin here,' she said in a slightly sharper voice.

'I do, indeed I do. But Tommy O'Hara has lots of connections in London. I be thinking he might have been helpful to ye.'

'He never suggested that.'

'So did ye have a job in Ireland?'

'A job, why yes.'

'And where did ye live then? With a relative, perhaps?'

'No, I didn't. I lived with . . . a woman who was kind and compassionate. I was a lady's maid.'

'Oh, that will be useful information for Mrs Wilson, I believe. What do—'

Moira cut him off sharply, 'No more questions, Blackie. I feel as if this is a version of the Spanish Inquisition. I don't understand you, asking so much about my past.'

Finn exclaimed in a loud voice, 'I agree with Moira. Stop it!' Looking at her, he said in a quieter tone, 'He's a nosy parker, that's what he is. Shame on ye, Blackie!'

A flush rose from Blackie's neck to his face, and he said swiftly, 'I'm very sorry, Moira. I didn't mean to upset ye. I'm just interested in your life in Ireland, sure and that's all it is.'

'Why?' she asked, still staring at him. 'Why is my upbringing so important to you?' Her voice had risen.

He half shrugged, suddenly embarrassed and feeling foolish, fully aware that his uncle was puzzled, even annoyed with him. And Jack had a disapproving glint in his eyes. Clearing his throat, adopting a conciliatory tone, he said slowly, 'Because ye are different to anyone I've ever met from round our way – back home in Kerry, I mean. Your way of speaking, and your lovely looks, and I feel ye are well educated . . .' He broke off. 'I didn't mean any harm, ye must understand that. Please accept my apologies.'

Moira nodded. 'I do, Blackie. Let us forget about this.'

Jack said, 'That's the best thing I've heard in the last twenty minutes. And we'd better get going.'

'I agree,' Patrick said. 'Let's pay the bill, Jack; we'd better make haste to City Square to catch the tram to Upper Armley. Mrs Wilson's expecting us at four o'clock.'

Once they were outside, Patrick took hold of Blackie's arm and, stepping out swiftly, he hurried his nephew forward.

When they were a little ahead of the others, Patrick asked in a low, stern voice, 'What on earth got into you, lad? Probing Moira the way you were. It was like pinning a butterfly to the wall. Poor girl, she was getting upset.'

'I didn't mean any harm,' Blackie protested, knowing full well he had been really stupid. 'She intrigues me, that's all.'

'Are you after her? Do you want to take her out? Start courting?' Patrick glanced at his nephew. 'She's a beautiful lass, no two ways about that. Any man would fancy her.'

'No, no, I'm not wanting to hook up with her, Uncle Pat! Honestly, I'm not. It's just that she's different from us—'

'In what way?' Patrick cut in.

'Her way of speaking. She doesn't really have an Irish accent. She sounds more English. And her clothes are of good quality.' He shrugged and let out a sigh. 'I expect I did go too far, but I couldn't stop myself, I swear.'

Patrick said, 'She is well spoken, you're correct there, but *I* caught an Irish lilt in her voice and, to be honest, I thought her dress was rather plain, nothing so special. But she is a little different; I'll grant you that, lad. But please, don't question *anyone* like that, not ever again. It's rude.'

'I won't, Uncle Pat, I promise, and I'm sorry I've upset ye. Shall I apologize again to Moira?'

'God, no! Leave it alone. Leave her alone.'

'Shall I come with ye to Mrs Wilson's?'

'Absolutely not. I am going alone with Moira. That is the proper thing to do. I got Moira the job, and we don't need a gang of men to accompany us.'

Blackie stole a surreptitious look at his uncle, and said in a hushed tone, 'Glad to hear that. Ye can't take your friend Jack with ye. He's been bowled over by her . . . he's stuck on her.'

Patrick eyed Blackie and couldn't help chuckling quietly. 'I'm afraid you've hit the nail on the head there. That's a fact. But he's a bit old for Moira – after all, he's my age.'

'How old do ye think she is?'

'I don't know, Blackie, maybe seventeen, even eighteen.'

'She could be older, ye knows, perhaps even twenty.'

'Oh come on, that's a bit of an exaggeration. Why do you think she could be twenty?'

'She's very grown-up. Mind ye, I think she's also well educated . . .' Blackie paused, and added, 'There's something *worldly* about her.'

'Do you mean sophisticated, perhaps?'

Blackie just nodded. After a second, he said, 'She's been under someone's influence, I feel that strongly.'

'Not necessarily bad, though. Good, I would say. Now let's close this little discussion. We're almost at City Square. When we're on the tram to Armley, Moira will sit with me. Once we arrive at Whingate Junction, I'll be off with her to the Towers. You will go with Finn and Jack down Town Street.'

'Jack might want to come with ye.'

'I'll make sure he understands he can't do that, Blackie. Leave everything to me, and don't utter a word to Moira, except a simple goodbye.'

TWENTY-FIVE

When he arrived home, Blackie was relieved his aunt had gone to bed for a rest. She always did this on Saturday afternoons; she usually helped out at the bakery in the morning and was tired. He worried about Aunt Eileen a little less these days. She was somewhat given to catching colds, ever since the bad illness she'd suffered just before he came to live with her and his uncle, but over the past few years the bloom had returned to her cheeks.

Immediately, Blackie went upstairs to his room, took off his jacket and boots and lay down on the bed. His mind was racing; he was filled with mixed emotions. Angry with himself, ashamed, and exceedingly embarrassed.

What a fool I am, he thought, focusing on the way he had questioned Moira. His Uncle Pat was right. He had been rude and over-inquisitive. No wonder Moira had been impatient with him. Worst of all, he had probably hurt her feelings. He knew Uncle Patrick was furious with him; he had made no bones about that. Finn and Jack were also irritated, and barely spoke to him when they walked down Town Street from Whingate

Junction. Finn had not even mentioned going to the dance hall, as they usually did on Saturday nights.

Blackie let out a long sigh. He didn't want to go dancing. He must find a way to apologize to Moira, but he would not seek her out. Anyway, it was more than likely he would run into her at Mrs Wilson's in the next week or so.

His thoughts turned to the Bank, that foul slum; it was hard to know why the town council allowed it to exist still. There were inspectors being sent in, he knew, and talk of razing parts of it to the ground, but no one knew what the fate of the desperate men, women and children who lived there, often in one or two rooms with no running water, would be. Blackie sighed, glad to be back in his safe little room. The world could be an ugly place, hard and dangerous.

His thoughts ran on, and he suddenly thought of Gwen, who had disappeared in the blink of an eye. Was he correct to think someone must have grabbed her? He wasn't quite sure, and yet what other explanation was there?

She had not come home, and the local police had not found her body in any of the local parks. A mystery, that indeed it was. It had really affected Alf, who was troubled and sad these days.

A cold chill trickled through him at the mere idea she could have been murdered or abducted. Not here. Not in Upper Armley. Uncle Patrick considered it one of the safest places in the entire world. But was any place *really* safe? He shuddered at the thought of danger hiding behind every corner.

Pushing aside these uncharacteristically gloomy meanderings, his thoughts turned to Angela. What a lovely woman she was, and so kind and generous. He had promised to go and see her next weekend, and he surely would. She made him feel happy, an emotion he had not been particularly familiar with so far in his life. He had felt content in the past few years, and grateful to his Uncle Pat, and he liked his life in Upper Armley, but this was something new.

His own life had been difficult in many ways, and he had taken on responsibility very young. And oh, the sorrow and the grief he had borne when his family began to die around him.

His eyes were suddenly moist, filled with tears, as he thought of his father and mother, William, his brother, and Bronagh. One after the other, they had passed away. Life had dealt them the hard blow of poverty, hunger and despair. They were taken by the rough land they lived in. Ireland, where death was all around.

Blackie pushed his face into the soft pillow, the only pillow he had ever had, and wept. He had not cried for a long time, and in a sense it was a great relief to him to shed his tears of a grief so intolerable it was almost impossible to bear.

A gentle tapping on the door awakened Blackie, who had fallen asleep. He sat up with a start, jumped off the bed and opened the door.

His aunt stood there, a gentle smile on her face. 'Won't you come down for tea, Blackie? Your uncle was asking where you were when he got in. And I've a lovely bite of tea for you both today. The pork pies you like from the bakery, and a sponge cake with cream.'

Blackie smiled at her; his aunt was so kind, and he knew it would upset her if he missed his meal. He nodded and went out onto the landing. 'I'll just wash me hands and come right down, sure and I will, Aunt Eileen.'

Although he expected his uncle to still be angry with him, Blackie knew he had to put up a warm front and take the flak if necessary. But Patrick greeted him in a kindly voice when he went into the parlour a few minutes later.

As usual, Patrick Kennedy was standing in front of the fire, warming his back. Even though it was summer, it had turned cool in the late afternoon, and Eileen had put a match to the fire. Blackie knew she always felt cold.

'Mrs Wilson asked me if you had finished your plans for her conservatory when I took Moira there,' Patrick announced. 'I told her I thought you had – almost, anyway. So what stage are they at?'

'They're more or less ready. I was hoping to show them to her this week. After ye've given me the go-ahead, Uncle Pat.'

'I'm impressed, lad, and I know you've worked hard on them. You can show them to me whenever you're ready.'

Blackie nodded and went into the kitchen to help his aunt bring the food to the table, knowing he was back in his uncle's good books. But he would be careful in the future not to ask people too many questions about themselves and watch his manners in general. His uncle was a stickler about that, after all his years in the military, and expected no less from his nephew. Blackie knew that Pat held manners, politeness and courtesy to be the way you got on in life.

Moira Aherne and Mrs Wilson took to each other at once. Moira, observant, quick-witted and highly intelligent, knew at once that Patrick Kennedy had chosen just the right employer for her. And without having met her until today. Good luck, perhaps.

The house in the Towers was a mansion, but small, and it had been well kept. Mrs Wilson – who looked to be in her early fifties, was attractive, well dressed, and had a pleasant demeanour – welcomed her warmly.

Almost at once, Patrick Kennedy had explained that Moira was happy to be employed as a parlourmaid, but that she had actually been trained to be a lady's maid.

To Moira's surprise, Mrs Wilson pondered this for only a moment, before saying that she would employ her as a lady's maid. Mr Kennedy said he would leave them alone for a moment to discuss Moira's wages and stepped onto the terrace. He was curious to see the area where Blackie planned to build the conservatory, as well as giving the women privacy.

'Please sit down, Moira,' Mrs Wilson said, 'and let's discuss your duties as a lady's maid.'

Moira did as Mrs Wilson asked, opened her reticule and took out an envelope. 'Here is a reference from my last employer, Mrs Wilson.' She gave it to her as she spoke.

'Thank you,' Mrs Wilson replied and took out the reference, and read it not once, but twice.

Moira noticed that Mrs Wilson seemed surprised, yet pleased, when she laid down the letter, which was written on headed stationery, and looked across at her. 'Lady Henrietta Fitzgerald Chandler. Why did you leave her service, Moira?'

'Sadly she died, Mrs Wilson. My parents had both died within a year of each other, three years ago now, and after her ladyship passed away, I was all alone. She wrote this for me while ill.'

'I see, I understand. This is a most favourable reference. Her ladyship does speak most highly of you. I think you will fit in perfectly here, and I had been considering hiring a lady's maid because I may have to travel with my husband in the near future. I see from the reference that you travelled with Lady Henrietta.'

'Yes, her ladyship lived in London part of the year, for the season, you know, and also in Galway. She had a lovely house just outside the town.'

'You worked for her for many years,' Mrs Wilson commented, glancing at the reference again, and then staring at Moira.

'I did. I lived with her as a child; what I mean is I lived in her two homes because my mother was her housekeeper and my father the butler for Lord and Lady Fitzgerald Chandler.'

'I understand,' Mrs Wilson murmured, and rose. 'Come along. I'll take you upstairs and my housekeeper will show you your room, and we will discuss your wages and other matters.'

'Yes, of course, Mrs Wilson.'

Once Moira was alone, she walked around the room which Mrs Wilson's housekeeper had told her would now – as a lady's maid – be hers. It was at the far end of the main bedroom corridor. Compact in size, it was nonetheless comfortable, with a single bed with a headboard, a chest of drawers, and a sturdy wardrobe, all made of a warm dark wood. There was a rug covering the wooden floor and a small chair near the fireplace. A large window let in lots of light and the long green-and-blue curtains matched the upholstery of the chair.

Moira put her carpetbag on the bed and carefully took out the few clothes. She then reached for the photograph frame wrapped in a nightgown. After unwrapping it, she took out the silver frame and stared at the woman in the picture. Tears sprang into her eyes and she went and sat in the chair, taking deep breaths.

'I miss you so much. I'll miss you all my life,' she whispered to the photograph. 'Until the day *I* die, and I come to you in Heaven.'

The tears rolled down Moira's cheeks and splashed onto the glass, blurring the woman's beautiful face. She reached into the pocket of her dress, took out a handkerchief, and wiped the glass, then held the frame close to her heart.

Moira closed her eyes, remembering . . . She knew then that she would always have these memories to draw on, to keep her sane in this awful world, to comfort her in times of trouble. She had belonged to them, and their imprint was on her, every part of her.

She had their manners, their way of speaking, and they had educated her, recognizing her fierce intellect, her love of books, her curiosity and cleverness. They had made her who and what she was . . . their creation in every way.

But now they were gone, and she would have to make her own way in the world.

After a while, Moira stood up and went to the chest. She placed the silver frame in the middle drawer, then covered it with her underclothes. Once she had unpacked the carpetbag, she put it away in a closet.

A small bathroom opened off the end of the corridor nearby. After washing her hands and face, and smoothing her hair, Moira went downstairs to meet Mrs Caulfield, the housekeeper, who would give her a uniform composed of a black dress and a small white lace collar. And then her new life would begin until she could find a way to change it. Permanently.

As she went downstairs, Moira thought of the young man called Blackie, who had probed, asked her about herself. She had been startled he had spotted how different she was. And so fast.

As for the older man, Jack, he had been nice to her and tried to be protective. But it was Patrick Kennedy who had been the true gentleman. There was no question in her mind about that.

Mmmm, she thought, pursing her lips, we shall see. We shall see.

TWENTY-SIX

I t was a mild Sunday afternoon at the end of June. The sky was pale blue, with puffball white clouds, the air balmy and soft.

A good afternoon for their mandatory walk after lunch, Patrick thought, as he and Blackie went up the hill, heading towards the moor and the Traveller's Rest pub.

There was a companionable silence between them on this particular day. Usually Blackie was talkative, full of titbits of information, local gossip, or his opinions about a book he was reading.

Patrick's thoughts turned back to their visit to the Ham Shank the day before. He still felt shocked himself by what he had seen: the filth, the horrific smells, the poverty, the soot-blackened houses packed together, the general air of despair and apathy about the place. A slum of the worst kind. Although his nephew's life in Ireland had been desperately poor, his uncle knew that Blackie's rural childhood had sheltered him from the crowded tenements and slums that were a stain on the cities, and for that Patrick felt very grateful.

As they reached the moor, Blackie took a few steps forward, hurrying up to a gate in front of a nice-looking house.

Patrick frowned, suddenly hearing the laughter that had obviously drawn Blackie to the gate. He increased his pace and joined Blackie at the white gate. Much to his surprise, Patrick saw a look of anger on the young man's face. Following the direction of Blackie's gaze, his eyes settled on two women sitting in chairs on the lawn.

Blackie was frozen on the spot, holding onto the gate, his body rigid. After a moment, he glanced at his uncle and said, 'I can't believe it! They *lied* to me.'

Patrick's brows drew together in a frown. 'I don't understand . . . do you know these women? And what did they lie about?'

Blackie did not answer. Instead he opened the latch on the gate and strode down the path in long strides.

Watching him heading towards the women, Patrick shook his head, still puzzled, and followed his nephew, now somewhat intrigued.

Sarah jumped up swiftly at the sight of Blackie, who had appeared as if from nowhere. To her astonishment she saw his uncle was not far behind him.

Running across the lawn, Sarah swiftly reached him, and as she came to a stop, she pushed a smile onto her face, and exclaimed, 'Blackie! Hello, hello, what a surprise to see you.'

When he didn't respond and was looking over her shoulder at Angela, who had risen from her chair, Sarah grabbed his arm.

'This is a misunderstanding,' she said, her voice calm. 'We only got here last night, and Angela's leaving shortly for Harrogate. I'm going to accompany her. She can't travel alone.'

'Ye both told me ye'd be in Harrogate this weekend.' He laughed. It sounded hollow. 'And now here ye are, Sunday afternoon, sitting in the garden. Why did ye lie? To get out of seeing me?'

'No, no, it's not like that at all,' Sarah cried, her voice rising. 'Angela suddenly needed some documents. For her solicitor in Harrogate. That is the reason we came to the house.'

Patrick drew closer and stood next to Blackie. He vaguely recognized the young woman Blackie was talking to in an angry tone, but could not place her, nor did he recall her name.

Sarah, relieved to see Patrick Kennedy now standing with Blackie, gave him a huge smile and thrust out her hand. 'Pleased to meet you, Mr Kennedy. I'm Sarah Clough. I live in the Edinburghs near you, just behind Town Street.'

After shaking her hand, Patrick smiled, then nodded. 'Of course, now I realize who you are, although I hardly ever see you around in our area these days.'

'No, I work in Leeds. I have a secretarial job at Andrews, the tailoring firm. And I am also here sometimes, with my sister.'

'I see.' Patrick glanced at the woman who was now standing on the terrace, thinking she was older than Sarah, and rather beautiful. He was about to speak to Sarah when he was slightly pushed aside by Blackie, who stepped around Sarah and loped across the lawn, heading for the terrace, determination in every step.

Sarah let out a small cry and swung around, gasping as she saw Blackie and Angela head into the house, talking in low voices.

Patrick, staring at her, asked, 'Does Blackie know your sister? Do you understand what this is all about?'

'I think so,' Sarah responded, and took hold of his arm for a moment. Then she said, 'Let's go and sit down for a minute or two, and I'll try to explain.'

'Very well,' Patrick answered, and strode along next to her as they crossed the lawn. There were white-painted wicker chairs on the terrace, where Sarah indicated they should sit.

Clearing her throat, she said, 'I told Blackie we'd not be here this weekend because Angela, that's my sister, had to be in

Harrogate, where she has to do some work for Lady Lassiter. Then everything changed. Unexpectedly. Angela's solicitor needed some documents, which were here. We came here last night to get them, and we're leaving soon, going back there. Blackie thinks we lied to him, about being in Harrogate, I mean.'

Patrick was silent. He stared intently at Sarah, who looked troubled, and he noticed she was twisting a handkerchief in her hands, and somewhat nervously so.

Carefully, Patrick said quietly, 'My nephew is involved with one of you. Otherwise, he wouldn't be so emotional. I suspect it's you, Sarah, isn't it?'

'Oh yes, yes, of course!' she exclaimed quickly, almost stumbling over her words, and then nodding vehemently.

Yet all of her gestures made Patrick wonder if she was speaking the truth. But would Blackie be of interest to Angela? After all, she looked to be the older of the two, presumably a married woman if this was her own house and she didn't live with Sarah. On the other hand, he had only seen her from a distance. So why had Blackie taken her into the house?

After a moment's reflection, Patrick gave Sarah a puzzled stare. 'I'm not sure I believe you, Sarah. What is Blackie doing talking to Angela? And whose house is this?'

Quickly seizing on the last question, Sarah explained, almost breathlessly, 'It belongs to Angela. She's lived here since she got married.' As these words left her mouth, Sarah felt like biting her tongue off.

Patrick picked it up at once. 'She's a married woman who—'

'No, no, she's a widow,' Sarah shot back, interrupting him. 'Her husband was in the Royal Navy and he was killed in the Boer War.'

'I see,' Patrick answered in a quieter voice. 'However, there is something going on here, and I aim to get to the bottom of it.'

*   *   *

When Blackie saw Angela cowering against the desk in the small library, with tears on her face, every ounce of his anger disappeared in an instant.

He knew not to make a move towards her, but instead to keep quiet for a moment, and to allow her to accept his presence. He felt foolish for acting up.

She stared at him with intensity and finally spoke. 'You called me a liar, and I didn't like that. I've never told a lie. Ever.' Her voice was soft and even.

'I'm sorry, Angela, so very sorry, and I apologize . . . sure, and it was a mistake on my part. I've no excuse for being suddenly angry . . . it's just that I was shocked. I thought ye were trying to trick me, that ye don't want my company.' He ran his hand through his thick, dark hair, his heart racing. What had he been thinking?

'I understand, in a way. You hadn't expected to see us, and here we are. We *did* go to Harrogate on Friday morning. When I spoke to my solicitor that afternoon, he told me he needed to see some legal documents. They were not in the house in Harrogate, but here. So we came back to get them last night, and we will return there in an hour.' She half-smiled. 'A simple explanation.'

Blackie let out a deep sigh. 'I'm a fool.'

She shook her head. 'No, you're not. You're a man, and men often jump to conclusions without thinking.'

He grinned. 'And women do that too, don't ye think?'

Walking forward, now smiling, Angela hurried towards him and took hold of his arm, then leaned against him, her head resting on his chest. 'Let us forget this silly incident, Blackie. I like you as my friend, and . . .' She paused, lowered her voice and added, 'More. As my lover. If your uncle were not outside, I'm afraid I would be tempted to rush you upstairs.'

Looking down at her, his black eyes sparkling, he laughed

quietly. 'I know what ye mean, but I don't have the courage to do that, though I'd enjoy it. I'd be afraid to get caught, so I would.'

At this moment, Sarah came into the library and hurried over to them.

'Your uncle is asking questions, Blackie. I think you'd better come up with some sort of explanation, about why you're in here with Angela. Why you're angry.'

Blackie frowned, and slowly released Angela, shaking his head. 'I don't have an explanation, sure and I don't.'

Angela murmured, 'Just make it a *partial* truth. You could say we'd asked you to supper, but then cancelled at the last moment because we'd had to go to Harrogate on Friday on an urgent matter. Unexpectedly, you saw us here. Then we, or rather I, just explained everything.'

'I think it might work . . .' He paused, wondering if it would. Patrick Kennedy was one helluva smart man.

Looking up at him, smiling, her blue eyes fixed on him, Angela said, 'Come to Harrogate next Saturday. With Sarah, and bring Finn if you wish.'

'Thank ye,' Blackie murmured, gave her a quick kiss on the cheek, and left, bracing himself to face his uncle.

TWENTY-SEVEN

'Sorry to keep ye waiting, Uncle Pat,' Blackie said, joining him on the terrace outside. He grinned. 'I'm afraid Sarah and Angela are both chatterboxes. I couldn't escape for a bit.'

Patrick simply nodded, and gave him a searching look. They turned to leave, when Blackie heard his name being called. As he swung around, Sarah was coming outside, followed by Angela.

Angela rushed forward and stretched out her hand. 'Hello, Mr Kennedy, I'm Sarah's sister, Angela Welles.'

He took her hand and found himself smiling back at her. 'Nice to meet you, Mrs Welles.'

'Can I offer you something . . . a glass of lemonade perhaps? It's such a warm day.'

'Thank you kindly, but we must be off. We've been out for a while; I must get us home.'

'Of course, I understand.'

Sarah said, 'I hope you can come with me to Harrogate on Saturday, Blackie. Finn said he'd like to join us . . . for a day out.'

'I'll try,' Blackie answered, wanting to escape. 'Are ye going in the morning?' He started to walk forward.

'Today probably.' Sarah gave him a big smile, and Angela said, 'You're welcome too, Mr Kennedy.'

'Thank you, but I'm busy next weekend.'

'What a shame,' Angela answered, and retreated to the house.

'Goodbye to both of ye,' Blackie said, and took hold of his arm. 'Let's be going, Uncle Pat.'

Patrick waited until they were out of the garden and on the street before saying, 'I must admit they're both very pretty girls . . . women.' His voice trailed off, and he didn't say anything else, leading his nephew along the path that led onto the moor. 'Let's sit down on this seat for a moment,' Patrick said. 'I need to talk to you before we get home.'

Blackie did not respond but sat down, waiting, wondering what his uncle would say. Tell him off, no doubt.

But he was wrong. Patrick shifted on the seat slightly and stared at Blackie. 'How far has this gone, lad?'

'Er-er – not sure what ye mean, Uncle?'

'Have you . . . been intimate with Sarah?'

Blackie was startled. His uncle obviously assumed he was entangled with the younger of the sisters. Not wanting to get Sarah into this mess, he improvised, 'No, I haven't.'

'All right, I'm glad to hear you've been cautious. But if it goes any further and you take that step, I want you to protect yourself. We don't need any babies out of wedlock. Go to the chemist shop tomorrow and sort out what you need. Just in case, so you're prepared. And remember what I said about behaviour. You need to be thinking about marriage if that's the way things are going. And don't ever force yourself on a woman. Let her show that she's . . . ready, willing and able. Understood?'

'Yes, Uncle Pat, ye know I always listen to ye.'

Patrick nodded. 'Sarah explained why you were angry. And in

a way, I suppose I don't blame you. Take my word for it, some women can be devious and manipulative. So be careful, be alert.'

'Thanks for the warning,' Blackie muttered. 'Shouldn't we be going, Uncle Pat?'

'Aye, we should. Let's go across the moor and down to Tower Lane. That's the quickest way to Town Street.'

The week became busy for Blackie. He had shown his plans for Mrs Wilson's conservatory to his uncle and to Mrs Wilson herself, and both sides had approved.

Patrick Kennedy was delighted when she signed the work contract and told him Blackie could start at once. And he did. He was measuring the space, visiting the glaziers, ordering quantities of glass, wood and paint. Then he went in search of terracotta slabs for the floor of the conservatory. He was thrilled, the fuss of the weekend forgotten.

In the middle of the week, he came home to find a note from Sarah, explaining he should go on his own to Harrogate. She had written down an address. She had also explained she would meet him there that afternoon. Unexpectedly, she had to work on Saturday morning and would go straight to the train station at noon, see him in Harrogate later.

There was no mention of Finn in Sarah's note, and so Blackie spoke to him the next day, when he finally went to the carpentry shop.

'I don't want to go,' Finn said in a quiet voice. 'I don't want to spend the money, and anyway . . .' Finn cut himself off, then whispered, 'I had a note from Moira. She wants to talk to me on her day off. And that's Saturday.'

Although Blackie was surprised, he kept his face neutral. 'And where are ye meeting her?'

'On the moor, opposite the Traveller's Rest. She said we might want to find a café, have a bite for dinner.'

'Then you'd better take *some* money with ye,' Blackie chuckled.

Finn said, 'I will. I've got a bit put away, just like you. But she said it's her treat . . . as thanks for seeking her out in the Ham Shank.'

Later that week, Blackie found the right time to talk to Patrick. He asked his uncle if it was all right for him to go to Harrogate on Saturday.

'You're going with Sarah, correct?'

'She has to work Saturday morning, but she'll be there, yes.'

'Is this an overnight trip?'

'I think so, Uncle Pat.'

His uncle frowned and paused for a moment. 'Then take some money from your savings and stay at a bed-and-breakfast place. More suitable, I think. More discreet. And be careful. Watch your step and keep your eyes peeled.'

'I will, Uncle Pat, I swear on the heads of the Blessed Saints, I will.'

Patrick simply nodded, went into his office and closed the door. As he sat down at his desk, he grimaced to himself, and wondered why he'd bothered to say those words. If those two want to sleep together they will, he thought. They won't be able to help themselves. Don't be so daft, Kennedy. They're young and involved, don't kid yourself.

TWENTY-EIGHT

S he was not home.

Blackie banged the brass knocker several times, and there was no response. There were no lights on inside the Harrogate town house that was home to Angela's aunt. Surprise assailed him.

Happy anticipation turned to disappointment. He noticed the side path and walked down to the back door. He tried the doorknob. It was locked. It was obvious the house was empty.

Suddenly, the woman in the garden next door came over to the wall, and said, 'Mrs Welles might be out shopping, yer knows. For the weekend. She usually does that when her aunt is away.'

'But I had an appointment with her at this time,' he explained quickly.

'Can I give her a message when she gets back?' the woman asked, offering him a smile. She looked him over quickly, and probed, 'What's your name?'

'Shane O'Neill,' he answered. 'I'll try to come back later.' He glanced up at the darkening sky, and said, 'It's starting to drizzle.' As he gave her a quick smile, he moved away from the wall, then paused and turned around. 'Can ye tell me where to get a sandwich, please?'

'The best place is Hettys Café, just down the hill from The Stray. Do yer knows The Stray?'

'I do, sure and I do. I be thanking ye, missus. Yes, thanks very much.'

As Blackie walked down the street, a myriad of thoughts rolled around in his head. Why hadn't Angela been there? She had said twelve o'clock at her aunt's house. Had she forgotten? Got caught up with her Saturday shopping? Changed her mind?

He had absolutely no idea and was suddenly irritated. This was the second time something strange had happened. Perhaps they were fated not to get together again. Or *she* had decided to drop him, perhaps? But why?

He had no answers for himself and felt angry at being made a fool of. Perhaps this is what happened when you became involved with women beyond your station. He should have stuck with a girl from the dance hall. He shifted his small bag to his other hand and increased his pace as the drizzling rain splashed on his face. He felt a rush of relief when he saw The Stray ahead of him. He began to run.

He was heading down the hill towards a clutch of shops, where he could see Hettys Café slap in the middle, when he heard his name being called.

'Blackie! Blackie!'

He came to an abrupt halt and swung around. Instantly, his face lifted with incredulity. Flying straight towards him was none other than his cousin Siobhan. He blinked in disbelief, and he dropped the bag and opened his arms to catch her.

As she fell against him, gasping, he gripped her tightly and held her close to him. 'Whatever are *ye* doing in Harrogate, mavourneen? Of all places, I should come here today. But I'm so happy I did. Faith and ye are a long way from home.'

Stepping back, she said, 'I'm here with her ladyship, Lady Lassiter. You know I became her lady's maid earlier this year, after Alice died.'

'I'd forgotten that, sure I had. A great chance for ye. Why didn't ye let me know ye were coming over?'

'I did. I sent you a note, but I don't suppose you'll get it now 'til Monday if it hasn't arrived yet. I posted it to your uncle's address in Upper Armley.'

Blackie wrapped his arm around Siobhan and smiled down, unable to believe his eyes. He hadn't seen his cousin in the flesh since he left Kerry four years earlier, but she looked just the same, if a little more grown-up. He squeezed her to him.

'Come on, we're getting wet. I'll take ye for a bite . . . to Hettys Café down the hill there.'

'I was going there, Blackie, to pick up a packet for Cook. But it's my afternoon off, so I don't have to hurry back. It's just lovely to run into you like this – I wrote that we should meet up, and here you are!'

'It is indeed – sure and I'm glad to see ye. How do ye like England? And how was the crossing? I'll bet you didn't come steerage.' He picked up his small carpetbag and tucked her arm in his as they hurried down the hill. And his mood changed, became much lighter.

Once they were settled in a cosy corner of the café, and the order had been given to the waitress, Blackie sat back and looked at Siobhan intently. 'So why is her ladyship in Yorkshire?'

'She usually comes to her parents' estate for the summer, before his lordship comes to Bolton Manor for the Glorious Twelfth – you know, the start of the grouse shooting. And naturally I had to come 'cause I look after her clothes as her lady's maid.'

'That's a grand rise up the ladder for ye, and I'm proud of ye. And how's Michael doin'?'

'He's happy now he lives up at Lassiter Hall in the servants' quarters. His life is better, and Lord Robert is glad to have him. He likes Michael's work, says he's a talented gardener.' She began to laugh, and then went on, 'I'll never forget when her ladyship came to see me at the cottage and was furious. She said, "This place is totally unsanitary! Dreadful!" And she took us to live in the servants' quarters at the Hall.'

Blackie grinned at her, and said, 'That's quite an imitation ye do of her. Ye are a good mimic. Mmm . . . that's a posh voice ye can put on.'

'So I'm told. But her ladyship is not a bad employer, you know. She's been good to us, even though some say she's cold and stand-offish.'

'I do know. Lots of hand-me-downs she sent me.' He leaned across the table and held his cousin's hand. 'You're a sight for sore eyes, sure ye are. I didn't know when I would see ye or Michael again.'

She squeezed his hand back and then the waitress brought their pots of tea.

'Anyway, why are you in Harrogate, Blackie?' Siobhan asked, changing the subject.

He thought for a moment and decided to tell the truth; there was no reason not to do so.

'I have a friend, a lady friend, and she invited me to come today. When I arrived at her aunt's house at noon, she wasn't there. Everything was locked. A neighbour said she might be back this afternoon. I decided I couldn't wait. Ye see, it had begun to drizzle, and I was . . . well, a bit put out. It's not the first time she's done something odd.'

'I understand, you *should* be annoyed. It's not nice to mess you around. So are you going back later, then?'

'Not on your life. I'm not going to be played for a fool.'

'So where are you going when we leave Hettys?'

'I'll have to try and get a train back to Leeds. I don't know when they leave.'

'Don't do that! I've got a better idea!'

'And what is it?' he asked, filled with curiosity.

'Come back with me to the house. Lord Robert will be glad to see you, and so will her ladyship.'

'But it's too far to go out to Bolton Manor, and then come back to Harrogate to catch a train,' Blackie pointed out.

'You can go back to Leeds on Sunday. There're lots of empty rooms in the servants' quarters. They won't mind, the Lassiters, I mean. They'll let you stay, I just know they will. Lord Robert often asks about you.'

'Are ye sure, Siobhan?' Blackie asked, sounding doubtful.

'Oh yes, I am. You were always a favourite.'

TWENTY-NINE

The drizzling rain had stopped, and sunlight filled the air with a golden glow. Suddenly it was a nice day.

'Sunshine,' Blackie said with a laugh. 'Nothing like Yorkshire weather! It changes in three shakes of a lamb's tail. It reminds me of Ireland.'

His cousin nodded, and then explained, 'It's not too far to Bolton Manor, about half an hour at a steady pace.'

'Oh, I thought it was further away than that, closer to Studley Royal.'

'No, nearer to Harrogate. His lordship likes it up here in July and August, when guests come to stay. You know, for the shooting in August.'

'Aye, a lot of people do that. Can't say I do . . . shooting little birds is not a pastime I'd go for. I find it a bit cruel in fact, Siobhan.'

'I know what you mean. But the toffs like it. The men anyway. Most of the ladies don't go roaming the moors with guns in their hands, murdering birds.'

Blackie didn't respond, and they walked on in silence for a while, lost in their own thoughts.

He was glad now he'd accepted Siobhan's suggestion to go back to the manor. Her ladyship and Lord Robert had helped him and his cousins out over the years back in Kerry. And he had no qualms any more about just turning up with Siobhan. He *would* be welcome, made to feel at ease, he was certain of that.

Siobhan said, 'All of this land surrounding us belongs to Lord Robert, and he owns lots of forests as well. Bolton Manor is on agricultural land and it's farmed. You know, it's a money-maker.'

Blackie nodded. He hadn't known that. In fact, he didn't know much at all about Bolton Manor, except that his lordship often stayed there into the autumn, sometimes until after Guy Fawkes Day in November.

He glanced about as they walked along, admiring the lovely countryside, the lush green fields, and huge trees that looked ancient. His eye caught sight of a flock of birds rising up into the sky. He followed their flight for a moment. He liked nature and was well aware that, in the fields and woods surrounding them, lived rabbits, hares, squirrels, foxes, and all manner of little scurrying animals. When he built his house one day, he would make sure he not only had lovely gardens, but also fields and forests. An estate, I want, that's it! And another dream was born in his head. And it would grow over the years.

Bolton Manor was Georgian in style, his favourite, and Blackie liked the look of it at once. He saw that it was square, with no 'bits' shooting off the sides, and there was a well-kept garden at the front.

'I like the house,' he said to his cousin. 'It was built well.'

'It's lovely inside,' she replied. 'We have to see Cook first, so I can give her the box of little cakes from Hettys, then I'll go and speak to her ladyship, explain that you're here.'

'Thank ye, Siobhan, but don't mention why I'm in Harrogate, or me lady friend, please.'

'I won't! Don't be so daft!' she shot back as she led him across the cobbled yard to the service entrance. Beyond was the stable block, and he could hear the sound of the horses' hooves and their snorting. They seemed restless, he thought.

As Blackie walked into the kitchen with Siobhan, his warm smile flashed across his face.

'Ah, and 'tis a grand place, this,' he said. Moving across the floor, he was heading for Cook, who had swung around at the sound of voices.

'And there you are, O'Brien,' she said. 'I see you have my box of little cakes. Carried them carefully, I hope, lass.'

'I did, Cook.'

'And who is this strapping lad tagging along with you?' she laughed. 'I can hardly ask, what's this the cat's dragged in? He's too brawny for that.'

Stepping closer, stretching out his hand, Blackie said, 'Shane O'Neill is me name, but most call me Blackie. It's Siobhan's cousin that I am.'

Cook gripped his hand, nodded and said, 'Irish, eh? Well, take the weight off yer feet, and I'll give yer both a mug of tea.'

'Thanks, Mrs Felton, but I just have to see her ladyship,' Siobhan said to the cook. 'I need to speak to her urgently.'

'Get along with you then, do your duty. Tea will be waiting when you get back.'

Siobhan nodded and ran out of the kitchen, smiling to herself as she heard Blackie complimenting Cook on the delicious smells floating around her kitchen. Hasn't he kissed the Blarney Stone she thought, as she crossed the stone hall.

THIRTY

They sat together on an iron garden seat in the back gardens of Bolton Manor.

Hatton, the butler, had suggested they wait there while he spoke to Lord Robert.

Siobhan, following the direction of Blackie's gaze, and then glancing at him, knew how he felt. He did not like the gardens, she could tell for sure. His face was full of dismay.

'They need a bit of work, don't they?' she said, her eyes on him intently. 'Poor gardens.'

'I'd say a lot of work,' he replied. 'They're a right mess . . . a muddle, sure and they are. No plan. Bushes, flowerbeds, the lawns, a fountain where it shouldn't be. And the lake obscured by more bushes.'

'I bet *you* could put it right?'

'Aye, I could that. But I'm not going to, Siobhan. I'm aiming to be a builder of houses, not a gardener now.'

'I know. But it's a shame. Maybe you could recommend somebody.'

'I can't,' he said brusquely, a tone not usual for him.

'Oh, here comes Lord Robert, down the terrace.' Immediately Siobhan stood up and so did Blackie, and they walked towards the terrace.

'Welcome, Blackie,' Lord Robert said. 'How nice it is to see you again after all these years.'

'Thank ye, and it is a real treat for me to see ye, too, Lord Robert.'

'A treat indeed. Hatton told me how you ran into Siobhan today. Quite by accident. A lucky accident, I'd have to say. Apparently you were able to have a bite together.'

'Yes, Your Lordship. And thank ye for letting me stay the night. Siobhan and me, well, we talked a lot, and I knew the last train to Leeds would get me in very late.'

Lord Robert exclaimed, 'You've always got a bed here, Blackie! Why, we've known you since you were a child. And there're plenty of rooms empty in the male servants' quarters. Just make yourself at home.' He hesitated, then added, 'Could you walk around these gardens with me? *You* could give me some sound advice, I feel sure of that.'

'Of course, m'lord.'

Blackie raised his eyebrows at his cousin as he followed Lord Robert down the terrace. Siobhan smiled and excused herself to go back to the kitchen to chat with Cook.

As they strolled around the garden together, Lord Robert pointed out things that genuinely troubled him. He thought the lawn wasn't trimmed enough, the bushes appeared cumbersome, and he disliked the flowerbeds, which were a mess.

Blackie, as always, listened intently, whilst noting many details that were wrong. When Lord Robert finally paused, Blackie said, 'Bolton Manor is pure Georgian architecture, *early* Georgian.

And it's perfect, well-built and quite grand. But, ye see, Your Lordship, a tradition from that period is gone. It's disappeared.'

'What do you mean exactly?'

'The Georgian tradition was to build a house on a hill and then create a lake at the bottom of that hill. A large man-made lake.'

'Of course! And the house would be reflected in the lake. It was considered to be a vanity, in a way.'

'These bushes block the view of the house in the lake, m'lord. That's wrong.'

'They have to go, don't they?'

'I'd say so, m'lord. And the gardeners have to cut the lawns several times a week. It always has to be flat . . . as a pancake . . . so, very short blades of grass. And all those flowerbeds . . .' Blackie stopped short, grimaced as he waved his hand at them, and finished, 'They all have to be dug up and replanted elsewhere.'

'I see,' Lord Robert murmured. 'But it will be a dull-looking area, won't it?'

'I be thinking the best thing there would be a parterre, Your Lordship. Elegant they are, and they would stretch right across, from that wall to the far edge of the lawn.'

Lord Robert stared at Blackie, a sudden look of comprehension entered his eyes, and he nodded vigorously. 'Of course! A parterre would be absolutely glorious. And how clever of you, Blackie, to solve my problems so swiftly.' He cleared his throat, and asked, 'I wonder, well, er, would you take it on, Blackie? I would see you are well compensated.'

'It would be an honour, Lord Robert, under normal circumstances, but I want to be a builder of houses now. Also, I start a new job on Monday, building a conservatory for a client of ours.' He straightened up slightly, and said in a solemn tone, 'My uncle's made me his partner.'

'Congratulations, Blackie. That is a wonderful promotion.

However, think seriously about working on these gardens. I'm sure with your innate talent you'd get them shipshape quite quickly. And I would pay you well. Extra money is always useful.'

'All right, m'lord, I'll think about it. 'Tis perhaps possible for me to fit it in. I'll have to let ye know. Could I come back in a few weeks to discuss it?'

'I'm afraid not, Blackie. I have urgent business in London and will travel there early tomorrow.'

Blackie felt a pang of disappointment. His thoughts turned to his cousin, and, wanting to see her again, he took a deep breath and ventured, 'Will her ladyship be coming to London also, m'lord?'

'No, probably not. She is only here at Bolton Manor very briefly and then will be staying at her parents' estate in Skipton. They're rather old, you know, and not in the best of health. However, I believe she will return here for the shooting in August.' He smiled a little grimly and murmured, 'Bolton Manor is not her ladyship's favourite place, and . . .' He paused, cleared his throat, continued. 'We do tend to lead separate lives and I'm afraid I do tend to be very tied up with my business.'

'I understand,' Blackie answered. 'But ye will be here for August the twelfth, won't you, Lord Robert?'

Lord Robert nodded, and they continued to walk through the gardens, now speaking about the trees. At the back of Blackie's mind, the word MONEY lurked temptingly. He hoped he hadn't passed up a great chance.

THIRTY-ONE

Moira Aherne sat on an iron bench on the moor opposite the Traveller's Rest pub, lost in her own thoughts.

Earlier on this Saturday, she had suddenly realized she might well have made the wrong move by coming to Leeds.

It might have been better to have gone to London after all. She had been drawn to this northern city because of its reputation, and because people had told her its streets were paved with gold – though she was bright and intelligent, and knew enough to understand that this was just an expression to convey that jobs were plentiful.

Also, she wanted to be close to Harrogate for a variety of reasons. And the last factor was Tommy O'Hara, who had pointed her in this direction, had offered her somewhere to stay, because she had told him she had relatives moving to Leeds. Another fib, but it worked.

Moira let out a sigh and sat up straighter, rubbing her aching back and deciding that for the moment she would remain put. Mrs Wilson was a nice woman, the work was not too arduous, though she was certainly tired now, and she paid her a decent wage. Most importantly, it gave her a roof over her head while she considered what to do next. How to start a new life.

Being in a pleasant atmosphere, in a well-decorated house, helped to make her feel at ease. Because it was what she was accustomed to, and had been, all her life. It gives me time to make my plans, Moira thought, and then waved as she saw Finn Ryan approaching.

He smiled as he came to a stop, and she returned it, then said, 'Right on time, Finn.'

Seating himself next to her, he said, 'I like to be punctual. And how have ye been?'

'I am doing very well, and Mrs Wilson is nice, a kind person. She's made me feel welcome and at home. So, are we going to have a bite to eat? Go into Leeds?'

'Yes. I am going to take ye to the Blue Door Café . . . where we went with Patrick Kennedy.'

'Oh, that's lovely, Finn. It was a nice place.'

Finn put his hand in his pocket and pulled out a letter. 'Mr Kennedy wrote a note to the waitress, Gladys, just to make sure she looks after us, does well by us.'

Moira nodded, stifling a smile. After a moment, she murmured, 'That was kind of him.' Her amusement still bubbled inside of her and she stood up, trying to quell it.

She could have handled everything quite easily; she didn't need a letter. Still, he had meant well, she thought, and said, 'Let us walk down to Whingate Junction, shall we? And take a tram into Leeds.'

'Right away!' Finn exclaimed, then jumped up, adding, 'I'm glad ye like the Blue Door enough to go back again.'

* * *

Moira preferred to sit on the lower level of the tram, and she explained this to Finn as they walked down the hill together. To their pleasure they saw that a tram had just pulled in from the city, and they began to run. They were laughing together as they jumped onto it alertly, slightly startling the driver, who scowled at them.

'Lead the way,' Moira said, and she followed Finn. He went along the lower level and stopped at a double seat. She slid in first, and he joined her.

'I will pay the fares,' he announced grandly, and took some change out of his pocket.

'Then I must pay on the return journey,' Moira said in a firm voice.

Within a few minutes, the tram set off. Moira settled back, looking forward to seeing the city. She had always had a thirst for knowledge, a curiosity about everything.

When she was growing up, she had had lessons every day with her half-brother, Lawrence; his mother had insisted on that. He was several years older than she, and so she got a head start very young. An image of Lawrence popped into her head. He would beat the estate near Bath now, where his late father had grown up. She thought of that lovely house, Waverly Priory, and a sudden rush of longing rippled through her, tinged with sadness. Until she had come to Leeds she had lived only there and on the large estate in Galway, which she had left so suddenly. Both had been her homes. Neither ever could be again.

Finn broke into her thoughts when he said, 'I'm sorry about Blackie, the way he pestered ye with questions. He was being very nosy, Moira, the other day.'

'I know that, and I did feel a bit persecuted . . .' She broke off, laughed. 'That's perhaps too strong a word to use, I suppose. But he did irritate me.'

'He meant no harm.'

'Perhaps not, but it was rather bad-mannered.'

Finn turned slightly in the seat, staring at her, and blurted out, 'But ye are different to us, Moira. Ye're posh, the way ye speak, and how ye look . . .' He broke off, wondering if he'd said the wrong thing, when he noticed an odd expression on her face.

'Not so different,' she said quietly. 'I'm a human being, just like you. We have the same emotions and feelings. Why, we are just like the Romans were, except we wear different clothes, live differently, because our civilization has changed over the years . . . hundreds of years.'

He was silent, gaping at her.

Moira said, 'I did grow up in a great house.' She paused, could have bitten her tongue off. Improvising with the lie she had told before, she added, 'I was a lady's maid, my parents in service there before me.'

He nodded, 'Well, then, that's what Blackie spotted.' He sat back, his mind racing, his curiosity about Moira Aherne aflame.

Once they arrived at the Blue Door Moira was tempted to prevent Finn from taking out the letter for Gladys. They didn't need it. But she stopped herself, thinking of Patrick Kennedy. Finn was bound to tell him what she had done, and she knew this would most likely embarrass Kennedy. Better to refrain from interfering, she told herself. He is a fine man, and I wouldn't want him to feel belittled or foolish. Anyway, I might need him . . . for something or other, one day.

Finn pushed the door open, and she entered the restaurant first, glancing around. Finn stepped up to her, and took out the letter, held it tightly in his hand, seeking Gladys out eagerly.

A moment later the waitress spotted Moira and came hurrying over, her face full of smiles.

'Welcome back!' she exclaimed. 'I have just the right table for you.'

Finn said, 'This is for ye, from Mr Kennedy.' He handed her the letter. She took it from him.

Gladys smiled at him. 'Hello, Finn. Welcome to you as well. Come along, there's a lovely table right here, the one Mr Kennedy likes, it just so happens.'

They both sat down, and Moira said, 'Thank you, Gladys. And perhaps you should read Mr Kennedy's letter.'

'Oh, yes, I will. In a minute. Can I get you something to drink, my lady? Tea? Lemonade?'

'Tea for me, please,' Moira murmured, smiling at her.

'I'll have the same, please,' Finn said.

'Right away, and I'll bring the menus.'

As Gladys disappeared, Finn looked at Moira, and asked with a frown, 'Why does she call ye *my lady*?'

'Oh, I don't know, Finn,' Moira muttered. 'Perhaps she just means lady.'

'Some waitresses call women *madam*,' Finn pointed out. 'And you're a *miss*, aren't you?'

Laughter trickled through Moira; she couldn't help it. He was a smart one, Finn. When she managed, finally, to calm herself, she said, 'She wants to be polite, that's all. Gladys is that kind of person. She wants to please her customers.'

He nodded. 'Well, how old are ye anyway?'

'A man must never ask a woman her age, Finn.'

'Oh, why not?' He sounded genuinely puzzled.

'Because it's a very personal question, and just a bit rude, bad-mannered.'

'I bet ye're seventeen or eighteen,' Finn shot back, squinting at her, obviously taking her measure, his eyes roaming over her.

Since she had nothing to hide about her age, Moira answered

in an amused tone, 'A good guess on your part, Finn. I was eighteen in May, early in May, in fact.'

Gladys returned with the tea and menus, and reminded them about the other dishes available, written on the blackboard in chalk on the far wall.

'Take your time,' the waitress said as she hurried away.

Moira picked up the menu and perused it for a while, not really feeling hungry. She wanted something light. She glanced over the menu, which was full of hearty dishes, when Finn said, 'Do ye knows what ye want?'

'I think I'll have some fish, with vegetables. That's it, yes, that's enough. I have a small appetite.'

'I see potted shrimps, I'll have that.'

Finn put down his menu, and said, with a grin, 'Mr Kennedy would say it's a bit of a fishy tea we're having.'

Moira smiled. He was a nice boy. She mustn't let him irritate her the way he did.

THIRTY-TWO

'So I suppose you've recovered from your adventures by now, haven't you, Blackie?' His uncle suddenly grinned. 'What a weekend of changing emotions for you, eh? Disappointment at noon, plus a dash of annoyance, I've no doubt. A joyous reunion with a loving cousin and walking the gardens of Bolton Manor with Lord Robert.'

Blackie couldn't help chuckling. 'You've hit the nail on the head, Uncle Pat. I can't believe she's in Yorkshire. It was so special to talk to her, to see her once more. Anyway, the best part was having a nice tea in the kitchen with Siobhan, before she went upstairs to do Lady Lucinda's hair.'

'The food always gets to you, lad,' Patrick said, a smile of affection on his face. 'But as Shakespeare said, "All's well that ends well." And what a stroke of luck that you ran into her in the town. How wonderful for you to see her again after all this time, and with her having been able to travel over to England with Lady Lassiter.'

'It was, and Lord Robert was as nice as always, and listened when I spoke about his garden. He even offered me the work!'

'And he gave you a shilling to boot, very generous indeed.'

Blackie nodded and took a bite of the fried egg sandwich. He was hoping he could see Siobhan again soon. 'I hope Aunt Eileen feels better now. Shall I go upstairs and ask her if she wants a cup of tea?'

Patrick shook his head. 'I'm sure she's sleeping. She was a bit off it all weekend, and I finally got her to go to bed just before you came home yesterday afternoon. Maybe it's a cold.'

Blackie took a sip of tea. Then looking at his uncle intently, he said, 'I measured the back garden at Mrs Wilson's today. Ye see, I need to know the size of the floor, to order the terracotta tiles. Floor first, Uncle.'

'You're gifted, Blackie. You have an inbred talent for building, and I must admit I was struck by the cleverness of your plans. It'll be a grand conservatory.'

'Let's hope so, Uncle Pat. I'll be handling a lotta glass again.'

'And with lots of glaziers, I hope.'

After they had finished their tea and washed the dishes, Blackie and Patrick sat down to read in front of the fire.

Patrick had his head in the morning newspaper, which he had not had time to read before. Monday was always a busy day for him.

Blackie was reading a book on engineering, this time about Brunel. But he couldn't concentrate. He felt confused by the situation with Angela, naïve almost. Had he misunderstood her interest? She was a widow with a nice house, perhaps she had never intended to see him again. He couldn't deny it stung. He had not been able to put her out of his mind. Should he write her a note? Or perhaps walk up to her house by the moors, speak to her if she was at home again? If the truth be known, maybe she had not been in at her aunt's house in Harrogate because of a sudden emergency, something he knew nothing about. He shouldn't blame her or make assumptions. Anyway, she might have just lost track of the time.

Sudden knocking on the front door startled the two of them. It was Patrick who rose at once.

When he opened the front door, he found himself staring at Sarah Clough. 'Good evening, Sarah,' he said with a wide smile.

She didn't smile back, but said curtly, 'Is Blackie here?'

'Well, yes, he is. Do you wish to speak to him?'

'I do.'

Blackie, hearing Sarah's voice and detecting a harsh tone, was already crossing the floor. In a split second, he was standing next to his uncle.

'Hello, Sarah, why are ye here? Do ye have something to tell me?'

'No, ask you. What happened when you saw Angela on Saturday?' She sounded angry.

'Nothing, because I never saw her.'

Patrick interjected, 'You'd better come into the house, Sarah. I don't want a commotion on my front doorstep.'

He opened the door wider, and Sarah walked up the steps. He noticed that the young woman was extremely pale. Chalk-white, in fact. Something was wrong.

Pulling out a chair, he said, 'Please sit down and make yourself comfortable.'

She did so. Patrick indicated to Blackie that he should sit opposite her, and then he himself took a seat.

'Now what is this all about?' Blackie asked, looking nonplussed, slightly troubled.

'You tell me,' she snapped. 'What happened on Saturday morning?'

'Nothing. I arrived at her house, at noon. She didn't answer the door. I went to the back. That was locked also. The neighbour saw me and said she thought Angela had gone shopping. I gave her my name and left.'

'She wasn't there, you say. But I know she was,' Sarah protested.

'No, no!' Blackie shot back. 'I asked the neighbour where I could get a sandwich. She told me to go to Hettys Café near The Stray. I did. It began to drizzle. I ran. On my way, I bumped into my cousin Siobhan. We went to Hettys Café and then to Bolton Manor, where Siobhan works as a lady's maid.'

'And after *that*?' Sarah demanded.

'I walked around the garden with Lord Robert. He said I could stay, sure and I did. There're plenty of male servants' rooms. But why are ye questioning me like this?'

She was silent, glared at him, her animosity apparent.

Patrick exclaimed, 'You've come here in an angry mood, flinging questions at Blackie, and it makes no sense. Are you accusing my nephew of something? Something bad?'

Sarah shook her head, and said, 'I had to be sure Angela wasn't lying about something that happened to her, to protect *him*, because she cares about him. Now I believe she was telling me the truth.'

Unexpectedly Sarah burst into a flood of tears, searching her coat pocket for a handkerchief.

The two men exchanged glances, and Patrick said in a soothing, rather sympathetic voice, 'What is wrong, Sarah dear? How can we help you?'

Eventually taking control of herself, she replied, 'There's nothing you can do right now. But thank you.'

'Tell me, what is this about? Ye owe me that,' Blackie exclaimed, his black eyes intent on her.

Sarah glanced at him, and nodded. 'It's true, I do owe you. I went to Angela's house in the afternoon. I told you I had to work on Saturday morning. She didn't open the door, so I found my key in my bag and went inside. I was terrified when I found Angela on the sitting-room floor. She was unconscious, and there was blood everywhere. She had been beaten, she was bleeding and her face was a mess.' Tears started again, and Patrick endeavoured to calm her.

Blackie cried, 'I can't believe ye think I would hurt a woman!' He was again suddenly angry, and had to take hold of his flaring emotions.

'Finish this story, please, Sarah,' Patrick murmured in a kind and encouraging voice.

Taking several deep breaths, Sarah nodded. 'I got an ambulance and she was taken to Harrogate Hospital. I stayed with her all Saturday and Sunday. She did eventually regain consciousness. She was able to talk to me. When I asked her who had done this to her, she said it was Barry Simmonds, a man she went to dinner with a few times last year. She broke off with him, and he left Harrogate . . .'

There was a pause, and she added, 'But he came back. Obviously.'

'And yet ye didn't believe her,' Blackie said in a harsh voice, his glance reproachful.

'I just thought she was protecting you because Barry had gone to London. To a new job . . .' Sarah did not finish her sentence, looked somewhat woebegone, and a little guilty.

Patrick, always the peacemaker, gave Sarah an encouraging look. 'How is Angela now? How long did you stay with her?'

'I left the hospital around twelve o'clock today, got back to Leeds and came home.' Tears began to trickle down her cheeks, and she was unable to speak.

Neither Patrick nor Blackie said a word. They waited until the tears stopped and she patted her eyes with her handkerchief.

'But she has recovered, or rather *is recovering*, isn't she?'

Patrick let his steady gaze rest on Sarah, aware that things were not right with her. 'She is on the mend, surely?'

'From the beating, yes, and the cuts and bruises have been properly treated.' Sarah cleared her throat several times, and finished a little unsteadily, 'However, during her general examination, the doctors found a lump on the side of her stomach. Angela has cancer.'

Patrick and Blackie were stunned, and it was Blackie who got up and went to Sarah, put his arms around her. 'I'm so terribly sorry to hear this, and I will help ye any way I can.' He kept calm, but he was reeling from shock, and filled with worry for Angela.

Patrick also stood. 'I'll go and put the kettle on, and make a pot of tea. Then we can talk a bit longer. I too will help you, Sarah, and help Angela as well.'

'Thank you, Patrick.' She looked up at Blackie, and asked, 'Can you forgive me, Blackie, for thinking it was you?'

'There is nothing to forgive,' he answered in a quiet voice. His anger had fled when he had heard this awful news about the beautiful woman who filled his thoughts.

Blackie was unable to sleep that night. He lay in his bed, his mind restless, his sorrow enormous. *Cancer.* The most dreaded of all diseases. Nobody ever spoke about it; they pushed it away, buried it deep inside. Everyone mentioned their fear of consumption, which some people called tuberculosis, and of pneumonia and typhus too. But never cancer.

He clenched his fists; his body was so tense it was rigid. How could Angela, of all people, have cancer? Surely it was a disease of the old? She was only twenty-four. *Young. Vital. Full of life.* There had been no sign of illness.

Grasping at hope, he thought for a moment that perhaps the doctors had made a mistake. Could the diagnosis be wrong? He pushed himself up in the bed, and put the pillow behind his head, thinking hard. Mistakes could be made. That he knew. She might not have it.

A deep sigh escaped him, and he slumped back down. Harrogate Hospital was one of the best, with good doctors . . . Could it be treated? This new thought gave him a quick rush of hope once more, then it slid away.

The problem was his ignorance. Because no one talked about it, no one had any information. Only doctors knew the details, and the cures, if there were any. Who could he ask? Where could he go?

He squeezed his eyes shut, and suddenly, in his mind, he saw her image. The shining light-brown curls, the wide translucent blue eyes, so full of warmth, her delicate features, her vivid smile, her happy laughter.

The tears rolled down his cheeks and he buried his head in the pillow, crying for her, for the pain she would be enduring, filled with a sense of loss.

Never to see her again, never to know her better, to be friends if nothing else was possible, just to see her sometimes. Angela was not going to live, he knew that. Sarah had made that clear. Blackie cried for a long time. He thought his heart was breaking.

Eventually he quelled his tears, and got out of bed, went to open the window. He sat on his bed, his thoughts whirling once again in his busy mind. Earlier, when Sarah had arrived, and accused him of attacking Angela, he had been enraged. He could not understand why someone who knew him would believe he could ever assault a woman.

He had been furious with her. But his anger had fled. Blackie knew that Sarah had leaped to a conclusion, not believed Angela's explanation, because she had realized Angela cared for him, might be protecting him even. Her sister Angela was sincere.

And now, in the middle of the night, as devastated as he was about Angela's illness, he knew one thing. And it was this . . . Angela had been emotionally involved with him, as he had been with her. And somehow this bit of knowledge gave him a little solace, something to cling to always.

PART THREE

Chances with Challenges
Yorkshire & London
1903

THIRTY-THREE

H e sat at his Georgian desk in his library in the house he owned and loved in Grosvenor Square, at the heart of Mayfair.

His attention was focused on his own name on the contract he was about to sign: Robert Marmaduke Allenwood Lassiter.

Lifting his sleek dark head, he looked across at his closest friend, Adrian Fraser, and said, 'I wonder what my parents were thinking when they burdened me with such a long name?'

Adrian chuckled, 'Family tradition, old chap. Marmaduke's been one of your male names for centuries, and, of course, your great-grandmother's maiden name was Allenwood, from which—'

'Our fortune sprang,' Robert cut in, also chuckling, his very blue eyes fixed on his friend.

'Correct. And don't forget, you've gone and burdened your eldest son with the same middle names.'

'Poor chap! I have done that, but Quentin doesn't mind. Anyway, here goes, I'd better sign it, get it done.' As he spoke he picked up his pen, signed the contract, and put the pen back in the inkstand.

Sitting back in the chair, he said, 'You asked me earlier why I was so intent on coming to town so quickly, to close the deal on these warehouses on the docks in the East End, when I'd only just arrived in Yorkshire. So, now, let me explain. I know that the docks are growing by leaps and bounds. England has become the greatest export country in the world. Our country is *powerful*, and shipping is on the increase—'

'So you're banking on the need for extra storage,' Adrian interjected.

'No, not really. I'm buying the warehouses to tear them down. It's the land they're standing on I want. To build on.'

Adrian looked taken aback. 'Will you build new warehouses? Is that your plan?'

'No. A large office building. Companies in the shipping business will need to be on the docks in permanent buildings. Some already are, but the need will rapidly increase.'

Shaking his head, Adrian exclaimed, 'I've got to give it to you, Robert, you're ahead of the game. As usual. You've made Allenwood and Sloane the most important property company in London. Congratulations.'

'Thank you, Adrian, you're too generous.' He laughed. 'Not bad for the snot-nosed lad you made fun of when we were at prep school.'

Adrian also laughed. 'What did I know then? You were always talking about business deals and property, and following in your father's footsteps, building the family fortunes like he did. I was always a bit puzzled that you knew what you wanted to do with your life at eight years old. And I had no idea about the future, *my* calling in life.'

'I guess it was drilled into me from a young age – you could say they all brainwashed me. But I do enjoy the wheeling and dealing, as I call it.'

'You certainly know how to make a lot of money. That's a

true skill. Do you ever think you might make some terrible error?'

'Every day, believe it or not. I start my day by asking myself how much I might lose, never how much I'm going to make. That keeps me on my toes. It starts when I'm shaving and only ends when I go to bed at night. But enough about all that. Shall we go to the club tonight, after that event?'

'What event?' Adrian frowned, sounded puzzled. 'Are we going somewhere tonight?'

'To the Strattons', remember? Caroline invited us. She's having a small gathering, to tell us about a charity she's starting.'

'Oh God! I'd totally forgotten about it. Frankly, it sounds quite ghastly.'

'It won't be. She told me she's serving champagne and canapés – a nice idea, I thought. She just wants us all to back her, by writing a cheque.'

'She said that?'

'More or less.'

'Bloody hell, she's got balls.'

Robert laughed. 'She always had balls. She's independent, and very self-confident. And the charity is a good cause.'

'What's the charity she's dreamed up?'

'Teaching underprivileged women how to learn a craft, especially battered women. Those who have come out of care homes. I'm going to give her five hundred pounds to help get her started. You should do the same.'

'Bloody hell! And aren't you being generous with my money!'

'Come on, old chap, you can afford it. You're the most successful banker in London. No, in England, I'd venture to say. You're rolling in dosh.'

Adrian nodded. 'Of course I'll give the same as you, and it *is* a good cause. I was shocked the other day when my sister told me how many women go to the safe home she supports with donations. Clarissa also goes there once a week to talk to them, tries to guide them into a new direction, gives them clothes. Battering defenceless women seems to be a growing hobby for some men. Bastards they are.'

'I know,' Robert replied, letting out a long sigh. 'I've heard the same stories. I told Caroline I would give her money for her charity on a continuing basis, but you don't have to, Adrian.'

'Of course I will, you know I'm always guided by you. What's that saying of yours? Anything you can do, I can do better.'

'Caroline will be pleased,' Robert murmured.

There were a few moments of silence. Adrian sat staring at his best friend, the closest person to him since their days at prep school.

Robert Marmaduke Allenwood Lassiter, Fifth Earl of Harding. Thirty-nine years old now. Handsome with a natural charm and an easy-going, almost casual demeanour. Yet these traits hid a brilliant mind and a fierce intellect. Adrian knew how trustworthy he was, that he had genuine ethics, honour, and great integrity.

A busy man, something of a workaholic, Robert divided his time between his family mansion in Ireland, Bolton Manor in Yorkshire, his favourite estate, which he loved to use for shooting parties, plus his London house. He kept socializing in town to a minimum. And although women tended to chase him, he was not a womanizer or a philanderer. In fact, he was rather aloof in certain ways, and somewhat traditional.

But Adrian knew Robert was vulnerable, although he never allowed this to surface. He had once told Adrian his motto: *Never display weakness, never show face.*

'You're awfully quiet, Adrian,' Robert said, looking at his friend curiously, aware of his eyes on him. 'What's rolling around in that busy mind of yours?'

Adrian sat up straighter in his chair, and answered, 'Are you sure you really want to go to the Strattons' "do" tonight? It's not like you.'

'Yes, I promised.' Robert's eyes narrowed. 'Why are you asking that?'

'It's that sister of Caroline's . . .' His voice trailed off.

'Sister? *Which sister?*' Robert demanded.

'She only has two. One lives in Paris, one here. Her name is Vanessa. You know her, Robert, 'course you do. I think she likes you. She can't take her eyes off you when we go there.'

'Don't be *daft*!' Robert exclaimed. 'She's a child, as I recall, about fourteen or so. And she hardly knows of my existence. Now you are being imaginative.' He sounded outraged.

Adrian leaned forward, staring at Robert across the desk. He said carefully, 'Maybe you haven't noticed her interest in you, but by God, I have! And she's not fourteen; she's about twenty-two or -three. Gorgeous-looking with all that russet-coloured hair and amber eyes. Tall and willowy.'

'I haven't really noticed her!' Robert snapped.

Adrian knew that this was true. Robert was often oblivious to the women who were attracted to him.

After a moment, Adrian said, 'I believe you, Robert. Honestly, I do.' He hesitated before adding, 'But she's smart, clever, intelligent, and determined. And she's interested in you.'

'I'm a married man, so you can rest easy. I do not stray,' Robert reminded him.

'About this marriage of yours. Let's discuss that. A heart to heart is long overdue.'

'Let's go to White's instead. I haven't been since I came to town.' Robert stood up, straightened his jacket, and then smiled at his friend of such long-standing that they were like twin brothers.

'Just keep your eyes peeled at the Strattons'. We can't go

directly to the club, we have to show up. We can't offend Caroline. She would be hurt.'

'You're right, I suppose.' He began to laugh. 'Just half an hour though. In view of the dire circumstances. Anyway, I'm not worried. I have you to defend me from any fearsome women, and – most importantly – from Vanessa.'

'You bet!' Adrian answered, also laughing.

THIRTY-FOUR

The two men could see the crowded drawing room from the large entrance foyer. They stared at each other in dismay. Robert said, 'It's packed to the nines already. Shall we scarper?'

Adrian shook his head. 'Better not. As you just said earlier, Caroline would be hurt.'

'All right. We'll make our appearance, stay only a short while, and slip out when we can. Beat it to the club, where we can relax.'

'Agreed,' Adrian answered, sounding relieved.

The two of them walked forward in step, and a moment later were greeted by Caroline Stratton and her parents, Bertram and Claire.

Caroline led the men into the drawing room, and both of them reached into their pockets and brought out an envelope.

'These are for your charity,' Robert said, giving her his dazzling smile.

'Oh, thank you, Robert, Adrian. Just pop them in that big bowl over there. That's what everyone's been doing.'

They did as she asked, and Robert, an expert on antiques, noticed that the bowl was of the finest Rose Medallion china.

Caroline said, 'I've got to stay here, you know, greet people with my parents. But you should both go into the room and mingle. You'll know lots of people. Many of your friends are here.'

'Righto,' Adrian said, and taking hold of Robert's arm he pulled him into the chattering throng. Within seconds they were separated. Adrian was caught by two women, one of whom he knew. Robert was pushed to the left and found himself near a wall, where he managed to slide past two men he vaguely knew from business and wanted to avoid.

Suddenly, he saw his chance to rush down to the far end of the room, where French doors opened onto the garden. It would be cooler.

He was halfway there when his way was blocked by a tall young woman wearing a beautiful purple silk evening gown, with a deep flounce to the skirt and ribbon trim against her bare shoulders.

She was in profile, and what immediately struck him was her marvellous hair. It was piled high on top of her head in curls, the style currently favoured by Queen Alexandra. It gleamed in the light.

He was a few feet away from her when she turned around. They were suddenly facing each other, almost eye to eye.

Both of them seemed surprised, and they stared. Neither could look away. Their bodies were frozen, blue eyes locked on amber eyes.

Robert caught his breath, and there was a tightening in his chest. Unexpectedly, he felt as if he had been turned upside down. He couldn't move, or speak. All he could do was gaze at the most stunning woman he had ever seen.

On her part, the young woman was truly dazzled by this tall, dark man whom she had glimpsed here from time to time, but had never been close enough to speak to. Although she had always wanted to meet him properly, talk with him, he had never noticed her.

Now, he had. The startled expression on his face showed her that.

She took a step towards him, and then another.

He smiled at her, and said, 'I'm Robert Lassiter,' and stretched out his hand.

She took it and felt heat running down her body. 'I know who you are, Your Lordship. I'm Vanessa Stratton.'

Although he was momentarily taken aback, he kept a neutral look on his face, and said, 'I'm very pleased to meet you, very pleased indeed.'

'I think you know my sister, Caroline.'

'I do. It was she who invited me. Can we walk down to the French doors and get a little air, do you think?'

'Of course,' she answered, and realized he was still holding her hand. She decided not to disentangle herself since he hadn't, and he led her to the end of the long drawing room without speaking.

Robert finally let go of her hand, and opened the French doors wider. 'There, that's better,' he said, turning back to her. A waiter was drawing closer, and Robert swiftly took two glasses of champagne from his tray, and thanked him.

Robert never took his eyes off her face as he handed her the flute. They touched glasses without saying a word, just gazed into each other's eyes.

Finally, it was she who spoke. 'I'm glad the crowd hasn't migrated down here. We're in a little bubble, lovely and quiet, aren't we?'

He laughed. 'That's a nice way of putting it. I'd no idea it would be such a crowd, so many people tonight.'

'Caroline doesn't keep track of whom she invites. That's why it's always like this. Eloise says she does it on purpose.'

'Who is Eloise?' he added, filled with curiosity about Vanessa.

'My eldest sister, she is *our* eldest sister. She believes Caroline likes crowds.'

'Is Eloise here tonight?'

'Oh no, she lives in Paris. She's married to a Frenchman, Jean-Claude. I go to see her quite often. She has a baby girl. And now she's happy.'

'Was she unhappy before?' he wondered out loud.

'Very. Jean-Claude didn't want children. You see, he's much older than Eloise. But she talked him into it.'

'How old is he?' Robert asked, wondering what this lovely-looking young woman considered *old*.

'He's forty. Can you imagine?' She grimaced.

'And how old is Eloise?' he murmured.

'She's twenty-eight. But she's . . . well, she's very grown-up and sophisticated. I enjoy going there, because I also like to go to the art galleries. I love Impressionist paintings.'

'So do I!' he exclaimed, forgetting about age for the moment. 'Who is your favourite, if you have one?' His eyes were still on her, but now they were filled with curiosity.

'Renoir, most of all,' Vanessa answered. 'But I also like Cézanne. And you? Who do you like?'

He smiled that dazzling smile of his, and said, 'Renoir and Cézanne.'

Vanessa laughed and raised her glass, touched it to his. 'There, you see, we have the same taste.'

As she spoke, she edged towards the French doors, and then looked at him. 'Let's go outside. It's cooler.'

'Good idea.' Robert followed her, realizing that they would also be totally alone out in the garden. Those amber eyes flecked with gold, the white skin like polished alabaster, the high forehead and prominent cheekbones, and the very sensual mouth. He longed to seize her hand, rush her out of this house, and take her away to another quiet place to be alone, talk to her.

These thoughts sent shockwaves through him. He had never felt quite like this about a woman. Not his wife. Not ever in his life before, and there had been a few.

'Are you coming outside, Your Lordship?' she called from the middle of the garden.

'I am,' he answered, walking forward, fully aware of the varied emotions running through him, surprising him, *unsettling* him.

She stood near a big old oak, and had put her glass of champagne on a garden table.

He joined her, and said, 'Why haven't I met you before? You said you'd seen me here, and I've been often.'

'Nobody bothered to introduce us, I suppose because I'm the youngest. Not so important. And people were always flocking around you. After all, you're the Earl of Harding, the great businessman everyone wants to meet.'

Her words took him by surprise, and he exclaimed, 'I'm not famous. I just get on with it, and do my work.'

'I decided I was going to meet you tonight, no matter what, and I planted myself down here because I get a good view of the room.' She gave him a small smirk of a smile.

He laughed, but made no comment.

She said, 'Can I ask you to lend me something? I promise I'll never ask you for anything else as long as I live.'

Robert gave her a rather puzzled look, wondering if she was teasing or flirting, but she appeared to be serious. 'What can *I* lend *you*, Vanessa?'

'A cigarette, please. I'm dying for a smoke. Aren't you?'

'Actually, I would like a cigarette, and, of course, I will *give* you one, not lend it.'

'My mother won't allow smoking in the drawing room, so don't be surprised if a few chaps step out here to have a smoke.'

He nodded, took out his cigarette case and offered it to her.

She took the cigarette, smiled at him sweetly. 'Thank you,' she murmured.

Robert took one for himself, and put it in his mouth, closed the gold case.

Vanessa, watching him closely, said, 'I bet that's from Cartier's.'

'You're very observant,' he remarked, and put the case in his jacket pocket, retrieved an elegant lighter and proceeded to light their cigarettes. They smoked in silence for a few seconds. Then he said, 'You seem to know what I do for a living, but I don't know *anything* about *you*. Want to fill me in?'

'I will, but there's not much to tell. I'm called a debutante, but I loathe being one, so I won't go through the motions. I want to be a writer, you see.'

'I do see, and I suppose your parents don't like *that* idea, do they?'

'No. But they don't pressure me too much.' She gave him a long look, her eyes on his, and continued, 'I wanted to be a war correspondent at one time, you know, like Mr Churchill when he covered the Boer War. But my father said that women weren't allowed to cover wars. So that was that.'

Robert nodded. 'I believe he was correct. It's a dangerous profession, even for a man.'

'I know, and I thought if I got killed—' She broke off, took a sip of champagne, glanced away.

Robert Lassiter was silent, endeavouring to truly understand what was going on here. He knew he felt as if he had been hit by a truck. This woman took his breath away, filled him with rampant sexual feelings. He desired her, wanted her, for always. As down to earth as he was, he knew, nonetheless, things like this did happen to men and women. The French called it a *coup de foudre*; he called it *recognition* – the moment when twin souls suddenly meet.

He had great insight into people, and he was pretty certain Vanessa had felt the same when they finally came face to face. But he needed to be sure.

She was light-hearted, flirting with him, playing him a little, and he was allowing it. And yet she had been quite blunt when she admitted she had wanted to talk to him on other occasions and had tried to seek him out. And she had made a plan to do so tonight.

'You're quiet,' Vanessa murmured, cutting into his thoughts. 'Is something wrong?' She sounded worried.

He shook himself. 'No, not at all. I'm just a little baffled, though, and perhaps you could enlighten me.'

'Of course I will. Tell me why you're baffled.'

'You said you'd seen me here several times in the past, had tried to get through the usual crowd of people in order to properly meet me. I'm right, am I not?'

'Yes. I did say it, and I did do it. But you were always surrounded by an admiring swirl of skirts or men out to pick your brains.'

His mouth twitched, he wanted to laugh, but he held it back. 'Why did you want to meet me?'

'Because . . . because . . . well, I . . . er . . . just did. After all, you're very good-looking, and charming, and . . . er . . .' Her voice trailed off, and she felt herself blushing. He had put her in a spot.

She was suddenly afraid to continue. To hide her embarrassment, she sat down in a garden chair and looked up at the sky, still light on this summer's evening.

He remained standing, leaning nonchalantly against the old oak tree, the flute of champagne in one hand, his cigarette in the other. Regarding her for a few moments, an unreadable look on his face, he finally said, 'I think you wanted to meet me properly, as you call it, because you were attracted to me.'

When she remained silent, he said in an even gentler voice, 'I want you to know *I* am attracted to *you*, Vanessa, very much so.'

She gaped at him.

He put the champagne flute on the garden table and stubbed out his cigarette, took several steps over to her, offering his hands to her.

She took them and he pulled her to her feet, brought her into his arms and held her close. She was trembling as she clung to him, and he himself was shaking inside.

After a while, he released her, and looked at her face, his eyes roaming over it. He lifted a hand and stroked her cheek, then said, 'Let's sit down. We have to talk.'

She did as he said, looked across the table at him, and murmured in a low voice, 'It's not going to be so easy, is it?'

'You're obviously very intelligent, and you are correct. It won't be easy if, and I say if, we did start . . . an affair. In fact, it presents many problems.'

'I can handle it,' she replied in a low voice, still shaking inside.

'I'm a lot older than you—'

Interrupting him, she said, 'I know your age. You're thirty-nine.'

'And you? How old are you, actually? Twenty-three, twenty-four?' He raised a dark brow.

'I'm twenty-two. You are seventeen years older than me, Robert, but you don't look it. And I don't care. Numbers are just that. Numbers. They don't matter.'

Robert had been slightly taken aback when she told him her real age. She had a certain sophistication about her, self-confidence, and she was rather forthright. Blunt even.

He took a deep breath, and said, 'Whatever you say, seventeen years is a huge age difference. You grimaced when you explained your brother-in-law is older than your sister.'

'Oh, did you notice that! Well, Jean-Claude is like an old man, behaves like one, and he's not drop-dead gorgeous like you.'

He chuckled, 'Oh, Vanessa, you do take my breath away. But to continue: there is an even greater impediment. I am married.'

'I know that. I know you have two sons, Quentin and Christian, at prep school. Your wife doesn't come to London any more. Much of the time you live alone at your beautiful house in Grosvenor Square, when you're not in Ireland or Yorkshire.'

'My goodness, do you have some sort of dossier on me?' he asked in a mild voice, rather pleased with her honesty.

'Of course not. And I've never asked Caroline or anyone anything about you. All I've told you is just common knowledge. After all, you are a very visible man.'

'I understand. I'll have to become less visible, I suppose.' He sounded droll.

Vanessa looked up at the house, where the noise of talking and laughter could be heard, then turned towards him on the bench. 'What are you going to do about me? About us? Are we going to see each other again, Robert?'

He was silent, looked miserable and worried. And his face was solemn.

She waited for a while, felt her heart sinking, certain he was going to reject the idea. This thought was unbearable.

Taking all her courage in both her hands, she said carefully, slowly, 'If a very nice, well-brought-up young woman invited you for tea at The Ritz, would you accept?'

Robert looked at her, a smile flickering briefly. 'It would depend on who that young woman was, whether or not I would go to tea at The Ritz with her.'

Vanessa did not say anything.

After a second, wishing to please her, to play her little game, he went on, 'For instance, if that young woman was anything like you, then I would accept that invitation with alacrity.'

'Oh, very good. She would like to suggest tomorrow. If it suits your schedule.'

'I can fit it in. At what time would I be expected to arrive?'

'At tea-time, of course, four-thirty p.m.'

'Then I think we have a deal.'

They were both startled and looked around when they heard Adrian calling from the French doors. 'Robert, are you out there?'

Robert jumped up, pulled her to her feet, then walked ahead of her to greet Adrian.

'I am, old chap. Came out to have a smoke. Found Vanessa doing the same. Apparently her mother doesn't like chaps smoking in the drawing room.'

Adrian said, 'I know. Oh, hello, Vanessa. How are you?'

'Hello, Adrian,' she answered, smiling at him. 'I'm fine. I ran into Lord Lassiter out here and we got to talking about Impressionist paintings.' She turned to Robert, and said sweetly, 'It was so nice to chat with you, and thank you for taking the time.'

Thirty-Five

The two men left the Strattons' house and hailed a hansom cab. Adrian gave the cab driver the address. 'Thirty-seven St James Street, please,' he said, getting into the cab, with Robert following.

'Right away, guv'nor,' the cabbie replied, his Cockney accent apparent. 'White's Club it is!'

Lord Robert and Lord Adrian sat back, and Robert said in an amused voice, 'Despite all the clatter of horses' hooves, wheels on cobbles and tooting motorcars, I think it's quieter out here than it was in there.'

'I couldn't agree more,' Adrian responded. 'I do believe Caroline outdid herself tonight. Too many people for my liking. I couldn't hear myself think, never mind speak.'

'I know what you mean. It was a bit horrific.'

Adrian glanced at his dearest friend, and murmured, 'I'm sure it was better in the garden, wasn't it?'

'Yes. But I was only outside a couple of minutes, having a quick smoke.' He changed the subject. 'I noticed Caroline's bowl of donations was filled to the brim with envelopes and promises.

I bet you she made quite a lot of money, enough to get her charity started in a proper way, certain of that.'

'I agree. She's always been quite enterprising, for as long as I've known her. I like her for her independent traits, her drive and ambition. She's what I call a modern woman, perhaps a bit before her time, in fact.'

Robert nodded, then asked, 'Are you going to invite her out again? You said you enjoyed your evening with her last week?'

'I am. I'm taking her to the opera on Saturday. I have a box, and I was wondering if you would like to join us.'

'Two's company, three's a crowd,' Robert said with a chuckle. 'Thank you, though.'

'You know a sackful of women, *you* can pick from a dozen. There must be *one* of them you could invite. It would be great to have you.'

'Thank you, Adrian, but I think I have to beat it back up north to Yorkshire. I haven't been there much this year. I have a lot of work to do with the new estate manager, Colin Wilson. Lucinda is only staying there briefly with the boys, then going on to her parents.' He tried to keep his mind off Vanessa Stratton.

'How's Wilson working out?'

'He's turned out to be absolutely bloody marvellous. Clever, hard-working, and full of innovative ideas for Bolton Manor. I wish I'd found him years ago. Much as I love it, the estate has been a bit of a burden, as I just can't be there enough, and he's brought me some relief.'

The hansom came to an abrupt stop, and the cabbie said, 'White's, me lords.'

Robert, then Adrian, jumped out; Adrian paid the cabbie, and together, in step as usual, they entered one of the oldest gentlemen's private clubs in London. First opened in 1693, its membership was aristocratic and Tory, and was considered the best amongst many others.

The steward greeted them both by name in the entrance foyer, and escorted them to the dining room and their preferred table. They had chatted with the steward, Smythson, politely. He had responded in kind and then departed once they were settled.

'I want a proper drink,' Adrian said, once they were alone. 'A Scotch and soda. I don't enjoy too much champagne.'

'Good idea, I'll have the same. I forgot to tell you, I was talking to Johnny Anderson last week, and he told me that the King now seems to be getting on well with Arthur Balfour. They've sort of . . . bonded. So much for all those chaps who said the King would never do that.'

'Everybody's got an opinion about the Prime Minister, so I don't pay much attention, as you know. Anyway, there's nothing wrong with that, as far as I can see.'

'I suspect *that* doesn't sit well with some folk.'

Their drinks arrived; they clinked glasses and said, 'Down the hatch,' in unison.

After a few sips of his Scotch and soda, Adrian stared at Robert for a long moment, before saying in a low but forceful tone, 'She got you!'

Robert returned Adrian's stare, his expression neutral, in total control of himself. He had known this kind of comment would be coming and was prepared to respond appropriately.

After a swallow of the Scotch himself, he said, '*Got you* is a rather strange expression. Does it mean, got you in her clutches, suggesting a bad thing? Or cornered me in a bad way? On the other hand, it could mean she's got you in a nice way. Such as having captivated me. Certainly she hasn't got me by my short hairs, if you were meaning that. Not at all. Quite the contrary.'

Adrian burst out laughing. Then, calming himself, he said, 'There's just nobody like you when it comes to words and explanations. You're a bloody marvel.'

'I knew earlier tonight that something peculiar would be forthcoming from *you*, old chap,' he replied, also laughing.

'So which is it?' Adrian probed.

'Can't you guess? Go on, have a go.'

'She cornered you, chatted you up and you fell for it . . . for her.'

'Partially true. I got separated from you when we arrived, and I made it down to the end of the room and the French doors. We kind of bumped into each other, and I was struck at once by her looks. Vanessa is stunning, you can't deny that.'

'I don't. But I think it was a bit calculating.'

'I would prefer to say she's *enterprising*. In any case, I felt as if I'd been hit by a truck. I couldn't take my eyes off her, and she reacted in the same manner. Finally, I took her hand and we went right down to the back of the room. Later, we walked into the garden to smoke.'

'*How* did you feel, really and truly?' Adrian asked quietly, understanding that this was a serious situation now developing right before his eyes.

'I'm smitten, and so is she, I'm certain. But before you tell me, I *know* it can't work because I'm a married man. But I'm in trouble, Adrian.' Robert smoothed his hand over his forehead. 'I have a wife. In name at least.'

'Finally, we can now discuss that bloody *dead* marriage of yours! Because you've brought it up, your feelings must be very genuine indeed.'

'They are. I don't want to hurt Vanessa.'

'You could have an affair with her. Would she go for that?' Adrian raised a blond eyebrow.

'I've no doubt she would. She wants to be with me.'

'So go ahead, enjoy each other whilst you can.'

Robert shook his head. 'I cannot. I don't want a quick affair with Vanessa. I want more. Something is different.'

'I wish I could think of a way to murder that bloody wife of yours—'

'Don't be so bloody daft!' Robert cut in sharply.

'Let me finish, Robert. I was about to add, *without getting caught*. But I can't. No woman is worth swinging for. We must find a way to get you your freedom. It's all gone on far too long. You have been living separate lives for—'

'Nine years!' Robert interrupted. 'That's how long ago it is that Lucinda told me she would never allow me in her bedroom again. I tried several times, because I did want more children after the boys were born. However, nothing worked. She's just about civil. However, she comes to Yorkshire less and less, and never to London now. When we're back in Ireland I barely see her. She's moody, reclusive, haughty with the staff. We effectively live separate lives.'

'You usually go to Yorkshire when she goes to Switzerland.' Adrian frowned and threw Robert an odd look. 'Come to think of it, *why* does she go trotting off to Zürich, and quite a few times a year? What's that clinic she goes to, the Medallion?'

'Yes. She claims she's not well, and their treatments help her nervous condition, and she likes to be in the mountains. The air helps her breathe better . . .'

Robert's voice trailed off when he saw the utter disbelief reflected on his friend's face, and he shook his head, appeared nonplussed.

'What a load of codswallop that is!' Adrian exclaimed, sounding very annoyed. 'She's not really ill, not in my opinion. She's faking it, and I wonder why? Do you have to pay all these Medallion bills?'

Robert shook his head. 'No, she does that, and sometimes she stays at the Baur au Lac, my favourite hotel, and yours. However, she does have her own money.'

Adrian now looked startled and said, 'I remember you mentioning the hotel ages ago, and thinking at the time that it was odd she was not actually in the clinic . . .'

He stopped speaking and stared into space, a reflective expression in his eyes. After a moment or two, he said slowly, 'Could there be another man in Lucinda's life? A man she meets in Zürich?'

'Or in Geneva,' Robert volunteered. 'She's sometimes there. I have to be kept informed of her whereabouts, because of the boys.'

'Here's my point. She can afford to do a lot of things, Robert. Everyone knows her father gave her a huge trust fund, and her brother Valentine as well. Money gives a woman a certain amount of freedom. *Could there be another man?*'

'Yes, of course. Or another woman. Or more than one man, maybe different men at different times. How would I ever know, since she's in Zürich, Geneva, or wherever? But I think she's lost her looks. She has become faded, and tired-looking. She *is* moody, certainly with me. I don't think a man would be interested in her sexually. She's lost it.'

'Except that she's rich, and titled . . . the Lady Lucinda Lassiter, and perhaps ready to play around when she's off her home base. And maybe she gets all dolled up.'

'What you say is true, and it's occurred to me, although I've never brought it up with you, my closest friend.'

'Why not?'

'Because marriages are private, and our sort don't discuss their marital difficulties. Also, I have no feelings for her now. Since you were my best man, you'll know I married her when I was twenty-nine. The boys were born within a couple of years. After that she lost interest in me and banned me from her bedroom. Eventually, I drifted totally apart from her. I'll never understand what I did to offend her, if anything.'

'I know you were always in London, and always with me. We've spent our lives together since we were eight, and I'll tell you this . . . I don't know how you've managed the way you have. You're a healthy man of thirty-nine, and you need a woman in your life – for love, companionship, tenderness and sex. And you're vulnerable at this moment in time. That is a certainty.'

'I realize that, and I'm so glad we've kept our long friendship. However, what I'm trying to say is I suppose at one level I don't care about Lucinda or what she does. However, I am beginning to see that she has become an impediment to my future, to my happiness.'

'Then we have to remove her from your life,' Adrian announced. 'Get you a divorce.'

Robert frowned. Divorce was still scandalous: difficult, expensive and messy. 'And how do you plan to do that, Adrian? I have no idea, believe me, I don't. She'll never agree. She likes being the Countess and she won't want the scandal.'

'I am going to hire a private investigator. And immediately, which means tomorrow. There are a number of good companies and I'll choose the best and foot the bill.'

'But—'

Adrian interjected, 'No *buts* or *ifs*. It's your only way out of a ridiculous situation, and it's my pleasure to pay the bill. So don't argue with me.'

Robert flashed his smile, and said, 'Thank you. We might be heading for quite a war, though.'

Adrian laughed. 'Into the valley of death rode the six hundred.'

Robert stared at him. 'Why are you quoting "The Charge of the Light Brigade"?'

'That's what is going to happen tomorrow. I am going to bring about another Charge of the Light Brigade. But *I'm* bloody well going to win. I'll bury Lucinda in her own dirt, because the more I think about it, the more certain I am she is covered in it. You'll soon see.'

'I hope so,' Robert answered, understanding that Adrian meant every word he said, and that he wouldn't leave any stone unturned.

THIRTY-SIX

Robert Lassiter looked briefly at the menu, and put it to one side. Glancing at Adrian, he said, 'I'm having potted shrimp, and whatever is on that large silver trolley over there.'

Adrian lifted his head and nodded. 'Same here. And I do believe it's a sirloin of beef on the trolley. The thought makes my mouth water. Do you want a glass of red wine?' He put the menu down on the table as he spoke.

'Why not, and you pick one.' He raised a hand and beckoned to the wine waiter standing nearby.

It was Adrian who asked for the wine list, and perused it swiftly, and then ordered a red burgundy he and Robert both liked.

Lighting a cigarette, Robert said quietly, 'I hope the firm you use to do the investigating will be discreet.'

'Oh, of course they will!' Adrian exclaimed. 'The one I've used at times for bank matters is exceptional. No one will know they're investigating Lucinda, not even she herself. They're experts at that sort of cloak-and-dagger stuff.'

Robert couldn't help himself, he burst out laughing. '*You* have a clever turn of phrase, old chap, as you say I do. And I hope there are no daggers around – as you said, no woman is worth swinging for. Certainly not Lucinda.'

'Funny how she changed, and so radically. And you're right, you know she has grown . . . *dowdy*. I think that's the correct word. She was quite glamorous when you got married, and for a few years after that,' Adrian said. 'Then she faded.'

'The only time she sort of bucks up is in Ireland. She enjoys Lassiter Hall, and the villagers seem fond of her, although she doesn't go out among them so often these days. Keeps herself to herself. Actually, I am going to make a trip back there in the not too distant future. I'll take Colin Wilson with me, and I'm pondering the idea of taking Blackie O'Neill along – that Irish lad, you remember? Or sending him ahead perhaps, with Wilson. I like the lad, think he's got something special about him. He could work wonders in the gardens there. I think they've been neglected lately.'

'From what you say, he's turned into a strapping lad, no doubt about that. Funny that you ran into him again recently, when he turned up at Bolton Manor with Lucinda's maid. Forgotten her name. Irish as well.'

'Her name is O'Brien, Siobhan O'Brien, and she's his cousin. A nice young woman, calm, hard-working, but I think she misses her brother, who still works at the house in Ireland. I think really she'd prefer to be back there.' Robert stubbed out his cigarette and smiled at Adrian. 'Our wine is about to arrive.'

Once their glasses had been filled, Adrian said, 'Here's to you, my dear old friend, and a new future, all shiny and bright and full of happiness with a stunning lady love called Vanessa Stratton.'

'Let's hope so,' Robert replied, a smile flickering slightly, his face suddenly changing, growing serious. 'If *you* can make it happen.'

'Don't you fret, Robert. It's about time you started to live a better life. No one deserves it more than you. Now, about Vanessa, you said she was willing.'

'*Willing?* What exactly do you mean?'

'To have an affair with you.'

'I don't want that, Addy. I really don't,' Robert answered swiftly, using his friend's childhood nickname. 'I want to be with her. Not as my mistress. To be able to marry her.'

'Getting a divorce can take a while, from what I know about chaps who have taken that step,' Adrian felt bound to explain. 'And you will need to prove cruelty, desertion or adultery.'

Robert returned Adrian's intense gaze, but remained silent, obviously fully digesting his friend's words.

Adrian said in a quiet voice, 'You might feel it hard to keep your hands off her, and I'm certain you'll go on seeing Vanessa, as I do my bit, so to speak, getting your freedom.'

'I might,' Robert agreed. 'However, I'll just have to manage it, be very controlled. I'll try hard.'

'What about Vanessa? She's already mentioned the word *affair*, according to you.'

'She has. There is a problem, however. I've nowhere to take her. My homes are full of servants. I can't have her meet me at a hotel. I would be recognized, and so would she. There are often reports about her in the society magazines, and I'm well known, somewhat *visible*.'

'All too true. But I can solve that problem for you quite easily, if ever you can't stand it any more,' Adrian announced, sitting back in his chair.

'In what way can *you* solve it, Addy? Your house is full of servants, too.'

Reaching into his trouser pocket, Adrian brought out a bunch of keys and selected one, then showed it to Robert. 'I would lend you this key.' Out of the corner of his eye, he saw their waiter approaching and put the keys back in his pocket.

Once the waiter had placed the potted shrimps in front of them and left, Adrian said, 'That key can be yours whenever you want it.'

'What door does it open?' Robert, filled with curiosity, was eyeing Adrian with interest.

'A house in Farm Street.'

'Whose house? Yours? A secret place?'

'No, not mine. It belongs to my brother, Julian, and it's actually his home. If you remember, he went to America a few months ago. He's now working at our New York office, learning about American banking. Julian will be gone for a year, and asked me to check the house twice a week, look at his mail, that sort of thing.'

'Doesn't he have help? You know, a housekeeper, for instance?'

'He's only twenty, Robert. No staff. Just a charlady. Nice woman. She goes in every Monday, so Monday is strictly *verboten*. To be avoided. That is the only day Mrs Weathers goes in, though.'

'Have you used it yet?' Robert asked, his face neutral.

'No, I haven't, and the key is yours whenever you wish,' Adrian responded.

'Thank you,' Robert replied, and stuck his small fork into the potted shrimp.

Adrian did the same, saying at one moment, 'I didn't have anything to eat today, other than breakfast. I'm starving. And these are good.'

'The same for me, and I must say I'm also enjoying the shrimp. Getting back to the key. Would Julian know? I mean, you wouldn't tell him, would you?'

'Of course I wouldn't; anyway, he's in New York. I explained that.'

'But you'll write to him, won't you?'

'Yes. And I'd never betray you. Surely you know that after all these years.'

'I know. But I doubt I'll use it . . . the key.'

'I realize that, Robert.' Having finished the first course, Adrian glanced around, and exclaimed, 'The club's rather busy for a Thursday. Usually all the married chaps are on their way to the country at this hour, off to be with wife and family. Mandatory two days before back to town and, for many, the life of Riley, as the saying goes.'

'Only too true,' Robert agreed. 'It's a man's world we live in, but then it has been for centuries. Always will be.'

'That's right,' Adrian agreed. 'We do what we want, and get away with it. Out at work, if we have a profession or business. Then palling around with men at night, going to dinner clubs, gentlemen's clubs like this, gambling clubs, variety shows, card games. Some go to Madame Paloma's, seeking entertainment of a more carnal nature.'

'What you say is true. To each his own.' Robert let his eyes roam around the room at White's and then he leaned closer to Adrian and said, 'I'd bet my bottom dollar that eighty per cent of the men in this room have mistresses. What say you, Addy, my boy?'

'I'd say ninety. Men have always had mistresses, since time began. It's *the* thing, the normal thing for men. And, as often as not, the mistress is a married woman. The preferred choice for most.'

'I've often wondered why that is so,' Robert confided. 'And I came to the conclusion that men prefer mistresses with husbands. They're safe in the long run; too much to lose if caught. So they are careful.'

'Were any of your mistresses married, Robert?'

'Several, although I'm not sure I would call any of them *mistresses*. They didn't last long at all.'

'I see what you mean,' Adrian chuckled, and went on. 'I often wondered how many men know *they* are being cuckolded.'

Robert shook his head. 'Can't answer that, I'm afraid, but some husbands are quite compliant, know about their wives' antics.'

'Do you really think so?'

Robert nodded. 'Look at Mr George Keppel. There goes a genuinely compliant husband. His wife Alice has been the King's mistress for donkey's years, since he was the Prince of Wales, in fact. So far, she's his longest-lasting mistress. And still there.'

Adrian took out a cigarette, and before lighting it he said, 'When he goes to visit her, the King, I mean, her children crawl all over him and call him "Kingy". How about that?'

'How do *you* know? That's my question,' Robert asked, a look of disbelief on his face.

'Because my father is a friend of King Bertie's, and advises him about money. That's as far as I can go with that, the money part. My father rather likes our head of state, thinks he works hard, has proved himself to be highly competent, and an unusually clever diplomat.'

'You sound admiring of him yourself,' Robert murmured, and added: 'The silver trolley is being pushed our way. We're about to enjoy a delicious piece of beef, with the best horseradish in town.'

Thirty-Seven

He awakened suddenly, as if he had been shaken, and sat up, disorientated for a moment about whether he was still at his house in Yorkshire. When he had gone to bed earlier, he had opened the long draperies covering one of the windows to allow fresh air to circulate. He preferred a cool room. Now moonlight streamed in as well. It was still the middle of the night.

Throwing back the bedclothes, Robert Lassiter swung his long legs to the floor and turned on the small lamp on the bedside table.

Thank God for the invention of electricity, he thought, as he hurried into the adjoining bathroom, where he turned on another light. It was still far from common to have electricity in domestic houses, but Robert was fascinated by all the technological advances that the new century was bringing, and was fortunate enough to have the money to indulge his interest.

He stood in front of the mirror, staring at himself, deciding he looked exactly the same as he had a week ago. Black hair, sleeked back, black eyebrows above bright blue eyes, pale cheeks, clean-shaven, and a full mouth.

This was *him*, all right, no doubt about that. And yet he felt completely different, not the same man at all. But of course he did. A change had been wrought the moment he had set eyes on Vanessa Stratton.

He was hopelessly smitten. And shaken up inside, and knew he was in trouble, because he was not a free man, could not pursue her. He had nothing to offer her. Certainly not an affair, which, incredibly, she was willing to embark on, and at once.

He had fallen for her, had never felt this way before. Oh yes, women there had been, but only infatuations; no relationship had lasted very long.

An unexpected smile curved his mouth as he pictured her in his mind, the image of her face very vivid, the abundant russet hair, the amber eyes, the alabaster skin. A precocious young woman who couldn't help being honest and a trifle blunt, traits which had instantly endeared her to him, since she was revealing her true self to him.

He didn't want to be in trouble. He never had been before, and trouble did not work with his lifestyle.

He was a man who loved the role in life that he had been born to, and his work, and he worked long hours. He liked order, needed to be in control of himself, his country estates in Ireland and Yorkshire, his property company, and this house here in Grosvenor Square, which was his haven, his place of peace and quiet. A town house, modernized to suit his requirements; a place where he was comfortable, able to work if he so wished, and to entertain when socializing was required. Lucinda hated London society now and had never spent time here. *Order*. That was the name of the game, his game anyway. No other one to play as far as he was concerned.

Turning off the light, Robert went back to his bedroom and

sat down in the armchair near the windows, lifted his legs onto the ottoman, his mind racing.

He would take total control of the situation as of this moment. He needed to work out his decisions, sort them into their proper order, and then put everything in motion. *Tomorrow*. Once his decisions had been made.

Closing his eyes, he settled back in the chair, focusing on the first problem, concentrating. One thing at a time, he reminded himself. That was his way. No muddle. Clear thinking.

Each matter that was a problem he worked through patiently, taking everything into consideration, selecting the wisest thing to do. It took time. Although he had always been a quick decision maker, he was never rash. He weighed the odds before coming to a final conclusion.

Dawn was breaking when he finally went back to bed, turned off the lamp and settled himself. He was filled with relief, totally calm. He had arranged everything carefully in his mind, in correct order. And tomorrow he would proceed, knowing his decisions, made with great exactness, would bring success. Failure was not a word in his vocabulary.

The following morning, Robert got up at the usual hour of seven o'clock. He went through his ritual of taking a bath, washing his hair, and shaving.

He then went to his dressing room and selected one of his suits, most of which had been impeccably tailored by the best firms in Savile Row. This morning he chose a more casual, single-breasted style, navy blue in colour, and took out a crisp white shirt. After putting it on, he chose a light blue silk tie. He dressed swiftly and stepped into black shoes. He had not brought his valet by choice for what had been intended as a quick visit to London. There was something annoying about another man fussing over his clothes. He'd given the man leave to visit his parents in Harrogate while he was away.

He went downstairs to the breakfast room where his butler was waiting.

'Good morning, m'lord,' Turnbull said, greeting him with a smile. 'I hope you had a good night's rest, Lord Robert?'

'Morning, Turnbull, and I did, thank you.'

Turnbull pulled out the chair in the middle of the round table, and asked, 'Shall I pour a cup of tea for you, m'lord?'

'Yes, do that, please, Turnbull. But I would prefer a light breakfast this morning. Just scrambled eggs and toast. That's about it, I think.'

'Yes, m'lord.' Turnbull went to the sideboard and lifted the lid off a silver tureen, put the eggs on a plate, took it to the table, brought a plate of toast, then poured the tea. He worked with quick precision, as he always did, knowing Lord Robert was in a hurry.

After thanking the butler, Robert asked, 'What's the weather like today – not our perpetual summer rain, I hope?'

'It's a nice day, m'lord. Sunny, in fact.' Turnbull cleared his throat and stepped over to a small table next to the door. He picked up a small silver tray with an envelope on it and carried it to the table. 'This envelope was delivered earlier this morning, sir.' As he spoke, he offered the tray.

Robert looked at the butler and raised a dark brow. 'Who delivered it, Turnbull? Any idea?'

'No, Lord Robert, I'm afraid I don't. It was pushed through the letter box.'

Taking the envelope, Robert said, 'Thank you, Turnbull. I'll ring if I need you.'

'Yes, m'lord,' he answered and departed.

Ignoring the food, Robert slit the envelope with his knife and quickly read the note. It was from Colin Wilson, his new estate manager, who was due in London today, and his eyes widened as he read. Following his instructions, Wilson had written to inform him that Lady Lucinda had left Bolton Manor yesterday morning. Not for her parents' estate in nearby Skipton as planned, but for Switzerland. She was travelling with a lady friend, and had not been accompanied by O'Brien, her lady's maid, the Irish girl they'd brought over with them, nor by their sons.

Bloody hell, Robert thought, as he digested the information. I did not foresee this – but perhaps my wife, without knowing it, has just made everything simpler.

THIRTY-EIGHT

When he had finished his breakfast, Robert went into the library. Seated at his large Georgian desk, he took the note from Wilson out of his pocket and read it again. Then he glanced over at the carriage clock on the mantelpiece. He had an hour before Wilson arrived, bringing him the accounts for the Yorkshire estate. He was grateful to have this intelligent and innovative man working for him.

Robert smiled at himself. It was young Blackie O'Neill who had told Wilson about the vacancy, his need for a talented estate manager. Apparently O'Neill had built a beautiful new kitchen for Wilson's aunt, pretty much run the project himself, and had met Wilson there, sent him along to meet the Earl. Now O'Neill was building a conservatory for her. The boy is certainly enterprising, Robert thought. He wondered if he could find a job for him, something to test out the talent he suspected lay beneath the cheerful and hard-working Irish labourer. He'd come a long way from the skinny youth who used to help out in the gardens sometimes at Lassiter Hall with his cousin Michael.

Wilson had done wonders with the Bolton Manor estate in a very short time. He was thirty-two, had an open, very genial personality and got on well with all who worked with him. He had a love of agriculture and the estate was prospering under his guidance.

Right from the start, Robert had been honest with Wilson about the fact that he was estranged from Lady Lucinda, and they lived separate lives, keeping up a civil front for the sake of their sons. He had told the new estate manager he needed to know the Countess's whereabouts at all times. Hence, the early note this morning; Colin Wilson wanted to alert him that Lady Lucinda had already left Bolton Manor – and England.

Robert leaned back in the chair, his mind racing. He knew that Adrian was having a meeting this morning with the head of the private investigating company.

Later they would have lunch together at the Fraser Brothers' private bank.

Adrian ran the Mayfair office on South Audley Street, and a new dining room had just been created so that important clients could be entertained at leisure in secure surroundings.

Robert rose and walked over to the window, stood looking out at Grosvenor Square, thinking, suddenly, how his life had changed overnight. In the blink of an eye.

He heard his father's voice echoing in his head, warning him that he should never waste a day, because that particular day would never come back. 'So live those hours to the limit,' his father had constantly reminded him. And often he would add, 'And always remember *you* are not in control of your life. Life is. All you do is control your behaviour and your day-to-day living, your friendships, your relationship with women, your colleagues, your parents and your children, should you have them.' And *he* had remembered every word, cherishing his father's wisdom. His father had also forewarned that his life could change in the blink of an eye, and now it had.

At precisely eleven o'clock, Turnbull showed Colin Wilson into the library as he announced his name.

Robert stood up and went to greet him, his hand outstretched.

'Good morning, Wilson,' Robert said. 'I'm glad to see you.'

'Good morning and likewise, Lord Robert. I trust you found the note I left here earlier this morning? On my way to Shepherd Market.'

'I did indeed, thank you. I suppose her ladyship herself let you know she was leaving Bolton Manor?'

'Yes, she did, and went on to add that she was travelling with her friend Lady Glendenning, that they were going to the clinic in Zürich. She mentioned that you were aware your sons were on the estate with their tutor.'

'Did she say how long she would be gone?'

'No, she did not, m'lord.'

Robert nodded. 'I always know where the boys are. They were supposed to be going to their grandparents with her.' He frowned to himself. 'I shall need to make some arrangements.' He paused and then indicated a chair. 'Now, down to business. Shall we go through the accounts first?'

Colin Wilson opened his briefcase and took out several files, explaining, 'We've had a record season, sir, and I believe you'll be pleased with the agricultural figures. Just one thing, Your Lordship, before we begin, I would like to discuss the dry-stone walls in the lower fields, as I mentioned when you were there last week. Some are in dire need of repair. I thought I ought to bring in the best stone-waller in Yorkshire, Sam Bell. What do you think, Lord Robert?'

'By all means, do get Bell in to tackle them. It's quite an art, building or mending those walls. No cement used, as you well know – just fitting the right stones together.'

'I will hire him immediately,' Wilson answered, and leaned across the desk and offered Robert the first file.

Lord Robert Lassiter cut quite a swathe as he walked out of Grosvenor Square, and headed down South Audley Street.

However, he was totally unaware of the admiring glances that passers-by gave him. As usual, his busy mind was preoccupied with thoughts of business, which pushed everything else to the side.

For the last few years, he had watched the enormous new building going up at Harrods, a department store in Knightsbridge. Fire had destroyed the original store, but what a success it had become, defying those who had predicted failure because it was so huge. Now he wanted to find an area to build a similar edifice, or a clutch of old buildings next to each other, which he could demolish.

He did not want to open and run the store. His desire was to design, build and sell it.

He was confident he would make a very high profit. In this instance, he knew he had nothing to lose, although he often pondered on that possibility at times. He was well aware he had to place the idea of loss in every equation.

Within minutes, he was entering the offices of Adrian's bank, and being shown to the second floor.

Adrian was waiting for him on the landing, and after warm greetings were exchanged, he led Robert into the new dining room where they would be having the midday meal.

Robert stood in the middle of the room and glanced around.

What he saw pleased him. Pine-panelled bookshelves on either side of the fireplace, and rose-brocade draperies at the two high windows, covering other walls, and on the chair seats.

A carpet filled with a mixture of pinks and reds covered the floor. In the middle of the room, a circular polished wood table was set for two, and on the back wall there was a beautiful Chippendale sideboard.

'Congratulations, Adrian!' Robert exclaimed, turning to his friend. 'Your team has done a wonderful job. It's fresh, very inviting. And, of course, it has elegance as well.'

'Thanks, I'm glad you like it. This room has looked faded and worn out for years, very Victorian. We're living in the Edwardian era now, an era of great change, and change for the better.' Walking over to the sideboard, Adrian continued, 'How about a spot of bubbly, or do you prefer a glass of white wine?'

'Champagne, please, Addy. It's lighter. You know I don't drink much, and especially during the day.'

Once they had toasted each other, clinking glasses, Robert gave Adrian a pointed look, and said, 'Colin Wilson's in town for our estate meeting, I asked him to come down rather than wait for my return. He popped a note through my letter box this morning on his way to breakfast in Shepherd Market.'

Reaching into his coat pocket, Robert took out the note and handed it to his closest friend. 'Read that.'

Adrian scanned the note and raised his eyebrows. Eyeing Robert, he said, 'This is a surprise. You could say we've got her by the short hairs.'

'Exactly,' Robert responded. 'You could also say she's fallen right into our hands. Or rather, the hands of one of your private investigators.'

'Damned right.' Raising his flute of champagne to Robert, Adrian said, 'Here's to an unexpected windfall.'

Robert grinned, took a sip of the Dom Pérignon. 'How did your meeting go this morning?'

'My private investigating firm has taken the job. Oh, and one of the operatives pointed out another thing. He said that desertion has been used as grounds for divorce by some men.'

Robert nodded. 'That occurred to me a couple of years ago, but I was in the middle of a huge business deal at the time, and pushed my marital situation to one side. And strictly speaking our paths still cross, so I think adultery is a safer option.'

'True, well, you've been avoiding the issue for bloody years, so now's definitely the time to jump into the fray, my boy, and with both feet.'

'I agree.' He hesitated, then said, 'By the way, I'm seeing Vanessa for tea at The Ritz this afternoon.'

'Wonderful idea.'

'Not mine, hers.'

'She's not shy in coming forward, is she?'

'No, she's rather outspoken, says what she's thinking, but I don't mind that bluntness of hers. It's refreshing.'

Adrian pulled his keyring out, and tapped one key. 'Do you want it?'

'Thanks, but no thanks. Not today.'

Rising from his chair, Adrian went to the sideboard and topped up his glass. He said as he strolled back to the table, 'I like the suit. New, isn't it?'

Robert nodded. 'Yes, and a new style: single-breasted, three buttons, and navy blue instead of black.'

'Savile Row, knowing you.'

'Hawes and Curtis, actually. My tailor told me the King started the style, with a light cream suit with a brown stripe, and creases at the sides instead of the front. Plus the new hat he designed, which is called the homburg.'

'I've seen the King in that – can't say I like it. Oh, here is Rollins, the butler for this room. With the menu, I've no doubt.'

Rollins greeted the two men, handing them a menu each.

After perusing them, Robert settled for pâté, to be followed by Dover sole, and Adrian selected oyster patties and poached salmon.

When the butler left, Adrian said, 'I'm so glad you've stopped going to your office on Friday, which means we can get together.'

'So am I,' Robert replied. 'I began to realize that by Thursday night I needed to get out of the salt mines.'

'I think you mean the gold mines,' Adrian shot back with a cheeky grin. 'You're not known as England's wealthiest landlord for nothing.'

'Must you always have the last word, Addy?'

'Yes. And I usually get it!'

THIRTY-NINE

I t had been a difficult day for Blackie O'Neill, and he was glad to leave Mrs Wilson's house at two o'clock.

He had finally laid down the large terracotta slabs that would form the conservatory floor on cement, and they had settled well. He had started at seven in the morning, and not even taken time off for a bite to eat – he who was always hungry. He just wanted to go home as soon as he could and have a rest. His head ached.

Pleased though he was about the way the conservatory was progressing at a good pace, he felt miserable because of all the things that had happened of late. His eyes, usually alight with merriment, were today mournful, his Celtic soul suffused with melancholy.

His thoughts turned to Moira Aherne. What on earth had she been doing in the Ham Shank, that stinking cesspit, he wondered again. His early life in rural Kerry had been harsh, and he had seen first-hand what poverty could do, but at least they hadn't been crammed cheek by jowl with hundreds of other folk. What a horrific slum it was, bad people amongst the decent, and men who boozed and hurt women, and probably their children, and started to booze again.

What a *mystery* she was, Blackie thought, although he didn't believe anyone else was as curious about her. How was it that her only friend in England had been a boy from Galway who sent her to relatives in Leeds?

Only today Mrs Wilson had come out to the garden, had brought him lemonade because it was a warm August day. She was kind that way.

After oohing and aahing about the terracotta slabs, she had stayed a bit longer to sing Moira's praises.

He was certain she was not who she said she was, claiming to be the daughter of the housekeeper and butler in the household of Lady Henrietta Fitzgerald Chandler. He had noticed her breeding – for that was what it was – which had stood out the first moment he had come face to face with her.

She had what he thought of as classical looks, and a speech pattern that was used by aristocrats, and although her clothes were plain, they were well cut and of good fabrics. She had a certain style.

Yes, Moira Aherne was hiding something, he was sure. She had no friends or relatives, no one she visited or wrote to. He got glimpses of her often at Mrs Wilson's little mansion in the Towers. And when they bumped into each other in the house or garden, she always spoke to him nicely and moved on swiftly. Somehow he felt she was out to make trouble. She was always too interested in what he was working on, and where he had been. But Moira Aherne was not really his problem, he acknowledged.

He sighed. He still thought too about the missing girl, Alf's girlfriend Gwen, even though that was not really his concern either. She had never come home, nor had her body ever been found. She must have been taken, snatched up by somebody bad who'd made off with her. Everyone knew the terrible tales about Jack the Ripper in London some years back, and Blackie just prayed the girl hadn't met a similar fate. Her poor mother was distraught and the whole Armley community were still talking about it.

Yes, the world could be hard and cruel, he reflected, but he could not change it.

Hardest of all, Angela was gone. She had died very quickly, lingering only a few weeks after her sister Sarah had told them about the diagnosis, when they learned that her old boyfriend Barry had beaten her up. The doctors at Harrogate Hospital had told Sarah that she was riddled with cancer; it had spread throughout her body.

Blackie had never seen her again. Only her sister and mother had been with her in Harrogate.

He had wept when Sarah had told him that Angela was no longer with them. Dead and buried in Harrogate and he hadn't even known. He would have gone to her funeral.

And now there was Aunt Eileen, not well at all. So fragile. Pale and wan, and Uncle Patrick was worried about her – he was well aware of that. He was always bringing her tonics home from the chemist or suggesting new foods. Yet she still managed the house, did the cooking, and looked after her two boys, as she called Uncle Pat and him. No working at the bakery on Saturday morning, though. His uncle had insisted that she stay at home, and he would not agree she could return when she felt better. Very simply, he did not want his wife to work any more.

Blackie sighed again under his breath as he continued down the main street in Upper Armley. He felt down in the dumps, depressed, and he didn't like being in this state of mind. Normally, he was cheerful and optimistic, looking towards the future with hope, driven by ambition and the desire to succeed, by his curiosity about the world and appetite for life. He sometimes longed for Ireland, for the green fields and rushing rivers he'd grown up with, for voices like his and people who knew his family. But he knew there was nothing for him there. No work. Little to eat. No way to make a lot of money.

He must shake off this sense of defeat, his preoccupation with the bad things that had happened to him lately. And he must stop being angry with Sarah, who had believed he had physically assaulted Angela. She had made a bad judgement, that was all. He must let it go, wipe it out of his mind.

When he arrived home, Aunt Eileen greeted him warmly, and hid her surprise that he was suddenly back. Normally, he came home at twelve noon for dinner, and then hurried off to work, returning at five. Why was he here at two?

'Is everything all right, Blackie lad?' she asked as he came in and sat opposite her, giving her a brief smile. She was mending Uncle Pat's shirts, sitting in the small sewing chair close to the window. She looked a bit brighter today.

'Sure and it is, Aunt Eileen, I laid the slabs in concrete this morning. Now they are settling, and there was nothing else I could do. So here I be. Any post today, Auntie?'

She shook her head, her eyes kind. She knew he was hoping that Lord Lassiter's estate manager might write to offer him building work at Bolton Manor, a chance at something bigger than her Pat, and Armley, could offer. But she feared he was hoping in vain. The rich stuck to their own and the Earl would have his own men employed to work on the estate.

Blackie nodded and hung up his coat. 'Shall I put the kettle on for a cuppa?'

'That's good idea. By the way, Finn came by earlier; he said I should tell you that Laura Spencer, who you said you met at the dance hall, has invited you both to a church picnic at Armley Park on Sunday. He wants to go, and he wants you to go with him.'

'I'll think about it,' Blackie replied. 'I do remember her; she had a lovely gentle smile. I thought she appeared to be refined, different somehow.'

'She is,' Eileen answered. 'I've met her once or twice with my friend Maggie Hargrove. She's a really kind person. Her house is near St Ives Mount. Her mother left it to her when she died just recently.'

Blackie nodded. 'I'm going to the kitchen to make that cuppa for us.'

She watched him striding out of the room, feeling sorry for him momentarily. She had seen how hurt and upset he had been by Sarah Clough, and she and Patrick had been annoyed with her as well.

How could anyone in their right mind think Blackie O'Neill could beat anybody up – least of all a young woman? Like many tall, well-built men, he was gentle in his ways, and gracious, kind and considerate. Why, he wouldn't hurt a fly. But it was terrible news about Sarah's sister.

And it was a shame his cousin Siobhan had been sent back to Ireland. She knew that had cast him down too. Lady Lassiter had gone abroad unexpectedly, without Siobhan, just when Blackie had thought he would have his cousin close by. She knew he was deeply disappointed. Siobhan's hasty note letting him know she was being sent back to Lassiter Hall, to work as a parlourmaid again, had arrived only days after the tragic news about Angela.

Eileen tucked the edge of the shirt seam under and secured it with a pin. It was a terrible thing to be at the beck and call of these rich folk.

She hoped Blackie would accept Laura's invitation. She was a lovely person, and he might just start a friendship with her. Which could lead anywhere. He needed female companionship, a bit of tenderness in his life, Eileen was sure.

It would be nice to see him courting seriously, and on the way to marriage. Settled. Eileen knew him well, and he was the kind of young man who would flourish with a loving partner.

FORTY

As he entered the area where afternoon tea was being served, Robert Lassiter saw her at once, looking truly beautiful in a cream dress and matching hat.

Immediately, he drew back, stepped behind a potted plant, so she would not spot him. Should he join her as planned? Or should he leave The Ritz, and send a message he was unable to keep their appointment? Sudden and unexpected indecision made him hesitate. Sending a message and then staying away from her would keep him out of trouble. Because trouble she was.

Joining her as planned would mean he would be ensnared once again by her beauty and personality, and his own intense emotions. In a sense, it would be a commitment to her. At least it would be in his own mind. And perhaps hers.

He wanted her. Not for a few months like other relationships he had enjoyed over the past nine years. He wanted Vanessa Stratton for the rest of his life. Why deny the fact that he had fallen in love with her the moment they met? And she with him, he was certain. Hadn't she made it clear?

Taking a deep breath, Robert stepped out from behind the

plant, and strode in her direction. At once, he noticed the worried, anxious expression on her face, and felt a rush of love for her. She thought he wasn't coming and was upset.

Hurrying, he made sure he was in her direct line of vision, but for a moment she had looked in her reticule, her gaze averted. A second later, when she looked up, she saw him at once and her entire demeanour changed. A radiant smile flooded her face and her eyes sparkled.

Robert felt his heart pounding as he drew closer, and that tight, tense feeling in his stomach was gripping him again.

As he came to a standstill next to the table, he leaned forward, took hold of her hand and kissed it, then immediately sat down in the chair opposite her.

'Hello,' he said, hardly able to get even one word out. He sat gazing at her, entranced.

'Hello! Yes, hello!' she exclaimed in a low voice, her excitement and pleasure made very clear. Her eyes did not leave his face. How handsome he was. How charismatic. His presence filled the whole room.

He found his voice at last, and said, 'I'm so very sorry I'm late. I got caught up at the last minute with a matter, and it took a while to extricate myself.'

'It's all right,' she murmured, a half-smile on her face. 'I admit that I did think you had changed your mind at one moment, though.'

'I'll never change my mind about you, Vanessa. Be sure of that.'

At this moment, a waiter approached and they fell silent, glancing at the menu.

Once the waiter had left, Vanessa said, 'I don't think I can eat afternoon tea, but it was quicker to accept his suggestion and get rid of him.'

Robert laughed, shaking his head.

'Oh, Vanessa, you are priceless, my darling.'

'Am I really *your* darling, Lord Robert Lassiter?'

'You are, very much so,' he answered, his voice now serious.

'For how long though?' She looked extremely hard at him.

'Forever, if you'll agree to that,' he answered, drinking in her beauty, her lovely appearance in the cream lace dress, with its frothy neckline, long sleeves and tighter fitted bodice. It struck him that her eyes looked more amber than ever this afternoon, slightly shaded by the hat.

'I do agree to it. I want you for always, too. I've had an idea whilst sitting here waiting for you,' she announced.

'Oh, are you going to share it with me? I'd love to know what it is. I presume it has to do with me. With us.'

She leaned across the table, her eyes dancing, and he instantly caught the scent of her – floral, lemony, green trees. It was a lovely freshness. He wanted to kiss her, but sat further back, listened attentively instead.

'I thought I could go to Paris to see my sister Eloise, and you could go to Paris and stay at the Plaza Athénée Hotel on Avenue Montaigne. I could come there to . . . to *be with you*.' Her eyes challenged him to be shocked.

He remained silent, totally taken aback by this suggestion, yet also understanding she was as anxious as he was to consummate their relationship. Needed it desperately.

'Well, what do you think, Your Lordship?' she asked.

'It would be wonderful to be with you in Paris, Vanessa, so very special and fulfilling, and I do admit I yearn for you. In fact, I would love to take hold of you right now and sweep you upstairs—'

'Oh yes, let's do it, Robert. Please. I want to be alone with you,' she interjected.

'I know, but we cannot do anything like that. Not here. Not even in Paris.'

'But why?'

'I want to have a really serious conversation with you, darling, and I ask you to listen to me carefully, to fully understand the plan I've come up with. A plan for us to get through a difficult situation as best we can. It is to ensure our future.'

'I will listen with all my attention,' she answered, understanding he was in deadly earnest. 'But I want to ask you one question first. Can I?'

'Please do,' Robert replied.

'Why didn't you get a divorce years ago?'

'It's just not the done thing. People in my position don't divorce. We simply lead separate lives. I'm afraid I let it drift, let my personal life slide by me. I was intent on several important undertakings, after my wife and I became estranged. I needed to keep my household, my boys and the family situation stable. I also wanted to make sure my business was not affected by that estrangement. Eventually, my wife agreed to keep up a civil front for the sake of our sons. And she has done so. To a certain extent.'

'I understand. Why was she so difficult?' Vanessa asked quietly, looking puzzled.

'I don't know. I could never get a proper answer from her. Perhaps I didn't try hard enough, consumed as I was with my business. Also, I didn't want to marry anyone else. There was no one I cared enough about, and of course divorce is not something anyone would undertake lightly.'

'No, of course. Why were you estranged in the first place? I hope that's not a rude question, Robert. Is it?'

'Yes. But you should know. It was my wife who terminated our marriage. Abruptly, after our second son was born. We've had separate bedrooms for years, and I never found out why.'

'Oh my God! I can't believe any woman would shut her bedroom door on you!' she exclaimed, horrified.

He had to laugh at the way she said this, and the look of total disbelief in her eyes. 'Well, she did. And I was rather stupid not to take steps to end the marriage properly, with a divorce. I've come to see the error of my ways recently. I'm rethinking a number of things.'

All of a sudden there was a burst of activity around them. Waiters appeared with sandwiches, a large pot of tea, milk and sugar on trays. Smiling, being polite, they placed everything on the table, and one of them stayed behind to pour the tea.

Once they were alone again, Vanessa took a sip of tea, and then said, 'Could I ask a favour of you?'

'Naturally you can. What can I do for you?'

She threw him a flirtatious look, and said, in a tantalizing voice, 'Oh many, many rather delicious things I won't go into now.'

'Please don't,' he shot back, a hint of laughter echoing in his voice.

'I would prefer it if you could refer to your estranged wife as Lucinda. She hasn't been your wife for years anyway and, well . . . it makes me feel jealous. There, I've said it . . . is it silly of me?'

He reached out and took hold of her hand resting on the table, held it tightly in his. Staring at her, his blue eyes intense, he said, 'No, it's not silly. There's something I must say to you now, Vanessa.'

'What is it? You sound so solemn,' she cried, noting the serious expression on his face. 'Don't make me think you don't want us to be together.'

'Adrian is going to help me get through this divorce situation. He believes he knows a way we should handle it. In the meantime, you and I cannot be seen again in public after today. There cannot even be the merest whiff of a rumour that I am with another woman. Do you understand that, Vanessa?'

'Yes. But we can have an affair in private, can't we?'

He was silent for a moment, and then said in a calm but firm voice, 'No, we cannot.'

'Why?'

'Because I don't want to have it . . . I can take you somewhere private, to another person's house. However, I don't want this relationship to begin in a stranger's bed. It's too shoddy for you, a little tawdry, darling. You and I will have to contain ourselves and wait.'

'Oh God, Robert . . .' Her voice trailed off. She was filled with dismay, disappointed.

He said, 'I sat up all night working everything out, and made all the decisions for both of us. I know you're a modern young woman, independent and confident. However, we cannot give Lucinda any reason to contest the divorce. We must be smart about this.'

'I understand that, and I don't think you're playing the general—' She cut herself off and gave him a knowing look, added, 'Well, not really.'

Robert had the good grace to laugh, and then took a sip of tea. After a moment, he continued. 'Obviously, we will have the need to see each other, and this is what I propose. We will have supper every week while I'm in town, and I'm now thinking I'll stay down here for longer, at my house in Grosvenor Square—'

'Your servants will see us,' she cut in.

'Leave the servants to me. To proceed, we will endeavour to spend part of Saturday or Sunday together. Your parents and Caroline go to the country on Fridays, don't they?'

'Yes. Actually they went early this morning. Why?'

'If they're not in town, do they know what you're doing anyway?'

'Not really. I'm usually with my friends or just at home. The housekeeper and several maids are in the house to look after me. I come and go as I wish, though. I rarely go to the country with them.'

'So we might drive down to the country ourselves to visit Adrian. However, just for the day.' He leaned forward and grasped her hand, staring hard at her. 'We can enjoy each other's company, can't we, Vanessa? And wait for each other?'

'Yes, of course,' she answered swiftly. 'I'll do anything you want, you know that. I want to please you always.'

'And I wish to please you too, darling. We'll make it work, I promise. As long as our relationship is a secret and we're not seen, all will be well. Now, I have a thought . . .' He smiled at her and squeezed her hand.

'What is it, Robert? You've got a strange look on your face.' She sounded puzzled.

'Are you free this evening, my dearest lady?'

'I am. What do you have in mind?' Excitement filled her voice once more.

'Supper at my house? Can you come? I can send my Daimler for you. My driver will take you back home later.'

'Oh, how wonderful! That will be lovely. What time shall I be ready?'

'Ten minutes to seven.'

'Will I be your only guest?'

'Most probably, unless Adrian stops by. Do you mind about that? Mind him being there?'

'Not at all. Does he know we were having tea? Know about us? The way we feel?'

'Yes. He's known me since I was eight, as he was then. We were at prep school together and then at Eton. He's the closest person to me, and I to him. And so I trust him implicitly. In fact, he's the only person I do trust.'

She gave him a penetrating look and asked in a quiet, serious voice, 'Don't you trust me, Lord Robert?'

'I do, actually.'

'You should,' she said, in that same serious tone. 'I have only your best interests at heart. I would never betray you or hurt you.'

'Thank you. One last question. Do *you* trust *me*, Vanessa?'

'With my life.'

'It's in safekeeping, I promise you that. Always.'

Vanessa arrived at the Grosvenor Square house at precisely seven o'clock, having been driven from her home in Curzon Street by Palmer. Robert's driver was quiet and only spoke when spoken to.

Vanessa couldn't help herself, she had to ask him all about the motorcar, and he answered her accordingly.

It was a short drive, and she soon arrived at Robert's house, where she was greeted by the butler, Turnbull.

'Good evening, Miss Stratton,' he said and, after closing the front door behind her, he led her into the library. 'Lord Robert is waiting for you.'

The moment he saw her, Robert jumped up from behind his desk, and walked forward, a welcoming smile on his face. After kissing her hand, he let it go at once, and asked, 'Would you like a glass of champagne, Vanessa?'

'That would be lovely, Lord Robert. Thank you.'

Glancing at the butler, Robert said, 'I'll pour it, Turnbull, thank you. And Lord Adrian will be arriving shortly.'

'Very good, m'lord.' With a nod and a smile at them both, the butler retreated, closed the door behind him.

Robert walked over to Vanessa, who was standing near the fireplace, and said in a tone of total admiration, 'You look positively gorgeous, Miss Stratton. Too beautiful for words.'

His eyes swept over her. Her appearance entranced him. She was dressed for dinner, wearing another highly fashionable gown, this one a soft, very pale green with a hint of silver thread in the weave. It was low-cut, tightly fitted across the bust-line and skimming her figure to her ankles. She wore chandelier ear-clips of small emeralds and pearls, but no other jewellery.

'My God, you are the most gorgeous woman I've ever known. And you are mine. You are, aren't you?'

'I am indeed. You're the only man I've ever wanted, since the first time I saw you at my parents' house last year.'

He smiled, nodded, and stepped away, saying over his shoulder, 'I shall pour us both a drop of bubbly, darling.'

Last year, he thought. A crush on me for a year. Is that possible? Why hadn't he known?

She watched him as he went to the drinks table near the door, and lifted the bottle out of the silver bucket, poured the champagne into two flutes.

Before he could walk back to the fireplace, she hurried to his side, and said in a very low voice, 'Is this the house where I'm going to live with you? Where we will make love and be together? Have a life of happiness?'

Turning swiftly, he nodded, and immediately put the bottle back into the bucket. He couldn't help himself and, without a second thought, he reached for her, pulled her into his arms and kissed her. She kissed him back, as passionate as he was. He held her closer, leaned against the door, his hands sliding down her back onto her buttocks.

They clung together for a few seconds, then he looked at her, his eyes filled with yearning, and bent forward and kissed her neck, her cheeks and her mouth. Their tongues touched, then entwined, and Robert thought he would explode with desire. He knew he must control this sudden urge to make love on both their parts. Otherwise, he would be undone. And she also.

He drew away, his back resting against the door, and said, softly, 'We must stop at this moment, you know. Adrian will soon be here.'

'I know. I just love being held like this by you, so close, so intimate in a way. Why are we leaning against the door?'

'To prevent anyone from bursting in on us. Unexpectedly.' He sighed and said, 'Can I kiss you just here?' He touched the top of her breast, and added, 'One last kiss.'

'Last kiss for the moment, Your Lordship,' and smiled at him. 'You can kiss me anywhere you want.'

A small, knowing smile flicked around his sensual mouth and then he bent his head and kissed her swiftly. Releasing her from his arms, he reached for the two flutes of champagne and handed one to her. They clinked glasses, and he said, 'To you, my darling Vanessa.'

'And to you, Robert.'

They walked across to the marble fireplace, and she now swiftly took in the room. Beautiful, mellowed wood furniture. A Georgian desk, big and grand, and perfect for him. Bookshelves filled to overflowing with burgundy leather-bound books, all matched.

Dark green velvet draperies at the windows, and the same velvet on the two walls on either side of the door. A parquet floor, covered in dark green rugs. A big sofa and an armchair upholstered in dark green brocade.

All this green was accented by lots of white. The door, the fireplace and mouldings. A masculine room, yet it did not over-whelm. She realized what good taste he had.

'I think you approve of the library, Vanessa,' Robert said, recognizing the expression on her face.

'I do! It's elegant without being pretentious.' She gave him a pointed look, and asked, 'Can I see the rest of the house, please?'

'Of course.' He led her to the door and out into the white

marble entrance foyer with its imposing crystal chandelier, and the double staircase leading upstairs.

'This is the drawing room,' he explained as they went inside. 'Lots of yellow as you can see. But it makes for sunshine on a rainy day. You'll be in the dining room later. It's blue and white, and I know you'll like it.'

'Can we go to your bedroom?' she asked a little coyly. 'I'd like to see it.'

'Not right now,' he said in that firm voice. 'I hear Adrian on the doorstep.'

And a moment later, Turnbull joined them in the foyer, nodded to her, and said to Robert, 'I do believe Lord Fraser has arrived, m'lord.'

FORTY-ONE

Mr Oliver Templeton hurried up Curzon Street, relieved he had left the hansom cab in Piccadilly. The traffic there was incredibly bad on this hot August Friday. Hansoms, drays, carriages, and that odd thing called a motorcar, all so crowded together, making movement virtually impossible. And so he had paid the driver and jumped out. On foot would be quicker.

Now, thankfully, here he was almost at Lord Adrian Fraser's private bank. He paused, took out his watch and smiled. It was ten minutes to ten. Actually, he would arrive five minutes early. South Audley Street was just ahead of him.

As the top private investigator at the Berkeley Private Detective Agency, Oliver was proud of the work his team had done, and with the most interesting results they had produced. It was quite a dossier and, in many ways, it had been easy to track the various individuals under investigation. He hoped Lord Fraser would be well satisfied.

Within a few minutes, Oliver was entering the bank and being ushered into his lordship's private office.

As Oliver was led in by a lady secretary, Lord Adrian walked towards him, his hand outstretched.

'Good morning, Mr Templeton,' he said. 'Come and sit over here.'

'Good morning, Lord Fraser,' Oliver answered. He sat in the chair opposite the desk, put his briefcase on his lap. He opened it, took out several folders, and placed the briefcase on the floor.

Oliver Templeton cleared his throat and, looking directly at the man who had hired him, he said in a clear, distinct voice, 'My team did an excellent job, in my opinion. And I think you have all the answers to your questions, m'lord. Certainly, they didn't leave a stone unturned.'

Leaning forward, he handed the two folders to Adrian.

Adrian said, 'You've done it fast, I'll give you that, Templeton. Just one week.' A questioning look crossed his face. After a moment's hesitation, he asked, 'And yet you say your team has answered all my questions. How can that be? I had quite a lot that I needed to know.'

'Good work on the part of my team. They are excellent, efficient and diligent. But they were in luck because no one was in hiding and went about their business in the usual way. Mind you, none was aware they were being watched and followed, I'll give you that.'

Adrian nodded, and opened the first folder, and read the pages rapidly. His face was inscrutable, but his mind was boggling. My God, he thought at one moment. Templeton does have a bloody good team.

The second folder provided pages and pages of details that would only thrill Robert. He must get this information to him at once.

Looking across his desk at Templeton, Adrian said, 'This is an extraordinary report, and very helpful. Significant. Thank your team for me and my thanks to you also.'

'It was a pleasure to be of service, Your Lordship. Can I be of further help?'

After a moment's thought, Adrian nodded. 'I think perhaps you can. I'd like to know more about that villa. You should keep your team on the job for another week.'

'I will do that, Lord Fraser, and thank you for your confidence in me.'

Hugging the large envelope to his chest, Adrian hotfooted it down South Audley Street to Grosvenor Square. He had an urgent need to get the package to Robert as fast as he possibly could.

It was a hot day, and he began to perspire, but he kept up the pace. And, a bit sooner than he had expected, he was suddenly there, lifting the brass knocker on the door of his friend's house.

Almost immediately, the door opened and there was Turnbull, welcoming him warmly in his usual way.

'I'm afraid I'm a bit early,' Adrian said after greeting the butler. 'I have to see his lordship at once, unless he is otherwise engaged.'

'Come in, come in, Lord Adrian,' the butler said. 'It's much cooler in here.'

Indeed it was; Adrian noticed that at once. 'Thank you,' he said, stepping into the foyer.

'I will let Lord Robert know you are here. Just a moment, please.'

Before Turnbull could go into the library, the door swung open and Robert stepped out.

'Adrian, old chap, you've made it over earlier than usual today,' he exclaimed. 'But I've finished my work. You could say I've just closed my shop.'

'I'm happy to hear that,' Adrian responded, walking forward

as Turnbull moved aside. Adrian and Robert embraced quickly and stood apart.

'What's that package you're hanging onto for dear life?' Robert asked, eyeing the envelope. Adrian had it pressed to his chest.

'It's for you actually,' Adrian said to his friend, following Robert into the library and closing the door. Handing the large envelope to him, he added, 'It's your freedom.'

'My freedom?' Robert repeated and frowned. Then it dawned on him what Adrian meant, and he exclaimed, 'It's the report from the private investigator, isn't it?'

'It is indeed.' Adrian sat down in the chair opposite Robert's desk.

Robert was still standing. Placing the envelope on the desk, he finally sat and stared at Adrian. 'Dirt? Hot stuff? The goods?'

'I should say so . . . the works! You're now holding the winning hand, so to speak. Wait until you read it all. It'll knock your socks off.'

Robert smiled. It was almost disbelieving, and then he said, 'Give me the gist of it now, a taste, and then I'll go through the folders later. I suppose there is another man, by the look on your face. Or is it many men over the years? Nothing would surprise me with her.'

'One man.'

'Who is he? Do we know him?'

'He's French, by the way.'

'You've got to be joking.' Robert was aghast.

'I'm not. He's a Frenchman all right and quite a famous one at that. From a very wealthy background. Married. Four children and, as a Frenchman and a Roman Catholic, obviously no divorce. Not ever.'

'How long has the affair been going on?' Robert gave Adrian a hard stare. 'By the look on your face, it's long-standing.' A sudden thought struck him and, before Adrian could answer him, Robert said, 'Not before my boys . . . my sons are *mine*, aren't they?'

'Of course they are! They're the bloody spitting image of you. Blue eyes, black hair and tall. Lucinda has been involved with the Frenchman for years, and I'm certain of that. It's in the report.'

'Hmmmm. A long time. Who is he? What's his name?'

'Léon Theroux. Forty-two years old. Very ordinary-looking, not a handsome man at all. But he *is* an important politician. He's a minister in the French government. Powerful, with a lot of clout.'

'That must please her. Lucinda is always attracted to powerful people and powerful men, in particular. Does she go to Paris to see him? Or does he come here to London?' Robert asked, filled with curiosity.

'Neither. All their shenanigans take place in Zürich, Geneva or the South of France. In a little town called Beaulieu-sur-Mer, just outside Monte Carlo. Apparently he prefers to keep her out of his home city of Paris.'

'I get it,' Robert said. 'And what about her at the moment? Or should I say them?'

'Oh, he's in Zürich, as we speak. Seemingly he's got it hard for her. Lucinda is at the Baur au Lac; he's in a smaller hotel nearby. But he always stays over. My private investigator got that titbit from the housekeeper at the hotel. Bed linen, you know. Don't ever forget *that*. It's a dead giveaway.'

Robert couldn't help laughing, and then said, 'Your private investigator goes in for all the details. I'll say that for him. Has Lucinda been to the clinic? Or isn't she ill? Is that also a story?'

'Not sure. She has been to the clinic twice. Not much information available from there. Hippocratic Oath, and all that. There has been a suggestion from one source that she might suffer from arthritis, has treatments for that.'

Robert nodded, leaned back in the chair, a thoughtful expression settling on his face.

Adrian, watching him, thought how calm, cool and collected his oldest and dearest friend looked. On the other hand, Robert had always been like that. And he could easily adopt an inscrutable expression, and frequently did.

Finally, Robert said, 'So with this information, I can sue her for a divorce on the grounds of adultery, can't I?'

'You can indeed. There's plenty of evidence in those folders and also photographs of them together. They seem to be quite open about their association, seemingly no hiding in corners.'

'And what about the Lady Glendenning? Is she Lucinda's travelling companion?'

Adrian nodded. After a moment, he said, 'She's got one too. A lover, I mean. Some Swiss fellow.'

Robert shook his head. 'Women!' he exclaimed. 'They get up to everything under the sun.'

'Just like men,' Adrian pointed out. 'We're not much different when it comes to sexual adventures.' He frowned and then said, 'You know it will cause a bit of a scandal though. And it'll be expensive.'

Robert stood up and walked to the window of the library, gazing out over the square. 'Yes. But I have no choice.'

FORTY-TWO

Whilst Robert absorbed every page of the private investigator's report, taking his time, digesting everything, Adrian read the *Morning Chronicle*.

Finally, Robert closed the last folder and, looking across at Adrian on the sofa, he said, 'There's enough evidence here for me to divorce her.' He shook his head. 'I can't imagine what she sees in this man. He looks like a nonentity, a nobody, Adrian.'

'You said it yourself earlier, Robert. It's the power.' He grinned mischievously. 'He probably has hidden charms, as they say of men or women without good looks. Perhaps he's great in bed.'

'Perhaps,' Robert said, and opened a drawer in his desk, locked the folders in it, and stood up. 'I think lunch must be ready. We're having our schoolboy favourite today.'

'I hope it's haddock and chips and not sausage and mash,' Adrian replied with that cheeky grin of his.

'Fish and chips,' Robert answered and, taking his arm, he led his best friend out of the library. 'Thank you for all the effort you've put into this matter, Addy. I appreciate it. And I can't wait to get my freedom. I can tell you that. Please ask your source to let you know if she rents that villa on the lake in Zürich.'

Adrian nodded. 'Will you mention all this to Vanessa?' he asked in a low tone.

'No, I won't. She has no need to know any details, just that you're helping me to get my divorce.'

'Smart of you, old chap. Best to keep it to ourselves. We don't need any leaks. We must take Lucinda by surprise.'

'Do you mean adultery would get more attention? In the newspapers?' Robert asked, sounding suddenly alarmed.

'I do. There are court reporters present in the courts of law, and you are a very visible, well-known member of the nobility, and well liked also. However, the press *will* cover the case, no doubt in my mind about that. I do know a couple of newspaper proprietors; still, I might not be able to influence them. Your divorce case will make news, especially since a well-known French politician is the co-respondent.' Adrian grimaced. 'Big headlines here. Gargantuan headlines in Paris, you bet!'

'It would ruin him, of that I'm certain,' Robert said, looking reflective. 'Perhaps my solicitor could point that out to her solicitor, and make a bargain, threaten or persuade her to go the quieter way.'

Adrian chuckled. 'That sounds like blackmail to me.'

'I know it does, but we need to be in control of this situation.' Robert sounded grim.

'Do you think she wouldn't care about a terrible scandal here?' Adrian asked, raising a brow.

'She doesn't care about the world, what people think about her, and what she does. Not at all,' Robert replied. 'On the other hand, if she really loves her Frenchman then she won't want his political career in tatters because of her.'

'So she would be compliant,' Adrian suggested.

'Hopefully, but you never know with her. She's very independent, lives by her own rules.' Robert sighed and added, 'I shall go and see my solicitor on Monday and give him the report. Let's see what he advises.'

A moment later, Turnbull came into the breakfast room, where Robert preferred to have his daytime meals.

The butler was carrying a platter of deep-fried haddock. Behind him was one of the maids, with another tray on which there were dishes of chips and mushy peas, parsley sauce and malt vinegar in a cut-glass bottle.

Turnbull put the tray on the sideboard and asked, 'Would you like two pieces of fish, Lord Adrian?'

'Thank you, Turnbull, I would. And I'll have chips and the peas. But no parsley sauce, thank you. I prefer vinegar.'

'Very well, Your Lordship.' Looking across at Robert, he went on, 'And you will have your usual portion, m'lord?'

'I will indeed, Turnbull. And please put the parsley sauce on the table with the vinegar. Thank you.'

'I will, Lord Robert.'

Once the food had been plated and served, Turnbull and the maid left the morning room. Within seconds, the butler returned with two pints of beer and put a tankard in front of each man.

Robert said to Adrian, 'I know you don't like wine with fish and chips.'

He thanked Turnbull and picked up his knife and fork. 'Neither do I.' He grinned and said, 'I've been looking forward to this meal all week.'

'Nothing like childhood food,' Adrian murmured. Now that they were alone, he said, 'I've never seen you like this before. Besotted, I think might best describe your condition.'

'True, I am smitten. I am going to marry her, Addy.'

'Do you want the key to the Farm Street house in the meantime?'

'No, I don't. I've told you that before,' Robert said.

'You have. But I also wonder how you'll manage over the next few months.'

'I will! And that's that! I've put off going back to Yorkshire for the time being, and I'm staying in town. Listen to me. You've known me most of our lives. Once I've made a decision, I stick to it. I rarely change my mind.'

'Enough said, old chap. Don't get your knickers in a twist. I will not mention the bloody house again.'

'Thank you,' Robert muttered, and concentrated on the food.

The two friends fell silent as they ate, both sinking down into their own thoughts.

Adrian's mind had suddenly leapt to a cemetery in Kent, where he intended to go in the coming week. Annabel, he thought, my beloved Annabel. He needed to go and visit her grave. How he had loved her. To utter distraction, even though she had been married.

And how he had grieved when she had died. Unexpectedly, suddenly of a heart attack. She who had never been ill, never had heart problems. Her death had been a mystery to him, and it always would be. He blamed her husband. A rotten sod. And a bishop at that.

Robert was also thinking of a woman: his estranged wife, Lucinda. She could be difficult, contrary, wilful and, deep inside himself, he knew with great certainty that she would relish a scandalous divorce. Clap her hands with glee, in fact.

His only hope was that Adrian's information might prevent it all becoming the talk of the town. That she might agree to go quietly.

A small sigh escaped, and he pushed the image aside. Instead he imagined Vanessa, the woman of his dreams, whom he had thought he would never find.

And in a way he hadn't, she had found him, viewed him from afar, had had a crush on him for a year. A year of longing and desire. No wonder she wanted to have an affair with him now. He wanted that, too, if the truth be known. However, he had vowed to himself that he would control his desire for her. And wait.

He smiled inwardly, thinking of her bluntness, the way she blurted things out to him, exposed her feelings and emotions. He had never known a woman like her. Undoubtedly, she was unique. And, to be truthful, he liked hearing her thoughts in the raw, enjoyed her open-heartedness. It had turned his life on its head. He couldn't think about returning to Yorkshire yet. He had written to his sons and to their tutor, and arranged for them to go to their grandparents as planned, at the large estate in nearby Skipton belonging to Lucinda's father. They would stay there for several weeks.

Next he needed to give Wilson some instructions for while he was away, including what to do about the neglected gardens. He wished he could have tempted Blackie O'Neill to work on them. He needed someone he could trust. Someone who would just get on with it.

The arrival of Turnbull and the maid brought Robert and Adrian out of their thoughts. Both men straightened in their chairs.

Looking at Adrian, Robert said, 'It's jam roll for dessert. With hot custard. I thought you'd enjoy that, old chap.'

As the butler and the maid took their plates away, and replaced them with clean ones, Adrian said, 'Ah well, memories of Eton, no less. And it is my favourite. You're obviously spoiling me. Do you want something from me?'

''Course not. You've given me my freedom, helped me to make

a new life for myself. I'll say it again, I'm really grateful to you, Addy, for taking this on. Such a big job for you.'

'What are best friends for? If they see a way to help, they do just that.'

Robert smiled his dazzling smile at his longest friend, who had been with him for thirty-one years, and made no comment.

It was at this precise moment that the sun burst out from behind the clouds and filled the breakfast room with radiant light. To Adrian, it was as if a spotlight had been shone on Robert.

For the first time in years, he saw him objectively, as a stranger might view him. The sparkling, very blue eyes, the sleek black head of hair, the chiselled features, the white teeth and the smile that captivated all. He's a truly *beautiful* man, Adrian suddenly thought, not merely handsome. And there is the charisma, the fierce intellect, the extraordinary business acumen. That in itself was unbelievable. The way Robert had taken a long-time family business – several centuries old, in fact – and turned it from a profitable venture into a gargantuan empire.

Lassiter Estates owned half of Westminster and Mayfair, Kensington and beyond, not to mention much of the East End and the docks. He had the mansion and family estate in Ireland, as well as Bolton Manor and its land in Yorkshire, and he oversaw all of it. He's a bloody marvel, Adrian thought.

And then, immediately, he understood it all. Everything there was to know about that estranged wife of Robert's, the difficult Lucinda.

She was resentful and bitter about Lord Robert Lassiter. Envious and mean-spirited. Because Robert was the star of the show. And she was a nobody. She couldn't bear it.

And so she had locked the bedroom door on him, and eventually found another man. Not a handsome man, but one who was plain, nondescript and seemingly did her bidding. She was with him because he had a certain amount of power. But it was she who shone in that relationship, with her silver-blonde hair, big bust and long legs. Like her lover, her face was not beautiful, but she had a certain flair with clothes. And with Léon Theroux, *she* was the star of the show.

Total and complete jealousy burning in that woman was the explanation for nine years of emptiness for Robert. And yet he believed she would never agree to a divorce. Punishing him?

Adrian wasn't sure of that. But he knew one thing, the dossier he had on her would ruin her. And free Robert Lassiter finally.

'You're looking rather solemn,' Robert said, breaking the silence. 'Are you worried about something? Or about me?'

Adrian shook his head. 'I'm not worried about you. You are going to be just fine. Actually, I was thinking about going to the cemetery next week. Would you come with me? I do think I'll need your company. At least on the journey. I'm all right to go to Annabel's grave alone, though.'

'I'd be glad to accompany you,' Robert answered. 'It would be a sad and lonely trip if you were by yourself. And I will send a note to Harry Peterson, ask him if I can drop by his house in Aldington. He's just come back from Paris, where he bought some paintings. Impressionists.'

'Did he really! My God, he must have quite a collection by now,' Adrian said, sounding impressed.

'One of the best in the world, I suspect,' Robert replied, glad he had averted the conversation away from the cemetery and Annabel. Adrian was convinced her husband had hurt her in some way, caused the heart attack, which Robert truly doubted.

After the butler had served the jam roll and custard and left, Adrian said, 'This is perfection, Robert.' He grinned and continued, 'You're definitely after *something*, spoiling me like this.'

Although he wasn't looking for a favour, he suddenly thought of one. 'Can I bring Vanessa down to Fraser Hall tomorrow, to spend a day in the country?'

'It would be my pleasure! You see, I was right! You do want something in return for the comfort food. And you can stay the night, the whole of Saturday and Sunday too.'

Robert merely smiled and began to eat the dessert.

FORTY-THREE

Robert Lassiter and his old friend Harry Peterson greeted each other with warmth, embracing and smiling. They were happy to meet again after Harry's long sojourn in Kent and Robert's in Ireland. It had been some months.

Taking hold of Robert's arm, Harry led him down the long hall of Avery Court, his Tudor house built when Elizabeth I was on the throne. It had always entranced Robert, who favoured Elizabethan architecture.

Harry said, 'I was so excited when I received your letter, because I was just about to write to you.'

'Really!' Robert glanced at him as they entered a small, rather cosy parlour in the middle of the hall. 'Why were you going to write to me?' His curiosity was apparent.

'I've had a little windfall. No, I shouldn't call it that, because it's quite a large one, actually. My bachelor uncle, Thomas Peterson, recently died. I was his sole heir. I've inherited everything.'

'Sorry to hear about your uncle. So he left you property, I suspect, if you were going to contact me?'

'He did, Robert. Quite a lot of commercial property in Croydon – shops, in fact; two theatres in the West End, and a very large house in Hampstead with a lot of acreage attached.'

'And do you wish to sell it all?'

'I do. I have my house in Charles Street, and that's enough for me. These days the Home Farm down the road here keeps me very busy. It's a great agricultural success.'

Robert nodded and went and stood with his back to the fire. 'I'm glad this fire's going. It's such a dull, damp day, more like December than August. I was really chilled driving down here.'

'I know; the weather has been rotten lately. I told Mrs Dillard to put a match to most of the fires earlier. These big old houses seem awfully cold at times.'

As he spoke, Harry sat down at a small round table and filled two cups with coffee from an elegant silver pot that the house-keeper had brought in. 'Sugar and cream as usual, Robert?'

'Yes, thanks, Harry.' Robert joined him at the table, and continued, 'Are you going to give me all the papers I need to sell your property today? Or do you wish to come up to town for a meeting?'

''Course not! No formalities between us, after all these years. I'll give you the papers after lunch. And incidentally, when is the Third Musketeer going to arrive?'

Robert laughed, and said, 'I asked Adrian not to stay at the cemetery for too long. He'll be here in time for lunch, don't worry.'

'He's never quite recovered from Annabel's death, has he?' Harry gave Robert a knowing look.

'Not really, in some ways,' Robert replied thoughtfully, his face now serious, his blue eyes darkening. 'Mostly because he won't let go of the idea her husband caused the heart attack. I haven't been able to convince him otherwise. Or to look at any other woman.'

'I don't think he hurt her either; and he is a bishop, after all.'

'I don't believe being a man of the cloth exonerates him.' Robert sat back in the chair and took a sip of the coffee. 'However, he is known as a man of good character, and he is popular. It's a pity Addy can't let go of this idea. It's wedged in his brain, and it's preventing him from moving on and finding someone new. Someone who would bring some joy and laughter into his life.'

'He was always like that at Eton. Stubborn, really. Anyway, he seemed cheerful enough when he dropped you off.'

'He is doing well now, and getting on with life in a good way. As for you, my lad, you're in fine fettle.'

'And so are you. By the way, I've something special to tell you . . .' Harry paused, took a deep breath, and said, 'Unlike Adrian, I have a new woman in my life, and I'm really taken with her.'

Robert grinned. 'Don't expect me to look surprised, because I'm not. You've always got a *new* woman on a string.'

'That's true, I suppose, but Marguerite is different. I'm going to propose to her this weekend.'

'Oh! So it's serious then?' Robert now sounded surprised.

'Very much so. I'm giving her my mother's diamond engagement ring, getting down on bended knee, and all that.' Harry glanced at Robert. 'So, what do you think?'

'Congratulations, Harry. I'm happy for you. One rarely meets the right woman . . . it takes time, I suppose.'

'I met Marguerite a few months ago, and I knew at once she's the one. She did too. And so I decided to take the plunge. *Now.* Why wait? Nothing's going to change. You see, I've fallen in love.' Harry took a swallow of coffee.

Robert stared back at Harry, whom he had known since their Eton days, and said nothing, thinking immediately of Vanessa, and wishing he was free to put a ring on her finger.

After a moment or two, Harry said, 'You've gone so very quiet. What's the matter, Robert? You look sorrowful.'

'I'm going to tell you something, but I must ask for your full confidentiality and discretion. What I'm going to say must remain a secret between us.'

'But it will be. Surely you know that after twenty-five years,' Harry shot back quickly. 'It will be our secret, I swear.'

'I'm in the same boat as you. I met a woman a few weeks ago and I'm madly in love with her. I want to marry her, but I can't. And you certainly know why.' Robert shook his head. 'I've been very neglectful. I should have divorced Lucinda years ago. Now I'm in a tough spot. I've got to rid myself of her.'

'Never a truer word spoken,' Harry responded. 'Long ago, when you were first engaged, I thought Lucinda was glamorous and very sexual. She seemed to have that "come to bed" look in her eyes. But she hasn't aged well.' Harry paused, shook his head, then said, 'Do you think she'll agree to a divorce now? She must like being a Countess and living separate lives. Has something changed?'

'Yes, it has. I've found out a lot about Lucinda, thanks to Addy, who is handling things for me. But I can't be seen in public with Vanessa, and that's why this conversation must be confidential.'

'I fully understand, Robert. You don't want Lucinda having any grounds to contest the divorce.'

Robert nodded, and finished his cup of coffee. 'Lucinda has a man. We've got the goods on her, so to speak.' Robert sighed. 'I can't wait to get my freedom.'

'Thank God, you *are* going to get it at last. In the meantime, you have your lady, your future wife, and you can certainly enjoy a cosy little affair with her until you can make it legal.' Harry gave him a knowing smile. 'That's always comforting.'

Robert, momentarily taken aback, remained silent. He stood up, walked over to the window and looked out at the garden.

The sky was overcast, darker clouds moving across the far horizon. It would start to rain soon. He couldn't help wondering why Harry assumed he was sleeping with his intended; he reminded him of Adrian, who had fully expected him to have an affair with Vanessa, was always offering that key to the house on Farm Street.

After a few seconds, Robert returned to the table and sat down. 'It's going to be raining cats and dogs shortly.' Clearing his throat, he said, 'Are you enjoying a cosy affair with your lady?' He raised a dark eyebrow questioningly.

Harry nodded. 'I am. She said she wouldn't marry a man she hadn't *tasted*, that was the way she put it, because marriage is forever, and she wanted to know what she was getting.' Harry chuckled. 'Marguerite is a bit blunt, to put it mildly.'

'I know what you mean,' Robert said, also laughing. 'But I made the decision to wait, even though Vanessa is also a bit blunt about what we should be doing until we marry. Modern women, I suppose, are like that.'

Before Harry could answer, Adrian was coming down the hall, calling out, 'Where are the other two musketeers? Where are you chaps?'

Harry got up and went out into the long hall. 'In here, Addy.'

Adrian embraced his old friend, and then said, 'I think there's going to be a thunderstorm. Maybe Robert and I should leave now. Try to avoid getting caught in a downpour.'

As he was speaking, there was a flash of lightning and the sound of thunder in the background.

Harry said, 'Stay for a meal, as planned. Usually the worst is over in an hour or so. Better to leave a bit later.'

Robert joined them, and said, 'Yes, we'll stay. But we will have to leave at three o'clock.' He grinned. 'I have a supper date with Vanessa tonight. And I don't want to be late.'

* * *

The three men had enjoyed the meal that Mrs Dillard, the housekeeper, had prepared for them. It was the kind of food they loved from their youth.

Shepherd's pie made of minced lamb, topped with a mashed potato crust, steamed vegetables from the Home Farm, and gooseberry fool. A feast, as far as they were concerned.

Over lunch Robert had asked Harry about the paintings he had recently acquired, and Harry waxed lyrical about his two Cézannes and a Renoir. Robert, who also admired those artists, said he would love to see them before they left at three o'clock.

And so, once the food had been devoured and enjoyed, Harry took them down the long hall and into the drawing room where the new paintings were hanging.

'I've changed things around a bit,' Harry explained. 'Moved several paintings to other rooms, to make space for the new ones. They deserve to be in here.'

Robert saw the Renoir immediately. It was hanging above the fireplace, and he hurried across the room. 'Oh my God, this is spectacular!' he exclaimed, drinking in the painting. 'A feast for the eyes. I love Renoir's women and men; they come to life. What I mean is that *he* brings them to life. How vividly *alive* this is, Harry.'

Adrian and Harry joined him, and gazed at the portrait of a woman dancing with a man in a garden.

Robert said, 'I've always wanted to buy one of his street scenes, as I call them. Renoir is so good at capturing everyday life. Just look at it, all his many lovely blues and pinks, and the girl's red bonnet, her fellow's yellow straw hat.' He turned to Harry, and added, 'What's the name of this painting?'

'*Dance at Bougival*,' Harry answered. 'It was painted in 1883, and it's part of a series he did, all of them outside in those gardens.'

Nodding, Robert went on. 'His colours are always so clear, so pure . . . just imagine, he suffers terribly from arthritis, yet he goes to his easel every day and creates such masterpieces as this. Paintings others can enjoy.'

'Oh, I didn't know that,' Adrian said, referring to the illness. 'That sounds like a true triumph over adversity – physical pain, to be exact.'

'It is,' Harry remarked. 'Renoir also has a sad and troubled life in many ways, but he still paints hundreds of canvases, each of them so uniquely *his*.'

Turning to face his old friend, Robert said, 'Congratulations, I'm glad you were able to get this. Renoirs are very popular at the moment, getting scarce. I have one in Yorkshire. I shall look for another right away.'

'I have a good dealer in Paris. He's always done well by me. Now, come over to this side of the room where I've hung one of the Cézannes,' Harry said.

Robert nodded, an eager expression on his face. He strode across the floor, his eyes lighting up as he gazed at the Cézanne. 'What a wonderful example of his outdoor scenes, all these greens mingled together . . . a forest that truly beckons you into it. I have a sense of its coolness, as well as its beauty, its calmness.' It reminded him of the grounds at Bolton Manor. He suddenly felt a pang of longing to be there, to breathe the clear Yorkshire air, gaze upon the dales that surrounded his estate, the woodlands that edged his land.

'It's called *Forest* and Cézanne began painting it in 1890, probably finished it in 1892, or thereabouts. I couldn't resist it. I feel peaceful when I look at it.'

'I understand why,' Adrian remarked. 'It's lovely. A good buy, Harry. You did well on your trip.'

'And where is the other Cézanne?' Robert asked, and then spotted it on the wall near the door. Once again, he hurried to look at it, and stared hard, at first liking it, and then, after only a short while, he was frowning, feeling suddenly puzzled.

The painting was of two women picking fruit, and he had seen photographs of it, knew it well. Again, as it usually was with Cézanne, there was a great deal of green against a blue sky. The women wore white, and one had her back turned.

After a few minutes, Robert said, 'What's the name of this Cézanne, Harry? It's about picking fruit. Oh, I've remembered, it's called *The Fruit Pickers*. It was painted about 1877, I believe.'

'You're correct. So you know it, do you?' Harry sounded surprised.

'Yes. Well, sort of . . . I've seen photographs of it, and I now recall that I saw it fleetingly in the Fauvre Gallery in Paris. Two years ago, along with a painting of nude women bathers.'

'Cézanne did several paintings of nude women in a forest with a stream. What I mean is several versions of the same group,' Harry explained. 'Over several years.'

Robert simply nodded and gazed at the painting again. 'I got a glance of *The Fruit Pickers* at his gallery . . .'

He let his voice trail off, puzzled still. Then he realized the painting wasn't right. He went closer, acknowledging to himself that it definitely was *not* right. Therefore, it was wrong. And in the parlance of the art world, if it was wrong, then that meant it was a fake.

How could this be a fake? Cézanne was still alive. In his sixties, probably, he thought.

Would anyone dare to copy one of his works of art and pass it off as the genuine thing? He doubted it. Perhaps he was being overly critical because the painting appeared to be different, not as good as he remembered it. But better to keep silent. He would not say a word to Harry because he needed another opinion, and he didn't have any friends who knew more than he did about the Impressionist painters. And, of course, he could be wrong. Perhaps his memory held a brighter, sharper painting than the one he was looking at now. Let it go, he warned himself. You're asking for trouble if you voice your doubts about its authenticity.

Adrian came over and said, 'I must remind you, Robert, we have to leave at once if we are to reach London at the time you wish to be there.'

'Oh, God, yes. We must leave!' Robert exclaimed, swinging around. Glancing at Harry, he added, 'What a treat to see your new acquisitions. Great choices, old chap. And I'm very envious that you own that fabulous Renoir.'

FORTY-FOUR

Robert and Adrian had used Adrian's new motorcar for the trip, driven by his chauffeur. On the way back the car was caught in a nasty downpour in Kent and then hit heavy rain in London. And thick traffic, carriages, gigs and carts, as well as some other motorcars, filled the roads as well. The trip had seemed endless to them both; they were cold and the car's seats uncomfortable. Despite the luxurious trimmings and the skill of the chauffeur, the journey was no faster than in a carriage drawn by good horses.

He insisted on dropping Robert off at the Grosvenor Square house first. 'See you shortly,' Adrian said as Robert alighted.

'Whenever you can get here,' Robert answered, and made a dash for his front door. Having told Turnbull he would be returning by six o'clock, he realized when the butler opened the door that it was much later, by the look on his face.

'A bad journey back I think, m'lord,' Turnbull said in a dour tone.

'Quite awful, Turnbull. I'd better get upstairs and change before Miss Stratton arrives.' He headed for the staircase.

'Lord Robert, she's already here. I showed her into the yellow drawing room.'

'She must be early, surely?' Robert exclaimed.

'No, my lord, she was on time. It's already ten past seven.'

'Good heavens! I knew we were delayed, but I hadn't realized it was so late. Please tell her I've gone to freshen up and select a pink champagne. I shall change out of these damp clothes quickly.'

'Yes, m'lord.'

'Thank you, Turnbull.'

Robert took the stairs two at a time, rushed into his bedroom and shed his damp jacket immediately, then took off his shirt and tie. He realized his trousers were dry, and let his braces dangle down against his legs.

He went into his dressing room, took out a clean white shirt and blue tie, selected a smoking jacket of deep blue velvet and a matching pair of house shoes with his family crest on the front.

When he heard the bedroom door open and close, he frowned, and went into his bedroom. To his utter amazement, Vanessa was standing there, looking around.

He was frozen to the spot.

'Vanessa!' he cried. 'Whatever are you doing here?' His surprise was evident.

'I couldn't wait to see you, so I decided to come and find you. You didn't even say hello when you arrived home.' She sounded disconcerted.

'I was wet, needed to get out of my clothes.' Suddenly realizing he was bare-chested, he rushed into his dressing room, took his white shirt off the hook, and put it on. He tucked it into his trousers and pulled up his braces.

Returning to his bedroom, he discovered she was standing in the same place, obviously waiting for him. He said, in the mildest voice he could summon, 'Vanessa darling, I think you should go downstairs. I will finish dressing swiftly and join you momentarily.'

'But why can't I stay here, wait for you?' she asked, teasing.

'Because it would *look* improper, and it *is* actually improper for a young lady to be in a man's bedroom, watching him put on his clothes. Come along.'

He walked across the room and took hold of her arm, and drew her towards the door. Instantly, she grabbed onto him and pressed her body against his. He felt a sudden flare of desire but controlled himself, and led her into the corridor. 'Ten minutes,' he said softly, a smile flickering.

She nodded her understanding, half smiled at him and went downstairs. Robert stepped back into his bedroom and locked the door, although he laughed to himself as he did this.

It didn't take him long to finish dressing, but as he did so he realized one thing. He was not too old for her. It was the reverse. She was too young for him. Twenty-two, a mere girl. Seventeen years *was* a big difference. Had he made a mistake? Should he terminate this relationship?

He was not sure what to do. All of a sudden he was at a loss, myriad thoughts running through his head.

Walking across the dressing room, he looked at himself in the cheval mirror, straightened his tie, adjusted the jacket, and went out and into the bathroom.

After combing his hair, smoothing it into place, he took a face cloth, ran cold water on it and pressed it against his cheeks. The coolness helped, and after a few seconds he dried his face.

At least I look presentable, he thought, glancing in the mirror again. He turned away, preoccupied with thoughts of Vanessa. She was so young, inexperienced, and innocent in so many ways. Her sudden and unexpected appearance in his bedroom had signalled all this to him, and now he was on the horns of a dilemma. It was time to decide.

* * *

He found her in the yellow drawing room, sitting in a chair. She looked forlorn, even a bit miserable, and his heart went out to her.

As he crossed the floor to join her, he was pleased the fire burned in the grate. The house felt damp, somewhat cold on this wet August evening, and he was still chilled.

Sitting down opposite her, he said, 'We must have a little talk, darling—'

Instantly, she cut in, exclaiming, 'Please don't be angry with me, Robert.'

'I'm not angry.'

'But maybe you're disappointed in me, that I barged in the way I did,' she cried.

'No, I'm not. Very simply, I was startled to see you . . .' He paused. His thoughts upstairs had made it clear to him what he needed to do. 'There's something I must say to you now, Vanessa.'

'What is it? You sound so solemn,' she cried, noting the serious expression on his face. 'Don't make me think you don't want us to be together.'

Robert knelt down by her side.

'Will you marry me, darling, once I am free? Will you be my *wife*?'

'Oh yes, I will. I love you so much,' she answered, her eyes suddenly brimming with tears. Sliding her hand out of his, she took a handkerchief out of her reticule and discreetly patted her eyes.

Robert watched her, loving her in a way he had never believed possible. And she was so guileless, so honest, it touched his heart. 'I assume those are tears of happiness,' he murmured.

'Of course,' she responded, laughing. 'I can't wait to marry you.'

'Now that is settled, let us move on.' He smiled at her warmly, and continued, 'Let us say that if my life were normal, and I was single, the thing I would do now is go to your father and ask for your hand in marriage. I am sure he would welcome me as a future son-in-law. We would become engaged, an announcement would be placed in *The Times*, and there would be an engagement party. After that we would wait a year, and then get married. Always a year, so there's no suspicion of a shotgun marriage.'

Vanessa nodded. 'I understand all that, but what are you getting at?'

'I don't believe engaged couples should indulge in an affair before marriage. Don't you agree?' Robert focused his eyes on her intently, waiting for an answer.

After a moment's reflection, she said, 'I suppose you're right, and what you're saying is we're not going to have an affair right now. Or ever.'

'You are correct, Vanessa, but I promise you I will do my damnedest to get my divorce as swiftly as I can, and that we will get married the day after I'm free.'

She stared at him, bedazzled by those vivid blue eyes, his charm, the wide smile on his face. She loved him so much she would agree to anything. She must never lose this remarkable man. Caught up in his powerful personality, she could only nod her understanding.

Before Robert could say another word to her, Turnbull hovered in the doorway, and announced the arrival of Lord Fraser.

Adrian hurried into the yellow drawing room, smiling, holding an envelope.

'Good evening, Vanessa, you look ravishing as always,' he said to her, bowing slightly.

'Good evening, Adrian, and thank you for your kind words.'

Going to Robert, Adrian embraced him, and said against his ear, 'I've got great news.'

The two men stepped away from each other, and Robert said, 'You made it back very quickly, Addy.'

'I did. I wanted to give you this.' He handed Robert the envelope. 'It was awaiting me when I got home.'

Glancing at it, Robert asked, 'Who is it from? Do you want me to read it now?'

'You can read it later. It's a letter from my agent in Switzerland.'

'Oh! Is it about your villa? The one you want to rent?'

'It is. But it's not for rent any more. The owner needs to sell it. I shall buy it, because the other person, who also wanted to rent it, can't afford to do that. You could say it's already mine,' Adrian explained in a slightly gloating voice, still smiling broadly.

'I understand what you're saying. You will buy it immediately, I assume.'

'I will. What's that old saying? Make hay while the sun shines.'

Robert put the letter in his jacket pocket and went to pour the champagne, saying as he did, 'How about a drink to toast your new acquisition, Addy?'

'Thanks. I'd like that.'

'I'm sure you would like a glass too, wouldn't you, Vanessa darling?' Robert said.

'Of course, Robert,' she answered, having found her voice again, and was filled with curiosity about the villa they had just discussed.

A few seconds later, he carried the champagne over to them, and they all sat down around the fire. After they had clinked glasses and taken a first sip, Robert said, 'I've decided to inform Lucinda she can no longer live at my house in Yorkshire. She must stay in Ireland or with her brother in town. I have put it off, but I don't want to stay away from my own estate. I need to be there; I have plans and responsibilities. And I hope I can go up there soon. I want you to come, Vanessa, along with Caroline as your chaperone, and you too, Adrian. Do you both accept my invitation?'

'Of course,' Adrian said, grinning at this suggestion and loving the idea of Lucinda being barred.

'I'd like to come,' Vanessa murmured, obviously flattered to be asked, a beatific smile on her face. 'And I know Caroline will enjoy it, too.'

Much later that evening, after supper and Vanessa's departure in Robert's carriage, the two men sat in the library, each holding a balloon of Napoleon brandy.

'How come Lucinda can't buy the villa?' Robert asked, his eyes searching his best friend's face, his interest apparent.

'She's been paying off her brother's gambling debts for years. He owes every gambling club in London. He's a drunk – a reprobate, actually – and he's bled her dry. Valentine is bad news.'

'How foolish of her. Is she broke?'

'More or less, and she certainly can't buy the villa, which she wants to buy. *Desperately so.* As a home for her and the Frenchman.'

'And we know all this from our private investigator in Zürich?' Robert asked.

'Yes. If I buy the villa next week, I will hand it over to you, and you then have a huge bargaining chip—'

'I must pay you for the villa!' Robert cut in peremptorily. Putting down the balloon of brandy, he got up and threw another log on the fire, pushed it around with the poker, then returned to his chair.

'If you wish, of course,' Adrian agreed. 'She will be given the villa by you as a gift, *if* she returns to England, so that she can be served the appropriate divorce papers. This is what you have to relay to your solicitor on Monday morning. And she has to agree to a *quiet* divorce. And everything has to be done with great speed.'

Adrian sat back in the chair and propped his feet on the brass fender, brought the balloon to his nose and breathed in the cognac. 'That's your task next week.'

'I will do everything you suggest, Addy. You have managed the situation so well,' Robert murmured. 'My only question is how do we get everything done with speed? I'm eager to marry Vanessa *soon*.'

'As long as Lucinda does as she's told, your divorce should be through in a few months.'

'Are you sure?' Robert said, doubt echoing in his voice. 'How can you manage that?' A worried look settled on his face.

'Money talks,' Adrian answered. 'And in your case, you've got plenty of it. We shall use it wisely.'

Later, after wishing Adrian goodnight, Robert sat for a few moments staring into the embers of the dying fire. He could never have imagined when he stood on the terrace at Bolton Manor, preparing for this trip to town, how much his life would have altered in just a few short weeks. That he could have met Vanessa.

His boys were with their grandparents and his wife was in Switzerland. It was time to take the steps to reclaim Bolton Manor as his own, and to make a new life for himself.

PART FOUR

Good Fortune Finds its Way
Yorkshire & London
1903–4

FORTY-FIVE

I t had been a lovely day for late September. Not a drop of rain. Instead, a pale blue sky, scudding white clouds and sunshine.

Now, early in the evening, the weather was still nice, and there was a light breeze as Blackie O'Neill walked up Town Street.

He was heading for Laura Spencer's house; she had invited him to join her for a bite of supper with other friends. Blackie was looking forward to seeing her. He had been to her home in St Ives Mount three times now, and had grown fond of her. She was a lovely-looking young woman, with fair hair filled with golden lights, and soft hazel eyes.

But it was her character he admired the most; she had a warm, welcoming personality. Also, she was calm and made him feel comfortable, and whenever he was with her, he was peaceful inside, and somehow felt safe, protected even.

Aside from the lovely weather, Blackie knew this had been a special day for him. Lucky. He had received a letter from Lord Robert Lassiter himself. He knew it was from the Earl before he even opened it. There was a crest on the back of the envelope.

Lord Robert had written to him to ask him to build a small guesthouse on the Yorkshire estate. Furthermore, he had requested that Blackie design it. 'Something of medium size, reflecting Bolton Manor,' Lord Robert had suggested, and had asked him to come over to Harrogate within the next week to discuss it with Wilson and him.

Uncle Patrick had been as thrilled as he could be. They had built garden sheds, greenhouses, and house extensions, and he himself had designed and built Mrs Wilson's conservatory. But they had never been hired for a project like this. Uncle Pat was so proud they had been chosen.

Thoughts whirled in his head, mostly architectural thoughts: Palladian? Georgian? Elizabethan? He settled on Georgian, which would match the main house and would suit Lord Robert's tastes well.

Turning into St Ives Mount, he grimaced. The whole street was filled with what he thought of as modern monstrosities, built during the boom of the past fifty years. Neat Victorian terraced houses with steps up to a front door. A parlour and small kitchen up those steps, with two bedrooms up narrow stairs.

Once he arrived at Laura's house, Blackie rapped on the door. She saw him through the window and waved. A moment later, she was opening the door to him, her face full of smiles, her eyes sparkling, obviously happy.

'Oh, how lovely to see you. Come in. Come in.' She opened the door wider, the smile intact.

'I'm early, I'm afraid,' he said, smiling back. 'But ye see, I never want to be late for ye, keep ye waiting, Laura.'

'I'm glad you are early, Blackie. You can keep me company while I finish making supper.'

As he followed her into the parlour, he glanced around, as he always did. As usual the table was already set. Tonight it was for six, and there were vases of flowers here and there. The room was divided in half, in a sense. The big wooden table was for preparing food; the circular table in the centre of the room was the divider. Beyond it were a sofa and chairs that created the feeling of a parlour. A fire burned in the hearth, and there were two high-backed chairs on each side of it. The air was filled with delicious smells of baking bread and meat roasting that made his mouth water.

'Would you like a cup of tea?' Laura asked, leaning against the wooden table. 'Or a lemonade?'

'Nothing at the moment, thanks anyway,' Blackie responded, and reached into his pocket. He took out a small box tied with a ribbon bow. Smiling, as he walked over to her, he then said, 'This is just a little something from Aunt Eileen. She made it for ye, and 'tis with pleasure she did it, faith and I knows that.'

'Why thank you, Blackie, how nice of her.' Laura took the little box from him, untied the ribbon, and lifted out a white handkerchief edged with a wide border of fine lace. 'Oh, my goodness, it's beautiful,' she cried, unfolding it.

'Look in one corner, Laura, and ye'll see an "L" embroidered by Aunt Eileen.'

'Oh yes, here it is. I shall treasure it. How thoughtful of her to make this for me.'

'She likes ye a lot, but then ye knows that, I do believe.'

Leaning forward he kissed her cheek lightly. 'Laura, me sweet mavourneen.'

'What does that word mean?' she asked, as she went to the table and started to cut a freshly baked loaf of bread. 'You've called me that before.'

'It's the Irish word for dear or darling. 'Tis a word of affection, Laura.'

She turned and nodded. 'That's what I thought,' she answered, smiling shyly to herself.

FORTY-SIX

After looking in the oven at the food she was cooking, Laura nodded to herself and turned it off. Everything was ready to serve, and she wanted to keep it warm until the other guests arrived. To her way of thinking, there was nothing worse than hot pies gone cold.

As she came back into the parlour, Blackie said, with a hint of admiration in his voice, 'Everyone says you're the best cook they know, and I agree.'

'Thank you.' Laura sat down in the other chair in front of the fire, and said, 'I'm glad your work is going well, Blackie, and with these connections you're forming with the big houses.'

'Well, now ye knows, mavourneen. I'm serious all right. I've some news, so I have. I've to build a guesthouse for Lord Robert at his estate in Harrogate, Bolton Manor.'

Laura stared at him, a look of pleasure mingled with surprise on her face. 'Oh, how wonderful for you!' she exclaimed, beaming at him. 'Congratulations.'

Blackie laughed. 'I can hardly believe it meself. But it's a good chance for me and Uncle Pat. It'll be a fine fee for us, too. Lord Robert is very fair.'

'I'm sure it will work well. You'll be busy and still taking on more.'

'I will that, lass!' he exclaimed and, leaning forward, he poked the fire, moved the logs around, then sat back, threw her a warm smile, enjoying this time alone with her.

'There's just something I want to say,' Laura began, and hesitated for a moment, as if wondering whether to continue.

Blackie stared across at her. In the firelight, her face looked serious, or perhaps solemn might be a better word, he thought. 'What's wrong?' he asked, suddenly feeling nervous.

'Nothing's wrong,' Laura responded swiftly. 'I won't hold any secrets from you. As my . . . as one of my best friends, you know everything.'

Blackie nodded. 'Thank you for telling me that. And I feel the same way. I'll always share me thoughts, and I won't keep any secrets either.' As he spoke, Blackie thought of one secret he'd hidden from his uncle, but he shoved it to the back of his mind. Don't think about *that* now, he warned himself, knowing he must keep his attention on Laura. She was such a fine young woman, and he'd grown to be fond of her, and couldn't imagine what his life would be like without friends like her.

They sat in silence for a few moments, lost in their own thoughts, but both of them sat up straighter when they heard voices outside and feet coming down the path.

Laura jumped up, turned on a light and went to open the door.

Blackie also stood, straightened his jacket, and joined her. Together they greeted Peter Lowrie and his girlfriend Sally Powers, old friends of Laura's. Blackie knew Peter well; he was a cub reporter on the *Yorkshire Gazette*, an evening newspaper his uncle read.

With greetings exchanged, Blackie led the couple down the room to the grouping of chairs and the sofa. He asked them if they would like a cup of tea or lemonade.

'Lemonade, please,' Sally answered, and Peter nodded. 'The same, please. It's still quite a warm day.'

Laura took out glasses, and asked Blackie to get the jug of lemonade out of the larder. He did so, and went over to the oak table. 'Here ye are, love,' he smiled, as he put down the jug.

Within seconds, the four of them were drinking lemonade, and chatting, enjoying each other's company.

'So what's the latest news, Peter?' Blackie asked. 'Ye must know what's going on all over the world, what with the tickertape and all that fancy equipment newspapers have.'

Peter laughed. 'I do usually. But not now. It's my day off. Nothing's happening as far as I know. And so that's good news, in my opinion.'

Blackie grinned, and Sally said, 'I don't know any local gossip, but if Sarah's coming, she will.'

Laura looked across at Blackie, a brow lifting. 'Is Finn bringing Sarah?'

'I'm not sure. Because *he* wasn't sure,' Blackie replied. 'But we'll know soon enough. He'll be here shortly. He's usually a bit late for some reason or another.'

Sally, who worked in a dress shop in Leeds, started to talk to Laura about clothes and the new fashions. And Blackie and Peter got into a long discussion about horses and horse racing. Blackie prided himself on his knowledge of horseflesh and thoroughbreds, and tended to show off a bit when speaking 'horse talk', as Laura referred to it. He thought he knew the most, more than anyone else, and couldn't help boasting. But nobody minded; Blackie was so well liked by everyone.

When steps outside and loud knocking on the door interrupted their conversations, Laura got up and hurried across the room. Blackie and Peter both stood up, ready to greet Finn and Sarah.

But, much to Blackie's surprise and dismay, Finn was ushering in Moira Aherne. His heart sank, but somehow he managed to keep a neutral look on his face. Despite her tremendous popularity, she was not his favourite. He still thought she was not who she said she was. There was something of a mystery about her. When he ran into her at Mrs Wilson's, he always said hello, but avoided conversing with her, just got on with his work.

Now he walked forward, smiling, and greeted her and his friend Finn with geniality. It was Laura who took hold of Moira's arm and drew her towards Peter and Sally.

Finn turned to Blackie and said in a low voice, 'Sorry, Blackie, but Sarah fell and sprained her ankle yesterday. So I asked Moira. Ye're not mad at me, are ye?'

'No. It's all right. I often run into Moira at Mrs Wilson's. We always chat for a minute,' Blackie improvised, knowing it was wise to hide his dislike of Moira. He knew Finn fancied her, but then so did Uncle Pat's friend, Jack Blane. He guessed most men liked her. She was beautiful, no denying that.

Despite his dislike of Moira, Blackie managed to hide it well, and he tried hard to make the evening pleasant for Laura's sake. And he succeeded, too, in spite of his earlier misgivings.

Laura had made Cornish pasties, with a big bowl of mashed potatoes and baked marrow. Moira and Sally helped her to put the dishes on the scrubbed wooden table, and everyone came and helped themselves to the different choices set out in front of them. There was gravy, other relishes, and mustard, plus a bottle of brown sauce for the meat. And a junket for afters.

Everyone enjoyed the food, and there was a lot of conversation and laughter, although Blackie himself was not as voluble as usual. From time to time, he joined in, but mostly he was a listener. And an observer. He tried not to study Moira, and managed to keep his eyes averted. But he knew she was not like them; she was fancy-born, no doubt in his mind about that. And unexpectedly, and rather oddly tonight, she reminded him of somebody he couldn't quite place.

Her outfit was plain, but well cut and handmade. A navy-blue slim-cut skirt skimmed her ankles, and her striped poplin blouse was trimmed with good lace. She wore a short navy jacket with a white collar and cuffs. Smart, as she usually was. She wore small pearl ear-clips and no other jewellery, and she did look lovely with her shining pale blonde hair and perfect skin. 'Quality' was the word that came into his mind.

It was her demeanour, her speech pattern, a sense of self-confidence which she exuded that told him she had been brought up in an aristocratic household. And those chiselled, classical looks, of course, told their own tale. She was not his type, but other men obviously flocked around her and were apparently spellbound, according to Finn, and wanted to court her.

What Blackie also noticed as they sat around the table, enjoying their supper, was the way Laura and Sally behaved towards Moira. They liked her, were friendly, even admiring of her.

His small sigh was muffled as he stood up and tapped Peter on the shoulder. 'Come on, let's get a second helping,' he said, picking up his plate. 'Laura made enough to feed an army.'

Peter and Finn both rose at the same time and headed for the table, where there was still plenty of food for them.

Blackie was addicted to mashed potato, especially the way Laura made it, and he took a spoonful, and returned to the table, still wondering who Moira reminded him of.

As the meal progressed, he tried to bury his dislike. When she suddenly spoke to him directly, he looked her fully in the face, half smiled, wanting to be pleasant to her.

She said, 'Mrs Wilson told me you're going to build a guesthouse for Lord Lassiter at Bolton Manor. That must be a most exciting project for you, Blackie.'

'Yes, it is,' he answered. 'I will be doing the draughtsman's work – the design – as well.'

'How wonderful!' Moira answered. 'Very many congratulations. Mrs Wilson told me you want to build houses more than anything else.'

'Yes, I do,' he said, and took a sip of water. 'I hope to build my own house in Harrogate one day.'

'In the meantime, when will you start on Lord Lassiter's house? And will Lord Lassiter be at his estate when you do? How often is he in Yorkshire?' Moira proffered him a smile, her curiosity apparent.

'I hope next month, before winter sets in,' he answered, and wondered why she was so interested in his work. He had no answer for himself. And he still considered Moira Aherne a mystery.

She didn't fit in. There was something about her that wasn't right to Blackie's mind, and he liked everybody. She was hiding something, and he didn't like that.

FORTY-SEVEN

'It's an Indian summer day,' Adrian said, glancing around as he and Robert walked down towards the lake at Bolton Manor. 'Better weather than we've had all year, don't you think?'

'I do, Addy, but it's often nice in October in Yorkshire. And it's been like this for several days, given me a chance to study the estate. You see, I'm going to build a guesthouse in the grounds, and I need to pick the right spot.' Robert's step was light as he took in his land, his heart glad to be home again.

'A guesthouse!' Adrian exclaimed. 'When the manor is so comfortable and spacious. I'm surprised you'd bother.'

'It might sound strange to you, but there's method in my madness, old chap. In-laws, another family suddenly in my life—'

'Vanessa's family,' Adrian interjected, glancing at his dearest friend. 'So you *are* going to marry her?'

'Did you ever doubt it? Surely not. You've just given me the papers for the villa in Zürich. I'll be buying it from you later today, and it will be my winning hand, as you call it. Lucinda does still want it, doesn't she?'

'She does. And the villa will give you your freedom. *If* you hand the villa over to *her*. As a gift. Don't forget that bit.'

'I think I would prefer my solicitor to give the deeds to her solicitor, if you want the truth. I've no desire to see that horrendous woman ever again. Now, here we are . . . look over there, Addy, at that little wood.' Robert began to walk faster, explaining, 'The guesthouse will be just to the left of it. A perfect spot, with a lovely view, and easy access to the main house. It will be perfect for Vanessa's parents, and Caroline. Incidentally, what's happening between you two? Do I detect a hint of seriousness in your relationship?' Robert gave him a questioning look.

Adrian came to a halt, and took hold of Robert's arm, a strained expression flashing across his face. 'Caroline? No, it's not quite right for me,' he said, a tenseness in his voice. 'I like her enormously, and she's good-looking, smart, modern, all the things a man likes. Yet I hesitate, and feel I should break off with her. Not that there's been any understanding between us; nothing has ever been voiced.'

'You're not in love with her, Addy, is that it?'

'You're correct. And by the way, there hasn't been an affair. I've been a perfect gentleman, not made a move in that direction.' Adrian stared at his friend and added, 'So you can wipe that smirk off your face, old chap.'

Robert laughed. 'I believe you. After all, you're the man with a key to a private place, so the odds were all in your favour if you'd wanted to go in that direction.'

Adrian chuckled with him, and they both walked on to the wood, letting the subject drop.

'I plan to have four bedrooms, and bathrooms, on the top floor, and two sitting rooms downstairs for general use, along with a small kitchen and scullery, just so their maid or valet can make them a tray of tea or prepare a light supper. I want it to be small but comfortable,' Robert told him. 'A kind of lodge.'

'It doesn't sound *small*,' Adrian muttered.

'Medium-sized, I suppose,' Robert replied. 'Young O'Neill is going to build it for me. He was here yesterday, to show me his drawings. I decided to give him a chance, try him out, and he's a darned good draughtsman, by the way, unusually talented. He is in partnership with his uncle, and they have taken the job, much to my relief.'

'When are you going to start on the project?'

'In about a week, I believe – it's up to O'Neill and his uncle Patrick Kennedy. They are now in charge. Anyway, do you like this spot?'

'I do, yes, as long as you don't put *me* in the guesthouse,' Adrian said, his tone jocular.

'Only if you ask for it, perhaps if you're with a lady friend,' Robert teased him back.

'None around at the moment,' Adrian answered. 'At least none I'm bowled over by.'

'Things can change in the blink of an eye, as I so recently discovered . . .' He paused, and then said swiftly, 'I see my butler, coming out onto the terrace. I think he must be looking for me.' Without another word, Robert hurried towards the long terrace above the lawns, leaving Adrian to follow. As he rushed forward, he called, 'Are you looking for me, Camden?'

'Yes, Your Lordship. A young lady has just arrived and—'

'Did you show her into a sitting room?' Robert cut in.

'No, Lord Robert. At least, I tried to do so, but she said she preferred to wait in the hall.'

'I see. Thank you, Camden.' Robert edged around the butler and went inside through the French doors.

The moment Robert saw her, his face changed, filled with shock. He strode down the hall, saying, 'Thank God you are here. I've been so worried about you.'

When he came to a standstill in front of her, she stood up

314

and stepped into his outstretched arms. He held her close to him, and then he stepped back, looked down into her upturned face.

'Thank God you're alive,' Robert said, his voice full of feeling. 'Nobody knew how to find you. I even wrote to that monstrous brother of yours, to Lawrence, but got no response. So, where on earth have you been, Moira?'

'In Leeds, Robert. But I've written to you. Twice. Once when I arrived in London. And again when I got to Leeds. You never replied,' she said, a hint of sadness echoing in her quiet voice.

'I never received your letters,' he answered. 'I did get the short note you wrote from Galway, and I did send you a condolence letter, and explained I was right in the middle of a very big property deal in London and couldn't leave for her funeral. Did you receive *that* at least?' Robert stared at her intently.

'Yes. But my brother behaved terribly badly. He had already agreed a sale on the Galway house, while Mother lay dying, and he ransacked the house, looking for Mother's jewels, which he never found.'

'I know she did have a special collection from your father, that he gave her when he was alive. Separate to any of the family jewellery,' Robert murmured. 'All diamonds, I believe.'

Moira nodded. 'Lawrence accused me of taking her jewels. I hadn't. Also, I was frightened by his growing animosity and his threats.' Moira swallowed, and felt a cold chill run through her. 'He threatened to report me to the constabulary for theft, and said they would come and arrest me. When I said I would come to see you, he struck me, shook me, and threw me down on a sofa. I was terrified, I thought he was going to strangle me – kill me, actually. He was so enraged. Then he locked me in my room.'

'But he's your half-brother, you grew up together, I simply can't understand why he behaved in such a brutal way.' Robert was incandescent with sudden anger, furious with Lawrence, and couldn't wait to confront him, take him to task.

'Lawrence has a violent streak. He's like his father, Lord Andrew Chandler. I lived through many of *his* rants with Mother. Anyway, when I mentioned your name again he told me you were all ashamed of me because I was illegitimate. He called me Mother's bastard, and that none of her cousins wanted anything to do with me, that you wanted me out of the family.'

Moira paused, and realized her eyes were moist. She brushed her hand against her face. In a low voice, Moira said, 'Lawrence told me that it was my misconception that anyone in Mother's family cared about me. He added that you didn't, that you couldn't stand me, and I was now alone in the world.'

Robert's face changed. Again a look of rage crossed it, and he exclaimed, 'I can't believe this. He lied! Henrietta loved you more than anyone in this world, except for your father, of course. It was unbearable to us all that she was already married to Andrew, then tragic when your father was killed. Lawrence knew how special you were to them. But I've always sensed hatred emanating from him. Lawrence has the air of evil around him, and I'm afraid he resented your place alongside him in the family.'

'You are right. The night he attacked me, and locked me up, I knew I had to leave. I was terrified he would bring the constables to arrest me. So I packed a bag during the night and left at dawn, climbing out of my window. Tommy, the son of one of our grooms, helped me – he was taking the boat to Liverpool.'

'Why didn't you come to me? Or to one of your mother's other cousins?' Robert asked, a troubled expression in his blue eyes.

'Because I believed Lawrence. I felt that, without Mother, I was an outcast, a stain on the family honour.' Moira's eyes had filled with tears. 'And I had almost no money, only a few pounds left after I paid the boat passage. It was much more expensive than I realized to come here. I was scared.'

Robert shook his head, sorrow floating across his face. He had always loved his cousin Henrietta, had watched this daughter of hers grow up, and he had promised his cousin he would look after her, knowing that her place in society was fragile and insecure, owing to the open secret of her illegitimacy. After a moment, he asked, 'Where on earth did you go?'

'Tommy has a cousin by marriage in Leeds. He took me to her house, but it was in a terribly poor area, the Bank, and I couldn't stay there for long, or find work around there. Fortunately, a friend of Tommy's, Finn, came and rescued me and arranged for me to live somewhere more respectable. I've been waiting and waiting to learn that you were back in Yorkshire. By great good fortune I became friendly with Blackie O'Neill, and I heard from him you had returned. I thought if I saw you in person I would know for sure if—'

Robert heard the French door close, and then there was a slight cough before Adrian decided to walk down the hall, his footsteps echoing in the stillness.

'Ah, there you are, Adrian,' Robert said, thinking quickly. 'Please come and meet Moira, my cousin Henrietta's daughter,' he exclaimed.

'I would love to,' Adrian replied, moving forward swiftly, struck by this young woman's beauty. She was stunning, with her silver-blonde hair, glossy and shining, and those large soulful greyish-blue eyes in a perfect face.

'Moira, let me introduce Adrian, Lord Fraser, my best friend,' Robert said to her, calming himself as he spoke, clamping down his fury about Lawrence.

Taking his hand, Moira said, 'I am honoured to meet you, Lord Fraser.' She spoke softly, pushing aside her pain.

'And likewise, Miss Aherne, and it is my pleasure indeed.' He dropped her hand after a long moment, stunned by her looks, her lilting voice. What a true beauty stood looking at him, her eyes wide and full of expectation, he thought. A knot of tension was settling in his stomach. Suddenly, he realized he was just gaping at her, and he moved towards the staircase. 'I mustn't interrupt you both, Robert, Miss Aherne. Please excuse me.' He inclined his head, looking at Moira, and smiled. 'Excuse me,' he said, sounding flustered.

'Tea at four-thirty, Addy,' Robert called after his departing friend, who was now mounting the staircase.

'I'll be there,' Adrian answered without looking around.

Robert took hold of Moira's hand, and picked up the carpetbag next to the chair. 'Is this all you have?'

'Yes. I can only stay one night.'

Robert was startled, and frowned, 'Why? What *is* going on, Moira?'

'I have a job—'

'You're working?' he cut in sharply.

'Yes, I am.'

'Doing *what*, for God's sake?' It was apparent he was taken aback.

For a moment, she thought of fibbing, but changed her mind. He had known her all her life, knew her inside out.

Taking a deep breath, she said, 'I'm a lady's maid.'

He stood looking down at her, obviously flabbergasted.

After a moment, he said, 'You are joking, aren't you? Pulling my leg?'

'No, I'm not. That's what I've been doing since I got to Leeds. I *am* a lady's maid.'

There was a moment of silence. Robert looked slightly stricken and, without another word, he led her into the small study he favoured, closed the door, and said, 'You owe it to me to explain everything.'

FORTY-EIGHT

Moira sat down on a chair and said, 'I'm sorry I've caused you anxiety. Please forgive me.' She looked at him pleadingly.

'There's nothing to forgive, and perhaps I should have tried harder to seek you out. But it was very unclear what had become of you, once the house was sold, and your mother's other cousins and I were at something of a loss as to who you could be staying with. And I've had a lot of business to deal with,' he explained with a rueful smile, sounding chagrined.

'You always do; you're tireless.' Opening her purse, she took out an envelope and handed it to him. 'My mother told me to give this to you.'

'Thank you. How have you been surviving? Do you have any money?'

'A little, enough to manage at the moment. Mother gave me all she had left before she died, but that was used on the travelling.'

He nodded, and said quietly, 'So tell me everything that has been happening to you, please, Moira.'

'It was Lawrence who put me off coming to you at Bolton Manor. He had managed to convince me you were all against me, because I'm illegitimate, and because scandal surrounded me. He said my mother and John Clairemont flouted all the rules of decency, and you were furious—'

'But that's not true!' Robert exclaimed, cutting across her. 'I loved Henrietta, and I knew she had had a difficult life with that husband of hers, Lawrence's father. He frittered her fortune away, and it was a relief for everyone when he died. Though he turned a blind eye to the love affair with John, he wouldn't release her from the marriage, and she couldn't leave you and Lawrence.' He let out a long sigh. 'Do continue, my dear.'

'Through the Irish friend, Tommy, I managed to get to Leeds, as I just told you. Eventually I was taken from the Bank to Mrs Wilson's house, who gave me a job and a roof over my head.'

Robert half smiled when he said, 'As a lady's maid.'

Moira laughed. 'A parlourmaid at first, and then I was lucky. She's a nice woman, and has treated me with kindness. That's the story, more or less.' Moira sat back in the chair, waiting for his response.

After a moment, Robert broke the silence. 'I expect you have other things to tell me, but let's leave that for later.'

He glanced at the letter in his hand, and recognized the handwriting of his cousin Lady Henrietta Fitzgerald Chandler. Turning the letter over, he saw the family crest above the red beeswax seal. He managed to remove the seal, and opened the letter.

My dearest Robert,
By the time you are reading this, I will be dead. I have a malign growth and the doctors have lost all hope of curing me. I accept my fate.

Many years ago, you promised me and my dearest Johnny that you would take care of our child, Moira. She is grown up now, but, nonetheless, I ask you to keep an eye on her and help her if needs be.

Moira has an inheritance. This is my jewellery collection. I am afraid it has been a little depleted over the years. I have had to sell pieces to pay for our living needs. But it is still very valuable.

The jewels are in a safety deposit box in the Montague Brothers' Private Bank in Piccadilly. Those who have designated access to the box are myself, Moira Aherne, and you, listed as Lord Robert Lassiter, Earl of Harding. The small key enclosed in the pages of this letter will open the box.

I gave Moira the spare key for safety's sake. You must accompany Moira to the bank to access the box and sign, along with her, for the contents you both remove, in order to sell or auction them.

The managing director of the bank is Mr Ethan Montague. He is an old friend and knows all the circumstances of the situation. He will assist you both in whatever you need. He is pleasant to deal with.

I repeat what I've just said, the jewellery collection is valuable, if a trifle depleted. Mostly it is composed of diamond pieces, and every piece was given to me by Moira's father, the Honourable John Clairemont, who eventually became the Duke of Lowencester, after the death of his elder brother, who was childless. As you know, Johnny died accidentally in an uprising in India some years ago, when he was there on family business.

The jewels were always intended for Moira. It was the only way Johnny could provide for her future security, because of the circumstances of his private life and his family.

You are a good man, Robert, and I know you have great

integrity. I trust you completely. I thank you from the bottom of my heart for being my dearest cousin and true friend. May you live a long, fruitful and happy life. God bless you.

With love from your cousin,

Henrietta Fitzgerald Chandler

Robert put the letter back in the envelope, then placed the key in a drawer of his desk and locked it. The letter had touched him deeply, and for a moment he could not speak, felt choked up.

Looking across at Moira, he spoke at last. 'Would you like to read the letter?'

She shook her head. 'I know what Mother wrote. She gave me the copy she had made, so I would know what she had done. She left nothing to chance.'

Robert was taken aback, and stared at her, then said, 'Obviously, she wanted to make sure nothing went wrong, protected you as best she could. Well, she was always organized. And so was your father.' He gave her a long, intense look, and asked, 'What are your plans?'

'I don't really know,' Moira admitted, speaking the truth.

He said, 'Well, your life can change now. You are safe and we have the secret to your inheritance in our hands. Thank goodness Lawrence never found it.'

Moira's eyes filled with tears. 'Thank you. Thank you so much, Cousin Robert. I am so grateful to you for guiding me, which is what Mother wanted. I've been so worried.'

'I can't leave Bolton Manor this coming week. I have builders arriving to start working here. However, we could go up to town on Saturday, and visit your mother's bank on Monday. You will stay at my London home, won't you?' Robert asked.

'Thank you, I will.' Moira wiped her eyes with a small folded handkerchief. 'About my plans, I think that perhaps now is the time to leave Mrs Wilson's employment, to become myself, to become who I really am.' She sat up a little. 'I feel very safe now I am with you.'

FORTY-NINE

B lackie always told the truth.
Dissimulation was not in his nature, and he always kept a promise.

At least until recently.

Now, on this cold Saturday in early February 1904, he pondered the fact that he hadn't been entirely truthful with Laura. He had hidden a secret from her, and it was beginning to bother him.

The two of them were sitting in front of her fire, drinking tea and munching on ginger biscuits. Laura had lit a couple of lamps, and the kitchen had a cosy feeling, as the sky outside grew darker, and dusk descended even though it was only late afternoon.

Laura cut into his thoughts when she said, 'I like this time of day. The gloaming, my grandmother used to call it, but most people think of it as twilight.'

'I've never heard that word before – *the gloaming*,' Blackie murmured, gazing at her, his affection reflected in his black eyes.

'I think it might be Scottish,' Laura replied. 'Anyway, whatever it's called I like this hour.' She cleared her throat and, changing the subject, she said, 'You've worked so hard on your drawings of the rooms today, have you nearly finished?'

'I *am* finished!' Blackie exclaimed, a wide smile settling on his face. 'When I put me pencil down half an hour ago, they were done. Thank ye for letting me work on your table, love, it really helped, 'cos I could spread out the papers, sure and I could. Faith, and I'm grateful to ye, lass.'

'It's my pleasure, Blackie. So will you be going to Harrogate next week?' she then asked, filled with curiosity about his plans.

'I aim to go and see Lord Robert, to show him these interiors, but I'd be going anyhow, to see how Uncle Pat's been faring with me builders. The structure was up, I told ye that, and when I saw it, I knew I'd picked the right spot for the guesthouse. I think I told ye I'd decided to move the guesthouse in front of that there copse of trees, and I was right. They make a nice backdrop, and they'll add shelter in the bad weather, shade in the summer.'

Always impressed by Blackie, admiring of his ideas and his understanding of architecture, Laura said, 'You're so clever the way you do things – and how you taught yourself to build houses, I'll never know. And this is truly such a wonderful opportunity for you.'

'Well, I did go to night school, ye knows that, but I think I just knows how to design buildings, sort of naturally, I suppose.'

'You were born with a gift,' Laura said with her quiet authority. 'Of that I'm certain.'

'Perhaps ye are right. And I'd say ye have a gift for sewing. That was a lovely piece ye were putting lace on. What is it ye are making, love?'

'A nightgown. I was given the lace, so I'm making something special with it.' She paused, smiled shyly at him, and added, 'Perhaps it'll be for my Bottom Drawer.'

Blackie stared at her, a puzzled expression on his face. 'What do ye mean when ye say *bottom drawer*, as if it's something special?'

'Well, it is. Every young woman who hopes to get married starts a Bottom Drawer, to put things in for her wedding, like nightgowns, petticoats, tablecloths, that sort of thing. Items women make to take with them into a marriage. I suppose it's a tradition, a custom. Anyway, this lace is too pretty for everyday, so perhaps I'll make a start, if it's not tempting fate.'

'Fancy that . . . I've never heard of it,' Blackie answered. 'But I do see how practical it is.' Putting down his tea, he leaned forward, and focusing his eyes on her, he said, 'I've a confession to make to ye, love.'

Laura sat up straighter, a look of alarm settling on her face. 'What kind of confession?' she asked, her voice suddenly worried.

'I kept a secret from ye, lass, and it was real stupid of me, faith and it was. So now I shall tell ye. Is that all right?'

Laura simply nodded, wondering what on earth he had been keeping from her. Could it be another woman? She hoped not. She sat rather tensely in the chair, expecting the worst.

Blackie said in a quiet tone, 'I took a job once, some time ago, and it was only for the money. Ye see, I wanted to build me nest egg, and I couldn't resist the offer. It were ten shillings a day, and—'

'But there's nothing wrong with *that*,' Laura interrupted, filling with relief.

'No, there wasn't,' Blackie said. 'Let me just tell ye, Laura, and don't interrupt me, or it'll never get told.' He stared at her intently.

She nodded and sat back in her chair, remained silent.

Blackie commenced. 'The money meant everything. But the hours were difficult, hard to keep from dawn 'til dusk. The job had to be rushed to meet the deadline, so the manager of the building came to me. He said, "In at four o'clock every morning, and finish at five o'clock. Five other builders to help ye. Ye'll be the foreman and ye'll live in lodgings in Leeds. No time for travelling home.'"

Blackie paused, took a sip of tea and went on with his story. 'All that was no problem for me. I'm strong, long hours don't bother me. But the lodging house did. It was in the Bank, the Ham Shank. The most dangerous place there is in Leeds. Still an' all, I risked it. I wanted the work – it were good building experience, more than Uncle Pat could offer at the time. And for the money, ye see. Work building the last top floor. An office building it were, near Briggate. And tough to do, but we made it.'

Again, Blackie paused and, as Laura started to speak, he held up his hand. 'Not quite finished yet, love. I lied to Uncle Pat. I didn't dare tell him about the job, and living in the Ham Shank, so I told him I had a chance to go to London, to stay with Tommy O'Hara, my old friend from Ireland. A little break from work, a short holiday, and he agreed. Ye see, I knew Tommy had gone back to Galway to see his sister, so I was safe . . . in lying, I mean.'

Blackie let out a long sigh. 'I never did confide in Uncle Pat, not to this day, not even when we went there to fetch Moira out. But oddly, keeping this secret from ye has been troubling me, Laura.'

'I'm glad you told me, and I do understand why you wanted to make so much money. It was great temptation. Still, the Ham Shank is known to be a very dangerous place. People get killed in there for no reason at all, so I've heard.'

'Aye, they do, and I were lucky, but I had me own little gang, ye knows, five other strong men. We went in and out together, faith, and we weren't harmed.' He finally sat back, relieved to have spoken out to her.

'I'm glad you've told me,' Laura said, her voice full of warmth, a sympathetic look on her face. 'And I will keep your secret. It's safe with me. I told you the other day that you can trust me. Always.'

'I knows that, love. The thing is, I still don't want to tell Uncle Pat . . .' His voice trailed off, and Blackie gave her a helpless look. 'I just can't.'

Laura looked thoughtful. He knew she was a Roman Catholic, the same as he had been brought up, and Blackie thought she might tell him to go to confession. Even though she knew he had lost his faith. He waited, then she said, 'There is no reason to tell your uncle. It happened some time ago, so leave it alone. You've unburdened yourself to me, and you'll see, you'll feel better in no time at all. Best to keep quiet, Blackie. Your actions were in the past. Bury them.'

'Thanks, Laura. I shall take your advice, so I shall.'

'I'm glad, Blackie. Telling your uncle now wouldn't do any good; it would only upset him. Can I now ask you a question?'

'Of course ye can, mavourneen. Ask away.'

'Thank you, Blackie,' she said in the same determined voice. 'You're a lapsed Catholic because of your awful childhood, aren't you?'

Blackie looked at her, momentarily taken aback by her comment. But then she really did understand him and who he was.

'Yes,' he said at last. 'There was no God around to help me when I was a child. I had Cook, though, and women like Mrs O'Malley. It was them who came to my aid. Not God. So it's them that are meaningful. I've no idea if God even exists.'

Laura was stupefied by his comments and had no words to answer him.

*   *   *

Blackie could see them ahead, standing at the edge of the lake, and, as he drew closer, everything clicked together in his head and made sense.

He smiled to himself. Now he knew who Moira Aherne reminded him of . . . Lord Robert Lassiter. Their colouring was different, but Moira had his chiselled features, slender nose, and they both had dimples in their chins. The family resemblance was clear as crystal, and especially when they laughed.

He suddenly felt a bit chuffed with himself. He had been right when he had spotted how different she was to them, and on their very first meeting. He had known she was an aristocrat, even though she had been sent to the Ham Shank, and then worked for Mrs Wilson as a maid. Breeding was hard to hide, he thought, as he crossed the lawn. It stood out like a sore thumb, or rather like elegance, he corrected himself.

Lord Robert turned to look at him, and said, 'Morning, O'Neill.'

'Good morning, Your Lordship.' Staring at Moira, he nodded, and went on, 'Hello, Miss Moira, nice to see ye.'

'Likewise, Blackie. I think your guesthouse is starting to take shape.' As Moira Aherne spoke, she was looking towards the copse of trees at the other end of the lawn. 'You're building a charming house, and it's in a perfect spot.' She spoke with a quiet confidence, returned to her rightful position in the world by the patronage of the Earl. She stood beside Robert, dressed in a luxurious soft tweed suit and polished brown boots, her pale hair pinned up under a fashionable hat.

'Thank ye,' he said, smiling. The building had really come on in the last few months, and he was glad Lord Robert had approved the change in position. He turned to address Lord Robert. 'I've brought all the drawings for the interiors, m'lord. They're on the dining-room table, and I wondered if we could go through them. If I'm not disturbing ye.'

'Excellent idea, Blackie. Let us go up to the house, and dig in.' Glancing at Moira, he said, 'If you will excuse me, my dear, I have work to do with O'Neill here. But Adrian is in the study with my old friend Harry Peterson, who arrived for a visit late last night. I'm sure they would appreciate your company.'

'I shall go and join them, Robert. See you later for lunch.'

Once Robert had removed the two silver candelabra and put them on the sideboard, Blackie spread the large sheets of paper across the table.

Slowly, Blackie walked him through the sketches of the rooms in the guesthouse, starting with the two sitting rooms at the back of the house, facing the lawns.

'I decided to reduce the sitting rooms, m'lord. I think two work well enough. Do ye agree, Lord Robert?'

'I do indeed. Good decision on your part, Blackie. And I do like these rooms . . . tall windows, each room with a fireplace, and I notice you've sketched in sofas and chairs. Excellent. Easy for me to visualize. You've done truly great work. The builders have made good progress over the past few months.'

'Yes, and me uncle is doing very well as the foreman.' Blackie cleared his throat, then said, 'I just want to remind ye that I won't be here next week, Your Lordship. At the beginning of this project, I did explain I had to be at Fairley Hall sometime in February. My uncle promised Squire Fairley that I'd take care of the job, as I'm the best one to do the stonework on the chimneys and other bits and pieces that they need.'

'Ah, yes, I do recall that, O'Neill. Very honourable of you to inform me, and, of course, to keep your commitment to Squire Fairley. I believe you said your uncle would be here in your place again. That is fine with me. He's excellent, good with the men.

So, we will continue, and I will await your return. And thank you again for your dedication, O'Neill.'

'It is my pleasure, Your Lordship.'

Lord Robert went into his library and strode over to his desk. He had many papers to deal with, but ignored them and sat back in his chair, lost in his thoughts. He was impressed by Blackie O'Neill, admiring the young lad's talents. Mostly self-taught, he was growing into a clever draughtsman and builder. A good lad to have working for him. No, not a lad, not any more.

Robert sighed. At eighteen, our young men are old enough to be sent to the front to fight in a war when necessary. That's what they always did – send their young to die in foreign fields. Cannon fodder, he muttered to himself. But it was the young who were fit, energetic and enthusiastic; they wanted to go and vanquish the enemy, joyful in their mission.

'Well, thank God, there are no wars at the moment,' Robert said out loud to the empty library.

There had been none since the Boer War, and the whole world was at peace for once. But for how long? he asked himself.

There was always one bugger who wanted to invade another country, seeking power, money and so-called glory. But, it seemed to him, there were none of those devils around at the moment. I pray to God this gentle peace lasts, Robert thought, getting up and going to the circular table near the fireplace. There were newspapers and magazines on it, and a book about the Boer War. He picked it up, took it over to the bookshelves, and put it back in its place. His eyes caught another history book, one about Wellington, who had defeated the Emperor Napoleon in the little Belgian town, Waterloo, in 1815. He had enjoyed reading it. Taking it out, placing it on the table, he would give it to

O'Neill later. He was well aware Blackie liked reading about great achievers.

Leaving the library, Lord Robert strolled down to his study to join Adrian, Moira and Harry Peterson, who had worries about his newly acquired Cézanne. This did not surprise Robert at all.

His eyes rested for a moment on Moira. He thought of her like a niece. Her position in polite society was less assured than most of his family, her illegitimacy an open secret, but with his backing and her inheritance, he knew she would be accepted in London society.

She would need a chaperone, and he would sponsor her, so that she would never again need to run to strangers for help.

Fifty

It was an icy cold February day, and Blackie wished he did not have to cross the moors to get to Fairley Hall. He had no alternative.

Squire Fairley was expecting him, and the latter had made a contract with his Uncle Patrick many months ago. He had been taught that his word was his bond, and he had promised his uncle he would tackle the job.

Because he was building the guesthouse for Sir Robert, Blackie had been able to push the Fairley job to one side for several months while they made a start on that project, and his uncle had agreed. But now the time had come to keep the commitment to the Squire. His uncle insisted on that. Over the past few years, the Squire had sent some good jobs their way for people he knew in Leeds. Uncle Pat would go to Harrogate to oversee Blackie's builders. He knew his uncle would be on top of things. No worries there. Bolton Manor was in safe hands.

Blackie glanced up at the long stretch of moors above him, dark, sombre and always windswept. A harshly beautiful, desolate, grim place all year round.

Not quite true, Blackie thought. In August, the heather bloomed and turned those rolling hills into a sea of purple. But for such a short time, he added to himself.

Yesterday, he had travelled to Shipley and spent the night in a small bed and breakfast. The owner, Mrs Craven, had told him to take the lower stretch of moorland, following the wide gravel path. This path would take him to the highest part of Fairley village where there were no houses, only several paths branching off.

'Just stay on the wide path,' Mrs Craven had warned him. 'It gets very misty around those particular moors. Yer don't want to get lost.' He had noted everything she had told him; others had alerted him about the fog.

It seemed to Blackie that it got chillier as he walked along at a steady pace, and at one moment, he put down the sack he was carrying, pulled off his cap and took off his scarf. After tying the scarf around his head, he replaced the cap and turned up the collar of his coat, feeling warmer almost at once.

Within twenty minutes, he found himself in clouds of mist and had to peer ahead to make out where he was. He really couldn't see anything, but his boots crunching on gravel reassured him he was on the wide path. It was not long after that he realized the crunching sound had stopped. Damn, he thought, I'm off the path. How did that happen? I'm lost!

This thought took hold as he walked on. He wasn't sure what to do. A moment or two later, his dilemma was solved. Peering ahead he saw another person further along the path. Man or woman? He wasn't sure. He plunged ahead, calling out, 'Wait! Please wait! Wait for me.'

Suddenly, the mist lifted slightly and, as he rushed forward, he realized it was a young woman in a long, worn-out coat, wrapped in shawls and with a scarf around her head.

She had hidden behind an outcropping of rocks, and looked terrified. 'Get away!' she yelled. 'Ye looks like a monster.'

'I'm not a monster,' he shot back. 'Don't be afeard, little colleen. I'm just a man who's lost, looking to get to Fairley Hall.'

'Fairley Hall!' she exclaimed, edging out from behind the rocks. 'Why do yer want ter go there?' She peered at the man, intrigued now.

Realizing he had caught her interest, and that she sounded less afraid, he moved towards her. 'Let me tell ye.'

'Get back!' she shouted. 'Don't move!'

'I be going to Fairley Hall to do some chimney repairs,' Blackie explained, gently now.

'Where did ye meet the Squire?' she asked cautiously, every inch of her alert.

Blackie had drawn closer, and he noticed she had the greenest eyes he had ever seen. And now they looked wary, and her face was stern. Yorkshire folk were suspicious, he knew. He said, 'I met the Squire in Leeds. He'd heard I used to be a navvy, working on the canals. This told him I was strong and a good worker. And he knew my uncle.'

The girl moved out from behind the outcropping of rocks, and said in a more controlled tone, 'I heard a navvy was coming ter the Hall. I'm going there, so yer can walk with me. What's yer name then? Or don't yer have one?' She sounded scathing, and just a bit haughty.

Blackie laughed a deep belly laugh. 'Sure an' I do, I swear on the heads of the Blessed Saints. Shane O'Neill's the name, but the whole world calls me Blackie.'

The girl looked up at him, trying to see him better in the vaporous mists. She decided he must be Irish, because of his name and the singsong voice he had, a sort of lilt in his speech.

'And what might ye be called?' he asked, breaking the silence.

The girl did not answer. She believed the less that people knew about you, the safer you were. And if they knew nothing at all, they could not harm you. And so she did not answer him.

'Come on, little colleen. What's your name?'

'Emma. Emma Harte's me name,' she finally said.

'So let's be a-marching, Emma. Devilish cold 'tis out here.'

'Come on,' she muttered, and hurried ahead of him, leading the way out of Ramsden Ghyll, and up onto a flat piece of land, a plateau of moors that led directly to the Hall.

Within a short while, the mist had cleared, and Emma stole a glance at Blackie, her curiosity getting the better of her.

To her surprise, although he was the tallest man she'd ever seen, he only looked about eighteen. She wasn't sure. But she *was* sure of one thing, his kindness. It had echoed in his voice when he had spoken to her in the Ghyll, and now it was reflected in his face. Instinctively, she knew he was a good man.

Blackie smiled back at her, taken by her pretty face and those emerald eyes. 'So, where is the Hall, colleen?' he asked.

'Yer can't see it from here. But it's not far. Just over the crest.' She laughed. 'I'll show yer,' she exclaimed, somewhat taken with her new friend.

'Do ye live nearby?' Blackie asked, as they headed towards the crest of moors in front of them.

'At the edge of the moors back yonder. In a cul-de-sac called Top Fold, the highest part of Fairley village. I'd just been walking five minutes when I heard yer blundering behind me.'

'I'm sorry I frightened ye, little colleen,' Blackie apologized. 'I *was* lost, though. Well, so I thought. Ye were a welcoming sight, I can tell ye that.'

'Never been on the moors before then?'

'No, I haven't.'

'So where do yer live?' Emma asked, riddled with curiosity about Blackie.

'Leeds. Do ye knows it?'

'No, I've never been. What's it like then?'

'Ah, 'tis a wonderful place, Emma. A great industrial city with wonderful buildings, a fine Town Hall – very imposing it is, to be sure. And there are shops, Emma, the best of them in arcades—'

'What's that? An arcade? I've never heard of it,' Emma said, looking at him intently.

'Ah, a place to feast the eyes, sure an' it is. An arcade is like a wide passageway between two big buildings, but it has a roof over it, and shops line each side, selling beautiful things. Jewels, handbags, silken scarves, woollen jumpers, all kinds of things for ladies. And for men too. And there are also restaurants in Leeds, for delicious meals, and theatres. I can go on and on talking about Leeds, on the heads of the Blessed Saints, I can. And they say the streets are made of gold. Imagine that.'

Emma stopped abruptly and stared at him, a startled expression on her face. 'Are they *real* gold?'

Blackie chuckled. 'No, mavourneen, they're not. It's just a saying folks have. What they mean is that there are jobs aplenty in this great city, and work for everyone. And 'tis the truth. I came to Leeds to live with me Uncle Patrick, and I learned to be a carpenter and a builder. Uncle Pat and me, well, we've got a lot of work. We're a success. I'm building a guesthouse right now for Lord Robert Lassiter of Bolton Manor.'

Emma, looking very impressed, and also extremely interested, asked, 'Could a girl like me make her fortune in Leeds then?'

Blackie hesitated. The city was no place for a scrawny young girl. He was about to answer negatively when he recognized the passionate gleam in her eyes, the ambition that burned fiercely. 'Sure an' ye could, mavourneen. But not now, Emma, not yet. 'Tis a fine city, but dangerous too, for a girl like you.'

'Hey, what's that word mean that yer call me . . . *mavourneen*?'

'Ah, 'tis just a word of affection, Emma, like luv, or dear. It's a nice name. I like ye, ye seem like a nice girl, and I think ye are probably clever, too. Yes, ye would easily get a job in the city. I can guarantee that ye could sell things in stores, for instance, or find work in one of the manufactories making the fine dresses.'

'If I came ter yer great metropolis, as yer call it, would yer show me the ropes?'

'Sure, on the heads of the Blessed Saints, I swear I would.'

Emma smiled at him, her green eyes sparkling, and it seemed to Blackie that there was a new spring in her step as they walked towards the crest.

An observer and a fiend when it came to detail, Blackie had taken everything in: the old, worn black coat which had obviously seen better days, but was neatly patched. The old black boots, highly polished, and the old shawls around her shoulders, darned here and there. But all were scrupulously clean. Her face beneath the shawl was scrubbed and shining, but it was those green eyes that caught his attention, and her lovely features. She had a thin, pinched look but, in a year or two, she would be a beautiful young woman. There was no question about that.

Filled with interest, he asked, 'And do ye have any brothers and sisters, Emma?'

'Aye, I do. Two brothers. Winston, who wants to join the Royal Navy, and me dad won't let him go yet. Me mam's not well, and Dad says if Winston runs off, it'll be the last nail in her coffin.' Emma let out a sigh, and finished, 'And there's me younger brother, Frank, who's clever. He'd like ter be a writer on a newspaper. One day. But I don't know how he'll manage that.'

'He could go to night school, like I did,' Blackie said swiftly, wanting to cheer her up. She suddenly looked so sad.

Instantly, a smile flashed across her face. 'Will yer tell me how ter make that happen later?'

'It'll be my pleasure, Emma. I want ye to know I'll help ye any way I can.' He looked down at her and added, 'I believe we're going to become good friends, and that pleases me.'

'And it pleases me, too. I've never had a *real* friend before, and I'm glad it's you, Blackie O'Neill.'

FIFTY-ONE

The two of them walked towards the crest of the hill in silence, lost in their own thoughts. Emma was dwelling on her mother's ill-health; Blackie was focusing on the repair work he had to do at Fairley Hall: chimneys, flues, and some outside walls between the stables. Five days' work and several extra, if needed. Good money though. That was important.

Unexpectedly, Emma laughed and started to run, shouting over her shoulder, 'I'm going ter yon gate.'

He smiled as he watched her flying across the field. When she arrived at the white-painted gate, she unlatched it, stood on it, and swung forward, laughing once more as she went backwards and forwards, enjoying herself.

When Blackie joined her, he said, 'Here, let me give ye a good push!' He did this several times, delighted that she was having fun in a girlish manner.

A few moments later, she jumped off the gate, and said, 'We got ter get moving, Blackie. I don't want ter be late.'

'How far is the Hall?' Blackie asked, striding out beside her.

'Ye'll see it in a few minutes, when we get ter that moor in front of us.'

Silence fell between them once again. Several times he glanced down at her and saw that her face was now set in more serious lines. And he thought she even looked a bit anxious. But he made no comment. After all, they had only just met a short while ago.

After climbing up the hill, they were finally on top of the moor which overlooked a small valley. Emma looked out across the River Aire below, and then turned to face Blackie. 'That's where *they* live!' she exclaimed, pointing to a house in the valley.

Staring back at her, he was genuinely taken aback by the expression in those emerald eyes. It was one of pure hatred, and her face was tense with controlled emotion.

He felt a small shiver running through him. She was more than likely badly treated by the Fairleys – well, perhaps some of them, maybe only one. But the hatred was a palpable thing, and he wondered what he would find inside the Hall.

Clearing his throat, staring down at the house, he exclaimed, 'What an awful-looking place that is, Emma! Chimneys and towers, add-on buildings, and no symmetry. A monstrosity, if ye ask me. And here I was, thinking it would be a grand house, Georgian, perhaps even Palladian in style. But this house, Fairley Hall, is just a muddled mess. A hodgepodge of styles.'

His words obviously pleased Emma, and she smiled, and said, 'And I knows yer right, 'cos yer an expert. It's not got nice gardens either. And they're awful people, the Fairleys, most of 'em,' she finished dismissively.

'How many Fairleys live there?' Blackie asked, his curiosity aroused more than ever.

'The Squire, Mrs Fairley, Master Edwin, the heir, his brother Gerald, and sometimes Mrs Olivia Wainright comes to stay. She lives in London, and she's Mrs Fairley's sister. She's nice,' she acknowledged.

'I'm wondering what the sons are like?' Blackie looked at Emma and raised a brow questioningly.

She answered swiftly. 'Master Gerald's a bossy lad, allus shouting and teasing Master Edwin, who keeps away from him when he can. I like Master Edwin; he is polite. The other boy is nasty.'

'And what about the others there? Surely there is a house-keeper, a cook and a butler?' Blackie was well aware of the need the rich had for servants, having spent so much time at Bolton Manor in Yorkshire and Lassiter Hall in Ireland. A big house, like the one they were now approaching, would require the same number of people to clean it and run it – probably more, in fact.

'Cook is Mrs Turner, and the butler is Mr Murgatroyd. The housekeeper, Mrs Hargreaves, is in Ilkley. She's gone ter look after her sister who's poorly,' Emma explained.

'No other maids like ye?' Blackie asked, surprised at the answer Emma had just given. To be so low on staff seemed odd to him.

'Just Polly, but she's got a bad cold. She's in bed. I have ter do her work.' Emma grimaced. 'Well, we're there . . . welcome to Fairley Hall,' she announced in a scathing tone.

'The Monstrosity,' Blackie muttered, and looked at Emma, then put his arm around her shoulder. 'What is it, mavourneen? Ye've got such a strange look on your face.'

'I'm frightened of this place,' she murmured. 'Like when I have ter walk past the cemetery at night.'

'Don't be afraid, Emma. It's just a lot of bricks and mortar. The house can't hurt ye.' As he spoke, he suddenly thought, but those who occupy it can. He shivered inside at the idea of the Fairleys or their servants hurting this lovely young girl.

* * *

The warmth of the kitchen, the sight of a roaring fire in the huge hearth, and the delicious smells of bacon frying and chicken broth bubbling, changed Blackie's dour mood immediately, his spirits lifting.

Following Emma into the large kitchen filled with sparkling copper pots and utensils, bunches of herbs, onions and sausages hanging on a big rack dangling from the ceiling, gave him an unexpected feeling of well-being.

Standing next to a huge black pot, holding a wooden spoon, was a little plump dumpling of a woman. She had apple-rosy cheeks and a bunch of greying hair piled on top of her head; she wore a dark blue dress covered with a huge blue-and-white pinafore.

'Late again, Lady Emma, I see,' the cook said. 'Best hurry and change, pet, afore Murgatroyd sees yer.'

'Right now, Mrs Turner,' Emma answered and dashed over to a large cupboard.

'And what's this the cat's dragged in?' Mrs Turner asked, her beady black eyes settling on Blackie, hovering near the doorway.

'He's the navvy come ter do the repairs,' Emma shouted from behind the cupboard door. 'I met him on the moors. He was lost.'

'Got a name have yer, lad?' Cook asked, still eyeing him somewhat suspiciously.

'I do indeed, Mrs Turner. Shane O'Neill's me name, but the whole world calls me Blackie. And I'm pleased to meet ye, Cook.'

'So don't stand there gawping like a sucking duck in a storm. Take yer coat and cap off, and come ter the fireplace. Nay, lad, yer looks right nithered. A cup of hot broth is what yer need. And yer, too, Emma. Come on yer ladyship, get a move on.'

'I'm dressed, just about,' Emma called, and a moment later emerged from the big cupboard.

Blackie stood gaping at her, totally surprised by the change

344

in her appearance. She now wore a navy-blue dress like Cook's, a starched white pinafore, and a white cap perched on top of her head. Her hair had been covered in a scarf until a moment ago, and now its gorgeous vivid auburn colour, shot through with gold, was visible. Her hairline came to a widow's peak in the middle of her broad forehead. Her hair was wound into a bun at the back. The effect, in general, was elegant. Her emerald-green eyes shone in the morning light.

Why, she's already a beauty, Blackie thought to himself, filled with amazement. Rousing himself, he went to the cupboard, hung up his jacket, scarf and cap, and joined Emma at the hearth.

Cook brought them both mugs of chicken broth, and they sat down to drink it, whilst warming themselves in front of the flames.

'Is Mrs Wainright coming today?' Emma asked, looking across at Cook, her expression eager.

'Aye, she is, and I'm right thankful for that, I can tell yer. She allus restores order here and gets things on an even keel, keeps things shipshape,' Mrs Turner said, more of an explanation for Blackie than anything else.

Emma looked pleased on hearing this, and then said to Blackie, 'Mrs Turner's husband was in the Royal Navy, and now so is her son. That's why she uses a sailor's words.'

Blackie grinned. 'I like 'em though. Shipshape is my favourite, because I like everything to be neat and tidy.'

Cook nodded in agreement, and then asked Blackie if he would like a bacon buttie before going outside into the cold weather to work.

He exclaimed, 'Faith, and that would be a treat, Cook. I thank ye. 'Tis generous ye are.'

Smiling, Mrs Turner went to the table in the middle of the kitchen and cut slices of freshly baked bread, asking Emma if she wanted a sandwich also. She slathered butter on the slices and added thick strips of bacon.

'Thanks, but I'm not hungry, Cook,' Emma said. 'I'd better get me cleaning stuff together before Murgatroyd comes in looking for me.'

'Aye, do that, lass, he's a bit on the warpath this morning. Got out of bed the wrong side, I 'spect.'

Emma knelt down in front of another cupboard, taking out different products, black lead, small brushes, and dusters, piling them in a bucket.

Mrs Turner said, 'It'll be a bit hard for yer today, luv, what with Polly sick and Mrs Wainright coming. You don't have ter blacklead the grates this morning, but set the fire in the morning room, and dust it too; run the carpet sweeper over the rug. Set the breakfast table like Polly showed you, then come back here to help me with the breakfast. Yer'll have the dining room, the library and Mrs Fairley's upstairs parlour to do after—' Cook broke off when the door burst open, and the butler came rushing in, a grim look on his face.

'Why aren't ye making the fires already?' he shouted at Emma, moving across the room, tripping over her bucket in his haste. After steadying himself against the table, he leaned over her and slapped her face. 'Yer never on time and yer never do owt right.'

Cook instantly put a restraining hand on Blackie's arm, as he jumped up and looked ready to punch Murgatroyd in the face.

Addressing the butler, she said in an icy voice, 'Stop that right now, *Mister* Murgatroyd! And just listen ter me. If I ever see ye so much as breathe on yon lass, I'll have yer guts for garters. And I'll be having a word about yer treatment of her ter some-body who'll make mincemeat out of ye. Not Squire Fairley, but her father. And I don't think yer'd like ter tangle with Big Jack Harte – yer might not be able ter walk ever again when he's finished with yer. Mark my words, Murgatroyd, and don't touch her ever again. And remember, the kitchen is *my* territory, not yours. So don't start being bossy in here.'

Murgatroyd snarled something at her which she didn't quite catch, and then looked at Blackie, his eyes cold and hard. 'You must be O'Neill, the navvy,' he snapped.

'That's me all right,' Blackie responded, walking over to the butler, his expression now neutral. He said, 'Squire Fairley gave me a list of jobs to do, and I have my sack of tools in yon cupboard.'

'Fifteen shillings for the job,' Murgatroyd said. 'Five days' work.'

'Five days, true. But the price is one guinea, *Mister* Murgatroyd,' Blackie replied.

'Fifteen shillings, not a penny more, O'Neill.'

Blackie chuckled as he reached into his jacket pocket and brought out a letter. Opening it, he read, 'One guinea for five days' work, plus board and lodgings at Fairley Hall. This letter is signed by Adam Fairley, the Squire here. If ye don't believe me, go and talk to your boss.' He waved the letter in front of Murgatroyd.

Murgatroyd grunted, and swung around, saying, 'Get yer tools and follow me. The yardman's in the stables. He'll show ye what needs doing and yer room above the stables, where yer'll be sleeping.'

Blackie put on his coat, cap and scarf, and picked up his sack. Turning around, he grinned at Emma and Cook, saluted them and followed Murgatroyd out of the kitchen.

Once they were alone, Emma said, 'He tried ter cheat Blackie.'

'Aye, he did that!' Cook answered in a worried voice. 'Murgatroyd's in a bad mood this morning. Stay out of his way, Emma. And just so yer knows, I shall tell Mrs Wainright that Polly should be sent home. Otherwise, we'll all be getting sick. She's got a really bad cold.'

'I think yer should say summat,' Emma agreed, and picked up her bucket. 'Ta-ta, Mrs Turner. See yer later.'

Mrs Turner nodded and watched her go, sighing under her breath. The girl was clever, intelligent beyond her years, and she was no longer the starveling creature of the moors as she had been three years ago. She had filled out a bit, and her beauty was flowering.

All those years ago, she thought, a long-ago image flickering in her mind. Oh my God, I hope it's not happening again. No, I couldn't bear it. But she'd seen them, whispering in corners, running out in the fields together . . .

There was a knock on the door. Mrs Turner jumped slightly, startled. 'Come in,' she said swiftly, moving towards the door.

A moment later, the door opened and Master Edwin stood there, smiling at her. 'Good morning,' he said.

'Come in, Master Edwin,' Cook responded at once, and instantly realized the table needed setting for breakfast. 'I will have yer breakfast in the dining room in a few minutes, sir.'

'Oh, that's perfectly fine, Cook. I just came to tell you Papa thinks that Polly should be transported to her family in the village. She's not well.'

'I agree, Master Edwin. I will arrange it after breakfast. Now I'll make sure Emma's set the table—'

'Oh, but Emma has set it already, Mrs Turner,' he said, cutting her off. 'I saw her doing it after she had started the fire.' He gave her a faint smile and added, 'I'm the first down this morning. So you do have plenty of time. Also, Papa asked me to tell you Mrs Wainright will arrive in time for tea.'

'Thank ye, Master Edwin. Now is there anything I can make especially for yer breakfast? I've got sausages, bacon, eggs, kidneys, grilled tomatoes . . . oh, and porridge.'

'A wonderful selection as usual, Mrs Turner. I think I'll have scrambled eggs and bacon. Thank you very much.'

'Will ye be waiting for the Squire and Master Gerald, sir?'

'Oh no. Papa told me to start, and I must admit I'm hungry.' He gave her a small smile and left the room.

Mrs Turner watched him leave, always admiring of him, his manners, his politeness, the way he addressed everyone the same way. A perfect gentleman, just like his father. More than she could say about his brother.

Gerald Fairley was a bully, bossy, an ignoramus, and uncouth too. None of the staff liked him, and neither did she. He didn't seem to fit in the family.

As she went out, across the corridor and into the morning room, she smiled with pleasure.

The fire was burning brightly in the grate, and the table was perfectly set. That Emma was a treasure. How she had managed to get all this done so quickly, Cook had no idea. But she did appreciate her help. She's a good girl, God bless, Cook thought, and hurried back to the kitchen.

Her task now was to get the food onto the sideboard as fast as possible. Master Edwin was waiting.

FIFTY-TWO

I t took Blackie only a day or two to understand how Fairley
Hall was run and also to figure out the people who lived
there. It was the longest he'd ever spent in such a grand house.

His favourite by a long shot was Mrs Olivia Wainright. Her
sister, Adele Fairley, was married to the Squire.

Mrs Wainright was a widow, personable, pleasant to deal with,
down-to-earth and practical. As soon as she arrived, she took
control of the household immediately without seeming to do so.
There was a sudden sense of ease, and certainly a feeling of
tranquillity in the air. The Squire, Adam Fairley, seemed a little
distracted in general, but he appeared to appreciate the arrival
of his sister-in-law. He worked hard running the Fairley mill and
the brickyard, and other interests. He appeared kindly enough
to Blackie, and Blackie wondered why Emma hated him so.

Mrs Fairley, thin, dark-haired and haunted-looking, was an
alcoholic. Not that Blackie had ever seen her drinking, but he
had smelled her breath. She reeked of liquor when she came
downstairs, even at noon. Later, in the evening, she seemed
wobbly on her feet.

Their two sons were as different as chalk and cheese. Edwin, the eldest, was a gentleman like his father. He was good-looking and proper in his dress. He was always polite with everyone, including the staff, who loved him.

Blackie had taken a genuine dislike to Gerald, the younger son, instantly. He had wanted to punch him when Gerald was nasty to Emma. He was a bully, and most likely a coward, as all bullies usually were. He had a tendency to be bossy, and he lost his temper a lot, shouting at everyone. It was obvious to Blackie that he was universally disliked in the Hall and in the village as well.

The butler, Murgatroyd, was also a difficult man. He had grown too comfortable in his job, no doubt, and lax in his duties. He had a grumpy expression and a cold voice, and could become enraged about nothing much.

But Blackie did like Cook. Mrs Turner was the salt of the earth and a mine of information. She was easy-going to a certain extent, and always smiling. But he'd seen her put her foot down with Murgatroyd and knew she ruled her territory with an iron hand. Her kitchen was her domain, and everyone was made to realize that. This aside, she was a splendid cook, and that was one good thing about Fairley Hall. He got the impression that the Squire was inclined to neglect household matters – and certainly his wife was incapable of involving herself in running the place; but ever since Mrs Wainright had arrived, her keen interest in all aspects of the Hall's management had had a profound effect. Cook was now buying the best of produce from the local suppliers, and her meals were delicious as a result.

The other thing Blackie admired about Cook was the way she looked after a little boy from the village. He had been recently orphaned, had no surviving family, and Cook had asked her married daughter, Delphinium, to take him in. During the week, he worked at the Hall as the boot boy. He was ten, and bright as a new penny. And of course, Cook made sure Kip, for that was his name, had the best of meals every day.

Very importantly to Blackie, Mrs Turner had confided in him about earlier years at Fairley Hall, and it had intrigued him no end. And so they were friends already.

Over these last few days, he had got on with the work outside and had just this morning been asked by Squire Fairley to stay for a few days longer. The Squire wanted Blackie to look at all the mahogany doors in the interior, because he thought they needed repolishing, new locks and new knobs. Blackie was pleased about this request because the Squire had said he would double the fee if Blackie stayed another five days. Not only that, he would be working inside in the warmth, protected from the cold weather. He could also get to know Emma a bit more. The girl intrigued him. He'd never met anyone quite like her – she was driven, for sure. Perhaps even more than him. She worked like a demon and returned to her home across the moors whenever she could. Mrs Turner said her mother was right poorly.

'Do yer want another mug of tea?' Mrs Turner asked, cutting into Blackie's thoughts.

'Thanks, I don't mind if I do,' he answered. 'Whatever time does Emma finish upstairs?' he now asked, sounding puzzled and frowning. 'I can't believe she's the only maid at the moment. It's brutal the way Murgatroyd makes her work.'

'Aye it is, lad. He's nasty. If I had my way, he'd be sacked. But at least Emma will get a bit more help from now on.'

'Oh yes, how's that?' Blackie asked, an eager expression on his face.

'Mrs Wainright has hired another girl, Annie Stead, from the village. She told the Squire it was ridiculous to expect Emma to do everything. Annie's being trained as an in-between maid.' She chuckled. 'It was me daughter, Delphinium, who recommended her, through me. And I'm right glad.'

'So am I.' He went and took the fresh mug of tea from her, and continued, 'Emma is a good young woman, a hard worker, dutiful, who never complains, sure she is. But she's also very clever, at least so I've noticed, and given half a chance she could go far.'

'I knows that; she took a plan she'd made to Mrs Wainright,' Cook explained. 'I suppose I should call it a *schedule* – it were a "timetable", she called it, for doing the housework in a better way. Mrs Wainright was right impressed, so Emma told me. It was then that Mrs W. found out about Polly being sick.'

'That must be her plan with a capital P, as she called it when she spoke to me.'

Mrs Turner chuckled. 'Aye, it was. She's a right one, that Emma.'

Murgatroyd arrived in the kitchen ten minutes later, carrying the empty dessert plates on a large tray. He took it to the sink, looked at Cook and asked, 'Where's the girl? She can wash these.'

His manner infuriated Mrs Turner.

'Nobody gives orders in my domain, *Mister* Murgatroyd,' Cook said in a stern voice. 'Emma is still finishing upstairs and it's almost two o'clock. She will sit down and eat summat when she finishes the bedrooms. And that's that. It's none of your business.'

'She'll be getting too big for her britches if you spoil her, Mrs Turner.'

Mrs Turner decided it would be wiser to remain silent. It would only bounce onto Emma if she wasn't careful. Moving across the kitchen floor to a small corner, she tapped the silver coffeepot with a spoon, and said, 'You can serve coffee now, Murgatroyd, and I'll see to the washing up.'

When they were alone, Blackie said, in a furious tone, 'I wouldn't mind running into him on a dark night. He wouldn't know what hit him if I got me hands on him.'

'Yer not the first ter say that, lad. Murgatroyd is a lazy bugger, and I think he's run his course here.' Lowering her voice, she said, 'Mrs W. will soon notice he doesn't pull his weight. She is not here for just a few days, yer knows. She's come ter stay, in my opinion.'

'Oh, do ye really think that's true?' Blackie gaped at her. 'How did ye arrive at that conclusion, Cook? Come on, ye can tell me, sure and ye can.'

'The luggage. A lot of it,' Mrs Turner said in a low voice. 'Also, the Squire likes having her here. For company. The missus is . . . three sheets to the wind most of the time,' she whispered the last few words.

'Sure and I know that,' Blackie whispered back, and sat up straighter as Emma walked into the kitchen.

FIFTY-THREE

The minute Blackie set eyes on Emma, he jumped up and rushed across the kitchen. She was carrying two buckets, and he took them from her immediately, worried by her apparent tiredness.

'Let me get you a cup of soup, Emma,' Cook said, also alarmed by the whiteness of the girl's face, the strained expression in her eyes. 'Ye look done in, luv.'

'I'm all right, Cook, and thanks, I will have some soup, please.' Emma smiled at Blackie. 'Thank yer for taking the buckets. One's full of ashes from the fireplaces; the other has my cleaning stuff. Pop them over there, and I'll take care of them later.' She hurried over to the fireplace and stood with her back to it, warming herself. 'It was a bit cold upstairs until I got the fires going in the bedrooms,' she said to Cook.

Joining her near the fireplace, Blackie looked at her keenly, and said, 'Ye are tired, mavourneen. Can't ye take a rest now?'

'She will if I have anything ter do with it!' Cook exclaimed. 'She needs soup and food ter keep her strength up. And how about you, lad? Yer must be starving by now.'

355

'I wouldn't say no to a bit of your fine grub, Mrs Turner,' Blackie replied, and then led Emma to a chair in the corner where they always sat at a small table.

Happy to see that a little colour was coming back into Emma's pale cheeks, Cook bustled around, ladling soup into two bowls and cutting thick slices of newly baked bread.

She took a tray out and put everything on it, and went to the table in the corner. 'When yer've had the soup, I will give you both helpings of my mutton pie. It's nice and light, but nourishing. How does that sound ter yer, Emma?'

'Thank yer, Mrs Turner.' She laughed. 'For once I feel quite hungry.'

'Glad ter hear that, luvey.' Cook sailed across the kitchen and opened the oven door. There was still a second mutton pie inside, left over from the family's lunch. It was warm; she could serve it now.

At that moment, Murgatroyd came into the kitchen and glanced around. Clearing his throat, he addressed Cook. 'Mrs Wainright's hired a young girl from the village ter come and work here. Did ye know that?' He sounded angry, and there was a nasty expression in his eyes.

'She mentioned it in passing,' Cook answered, closing the oven door with a bang, not happy to see him.

'We don't need 'er, waste of money—'

'It's not yer money, Murgatroyd, so yer don't have to worry about it,' Mrs Turner interjected, glaring at him. 'And I'd watch yer step. Mrs W.'s a very practical woman, knows the world, and she was right put out, that she was, when she discovered the house was short on help. Right *mad*, if yer wants my opinion. I wouldn't try *her* patience, oh no, not at all.'

'The Squire runs this house. It's what he says that goes.'

'No, it's not. He defers to Mrs W. That's why he brought her here.'

'Mebbe for other reasons as well,' Murgatroyd muttered, a malevolent look in his eyes.

'What did yer say?' Mrs Turner snapped, rounding on him. 'Shut yer gob right now, mister, or I'll make sure yer don't work here after today.'

He laughed at her, and then glanced at Emma eating with Blackie. 'She should be working, not stuffing her gob—'

'Murgatroyd, I give you one second to shut up. And leave my domain. And I warn yer, if yer attempt ter make any trouble I *will* go ter the Squire. I've worked here for thirty years, since I was a girl, and Squire Fairley *listens ter me. And he'll take my advice.* Understood? So don't try ter play top dog with me. It won't get yer anywhere except outside on yer backside.'

Swinging around, Murgatroyd stomped out, banging the kitchen door behind him so hard the copper pots on the rail rattled.

'Good riddance ter bad rubbish,' Mrs Turner said, and took the pie out of the oven. As she carried it over to the big table, she remembered Kip. She hadn't seen the boot boy for quite a while. Now where was he?

Looking over at Blackie, she said, 'Can yer nip downstairs ter the top basement? I haven't seen young Kip for a bit. He must be hungry by now. Bring him to the kitchen, please?'

'Right away,' Blackie answered and jumped up. 'Back in a minute, Cook.'

Emma said, 'Kip's such a nice little boy, but why doesn't he live with Delphinium all the time?'

'She teaches at the little kindergarten in the village, and she also does a lot of sewing for the ladies in this area. Busy she is. But she has him at weekends.' Dropping her voice, Cook said, 'And the Squire gives him money for cleaning all the riding boots and shoes. Right kind, that's Adam Fairley. Allus helping others less privileged.'

'I see,' Emma murmured, her voice flat, and then smiled warmly at Kip as he walked in holding Blackie's hand. The blond boy grinned at her; they liked each other.

'There yer are, Kip. Whyever didn't yer come up ter eat something before, my lad?' Cook asked, her voice warm.

'I wanted ter finish the boots. And I just have. And here I am,' Kip answered.

Mrs Turner laughed, and said, 'Go to the sink and wash yer hands. Then come and sit by me. I've got a big bowl of soup on the ready for yer.'

'Thank yer, Cook,' Kip said and ran over to the sink.

Blackie leaned closer to Cook, and asked, 'What happened to his parents, his family?'

'His father was in the army and was killed in the Boer War. His mother died, a while ago, of rheumatic fever. Young she was, too. No brothers or sisters, no grandparents, so I took him in. He lives with me daughter at weekends.'

'And he's here during the week? In the servants' quarters, I suppose.'

'That's right, Blackie. And just so yer know, he's in the room next ter me. Emma on the other side of him. And with Squire Fairley's permission.'

'Ye are a good woman, Mrs Turner.' Blackie squeezed her arm. 'And a brilliant cook . . .' Blackie stopped talking when Kip came back to the big oak table in the centre of the room.

After a week at Fairley Hall, Blackie had come to understand all the occupants of the house. Except for Emma Harte. In certain ways, she was an enigma to him, although he liked her very much.

Now, as he lay in the bed in the attic, musing about his time here, he decided she might always be a bit of a mystery to him.

She was like a chameleon, instantly changing right before his eyes. One moment swinging on a gate, filled with girlish laughter, the next serious and quiet as she went about her work in the house.

He realized she was always cautious, wary and careful when she was working, and kept herself very much to herself during the day. They ate their dinner together at two o'clock, and then later they had a snack in the evening, after the family had been served supper. And this was when they chatted.

She had confided in him about her worries, particularly her mother's failing health and her brother's dream of going off to join the Royal Navy. She was friendly, bright, and very frequently made him laugh with her pithy comments and sarcasm at times. She laughed with him; they enjoyed each other's company.

Earlier this evening she had told him she would miss him, and seemed sad that he would be leaving in a couple of days. And then she had brought up the idea of perhaps coming to Leeds one day.

He worried about how a girl like her, from the country, would cope in the city, would find work that wasn't soul-destroying or dangerous. But he had reassured her that he would be there for her, if she ever made that journey. And this had pleased her.

His thoughts turned to Lord Robert Lassiter and the guesthouse, the work he would be back doing next week. Quite suddenly he realized he was excited about working on the new building once again, completing the guesthouse. It was his big chance. He hoped that if it went well his lordship's patronage might extend to more projects.

Then Laura was there in his head. He would soon be seeing her, and the thought of her gentle kindness sent a wave of warmth rushing through him. She was so special to him. Shy at times and reserved, she was a sweet friend.

And yet so was Emma unique and, in many ways, she had

captivated him. Her beauty seemed to become more vivid and vital every day. Certainly, her emerald eyes were stamped on his brain. He knew he would never forget that look of pure hatred in them when she spoke of the Fairleys, or the laughter sparkling there when she was happy, and the genuine sorrow when she spoke of her mother. Once, a long time ago, Aunt Eileen had told him that the eyes were the mirror of the soul, and he believed that. And most especially, it was true of Emma's eyes, because they were so expressive, so large and so green. Like the sea around Ireland, he thought, as he blew out the candle on the small table near the bed.

He pulled the blankets up around his shoulders, settling down for the night. He was wondering how he could be so drawn to two women at the same time. He had no answer, and within minutes, he had fallen asleep, tired out from a hard day's work.

PART FIVE

Other People's Lives
Yorkshire
1905–6

FIFTY-FOUR

'Here we are then, lass,' the tinker said, bringing his horse and cart to a stop. 'There it is, The Mucky Duck.'

Emma looked at the sign hanging outside the public house, and said, 'But it says The Black Swan.'

The tinker and his wife laughed, and he said, 'It's a local joke, luv. Don't yer get it? Just another play on't name.'

'Oh, yes, I see,' Emma replied. 'Thank you both for giving me a lift to Leeds. It was so very kind of you.' She enunciated her words carefully, copying the way Olivia Wainright spoke. She had been practising for months, wanting to improve her speech.

After carefully getting down from the cart, she took hold of her suitcase, which the tinker had lowered to the ground. Smiling up at them, she said again, 'Thank you very much,' and waved her hand.

The tinker's wife gave a little wave back and said, 'A beautiful young lady like yer will find Leeds a good place ter be.'

The tinker nodded, grinned, and flicked the reins, and the two horses started to move away from the pub, their hooves clattering against the cobblestones.

Emma stepped onto the pavement and went into the pub, and hesitated. One door said Saloon Bar; another Tap Room; and the third said The Snug. Deciding the right one must be the bar, she pushed the door open and went inside.

It was bright inside, and she could hear someone humming, yet obviously out of sight, because the bar was empty. Then she noticed a blonde head reflected in the mirror behind the bar.

As she walked closer, she called out, 'Hello! Hello! Is there anyone here?'

By the time she reached the bar itself, the blonde head had become a pretty face as the woman had stood up. 'Good day ter ye, miss. What can I get ye?'

'Oh nothing, thank you. I am looking for a person, not a drink.'

'And who're yer lookin' for then?'

'Miss Rosie. Do you know her? It's important I find her. Very important.'

'Yer have, luv. I'm Rosie. The one and only. And why are yer seeking me out? I don't know yer, do I?'

'Oh Miss Rosie, I'm so pleased I found you,' Emma gushed, the Wainright voice intact. 'It was Blackie O'Neill who told me to come here, because you would know where he was. And I do need to find him today.'

'Oh, luvey, yer've just missed him, and only by a few days. He's gone to Liverpool, to take the boat to Ireland. I'm sorry.'

Emma couldn't help it, her face fell, and she could not speak for a moment. She was shocked. It had never occurred to her that Blackie would not be here. He'd come back to the Hall in early April 1905, bringing her a beautiful green brooch – 'the colour of your emerald eyes, sure and it is' – as a present. It had been on that same day, which had started so wonderfully and ended so terribly, that Frank had run to the Hall to fetch Emma to her mother's deathbed; the day her mother had finally been released from all her suffering and returned to the moors she so loved; back to the Top of the World.

Now, all Emma could think of was that she was in a huge city she didn't know, and without a friend or even an acquaintance in sight. And nowhere to go.

Looking at her intently, Rosie, wise to the ways of the world and those who occupied it, knew this young woman was upset. In fact, she had a stricken expression in the most beautiful eyes she had ever seen. Very green, truly emerald eyes. And a pretty face and posh clothes. What had that Blackie boy been up to? Certainly he wouldn't have been able to resist this lovely. She was no doubt irresistible to men, with that face and figure.

Rosie finally said, 'Summat about going to see an old priest who was very badly, mebbe dying.'

'Oh no!' Emma cried out before she could stop herself, clutching the edge of the bar. Her heart sank. Whatever was she going to do? The possibility that Blackie would be away had never occurred to her. She was so shaken she found it difficult to speak.

'What about Blackie's Uncle Pat? Could I go and see him and find out when Blackie is returning? He is, isn't he?'

'Oh yes, luv, but it won't do yer any good going ter see Pat. He's away in Doncaster on a right big building job.'

The girl was obviously troubled.

'Nay, luv, don't get upset about it. Mebbe I can help yer in some way. What do yer need? And what's yer name?' Rosie asked, leaning on the bar.

'Oh goodness, how rude I've been, Miss Rosie. My name is Emma, Mrs Emma Harte.' She stretched out her right hand and offered it to the barmaid. Rosie took it, and said, 'Pleased ter meet yer, and I like yer crocheted gloves.'

'Thank you, Miss Rosie, and I need a place to stay, lodgings, or a boarding house. And I don't know Leeds at all or anyone here.'

'First, let's drop this Miss Rosie stuff. Everyone calls me Rosie.' Rosie eyed her shrewdly, her mind ticking. There was no way Mrs Harte could stay round here. 'And secondly, I have just the right place for yer to stay. It's some streets away, but not too far away if yer needs me. Mrs Daniel has a respectable boarding house, and she'll tek yer in. I knows that.'

'I do hope so. Where is her house, actually?' Emma was surprised she had used that word, *actually*, a favourite of Mrs Wainright's. And then a small smile flickered; she was pleased with herself and the way she was speaking.

Rosie said, 'I'll write her address on a bit of paper. But yer'll find it easily. Walk ter the end of this road, cross the side street and keep going for nine more side streets. Her house is number five. Yer can't miss it because it is a tall house, with a brass knocker, and it has white lace curtains.'

'Thank you, Rosie, for being so helpful. I'll come and see you again.'

'Yer'd better do that,' Rosie answered and smiled. 'And the minute Blackie O'Neill walks in here, I'll tell him where yer living.'

Emma found Mrs Daniel's house at last. It was narrow, wedged between others, its Victorian walls blackened by factory soot, but there were indeed crisp lace curtains and a gleaming brass knocker on the door. She lifted it, then dropped it.

A moment later the door was jerked open, and a thin, grey-haired woman was staring at her. 'Trying to break the door down, are yer? And what do yer want?'

'I'm so sorry. It did make a rather loud bang,' Emma said, sounding apologetic. 'I hadn't realized it was so heavy.' She offered her biggest smile and went on, 'I'm looking for Mrs Daniel.'

'I'm Mrs Daniel. What's yer name?'

'Emma Harte.'

'Why are yer on me front step, miss?'

'I was told by Miss Rosie at The Black Swan that you run a lodging house, let rooms.'

'Not to women I don't. Women create problems. I only take in gentlemen lodgers. Yes, single women are a nuisance and—'

'I'm not single, Mrs Daniel,' Emma said, interrupting her. 'I'm *Mrs* Harte.'

'Oh aye,' Mrs Daniel answered pithily. 'And where's the mister then?'

Emma had a well-prepared story she had created for herself, and she launched into it in a pleasant tone.

'My dearest husband, Winston Harte, is in the Royal Navy, and at this moment he is sailing in his ship on the high seas. He will be gone for six months. I have moved to Leeds in order to work, and I shall be looking for a permanent home for us. And I need to rent a room, Mrs Daniel, if you will agree to that, please.'

Whilst Emma had been speaking, Mrs Daniel had been weighing her up, scrutinizing her intently. And she had noticed the quality of the young woman's clothes. The black dress was of fine black satin, a little dated, but in good shape. Her cream bonnet was definitely real Leghorn straw and the flowers decorating it were made of silk. Gertrude Daniel thought the crocheted gloves were a nice addition.

She's quality, the landlady decided, and posh. Her speaking, her voice, the ways she said things denoted upper class. There was something about Mrs Harte that unexpectedly captivated

Mrs Daniel. She found herself saying, 'Well, yer'd better come in, Mrs Harte. Better to do business inside and not on the front steps, where all the neighbours can see us.'

Gertrude Daniel opened the front door wider, and Emma, holding the suitcase in one hand and her reticule in the other, stepped inside.

Glancing around, Emma was overwhelmed by the decoration in the sitting room. A pure shrine to the style of the late Queen Victoria, with black horsehair sofas and chairs, what-nots and small tables here and there, and a plethora of potted aspidistras in brass pots. The copies of famous paintings were horrid, hung on walls covered with bright red flocked-velvet wallpaper.

Swallowing her distaste, Emma exclaimed, 'Oh, what a handsome room, Mrs Daniel. You do have a flair for decorating.'

Mrs Daniel stared at her. 'Why, thank you very much, Mrs Harte.' Her face softened and Emma seized the opportunity to open her bag.

'Mrs Daniel, won't you rent me a room, please? I would pay in advance.'

'Since yer've nowhere else to go at the moment, I'll show it ter yer. Mind yer, it can only be for a few weeks,' Mrs Daniel said. 'I'll take yer up ter the attic. It's small, mind, but clean.' She motioned for Emma to follow her.

FIFTY-FIVE

The attic room was a bit bigger than Emma had expected, and neat, as Mrs Daniel had said it was.

Emma was relieved to see that while it had not an ounce of Victorian bric-à-brac, it appeared spotlessly clean. There was a single bed, with a darned, well-worn cream chenille quilt, a washstand under the tiny window in the eaves, a chest, a chair and a small round table. The walls and sloping eaves were covered in faded wallpaper, patterned with small bunches of forget-me-nots.

'Here's a nice big wardrobe,' Mrs Daniel said, glancing at Emma, opening a door. 'Come over 'ere and look.'

Emma did as she asked, and looked into the cupboard at Mrs Daniel's urging. Again, she was pleasantly surprised. There were hooks, a rail holding coat hangers, and several shelves. Plenty of space for her treasured clothes.

Turning, Emma gave her new landlady the benefit of a huge smile. 'It's perfect for me, and so tastefully done, Mrs Daniel. Just what I've been looking for. Thank you for allowing me to rent from you.'

'Now, the rent is three shillings a week, and I don't provide meals.' Clearing her throat, she found herself adding, 'But yer can use the kitchen.' This last comment surprised her more than it did Emma.

'Thank you, Mrs Daniel.' Opening her reticule, Emma took out a purse and counted twelve shillings, placed them on a nearby table. 'A month in advance, Mrs Daniel. And thank you very much for renting to me.'

Unsure that she wanted this girl in her home for a month, Mrs Daniel looked at the money on the table. Flustered, she said, 'I'll go and get yer case, bring it up.'

'Oh no, I can do it,' Emma said, taking a step forward.

'Nay, lass, I don't think yer strong enough. I'm used ter hauling up the gentlemen's cases. Back in a tick.' And she disappeared through the door.

Emma, still clutching her reticule, now put it on the table. She loved the black leather bag with the tortoiseshell frame. Olivia Wainright had given it to her. Also, it contained all the money she had in the world and bits of jewellery, once her mother's treasured pieces.

She sat down on the bed. She was happy the mattress was comfortable. Quite unexpectedly, she felt safer now, more secure because she had a roof over her head, and a list of places to find work, written out for her by Rosie. Tomorrow she would go in search of a job in the streets the barmaid had suggested.

Mrs Daniel reappeared in the attic with Emma's suitcase, heaving it in and dumping it near the door.

'Bit heavier than I expected,' Mrs Daniel explained, out of breath and flushed. 'Don't think I've ever lifted a real leather case afore. Only imitation. This is the genuine thing, it weighs a ton, I don't mind tellin' yer.'

'I know,' Emma replied. 'Thank you so much for bringing it up.'

'It must be yer father's,' Mrs Daniel said, eyeing the case again.

Emma seized on this, and said, 'It is, yes.'

'Is he still alive? Or did yer inherit it?'

Emma, cautious, wary, suspicious and self-protective, did not answer at once. As was her clever way, she weighed the odds. If she said he was dead, it left her vulnerable to a certain kind of person. If she implied he was alive, it might encourage too many questions.

Mrs Daniel exclaimed, 'Oh dear, ye must think I'm a nosy parker—'

'No, no, I don't!' Emma exclaimed, grabbing the moment. 'My father lent it to me.'

'Oh, I'm glad yer dad's alive, Mrs Harte. So, where does he live then?'

Caught unawares, Emma hesitated, but only for a split second, and said, 'Harrogate. He lives in Harrogate. With my aunt and her family.'

'That's a real posh place,' Mrs Daniel announced in an awed tone, inwardly congratulating herself. She had been right in her assessment of Mrs Harte, in believing she was quality. *Of course*, she came from Harrogate. It was written all over her. The clothes, the black leather reticule, the bonnet, and the suitcase. All spelled money. Old money, at that. She could tell that from the young woman's voice and her manners. In fact, it was obvious she was to the manor born. Very upper class, maybe even gentry.

Mrs Daniel walked towards the door, but before leaving she said, 'I'll bring yer a jug of water and a glass.'

'Oh but I—'

'Back in three shakes of a lamb's tail,' the older woman answered as she went out.

Emma sat back on the bed and sighed, a feeling of tiredness creeping through her bones. It had been such a long day. She wasn't sure if she had the strength to unpack, although she was aware she must. Her clothes needed to be hung up, the chest filled.

True to her word, Mrs Daniel was back in the attic in a few minutes, carrying a tray. 'Here I am, Mrs Harte. I've brought yer a cuppa, and a right nice ginger biscuit I made meself. I thought yer looked a bit pinched, yer face drawn. Tea'll pick yer up. And there's water as well.'

'Oh, how very kind of you, Mrs Daniel.' Emma stood up and went over to the table, touched by the thoughtfulness of this woman, who had endeavoured to send her running from the front steps. Charm does it all the time, Emma thought, remembering Mrs Wainright's words. So many lessons from that lovely compassionate woman, and how eternally grateful she was to her. She was also glad she had bothered to listen, asked questions, and learned.

Emma sat for a long time, eyeing the suitcase from time to time, and relaxing. The tea and ginger biscuit had refreshed her, and some of her strength was coming back. It really had been a long day: up at dawn, leaving Fairley, hitching a ride to Shipley on a farm cart full of produce and then doing the same thing with the tinker and his wife who were going to Leeds. She considered herself lucky to have found these lifts.

Her mind flew back to the events of the summer. The love-making in the cave and the all too predictable consequence; Edwin's abject cowardice when confronted with the news that Emma was expecting their baby.

Edwin Fairley had put the suitcase in her room with five pounds in it. As she had done when she had first seen the money, she now smiled somewhat ironically. All the money he had in the world, he had told her. How surprising that she was richer than him. Over the years she had managed to save fifteen pounds.

Money. That was the key to everything. She intended to make a lot of it. To become a woman of substance. Then she would have control, power, the ability to protect her unborn child and herself. That was her aim. Safety, security, *and* independence.

Better unpack and put the money in the suitcase, she decided. She went to the table. Opening her handbag, she took out the money wrapped in paper, and put it under the pillow on the bed.

Pushing her hand down the front of her dress, she found the ribbon around her neck and pulled it out. The key to the suitcase was attached to the middle of it.

Once she had taken out her clothes, all altered hand-me-downs from Mrs Wainright, and hung them up, she filled the chest with her underclothes and other small possessions. Then she put the money in the case and locked it. She put the ribbon around her neck and tucked it inside the bodice of her frock.

Feeling a little exerted, she went to lie on the bed, but was partially upright with the pillows behind her head.

The suitcase was in view once more. She would throw it away once she had enough money to buy one of her own.

There Edwin had stood, in the rose garden at Fairley Hall, looking for all the world like a grown man in his suit and fancy silk tie, all set to go to Cambridge University. But he was just a boy, and a weak boy at that. He had crumbled, become frightened when she had told him she was pregnant. He exclaimed it was a catastrophe, that his father would be in a rage, and would kill him.

She remembered her swift retort, 'Mine will, if yours doesn't,' and she had reeled slightly, as disappointment, apprehension and fear for her future rushed through her. Looking back only a few days, she recalled leaning against a garden seat, wanting to sit down, her legs weak. But she didn't. Never display weakness, never show fear, she thought. That became her motto for the rest of her life.

As she had watched Edwin dithering and continuing to rail on about his father disowning him, she had suddenly realized she was filled with hurt and grief, and she was trembling.

Suddenly, he had pulled himself together and had asked in a slightly calmer tone, 'What will you do?'

Instantly furious, she had shouted, 'Don't you mean *we*?' He had gazed at her dumbly, remained silent, and had then suggested he would help her find a doctor, the kind that could get rid of an unwanted baby. And he would sell his watch to pay for the operation.

Her fury knew no bounds, and her grief turned to hatred as she accused him of betrayal, of being willing to put her in the hands of a quack, who might butcher her to death. 'You're to blame for this as much as I am,' she had shrilled, drawing herself to her full height.

She had known she had to get out of the rose garden at that moment; the sweet scent of the flowers filled her with nausea, overwhelmed her.

Moving away from the garden seat, she had stared at him, and said in a chilling tone, 'I will never set eyes on you again, Edwin Fairley. Never, as long as I live.' And as she had walked away, gone out of the rose garden, her heart had hardened, had turned to stone.

She had heard him calling her name, begging her to come back, but she had paid no attention and walked on with dignity.

Although she had no way of knowing it, a terrible feeling of hollowness had settled inside Edwin Fairley. And neither did he know, at seventeen years old, that this wretched hollowness would stay with him always, until the day he died. In denying Emma, leaving her to her fate, Edwin Fairley had ruined his life, for he never stopped loving her, forever filled with genuine regret. Even his last words to his grandson would be for Emma.

Suddenly pushing thoughts of the last few days away from herself, Emma got off the bed, took the suitcase and put it deep inside the wardrobe, where it was hardly visible. Pushing it behind the clothes, she said under her breath, 'I will ruin the Fairleys, do whatever it takes to destroy them, to have my revenge.' Her green eyes were glittering with icy hatred.

FIFTY-SIX

Every morning Emma went out early. Her plan for each day was to visit the arcades and hopefully find a job in one of the ladies' clothes shops.

Her eyes widened in delight as she stared in at gleaming plate-glass windows, fascinated by the beautiful dresses, coats and two-piece suits. The hat shops held her interest for some time, as did the windows where jewellery was displayed.

Often, she went into a shop she liked the look of, asking if they could hire her. Inevitably, the answer was always the same: no vacancies right now.

At the end of the week, Emma began to feel despairing. She made her way to Leeds Market. Rosie had told her to go there, had added that the market was worth a walk-through anyway. Lots of goods available.

Feeling intrigued, she wandered through all the food stalls, and then headed for the other side of Leeds Market, marvelling at its size and the fact that it also sold clothes, shirts, underwear, shoes, hats, bicycles, china, linen, leather goods – almost every-thing under the sun. It had high stone walls around the huge space, and a high-flung glass roof. Shopping could continue six days a week, even if it rained.

Her thoughts turned to Blackie. He had been the person who told her that Leeds held all kinds of shops and opportunities. She wondered how he would greet the news of her coming to the city. He had told her it was no place for a young girl. But she had had no choice.

One stall suddenly caught her eye, and she came to an abrupt stop. Many small items of clothing were displayed on the stall. But it was the sign that was most significant to her. It read: *Don't ask the price, it's a penny!*

How clever, Emma thought, as she studied everything. A way to pull in customers at once. She glanced at the name above the stall – Marks and Spencer – and made a mental note of that catchy line. She also reminded herself never to fill a window with too many items. It looked too muddled, was distracting to the shopper.

When I have a shop, I'll put just a few things in the window . . . The thought slipped away and she stood perfectly still, startled. *When I have a shop*, she murmured to herself wonderingly, and then a small smile flickered on her mouth. Of course, that was *it*. She was going to be a shopkeeper, go into retail. TRADE. The word loomed large and so did her future. She loved clothes and was adept at sewing, alterations and even designing. She had sketched many a gown for Olivia Wainright and had made blouses for her.

It had turned two o'clock, and the moment Emma saw the fishman's stand she hurried over to it. She was desperate to save every penny, but she had to eat. After eating a plate of winkles and mussels covered in vinegar, she felt better. These days she craved spicy food, and put vinegar on almost everything, and pepper as well.

Back outside she set off towards North Street. There were

many tailoring factories in that area, and one of the girls from a dress shop she'd enquired in had suggested she might find a job in one of them, especially the smaller tailoring shops.

It was a boiling hot day, the heat rising from the dusty pavements in waves. Tram cars rumbled past, fine carriages carrying the gentry, carts with produce all filled the streets. Prosperity, that sense of self-help and independence, non-conformity, hard-headed Yorkshire shrewdness and industriousness were endemic. The rhythm and power of the city only served to buttress these very same characteristics so intrinsic in her. She was, without knowing it, the very embodiment of Leeds.

Emma opened the collar of her good cotton dress and fanned her face. She just needed enough money to support herself until the baby was born. After that she would work night and day if necessary, to get the money for the first shop. I'm going to have a shop. I'm going to have a shop . . . that thought rolled around in her head as she tramped the streets to York Road, where North Street was located. A lovely trickle of triumph made her stand up straighter, her head held high.

After walking around North Street and going into three different tailoring shops, Emma was ready to drop. She decided she had done enough for one day. She would go home to her attic. She had a heel of bread and some dripping for her supper. An early night would do her good. She would start again tomorrow.

Emma suddenly glanced around, as she heard shouting and running feet. A stone hit her shoulder. Great yelps and ugly words filled the air, and she was startled.

Turning a corner, she was horrified to see an older man hunched against a wall, covering his head with his arms.

He was protecting himself from two young ruffians, who were

throwing stones at him and shouting nasty things, swearing at him angrily.

Filled with sudden fury, Emma ran towards them, shouting, 'Stop that! Stop it! I shall fetch a bobby and he'll arrest you at once. Stop it, I say!'

The boys looked at her, laughed in her face and continued to hound the man, hurling stones unrelentingly.

Emma picked up two stones and, running closer to the ruffians, she threw a stone at one of them which hit its mark. She then pitched the other at the taller boy. It struck him between the shoulder blades and made him cry out in pain.

Again Emma raised her voice, 'There are more stones I can throw at you. Stop it, both of you. Get going!'

Without giving a thought to herself or the baby she was carrying, Emma ran across to the man, still hunched against the wall. Before speaking to him, she swung around and shook her fist at them.

'I mean it. I'll fetch the police!' She moved forward. 'I'm going right now if you don't leave,' she added in a threatening voice.

Obviously, she had been effective. They dropped the stones they were holding and slunk away, their tails between their legs, looking like the cowards she knew they were. Bullies, each one of them.

Emma now bent down and touched the man's shoulder. 'I will help you. Have they hurt you?' She then noticed the bruises on his cheek and forehead, and pushed down her anger at the hooligans. Good riddance to bad rubbish, she thought.

'I think I am all right,' the man finally said, lowering his arms. 'It is only a scratch or two, I believe.'

'Let me help you up,' Emma said, and managed to get him to his feet. He leaned against the wall, and said, 'Thank you, young lady, for coming to my aid. I am grateful.'

'I'm glad I was nearby,' she answered, and noticed the man

was looking down at the pavement. 'I seem to have lost my spectacles,' he muttered, sounding anxious.

'Oh, I see them.' Emma went and picked them up. She also noticed a brown paper bag with things in it and what looked like a twisted loaf of bread. She picked it up, saw some dirt on the loaf, blew on it and dusted it with her hands. Then she put it in the brown bag and fastened the bag tightly by rolling down the top.

The man had found his small black skull cap which he put on the back of his head. He smiled at her as he accepted his spectacles and the bag. He inclined his head and thanked her yet again.

He began to move, and said quietly, 'I must be going . . . home.'

'Goodbye,' Emma said, and then ran to him as he staggered and almost fell. He propped himself against the wall of the building.

Emma realized he was not well at all, out of breath and trembling. 'I will walk with you some of the way,' she insisted, ignoring his protests.

They had not been walking very long, when Emma, filled with a mixture of anger about the cruel and brutal boys and her intense curiosity, asked, 'Why were those horrible lads throwing stones at you? They could have really hurt you.'

There was a moment or two of silence before the middle-aged man spoke up. He said, in a quiet tone, 'Because I am a Jew.'

Emma said swiftly, 'Oh, I see.' But she didn't; she was mystified, at a loss. What was a Jew? And why would being a Jew incite such violence?

The man, intelligent and discerning, immediately knew she had no idea what he was talking about.

He glanced at her, took in the well-groomed auburn hair, the black dress, made of cotton but nicely cut, and her air of quality. And of course, there was her self-confidence, courage and compassion to be taken into consideration, all displayed when she had rushed at the hooligans, waving her fist and shouting at them. She had not displayed an ounce of fear and had shown she was in command of the situation. He decided he must explain who he was in more detail, explain Judaism.

He said, 'You are not from Leeds, I do believe. You are from the rural area, aren't you, miss?'

Emma answered at once. 'I am from Ripon.'

'Ah, yes, well, that does indeed explain it.'

'Explains *what*?' Emma asked carefully, regarding him with quizzical eyes.

'That you do not know that there are many, many Jews like me in Leeds, a whole population, mostly living in the Leylands area. And I do believe you don't know exactly what a Jew is. Am I not correct, young lady?'

Although Emma always wanted to appear well-educated and filled with knowledge, she had no choice but to tell the truth. Clearing her throat, she replied, 'I don't really understand, actually. Won't you tell me, please? I like to learn about many things, sir.' She felt slightly embarrassed, having shown her ignorance, always wanting to appear well-informed and cleverer than most.

The man began to speak in a soft, gentle voice. 'The Jews are a people descended from the Hebrews and the Israelites, from the tribes of Israel, in fact. Our religion is called Judaism. It was founded on both the Old Testament and the Torah.'

Emma was listening, giving him all her attention. The man noticed this, beheld the quickening interest in her eyes, the intelligence written all over her face. He also knew she harboured a sympathetic attitude, which she had proved by her actions.

Taking a deep breath, he asked, 'Have you read the Book of Exodus? Do you know the Ten Commandments?'

'Yes, some of it.'

The man continued. 'The Ten Commandments were given to our people by Moses when he led us out of Egypt and created the Jewish nation. Christianity itself is based on Judaism. Did you know that?' He peered at her intently.

'No, I didn't,' Emma answered, knowing she must be truthful with him.

'Jesus Christ was a Jew, and think how Jesus was persecuted.' The man sighed and his black eyes appeared to be full of sorrow. 'I suppose we Jews appear to be strange to some. That is because of our dietary laws, customs and forms of worship. We are not the same as Gentiles; our ways are a little different.' He paused, shook his head, and added, 'But I do believe we are not so very different when you stop to think about it. We are all human beings.'

Emma gave him a swift look. 'So you come from the land of the Jews, sir?' she said, realizing he had a slight accent that echoed in his speech.

'No. You see, the Jews scattered throughout the world over the passing centuries. They went to Spain, France, Germany, Russia and Poland, plus many other countries. I came from Kiev, in Russia, running away from the pogroms which were directed against the Jews, and our own harassment. It is good to be in England where we have freedom. I always say, every day, "God bless England, the land of the free" . . .' He broke off, staggered and leaned against a wall, looking stricken.

'Sir, you are ill!' Emma cried. 'I should get you home.'

The man caught his breath, sighed and stood stock still. After a moment or two, he seemed to regain his composure, but the eagle-eyed Emma, who never missed a trick, saw that his face was white and covered in perspiration. He looked drained. Her green eyes narrowed when she noticed the blue tinge to his lips. He was obviously in discomfort. He held his hand to his chest. She wondered if he had had a heart attack.

Now deciding to really take charge, Emma went to him and took hold of his arm tighter. 'I am taking you home,' she announced somewhat forcefully.

'You've already done enough for me. Please, I am all right. I can manage,' he murmured.

Ignoring these words, she said in a firm voice, 'Where do you live?'

'Imperial Street.' A small smile flickered on his tightly drawn face. 'An unfortunate name really for that poor little street, not a bit royal at all.'

'Where is it?' she asked, starting to lead him away purposefully, definitely now in charge.

'In the Leylands, I'm afraid.'

Emma shivered on hearing this name, and her heart sank. She had been told it was dangerous, the ghetto. However, she swallowed her fears and put on a brave face.

They continued to walk together, totally silent. After a short while, the man stopped and turned to face her. He said in a warm and grateful voice, 'I've never known such kindness from a stranger, least of all a Gentile. I thank you for being so solicitous, thoughtful and kind.' He thrust out one hand. 'My name is Abraham Kallinski. Would you do me the honour of telling me yours?'

Emma took his hand. 'It's Emma Harte.'

He noticed the silver ring on her left hand. 'Mrs Harte, I assume.'

Emma nodded, but did not say anything else. As usual, she kept silent, following her own rule: the less people knew about you, the safer you were. Like the north-country adage, 'A still tongue and a wise head.' Little did Emma know that meeting

383

Abraham Kallinski on this hot summer Friday afternoon would prove to be her lucky day indeed. Almost immediately, her life would change for the better, her feet on the path to the success she craved.

FIFTY-SEVEN

'Please, do come inside for a moment,' Abraham Kallinski begged. 'I want my wife to meet you. She will wish to thank you for coming so promptly to my rescue.' They had stopped in front of a terraced house at the end of Imperial Street, well-kept with wooden shutters and starched lace curtains. Abraham Kallinski's face had relaxed, joy in his eyes at reaching his home.

'I really think I must get back, time is passing. I don't like to walk home in the dark, not in these parts,' Emma explained, being absolutely truthful.

'Just one second, and you can be on your way,' Mr Kallinski said, then thought to add, 'My two sons come home around this time of day. They will escort you to your home.'

Against her better judgement, but understanding *she* could make it only a minute at the most, Emma agreed to his request. She was terribly thirsty.

As Abraham Kallinski led her into the house, Emma experienced a feeling of welcome, kindness and peace.

They entered the main room, which was large and

comfortable, an all-purpose room. The air was filled with delicious smells of food cooking.

Janessa Kallinski swung around at the sound of Abraham returning. She was tall, with jet-black hair and large pale blue eyes below dark brows. The welcoming smile on her face slipped, to be replaced by one of concern. She hurried to her husband, exclaiming, 'What has happened to you, Abraham? Your clothes are dirty and you have bruises on your face. Are you hurt?'

'It was nothing, really. I fell down and two hooligans threw stones at me, you know what that sort are like. It was Mrs Harte who came to rescue me. She frightened the boys so much they ran away. And then she kindly helped me to come home.'

Janessa swung around and took hold of Emma's hands, thanked her profusely, then said, 'Sit down in this chair, Mrs Harte. You look tired and hot. Let me get you some refreshment.'

'Thank you,' Emma answered and sat down with some relief. She did feel exhausted and thirsty. 'Could I have a glass of water, please, Mrs Kallinski?'

'But of course.'

Emma relaxed in the chair, as Mr Kallinski came over to her and said, 'Excuse me. I must go and tidy myself up.'

'I understand,' she said, smiling at him. A moment later Mrs Kallinski brought her a glass of water, which Emma drank immediately. She then settled back in the chair once more, enjoying the peace and quiet.

Her legs ached and she had a pain in her back. Too much walking the streets this week, she thought. She had tramped around looking for a job since Monday. Now it was Friday. A little rush of anxiety made her think of the baby, and how worry for her child was prominent in her always busy mind. She needed money. She must find a job.

Suddenly, Mrs Kallinski was beside her again, handing her a

glass. 'Here is some hot tea with lemon, Mrs Harte. You'll enjoy it, and it's better than the water.'

'Thank you,' Emma said and began to sip the tea. It was sweet, and she liked the taste of lemon. She had never had lemon tea before, but she did not say that. She always wanted to behave like a young woman of quality, who would certainly have had this kind of drink many times.

When Mr Kallinski returned, he joined her at the small table near the window, and accepted a glass of hot lemon tea himself.

Janessa looked at the clock on the mantel, and then at Emma. 'Do you live far from here, Mrs Harte?' she asked, a hint of worry echoing in her voice.

'Quite a way. Do you know The Mucky Duck in York Road?' Emma asked, looking at them. It was Mr Kallinski who nodded his head. 'Well, I live about half an hour's walk from there.'

'I see.' He too glanced at the clock. 'It's getting late. My sons will be here soon now. They will escort you home the moment they arrive.'

About to decline, wanting to leave now, Emma found herself agreeing with him. She saw the common sense of it.

Going to the oven, Janessa opened the door and looked inside, then peered into the pans on the stove. After replacing the lids, she sat down again.

'It is the least we can do,' Janessa interjected. 'We don't want your husband worrying about you, now do we?' She then continued, 'And no doubt you are anxious to prepare your evening meal.' A good-hearted woman, she smiled at Emma, her face full of warmth and understanding. It was obvious she had taken to Emma.

Cautious as she was, always afraid of revealing too much, Emma found herself saying, 'I don't have to prepare supper for my husband. You see, he is a sailor; he's in the Royal Navy. When he is at sea, as he is now, I live alone.'

'Alone!' Janessa exclaimed, sounding alarmed. 'Don't you have any family?' The thought of this young girl being alone in Leeds appalled her; that was quite obvious.

Shaking her head, Emma replied, 'No. My husband's grandmother recently died. I live in a respectable boarding house. I rent a room from a nice woman.'

The Kallinskis exchanged knowing glances, and Janessa now leaned forward, her face shining with hope and expectancy. 'If you don't have a pressing reason to leave, won't you stay and have Sabbath dinner with us? It would be our pleasure to welcome you.'

'Oh, I couldn't!' Emma exclaimed, sitting up straighter in the chair. 'It's so very kind of you, but I couldn't. I don't want to intrude.'

'You would not be intruding,' said Abraham. 'And just think of what you did for me today. You could have been hurt. Please stay for Sabbath dinner.'

When Emma remained silent, Abraham noticed the baffled look on Emma's face. '*Our* Sabbath is on Saturday. It commences at sundown on Friday. This is when we celebrate the beginning of the holy day with our Friday dinner.'

'I see,' Emma murmured, and couldn't help glancing at the clock herself, as they had done.

Abraham noticed this and exclaimed, 'Don't worry, don't worry. My sons will take you to your home after supper. David is nineteen and Victor sixteen; they are strong. You really will be safe with them, even if it is dark.'

'But I—'

Janessa cut across her. 'It is settled, Mrs Harte.' She smiled and continued in a gracious manner. 'You look tired, undoubtedly because of those hooligans. The food will nourish you, give you energy. You will enjoy it, I know.' She reached out and patted Emma's arm. 'We have more than enough for an extra person, an honoured guest, and when David and Victor arrive, they will welcome you too.'

Emma gave in, induced to accepting by Janessa's persuasive, good-natured pressure. She realized she was hungry, had not eaten much this week, and the bread and dripping had lost its appeal. Furthermore, the pans bubbling on the stove emitted delicious, mouthwatering aromas.

Finally, she said, 'Thank you. I will be happy to join you.'

Janessa beamed at her, as did Abraham. Janessa said, 'I am quite sure you have never eaten Jewish food before, but you will enjoy it. First, we will have the chicken soup with matzo balls. They are like Yorkshire dumplings, but smaller. Then a crisply-roasted chicken, golden brown and moist, with carrots and other vegetables from the soup. We will finish with honey cakes and lemon tea.'

'It sounds delicious,' Emma said, her appetite reviving even more. She could hardly wait for dinner. Earlier she had noticed the table at the other end of the room. It had been covered with a pristine white tablecloth and set for four. Now she watched Mrs Kallinski adding more cutlery and placing another chair for her. She suddenly felt at ease and very welcome in their home.

David and Victor Kallinski arrived home ten minutes later. Both of them were surprised to see a lovely-looking young woman sitting there, and also were instantly concerned about their father's bruised face.

After introductions had been made, and their father had explained how two ruffians had thrown stones at him and how Emma had rescued him, things settled down.

Janessa asked her sons, Emma and her husband to come and

wash their hands in the kitchen sink. As they did so, she ladled chicken soup into bowls and put them on the table.

'Come to the table, please. It's almost sundown.'

They all stood around the table. First, Janessa lit the two white candles on the table and blessed them in a language Emma did not understand. Then Abraham blessed the wine; he broke the bread and blessed it, again in the language Emma could not fathom. Later she discovered it was Hebrew.

Finally they all sat down; David courteously pulled the chair out for Emma and Victor for his mother.

As they ate, Emma became aware of the harmonious atmosphere in this house, and an immeasurable love that existed in this family. She began to relax even more. Everyone was so warm to her, congenial, and so she was made to feel completely at home. At one moment, she was so overwhelmed with gratitude, her throat thickened with unexpected emotion. And she kept thinking: *Why are the Jews hated? They are loving and gentle people, kind and considerate. It is despicable the way they are treated.*

And this was the way Emma Harte was to feel all of her life, staunchly defending her Jewish friends, constantly shocked and grieved by the excesses of naked racism that infected Leeds like the blight for many years.

After the soup, the chicken was served, and Emma enjoyed every morsel, understanding at once that she could not neglect herself and vowing to have a decent meal every day.

There was a lot of conversation at the table, and it was the family who did most of the talking; many diverse subjects were discussed. Emma just listened, fascinated by them all, but David in particular. He was articulate, full of knowledge, extremely intelligent and opinionated. Many of the things he said Emma silently agreed with. She admired him.

Suddenly, Janessa stood up and began to clear the plates. Victor and David helped her to take them to the sink.

Emma stood up to join them, but Janessa said, 'It's all right, Mrs Harte. The boys are used to clearing up.' A smile filled her face. 'I think you enjoyed our Jewish food, didn't you?'

'I did, very much so. It was delicious,' Emma responded. 'And please call me Emma.' Her eyes swept around the table. 'All of you, please.'

'We would be honoured,' Abraham said in his gravely courteous way.

It was when they were drinking their tea that David's bright blue eyes settled on Emma, who sat next to him. Like everyone who met her, including his family, David had noticed her well-bred air, her good manners, her dignity. Her dress was of cotton, but it was well-cut. He was very curious about her, interested in her.

After a moment of silent speculation, he said, 'I'm not meaning to be rude or nosy, but why was a girl like *you* in North Street this afternoon? What were *you* doing *there* of all places? Thank goodness you were, for my father's sake, mind you. However, it is not such a pleasant area to be wandering around in.'

Emma was momentarily taken aback, and returned his piercing glance with one equally brilliant. 'I was looking for a job,' she said in a calm voice.

The entire room was silent, but four pairs of Kallinski eyes were focused on Emma. It was Janessa who broke the silence. 'A girl like you looking for work in that awful district!' she gasped, totally thunderstruck.

'Yes,' Emma answered. They were all gaping at her in amazement, so she had no alternative but to explain her need for work, and how unlucky she had been in the arcade and the small tailoring shops. 'I hadn't found a job at Cohen's and was on my way home when I saw those cursed boys assaulting Mr Kallinski.'

Janessa spoke up at once, 'Abraham! Abraham! *You* must do something for Emma.'

'Of course I will,' he replied, smiling at Emma sitting next to him. 'You do not have to look for a job any more. I will give you one. On Monday morning, at eight o'clock sharp, come to my tailoring shop and I will take you on. I am sure we can find something suitable!' He looked at David. 'Don't you agree, son?'

'Yes, Dad. We can start Emma off as a buttonholer. That's not so hard,' David responded, thinking she was clever and would soon move on to a more important job.

Emma was speechless in surprise, but instantly found her voice. 'Why, thank you, Mr Kallinski! That would be wonderful.' She gave him an intent look. 'I learn fast and I will work hard. I didn't know you had a tailoring shop.'

Abraham couldn't help chuckling. 'How could you? Anyway it's in Rockingham Street, near Camp Road. David will write down the exact address for you.'

'I certainly will,' David said, unexpectedly filling with excitement about this young woman coming to work with them.

He had no way of knowing that night that he and Emma Harte would become business partners and that their partnership would add to their growing success and wealth. Or that it would last for half a century.

FIFTY-EIGHT

I t seemed to Emma that the months flew by. August had been boiling hot, but now, in October, the weather was cooler, and she felt better.

She was now four months pregnant, but she was so clever with clothes, she did not show yet. She went to Kallinski's every day and could now make a full-piece suit. Emma had always enjoyed sewing and was adept with a needle and had focused her tremendous energy on becoming good at the job fast. A sewing machine in a tailoring shop was easy for her too. David Kallinski was a delight to work with, training her well, first to cut sleeves, lapels, then jacket fronts and backs, and finally trousers out of the fine Yorkshire cloth that the mills produced. Quickly Emma turned her hand to new skills, lending a hand when the small factory was running behind with orders. Abraham Kallinski could not believe her capacity for work, but while she was friendly with the other factory girls, she was never quite one of them, meeting with a polite smile their teasing about her cut-glass accent.

But today she was happy because Blackie O'Neill had finally

returned to Leeds. He had left a note for her with Mrs Daniel, and she had gone to meet him at The Mucky Duck, where she had seen a different side to her friend. When she walked in, he was standing at the piano, his powerful baritone ringing out with the words to the 'Minstrel Boy'.

Emma had been moved almost to tears, her throat tight with the bittersweet sadness she experienced when she heard him sing.

Now, as she sat sewing in her attic, she began to laugh to herself. Blackie had been so astounded at her appearance, he had been thunderstruck. She'd never forget his words. 'Mary, Mother of Jaysus, whatever have ye done, mavourneen? Ye don't look like yeself any more.'

She now recalled how she had been annoyed and had asked him what he had meant, that he was being rude. 'No, I'm not, Emma. By God, if ye don't look more fetching than I ever did see ye. As elegant and as beautiful as the Queen of England,' he had announced.

Immediately, she had smiled, and explained, 'Oh, I see what you mean. It's just my hair. I copied Queen Alexandra's style. And the clothes I had from Mrs Wainright.' Emma knew she was looking her best, in a grey woollen suit she had cut down, with a blue silk blouse Olivia Wainright had discarded long ago. She had pinned the green glass brooch Blackie had given her – to match her emerald eyes – on the lapel. And they'd laughed together, and talked, and it had been wonderful to see her friend. And eventually, she had told him about the baby.

He had been shocked, stunned even, but he hadn't been judgemental. After all, if anyone knew about the traits and foibles of humans, it was Blackie.

He had been worried about her, wanting to know who the father was and why he wouldn't marry her, working himself into a terrible fury about it. He had even offered to marry her to keep her safe. She had seen something in his eyes, something about his appreciation of the woman she was now, and for the first time since she had left Fairley she had broken down in tears, touched by his loving and unselfish gesture. Shaking her head, with the tears spilling down her cheeks, she had refused his offer.

'You have your plans, after all. You're going to be that toff, that millionaire. You don't need the responsibility of a family. I couldn't do that to you, Blackie.'

He had accepted her refusal reluctantly, aware she was adamant, but Emma hadn't been able to read the expression on his face.

Because she was constantly busy when she was not at Kallinski's, Emma had bought herself a small second-hand watch from a pawnshop, with money taken from her savings. She looked at it now. It was four o'clock in the afternoon. Blackie was coming to get her at Mrs Daniel's house to take her to eat in a café and then go to the City Varieties again. She must put away her sewing and get ready. After all, he expected to see her looking like the Queen of England.

Blackie took her to the Blue Door, his favourite place to eat in Leeds. They were greeted with great enthusiasm by Gladys.

Now she said, as she seated them, 'You look so lovely, madam, and I like yer purple blouse.'

'Why thank you,' Emma murmured, smiling at the waitress, her face radiant.

Blackie ordered two lemonades and, after the waitress had hurried off, he turned to Emma and said, 'Ye do look beautiful tonight . . . and your eyes seem greener than ever.'

'It's the purple blouse. It's a colour that always emphasizes green, and thank you for your compliment.'

Blackie chuckled. 'Ye still look like the Queen with all them curls on top of your head. I don't know how ye manage to do it, lass. I swear on the heads of the Blessed Saints, 'tis a wonder to me. But then I'm just a man.'

Emma merely smiled and said, 'I was a lady's maid for Mrs Fairley, remember, Blackie. And I'm good with a needle.' She looked at the menu. 'It's a treat to be here, thank you, Blackie.' She had eaten in a café only once since coming to the city, never wanting to squander her carefully saved shillings. 'What are you having?'

'A steak pie, Emma. I'm a growing boy.' He winked at her.

Once their orders were given to Gladys, Blackie said, 'There's something I forgot to tell ye. When I was in Ireland to see my old friend, the priest, who was dying, and to see Siobhan and Michael, I met Lord Robert Lassiter. He wanted me to do a bit of work at Lassiter Hall. I felt I had to oblige, 'cos he's been very good to me, giving me work like the guesthouse.'

'Yes, he has. I'm glad you stayed on. I think it's important to be loyal.' She squeezed his arm. 'As you are to me.'

'I'm always here for ye, Emma. And I'll help ye when the baby comes. Make sure I'm available, like. Tell me again, when is it due?'

'It's due in March, and I can't wait to have it, I can tell you that. I do want to work at Kallinski's as long as I can. You know how good they are to me. They've become family in a way.'

'Aye, I know that, lass.' Blackie frowned. He didn't like the idea of her working so long. 'Ye know David admires ye a lot.' He gave her a pointed look.

Emma stared at him, surprised at his tone. Was he jealous of David Kallinski?

Blackie noticed her face changing, becoming reflective, and cursed himself under his breath. But David's presence in her life did trouble him. Blackie had discovered on his return from Ireland that, much to his surprise, he was no longer sure how he felt about Emma.

He had been out of Leeds when she had arrived from Fairley, and he had not seen her since her mother had died. How she had changed in that time. She had become a young woman with striking looks, an air of confidence, and lots of charm. Very desirable indeed.

Blackie knew he admired her, liked her, was fascinated by her. But the young girl he had felt protective over had disappeared. He could not describe how he felt about the woman sitting before him. He truly was baffled.

Emma said, 'What are you brooding about? You're looking very serious.'

'Just pondering on a few things – nothing serious, mavourneen.'

Gladys arrived with their plates of food, and said, 'Would ye like a basket of bread?'

'That's a good idea.' Emma then asked, 'And could I have a bottle of malt vinegar and pepper, please, Gladys?'

'Coming right up, madam,' she answered and dashed away.

Emma said, 'You spoke about David Kallinski, who is just a friend, as I told you. But what about your friend Laura you've told me about?'

'Oh, don't be daft, lass. We're just friends like ye and David.'

'Oh, I see . . .' Emma's voice trailed off and she looked thoughtful.

Gladys returned with the bottle of vinegar and the basket of bread. Emma picked up the bottle and covered her fish and chips with it, added pepper.

Blackie stared at her. 'That's very acidic for ye, Emma. Ye shouldn't put so much on your fish, ye'll be killing the taste.'

'I'm afraid I have a craving for spicy things these days,' Emma murmured and started to eat.

Taking up his knife and fork, Blackie pushed these thoughts aside and tried to enjoy his steak pie. He trusted Emma not to repeat her comment about Laura. His mind turned to the show ahead and to ensuring Emma enjoyed herself on a rare night out.

FIFTY-NINE

O n a Tuesday evening, towards the end of March in
1906, Emma knew the baby was coming. She had
moved in with Blackie's friend, Laura Spencer, early
in the new year; it had been Laura who took her into St Mary's
Hospital at Hill Top. Emma was in labour for ten hours, before
giving birth to her child. It was exactly a month before her own
seventeenth birthday in late April.

Much to Emma's joy, it was a girl, and when she held her in
her arms for the first time and looked into that sweet little face,
she wondered how she would find the strength to entrust her
to her cousin Freda in Ripon to bring up. Deep down, she
accepted, she had no choice. She had to work to provide for her
daughter and, at least with Freda, the little girl would be safe
and well taken care of. That was the truth, a certainty, in fact.

Now, on this blustery afternoon, Emma sat in Laura's parlour
in her house in Armley. It reminded her of Janessa Kallinski's
home, with comfortable chairs and a sofa at one end, and this
spot in front of the fireplace.

Emma was wrapped in a shawl, happy to be in front of a

roaring fire, warm and safe, but an air of dejection, abnormal for her, enveloped her. She glanced down at her daughter, just four days old. She knew she could not keep the baby with her, even though she longed to. The baby lay in a makeshift cradle, fashioned by Laura. It was actually a drawer from a chest that Laura had lined with thick blankets and downy pillows. In the firelight, the baby's fluff of silver-blonde hair shone brightly, and her cheeks were pink as she slept in perfect peace.

This lovely child was hers. *No sacrifice she could make would be too great if it ensured the well-being and security of this baby.* 'I won't let anything happen to you ever,' she whispered softly but with some vehemence. 'And you'll have the best that money can buy. I promise you that!' Emma meant every word.

Many diverse thoughts were suddenly running through her head. She would not countenance the idea of adoption or the orphanage. But her heart ached at the thought of giving the baby to her cousin Freda, in Ripon, as she had arranged, and only visiting at weekends. Should she go back to Leeds every day to work for the Kallinskis? Laura had arranged for her to work three days a week at Thompson's mill, nearby, learning to weave. But the Kallinskis were unique. She missed them, especially Janessa, who had mothered her, shown her such affection and love. Blackie was against it. He believed she was better off in Upper Armley, and had asked her in January where she would live in Leeds, if she stayed there. 'Not in that attic!' he had exclaimed. He had been annoyed on that cold January day, when she had told him she didn't want to live with Laura, share her house. And at first she had refused to go on the tram.

He had exploded in temper, which was not at all like him; he had badgered her and bossed her until she had given in. Emma had stayed virtually silent on the tram ride to Whingate Junction, while Blackie had done his best to bring her round to the idea of moving out to Upper Armley, painting a rosy picture of its shops and park and amenities.

But it had been Laura's character and lovely warm personality that had made Emma change her mind. She thought of that now. She had never met anyone like her before. So gentle, sincere and compassionate, with the face of the Madonna. Peace and calm seemed to shine all around her, like a halo. And she was welcoming, insisted on helping her to unpack. Settling her in the room upstairs that had been her parents' room, with its comfortable brass bed.

Emma let out a deep sigh. She was genuinely relieved she was living here, glad that Blackie had ranted and raved at her, made her come. Upper Armley also offered safety. *And shops.*

Yes, here she would have her first shop, perhaps even her second and her third. She would work every minute of every day to achieve the success she craved. Success equalled money. For her little daughter. She must protect her always.

Unexpectedly, she thought of Edwin Fairley, and looked down at the baby. She was also part of him, the weakling, the coward who had deserted her. No, *them.* Because the baby was his. She cursed him under her breath, and then abruptly stopped. She must put Edwin out of her mind. Now and forever.

The baby was innocent, and she could not let bad feelings about *him* cloud her judgement. I'll never think of *him* again, she promised herself and, as it was, she kept that promise.

'Hello! Hello! Anybody home?' The loud voice and knocking on the door made Emma sit up with a start. She had been dozing.

Blackie came marching in, his hair looking blown about by the wind, a giant smile on his face.

'Here I am, me darlin' Emma, bearing a few gifts for the wee bairn.'

It was true. His arms were full of packages which he put down on the kitchen table, before taking off his topcoat.

'Blackie! You're early. I didn't expect to see you so soon!' she exclaimed.

'Well, ye knows I can't resist the new addition to our little family. So I came galloping over without giving it a thought.'

'I'm glad you did. Just go and take a peek at her, sleeping peacefully. A perfect little girl, Blackie.'

'Aye and sure she is. For doesn't she take after her beautiful mother?' He strode over to look at the baby in the cradle, smiled, and then headed for the table. 'Come on, Emma, come and look at the bits and pieces I picked up for Tinker Bell.'

Emma laughed. Blackie had taken to calling the baby Tinker Bell well before it was born; he was already certain – because Emma herself was – that it would be a girl.

Blackie grinned back and began to unwrap the presents. 'Help me, mavourneen.'

Emma tore the paper off one parcel and discovered a pink wool coat trimmed with pink ribbon. 'Oh, Blackie, it's lovely. Thank you.'

'And here's the matching bonnet and a little pair of booties. I hope they'll fit the wee mite. I had to be guessing the sizes.'

'They're perfect, Blackie, but you should not be spending your money on Tinker Bell.' She smiled as she used his name for her daughter. 'You should be saving it to build that house of yours in Harrogate.'

'Ah, by God, I will do that one day, on the heads of the Blessed Saints, I will do that. But me and me Uncle Pat are doing well; sure and I can spare a few bob for Tinker Bell.' He paused and handed her the last parcel.

Emma opened it and found a fluffy white lamb in her hands. 'Blackie, thank you again, you're spoiling her already. She can cuddle this.'

'She deserves a toy, ye knows.'

Moving to the kitchen, Emma took the kettle, filled it with water and put it to the stove. 'I'll make us a cup of tea. Are you hungry, Blackie? Do you want something to eat?'

'Ah, no, mavourneen. Tea will be just fine.' He began to pick up the paper and threw it onto the fire. 'Tinker Bell has to have a real name, ye knows. So, Emma, what are ye going to call her?' he asked.

'I don't know,' she answered quietly, and stood waiting for the kettle to boil, suddenly looking plaintive. After filling the teapot, she sat down at the table, waiting for the tea to mash.

Blackie went to the cupboard, took out two cups, and sat down opposite her. He noticed at once that she was looking sad. 'Hey, Miss Emma, what's troubling ye?'

'Well, it's just . . .' She paused, stared at him, her worry now most apparent. Finally, she answered him. 'I'm just a bit concerned about the baby not being christened.'

Blackie was thunderstruck, stared at her, obviously uncomprehending, and then he began to laugh. Eventually, he calmed himself. 'Why should that matter to ye? After all, ye've been telling me for months that ye are an atheist.'

'I am!' Emma cried. 'But I don't feel quite right about it, and the baby might believe in God when she grows up, and she might be angry with me if she finds out she wasn't baptized.'

Realizing she was being genuine, in earnest, Blackie said, 'Go and see the vicar at Christ Church.'

'Oh, I can't!' Emma replied. 'The vicar would want her birth certificate. That is the custom. And since I don't have one he'll realize Tinker Bell is illegitimate. He cannot know that. No one can! Promise me you'll keep my secret, Blackie, *please*.'

'Sure an' I will, but are ye going to say Winston, your husband, is the father? 'Cos he's far away on the high seas, according to ye.' He raised a dark brow questioningly.

'Of course not, but I could. I *was* pregnant when I came to Leeds, remember.'

'Aye, I did forget for a moment. Let me put me thinking cap on, mavourneen. Meanwhile, could ye pour the tea, please?'

She did so, biting her inner lip, suddenly growing more worried. Why hadn't she thought of this before? One thing was certain, she wouldn't put *his* name on the birth certificate. She did not want her child ever to be linked to the name Fairley.

The two of them sat in silence, drinking their tea. Suddenly, Blackie sat up straight, as an idea came to him. 'I've got the solution! We'll have our own christening, I am thinking,' he shouted in a cheerful voice. 'Bring me a bowl.'

'I don't understand what you mean.' Emma's brow came together in a frown. 'Our own christening?'

'Since ye are so troubled about the bairn not being christened, I am goin' to do it meself.'

Disbelief flickered in Emma's eyes. 'Would it be proper? Would it be a real christening, I mean?'

'Sure and it would. I can do just as good a job as a vicar or a priest, for that matter. Though I'm a lapsed Catholic, I still believe in God, ye know. God lives within us, Emma. Nowadays I feel Him in me heart. I feel His love and His presence.'

Emma was absolutely astounded, so much so she remained silent, yet she knew he meant every word he said.

Blackie spoke again. 'He will accept her as one of the blessed children, sure and He will. Believe me, it's the baptism and the spirit of love behind it that counts – not the man that does it or where it's done. Bring me a bowl of water, please.'

'I believe you,' Emma said as she went to get a bowl. 'I want you to christen my baby. I'm so grateful to you.'

'That's my girl.' He took the bowl from her and went to the sink. 'Now, mavourneen, can you get me a small towel, please?'

She did so and looked at him. 'Shall I get the baby out of the cradle now?'

'A fine idea,' Blackie answered, filling the bowl with tepid water.

Emma went to the fireplace and lifted her baby out of the makeshift cot, cradled her in her arms, cooing to her. 'Oh, my sweet little girl,' she said, entranced with her child. Unexpectedly, Edwin's face flashed before her eyes, and so did Adam Fairley's and, having vowed never to think of them ever again, she was horrified. And her guard went down; suddenly she was distracted and aghast, actually flustered.

'Bring the baby over to the sink, mavourneen.'

'Just a minute, Blackie. I haven't got her quite right. Let me move her a bit.'

Emma turned her back and swallowed, endeavouring to retrieve her composure.

Blackie was calling from the sink. 'And what will ye be calling Tinker Bell then? Have ye thought of a name?'

Emma, so upset and preoccupied, did not have time to think. Edwin's face was in her head, his name on the tip of her tongue. She said automatically, thoughtlessly, 'Edwina—'

As she heard herself saying that name, Emma froze, so furious was she with herself, and her own carelessness. Why had she said that name? She felt as if the blood was draining out of her. What a fool I am, she thought.

Blackie's jaw had dropped open as he was staring at her back. Without having to give it a second thought, he knew who the baby's father was. Why had he not realized that before? Especially since he had been suspicious about her story from the beginning.

He realized she had not meant to call the child Edwina. Emma was far too canny for that. Why would she spell it out to him? No, it was a mistake, and one she could not really correct now.

Adopting an unconcerned tone, he said with a show of gaiety,

'And what an elegant name it is for wee Tinker Bell. I like it, sure and I do.'

Emma walked over to him, not trusting herself to speak. Blackie fussed with the towel, draping it over his arm, giving her time to regain her composure, feeling sorry for her.

'I'm ready,' he said with a very bright smile. 'Hold the baby forward, Emma. Yes, that's good, mavourneen.'

Emma, always swift to recover, said, 'Her full name is Ed . . . Edwina.' She almost faltered, then went on with more steadiness, 'Laura Shane—'

'Shane!' Blackie exclaimed, his surprise obvious.

'After you, my dearest friend. I can't call her Patrick or Desmond, now can I? And Blackie would be odd, most certainly.' She managed to force a smile onto her face.

Blackie had to laugh, and he was relieved she was more like herself. 'That's true, very true. And I am flattered, Emma, but let us now commence.'

He dipped his fingers in the bowl of water and, with a bit of a flourish, he made the sign of the cross on the baby's forehead.

'Please, Blackie, stop!' Emma exclaimed, her eyes wide and staring. 'I'm not a Roman Catholic, and neither is the baby. In the Church of England, the vicar just sprinkles water on in little drips. He doesn't make a cross on the baby's forehead. We must do it properly. We must start again, please.'

Blackie did his best to stifle the laughter bubbling up in him. For a so-called atheist, she was being mighty particular. 'Sure and I will, Emma, I understand.'

He wiped the water off the baby's brow, dipped his large fingers in the bowl, and sprinkled a few drops on the baby's brow. The baby stared up at him unblinkingly.

'I christen thee Edwina Laura Shane Harte. In the name of God the Father, the Son and the Holy Spirit.' Blackie crossed himself and then bent over the baby and kissed her.

'There you are, it's all done. But I have a question for ye, Emma. Whose name will be on the birth certificate?'

Emma's expression of happiness evaporated at once. 'I haven't quite worked that out yet,' she admitted a little dolefully.

'Then I shall do that for ye. It can't be left blank. That would be terrible. So ye will put my name on it. I want that . . . I would be more than proud to be listed as Edwina's father.'

'Oh Blackie, I can't! I mustn't saddle you with that . . . it's a responsibility,' Emma cried, shaking her head with some vehemence.

'Yes, ye will do it! I want it, and I just christened her. I will always be there for her, and I will protect her as if she were mine. We will go and see the registrar in Leeds next week. And that's that.'

Emma recognized that obdurate look on his face and knew she had no choice. 'Thank you, Blackie, you're so kind, my best friend, and I appreciate what you did today, and are doing.'

She stared into the fire. 'Laura must never see it.'

Blackie leaned forward and asked, 'What was that?'

'I don't want Laura to be hurt. She would be, if she saw your name on the certificate. She might believe you really were the father.'

'So what?' Blackie demanded, further bewildered.

'Laura loves you, Blackie. I bet if you asked her, she'd marry you.'

Blackie was stunned. A peculiar look settled on his face. One that Emma could not read.

By April, the baby was comfortably settled with her cousin Freda in Ripon. If she had been surprised at Emma's unexpected arrival on her doorstep, or shocked at her story, the loving and compassionate Freda had not shown it at all. Emma was content to know that Edwina had been left in capable hands, and that she would be looked after and cherished with complete devotion.

As soon as she was able, Emma had made her long-awaited trip to Fairley village, brimming with happiness at the thought of seeing her father and her younger brother Frank again, carrying thoughtfully chosen presents for them both and a bunch of spring flowers for her mother's grave. She had bumped into her brother Winston on her way to the cottage; he'd been coming out of the pub and looked tall, handsome, and resplendent in his naval uniform, on leave from duties in Scapa Flow.

Frank was dumbfounded to see his older sister, and overcome with emotion. He sped across the room, flinging himself into Emma's outstretched arms with such velocity he almost knocked her over. She held him close to her, stroking his hair. He began to cry, sobbing as if his heart would break. She was at once startled and baffled, and she tried to soothe him.

'Frank, lovey, don't cry so. I'm here, safe and well, and with presents for you, too.'

He raised his freckled and damp face to hers and said, with a snuffle, 'I've missed yer, Emma. Ever so much. I thought yer'd never come back. Never, ever again,' he wept.

Emma tried to comfort him. 'Don't be silly. I'll always come back. I've missed you, too. Now come along, stop crying, and let me take off my coat. These are for you, love,' she said, handing him socks, a shirt and writing materials, and a copy of *David Copperfield*. 'I'm sorry, Winston, I didn't know you'd be home so I didn't bring you anything,' she told her elder brother.

Busying herself at the Welsh dresser, taking out the other items, she said, 'These are for Dad. Where is he?'

She glanced from Winston to Frank, a look of joyous expectation on her face.

Winston's eyes dropped to the floor and Frank stood

gazing at her vacantly, clutching his presents. Neither of them spoke.

'What's wrong? Why are you both so quiet? Where's our dad?' Emma asked again. Fear began to trickle through her veins.

She sat down and Winston lowered himself into the chair opposite her. He took her hand in his and held it tightly, watching her with concern and saying very gently, 'He's with our mam, Emma.'

Emma seemed uncomprehending. She looked from brother to brother, at their distressed faces and tear-filled eyes.

'Our dad's dead,' Frank told her, with his usual childlike bluntness. His voice was leaden with sorrow. 'He died five days after you left, last August.'

'Dead,' whispered Emma, choking back a sob. 'He can't be dead. It's not possible. I would have known if he had died. I would have known inside. In my heart. I just know I would.' And as she uttered these words, she realized from their grim expressions that it was true.

She stared into space and finally managed to ask, 'How did he die?' Her voice was drained.

'There was an accident,' Winston said. 'We didn't know where to find you, Emma. We kept thinking you'd be back in a few days . . .'

Emma was silent. She had no excuses. A sick dismay lodged in her stomach, and guilt mingled with her grief, which was absolute. 'What kind of accident?' she whispered.

'Well, yer see, Emma, that Saturday yer left, there was a fire at the mill and me dad got burned. And he breathed a lot of smoke. He survived but me Aunty Lily said he didn't want to live any more, he wanted to join our mam. He died peacefully in his sleep that night.'

Emma said, with a strangled sob, 'Did he understand that I hadn't returned from Bradford, and that's why I wasn't there, Winston?'

Her brother nodded. 'Yes, and he wasn't upset, Emma. He said he didn't have to see you, because you were locked in his heart forever.'

Emma closed her burning eyes and leaned back against the chair. 'Was anyone else injured?' she asked eventually.

'No, only me dad,' Frank told her. 'Me dad was crossing the yard and spotted Master Edwin going in ter the warehouse. Me dad ran after him, warning him it was ever so dangerous. A blazing bale was falling from the gantry, so me dad threw himself on top of Master Edwin, ter protect him. He saved Master Edwin's life, and with selfless courage, so the Squire said.'

Emma went icy cold all over. 'My father saved Edwin Fairley's life!' she cried with such ferocity that even Winston was brought up sharply, aghast at her tone. 'He died to save a Fairley! My father sacrificed himself for one of them!' She spat out the words venomously, and a sick, fulminating fury rose up in her.

And so it began, something Blackie had never seen in his life ever before. The most relentless pursuit of money ever embarked upon, the most grinding and merciless work schedule ever conceived and willingly undertaken by a seventeen-year-old girl.

Blackie and Laura worried about Emma as days turned into weeks, weeks into months. They even tried to make her ease up on herself, to relax a little, go with them to Armley Park on Sundays to hear the brass band playing the popular tunes. But she wouldn't hear of it. Occasionally, she promised to come but never arrived.

Her schedule was brutal, but it was of her own creation. By day she worked at the mill; at night, after a quick supper, she retired to her bedroom where she designed, cut and sewed clothes for a rapidly growing clientele of local women, informed by the loving Laura of her flair with a needle. And her reasonable prices. Everyone raved about the clothes she created.

Once a month, on a Saturday or Sunday, she went to visit her baby daughter in Ripon. The rest of the time she made all kinds of pies, tarts, cakes and custards, trifles and jellies. Many of them were from recipes given to her long ago by Olivia Wainright.

She made jams of every kind; raspberry, strawberry and plum were everyone's favourites. She bottled apricots, plums, pears and various vegetables. The list was long; all were relished.

The pies and fancy pastries were sold at once. The bottled fruits and vegetables were stored in Laura's cellar for future sale. Everything she did was well thought out, and by the end of the year, she knew she had enough money to find her first shop. There was enough to pay the rent, buy fixtures and fittings, and display stands. And more money to purchase the stocks.

Emma was dogged, ruthless with herself. She scrimped and saved, worked seven days a week, and seven nights as well.

Her first goal was her first shop in Upper Armley if she could find one. And after that, more shops until she had a chain of them, just as Michael Marks had a chain of Penny Bazaars. But hers would be elegant stores, which would cater to the carriage trade.

SIXTY

Blackie stood with Laura in front of the altar in the church in Bolton Manor village.

They were looking at the flower arrangements the servants had created yesterday, finishing their final touches this morning. All the flowers were white: roses, carnations, lilies, orchids, hollyhocks and tulips. Not a single spot of any other colour was visible.

It was Laura who spoke first. 'Although I expected it, I think they have done a wonderful job.' She smiled. 'The whole church looks beautiful, you do know that, Blackie?'

'Thank ye, me darlin'. I think Miss Moira will be pleased the way they've banked them up on each side of the organ and down the steps to the nave.'

'Not to mention around the back of the pulpit. And what about the alcoves and windowsills, Blackie? I love the vases of roses and carnations against the stained-glass windows, as well. *Perfect.*'

Blackie nodded and took hold of his friend's arm. 'Let's sit down a moment before we go back to the manor to change our clothes, enjoy the peace and quiet in here.' He led her to a pew.

'It's wonderful ye can be here today at Miss Moira's wedding to Lord Adrian.' He smiled down at Laura.

'I am too, and I'm happy for her. She's always been so nice, if we met up in Armley or that time when she came for tea when she was working for Mrs Wilson.'

'Aye, she was that, I agree.' Blackie chuckled, and said quietly, 'When I first met her, I was always suspicious of her, though, so a bit wary.'

'Why would you be like that?' Laura asked, sounding taken aback. Her brows came together in a frown, and she shook her head, baffled.

'Because I knew she weren't like *us*, me and Finn. We're working-class folk. I knew deep in me bones that Moira Aherne was patrician, totally different. I didn't understand why she was . . . well, playing it down. Ye knows what I mean, pretending to be like us.'

Laura nodded. 'Whatever, she's always been friendly to me when we spent time together.'

'Aye, she is friendly, but don't mistake friendliness for *friendship*. Most aristocrats have a gift for being *friendly*, but it's never their *friendship* they're giving. And that's just the way they are.'

'Do ye really believe that, Blackie?' she asked, scepticism in her tone. 'I think Lord Robert *has* been a friend to you, a real friend. Look at the work he's given you and your uncle.'

'Ye're right, he has been a patron, 'tis true, sure and it is. But ye see, Laura, Lord Robert is different to most aristocrats. He's a rarity. Nobody like him that I know of, and that's a fact.'

'I'm glad you appreciate his lordship.'

Blackie nodded. 'I do, I promise ye.' He stood up. 'Best we get back to the manor and change.' He glanced at the altar again. 'Miss Moira wanted all white flowers, like they did for Lord Robert's marriage in March. And we've certainly done that, don't ye think? Done her proud?'

'We have, and we've had a much better choice of blooms because it's May. She'll be nicely surprised.'

Several hours later, on this lovely May Saturday, a group of men gathered outside the church.

All of them wore Savile Row-tailored morning suits, each with a white rosebud pinned to their lapel. They waited, chatting and smoking, for the arrival of the bridegroom.

One of them, Harry Peterson, was the best man, the others ushers. All had been friends for years.

Harry said, with a chuckle, 'It's like the gathering of the clans yet again. We were here in March when Robert married Vanessa. Now it's Adrian and Moira today. Do you think there will be a third soon?'

Jack Fields grinned. 'I don't even have a girlfriend, never mind a fiancée. But I am on the lookout for a cracking young lady if you have any contestants.'

They all chuckled, and Harry said, 'I'm enjoying my freedom for the moment, since my last lady love has just dumped me, shall we say. But I don't care. I'm just thrilled I've survived the disaster of my Cézanne painting. That's a huge relief.'

Nelson Weatherby, a long-time friend of Robert's, said, 'Thank God for that, Harry. I just heard about it from Robert. The London gallery behaved well, I understand, and repaid you in full. And you got to keep the painting.'

'I got the money *and* the painting, yes. But I only kept the money. The Cézanne had to go.'

'What do you mean?' Weatherby asked.

'In France, when a painting is deemed a fake, it has to be destroyed. *Immediately*. That is the French law. And my art gallery in London, where I bought it, was a stickler about doing the proper thing. They insisted we follow the law to the letter.' He grimaced. 'When I say *we*, I mean myself and the London gallery's owner.'

'So how did you destroy it?' Jack Fields asked, filled with curiosity.

'I slashed it with a sharp knife. You see, no one should leave a fake in good shape. It could get sold again for a lot of money.'

'I'm even more curious,' Jack said. 'How did you discover it was a fake in the first place? I mean, when you bought it, you must have thought it was really a Cézanne, as the gallery obviously did also. So, what's the story? Do tell us.'

'It was Robert . . .' Harry began, and hesitated as he caught sight of the bridegroom heading towards the church. 'I'll tell you quickly. Adrian's on his way here. Robert saw the Cézanne at my home in Kent, and he thought it was *wrong*, the word used in the art world. When it's *wrong*, it's not *right*, which means, in their language, it's a fake. Robert kept his thoughts to himself for a long time, but one day he told me what he felt about the painting. I took it from there. I knew he was sincere and serious. It was on his conscience.'

'So all's well that ends well,' Jack said, with a faint smile.

When Adrian stopped in front of his ushers, Harry took hold of his arm and said, 'Come live with me and be my love, and we will all the pleasures prove.'

Adrian laughed. 'Quoting Marlowe's romantic poem to *me*! Those words are meant for a girl.'

'Not necessarily,' Harry responded swiftly. 'And I was just predicting your future. Pleasures with your love for a lifetime.'

The village church was packed to overflowing. All of the locals had come, and some of the servants from Bolton Manor. A number had stayed behind with Cook to make the wedding supper, and were happy to do so.

All of the front pews were filled with the bridegroom's friends and family, and the Strattons, now that Vanessa was married to Robert Lassiter, and a few of Moira's friends were there as well. Everyone was dressed in their best finery, especially the women.

Blackie and Laura were seated towards the back of the church with the locals, all wearing their Sunday clothes. After the wedding ceremony, they were going to the party in the church hall that had been arranged, and paid for, by Lord Robert for the villagers. It was a Lassiter family tradition.

Suddenly there was the sound of music as the organist began to play. Silence reigned as everyone stopped chatting and turned in their pews. Their eyes on the front door of the church.

Blackie glanced at the altar and saw Lord Adrian, the bridegroom, standing with his best man, Harry Peterson, both of them looking somewhat anxious as they waited for the bride.

Swinging around, Blackie focused fully on the entrance now, as Mendelssohn's 'Wedding March' filled the church to the rafters with soaring music.

And then there they were: Moira on the arm of Lord Robert Lassiter, her second cousin, who was giving her away. Blackie let out a small gasp as he stared at them. Lord Robert, so handsome in his morning suit, with a white rosebud pinned on his lapel, and Moira, looking like a fairy-tale princess. She was very beautiful in a white satin wedding gown, well-cut and somewhat tailored, with a low neckline, long sleeves and a straight skirt that was draped into a train at the back.

A diamond necklace and dangling ear-clips sparkled around

her face, and a fabulous coronet of diamonds held her long lace veil in place.

Blackie had originally believed Lord Robert was bringing out family heirlooms for his cousin to wear. Then later he had heard that the diamond pieces had belonged to Moira's mother, Lady Henrietta Chandler, much to his surprise.

Together, they moved slowly down the aisle, perfectly in step, and most people were a bit awed by them and the way they looked. Still, everyone gasped or sighed deeply at their elegance and aristocratic bearing. That Robert and Moira were related was patently obvious today.

Behind them walked Vanessa, the matron of honour, and two of Adrian's younger cousins who were the bridesmaids. All three wore pale blue gowns and coronets of white flowers in their hair.

When Robert and Moira arrived at the altar, Robert placed Moira's hand in Adrian's and stepped to one side and sat down in the first pew. The bridesmaids followed suit, along with Vanessa. A moment later, the best man passed the wedding ring to Adrian.

There was a sudden stillness in the church, a moment of intense quiet. Then the vicar's voice rang out as he began to say the marriage vows.

Within a few seconds, Adrian was sliding the wedding ring on Moira's finger as she smiled up at him, her face radiant with happiness.

His voice was strong and clear as he began, 'With this ring I thee wed . . .'

Crowds of villagers were waiting outside as the newly married couple came out of the church, both of them full of smiles.

Rose petals and confetti were thrown at them in handfuls and they ducked. They looked at each other lovingly as they made their way to the open carriage awaiting them.

As the horse and carriage set off for Bolton Manor and the wedding reception, tin cans tied to the back of the carriage rattled and a large sign read: 'Newly Wed'.

SIXTY-ONE

It was a flawless sunlit day. The wide arc of sky was vividly blue, no clouds. Shimmering light filtered through the leaves on the trees, a light breeze making them rustle gently. No hint of rain.

It was Sunday afternoon, Blackie's favourite day of the week, and he was in high spirits as he stepped out into Town Street. As always on Sundays, the traffic had disappeared, all was still, peaceful. No carts and horses bringing in produce, no drays, no hansom cabs. Just a few open landau carriages taking people to different places in the area.

That's what he liked about Upper Armley on Sundays, the feeling that it was a country village. As he walked along at a steady pace, he saw a few acquaintances walking down, obviously going to Armley Park for the band.

He smiled and nodded, and they did the same as they went on their way. How smart the men were, in their suits or jackets and ties, shirts starched and pressed. And the lady companions in long summer dresses and pretty hats looked lovely. All were dressed in their Sunday best for the concert. Blackie liked that, approved of the effort they had made.

Within minutes he was walking down St Ives Mount, going to pick up Laura and Emma to escort them to the park for the concert.

He smiled to himself when the front door opened before he had even knocked. Obviously Laura had been looking out of the window, waiting for him, hidden by the lace curtains.

'Well, aren't ye the bonny lass this afternoon!' he said, stepping into the house, his eyes on her. She wore a pretty pale pink dress, with a scooped-out neckline, long sleeves, a tight bodice and a pleated skirt that fell to her ankles. 'What a lovely dress, Laura.'

She blushed and said, 'Thank you for your compliment, Blackie. Emma made it for me last week.'

'She's clever, to be sure, and everything she makes seems unique,' Blackie said, putting an arm around Laura and leading her into the parlour.

'Just let me put on my hat,' Laura said, picking it up from a chair and going over to a mirror. 'She trimmed this too.' Turning around, Laura smiled. 'Do you like it?'

Blackie nodded, taking in the wide-brimmed straw hat decorated with pink roses on the band around it. 'My English rose, Laura, that's what ye are.' He went over to her, held out his arm for her to take, and smiled down at her. 'I've missed ye, sure and I have, and it's grand to see ye.'

'We've missed you too,' Laura said, shyly. She stepped away, went to a side table and picked up her reticule and a pair of lace gloves. 'We'd better go. You know you like to sit in the front seats.'

'Where's Emma?' he exclaimed. 'Is she still getting ready?'

Laura cleared her throat and after a moment she said, 'Emma's not coming, Blackie. She has a dress to finish for one of her ladies in the Towers. She says she must work.'

Blackie was taken aback. 'But she promised David Kallinski she would meet him there! She shouldn't do this to him. It's not nice!'

'I know. I also know work comes first with Emma. She'll never change.'

'I'd like to speak to her,' Blackie said. 'Right now.'

Laura nodded and went to open the door leading upstairs. 'Emma,' she called, 'Blackie needs to have a word with you.'

'I'll be right there,' Emma answered, and a moment later she came down the narrow stairs.

'Hello, Blackie,' she said. 'You look smart in your suit. I bet it's one of the new ready-mades, in't it?'

'It is. Look here, Emma, ye have to come to the concert, ye promised David. Ye can't stand him up like this. He'll be hurt.'

'I must finish the gown,' she said calmly. 'I thought I could do it by last night, but I haven't been able to get it done, I'm afraid.'

'Surely ye can be a few days late,' Blackie said, staring at her. As he looked at that beautiful face, now somewhat pinched and tired, he noticed a sudden obdurate expression settle on it; her green eyes were steely. His heart sank. He knew how stubborn she could be, and that once her mind was made up it wouldn't change. She had a will of iron, which she exercised often.

A rush of anger mingled with impatience rushed through him but he held his temper down. 'What shall I say to David?' he asked in a clipped tone, glaring at her. 'What excuse shall I give?'

'Tell him I'm sorry I can't come, but I will make it up to him, and have supper next week,' Emma answered, still in her steady, calm voice. 'Say that's a *promise*.'

*   *   *

Blackie and Laura walked down to Armley Park together, taking the Ridge Road route. Laura's hand was tucked into Blackie's arm, but both were silent, lost in their own thoughts, preoccupied.

Blackie was fuming inside, still angry with Emma; Laura was upset for David, whom she knew was enamoured, had a real crush on Emma, even wanted to marry her. He would be disappointed when they arrived without her.

By the time they reached the gates of the park, Blackie had managed to shake off his anger and he turned to Laura and smiled at her.

'Do ye want a lemonade, mavourneen? Or a cordial? Or another sparkling drink?'

'Thanks, Blackie, a lemonade would be nice.'

'I'll have one too,' he said, going up to the drinks stall outside the gates, putting his hand in his pocket for the pennies, chatting to the stallholder in his usual jovial manner.

Once inside, Blackie's dark eyes sparkled. 'Look at this, Laura, we're early, and there are plenty of seats at the front. Come on, mavourneen, let's get settled before the rush starts.'

The two of them headed for the second row in front of the bandstand, where the musicians were starting to get set up. One of the musicians bumped into the cymbals, which made a clatter, while another was testing his brass trombone. Noise, but good noise, and expectations of a wonderful afternoon.

Blackie was in his element as he and Laura sat down. He loved music, and he tried not to miss these Sunday concerts. They soothed his soul. He loved being in the park, full of trees and lawns and flowering bushes. He took a few deep breaths now, savouring the fresh scents of the grass, the leaves and the flowers. Peace here, he thought. A place to relax, to be at ease, to forget any problems and travails.

Laura broke into his thoughts when she said, 'Don't stay angry with Emma, Blackie. She just can't help herself. And it's that drive and ambition that makes her so stubborn. She's a good person, and she'd give you the coat off her back.'

Blackie turned slightly in his seat, and looked at Laura, her trusting face turned up towards him. He was filled with a rush of emotion, so strong he was startled.

'Aren't ye the one? Always seeing the best of people, always being so fair, never condemning. There's just no one like ye . . .' His voice trailed off and he glanced around. People were coming in slowly, and they were still alone at the front of the row of seats.

Before he could stop himself, he blurted out, 'Laura, I do believe I am falling in love with ye, mavourneen. Really and truly. It's friends we are, but I know I feel better when I'm with ye . . .'

Laura's eyes shone. 'I'm in love with *you*, Blackie,' she whispered. 'I have been since the first time we met. I thought it was obvious.'

Blackie's face filled with happiness, his black eyes warm as he said, 'Can we go steady? Can we think about being together?'

'What do you mean when you say "being together"?'

'Walking out, and perhaps something more.'

'Are you . . . are you proposing to me, Blackie?' Laura asked carefully, her eyes riveted to his face.

'I think I am, on the heads of the Blessed Saints, I swear I am.' He let out a shout of laughter. 'Don't ye know I love ye?'

'Yes, I do. I feel the same.' She smiled, joy in her face, and touched his cheek gently. 'We shall go steady, enjoy our court-ship, and one day, in the not too distant future, we'll get married, and perhaps even start a family.'

Filled with excitement, he pulled her into his arms, crushing her against his jacket. Gently Laura extracted herself from his arms, and said, 'We must stop now, my dearest Blackie.' She laughed. 'The others will be here soon.'

He nodded. 'I knows that.'

'I want to go steady, be your girl, but let's just keep it to ourselves for a little while. And let's not display too much in front of other people. I don't think that's proper, do you?'

'No, it's not, I agree.' Leaning forward he kissed her cheek lightly. 'I shall behave meself, Laura, me sweet mavourneen.'

She smiled. This dear kind man was hers for keeps, she was now sure of that.

Suddenly Blackie spotted David Kallinski walking towards them, and he sat up straighter and said to Laura, 'David has arrived. Not a word today then, me darling.'

Emma was filled with excitement. Once Blackie and Laura had gone to listen to the band in Armley Park, Emma changed into a crisp silk dress and put on her Leghorn bonnet. In her reticule were sixty pounds she had taken out of the black tin box that contained her savings.

Quite by chance, yesterday, she had seen the words TO LET on a shop window on Town Street. It was part of a row of three, and a small notice gave the name of the landlord. A Mr Joe Lowther, who lived in another area of Armley.

She set out, filled with confidence and determination. She would get that shop, no matter what. Success was in the air, so she believed.

Emma soon found the street where he lived, went up the stone steps resolutely. She knocked hard, and waited.

A few minutes later the door was opened by a tall young man, with a pleasant open face and fair hair. He stared at Emma. 'What can I do for you, miss?'

'I'm here to see Mr Joe Lowther.'

'I'm Joe Lowther. What can I do for you?' he asked again.

'I want to rent the shop on Town Street. Perhaps I should speak to your father?'

Joe Lowther looked at her, his eyes narrowing. 'That would be difficult. He's been dead six years.'

Suddenly realizing her mistake, Emma gave him her most radiant smile. 'Oh, well, then, obviously it is *you* I must talk to, Mr Lowther.'

'It is. Are you here on behalf of your mother?'

'No, myself, I—'

'You look a bit young to rent my shop,' Joe Lowther muttered, sounding suddenly annoyed.

'Could I come inside, please, Mr Lowther? I don't think we should be doing business on your front steps. The neighbours might be watching, don't you think?'

'Perhaps you're right. So come in then.' He opened the door wider, and Emma went inside.

After closing the door, Joe Lowther said, 'I don't do business on a Sunday.'

'Well, there's always a first time for everything. Mr Lowther,' Emma answered in a gracious voice.

'Please sit down,' he said, staring at her, now suddenly aware that she was a beautiful young woman. His chest tightened and he stepped back.

'I prefer to stand. Thank you, though. I want to rent your shop, and you should know I have a growing business I run from my home. I will make a go of your shop; I can reassure you of that.'

'You look a bit young—'

Emma cut him off when she said, 'I would be willing to pay you several months in advance, Mr Lowther.' Emma knew she had the winning hand, because she had cash. Everyone loved cash.

'How many months?' Joe ventured, feeling suddenly

uncomfortable and hot around the collar. This girl had stunned him, her emerald eyes totally focused on him.

Emma, fully aware of the effect she was having on him, smiled at him. 'I'm not sure what the rent is, but I would be prepared to give you six months in advance. Surely that shows my good faith, and also my belief in myself.'

Joe was obviously taken aback. '*Six* months?' he repeated, his voice rising an octave.

'Yes. And I am being very rude, Mr Lowther. I haven't introduced myself. I'm Emma Harte.'

'How do you do, Miss Harte.'

'It's *Mrs* Harte,' Emma corrected him, with another smile.

He nodded, wondering why he was filling up with disappointment.

Emma, seeing his confusion, knowing he was attracted to her, went in for the kill. Opening her reticule, she took out the bundle of cash and began to count the money. 'Now, how much is the rent?'

Joe, to his surprise, told her, 'A guinea a week,' he answered.

'Well, that makes it four guineas a month,' Emma said, as always fast with numbers. Paying no attention to Joe, she peeled off the notes and laid them on the table. 'I think we have a deal, don't we, Mr Lowther?'

'I suppose we do.' Joe nodded, thinking this extraordinary young woman had somehow got the better of him. But had she really? Glancing at the bills, he knew he hadn't done badly himself. He said, 'I'll just go and get you the rent book, Mrs Harte, and the keys to the shop.'

'Thank you, Mr Lowther.'

Emma smiled at his back as he went out of the room, almost delirious with happiness and excitement. She could hardly contain herself.

When he returned and handed her the rent book and keys,

she took them from him with a wide smile on her face. 'Thank you, Mr Lowther.' She glanced at the money on the table. 'Aren't you going to count it?'

'I trust you,' he said.

Emma thought she was floating home on clouds. Her step was firm and swift as she hurried back to Laura's, chuffed and full of excitement. She couldn't wait to tell Blackie and Laura. But when she went into the cellar kitchen, only Blackie was there. He was reading the racing sheet he favoured.

He put the paper down and jumped up, went to greet her. After hugging her tightly, he smiled. 'I don't know where ye've been but I've never seen ye look so . . . elated.'

'I've just rented my first shop, Blackie.'

He held her away from him, looking genuinely surprised. 'Have ye really?'

'I have. Where's Laura? I want you both to come and see it. It's only a few minutes away on Town Street.'

'After the concert Laura went to the church to help the priest's housekeeper for an hour. Something about a charity affair.'

'Will you come with me? *Now*?'

'Wild horses wouldn't keep me away.'

Emma and Blackie stood outside the shops. 'It's this one,' Emma told him. 'With the whitewashed window. The third in the row.'

He looked at her, filled with pride that she had accomplished what she had set out to do a year ago. She was miraculous in a certain special way. There was no one like her. She was a winner.

'Congratulations, Emma. I'm as thrilled as ye are. Well done, mavourneen.'

'Thank you. It's getting dark. Let's go home,' Emma said. 'And thank you many times over, Blackie. You've been so loyal to me, never faltered.'

He merely smiled, and she put her arm through his affectionately.

As they walked up Town Street neither of them knew then that they had embarked on a journey that would lead them to more success than they had ever dreamed possible. Or that their friendship would be so enduring it would last a lifetime.

ACKNOWLEDGEMENTS

A writer's occupation is solitary by necessity. But once the manuscript is finished, other people become involved. All of them help to get the manuscript ready for publication. I would like to thank those who do this job so well for me.

In New York my editor is Jennifer Enderlin, who is President and Publisher of St. Martin's Press. Despite all of her responsibilities, Jen finds the time to work with me on the books. Thanks to her and also her team: Brant Janeway, Marketing Director; Tracey Guest, Publicity Director; and Elizabeth Curione, Production Editor.

In London, my editor is Lynne Drew, Publisher. Lynne has a great sense of drama and character, and I appreciate her suggestions and ideas; thanks also to Lucy Stewart, Editorial Assistant, and Penelope Isaac, my copyeditor.

My team at HarperCollins also includes Kate Elton, Managing Director; Roger Cazalet, Associate Publisher, and Lucy Vanderbilt, Group Rights Director. I thank them all. Elizabeth Dawson, PR Director, deserves many thanks from me for her promotion and publicity endeavors once the book goes on sale. And for always keeping me laughing on the road.

I am grateful to Charlie Redmayne, CEO of HarperCollins UK, for his enthusiasm, encouragement and continuing support for my novels.

Although I do a lot of my own research, sometimes I use other people to help me. For this book, I was happy to use Sheron Boyle, who took on the task of researching Leeds in the 1800s and early 1900s. Some of her research helped me to understand the influx of the Irish in those years, as well as the condition of the city of my birth. I was genuinely pleased with her discoveries, some of them surprising.

I have a dear friend in London, John Scanlon, who works for the Dorchester group of hotels. He is Irish, and I knew he would be able to enlighten me about his country of birth. He did, and his knowledge and insights were very pertinent to me when I was writing the first parts of the book. I can never thank him enough for the help he gave me.

Maria Boyle has been my personal publicity representative for many years, and also represented my late husband, Robert Bradford, and his movies of my books. Maria still works with me, and she also gave me many insights into the Irish in Leeds. I owe her thanks for that and the other work she does.

Finally, but by no means least, I must give very special thanks to Linda Sullivan. For years, Linda has typed my manuscripts, and sometimes has also pointed out an error or made suggestions. I am appreciative of this dedication she shows. And my editors, like me, love her beautifully typed manuscripts.

If you've enjoyed *A Man of Honour*, why not follow
the story onwards with the original
multi-million-copy international bestseller,

A WOMAN OF SUBSTANCE

A WOMAN'S AMBITION . . .

In the brooding moors above a humble Yorkshire village
stood Fairley Hall. There, Emma Harte, its oppressed but
resourceful servant girl, acquired a shrewd determination.
There, she honed her skills, discovered the meaning of
treachery, learned to survive, to become a woman, and vowed
to make her mark on the world.

A JOURNEY OF A LIFETIME . . .

In the wake of tragedy she rose from poverty to magnificent
wealth as the iron-willed force behind a thriving international
enterprise. As one of the richest women in the world Emma
Harte has almost everything she fought so hard to achieve –
save for the dream of love, and for the passion of the one
man she could never have.

A DREAM FULFILLED – AND AVENGED.

Through two marriages, two devastating wars, and genera-
tions of secrets, Emma's unparalleled success has come with a
price. As greed, envy, and revenge consume those closest to
her, the brilliant matriarch now finds herself poised to outwit
her enemies, and to face the betrayals of the past with the
same ingenious resolve that forged her empire.

Follow Barbara on Facebook or sign up
to her newsletter to keep up to date with the latest news . . .

f /BarbaraTaylorBradford
www.barbarataylorbradford.co.uk

Barbara is proud to support the National Literacy Trust, a UK charity that changes the life stories of disadvantaged children and families, focusing on the most deprived communities. One in six adults in England have very poor literacy skills. This affects every aspect of their life: their job, their relationships, their health and even their life expectancy. By improving the reading, writing, speaking and listening skills of those who need support, the National Literacy Trust offers a route out of poverty and transforms their future.

The National Literacy Trust relies on donations for their vital work. A small amount of money each month enables them to give a child a book of their own to keep, fund a skills workshop for teenagers to give them a better chance of getting a job, or support a family's literacy and break the cycle of disadvantage.

You can find out more and donate at
literacytrust.org.uk/donate